MEET ME
AT THE
LAKE

MEET ME
AT THE
LAKE

Carley Fortune

BERKLEY ROMANCE
NEW YORK

BERKLEY ROMANCE
Published by Berkley
An imprint of Penguin Random House LLC
penguinrandomhouse.com

Library of Congress Cataloging-in-Publication Data

Names: Fortune, Carley, author.
Title: Meet me at the lake / Carley Fortune.
Description: First Edition. | New York: Berkley Romance, 2023.
Identifiers: LCCN 2022041943 (print) | LCCN 2022041944 (ebook) |
ISBN 9780593438558 (trade paperback) | ISBN 9780593438565 (ebook)
Subjects: LCGFT: Novels.
Classification: LCC PR9199.4.F678 M44 2023 (print) | LCC PR9199.4.F678
(ebook) | DDC 813/.6—dc23/eng/20220902
LC record available at https://lccn.loc.gov/2022041943
LC ebook record available at https://lccn.loc.gov/2022041944

First Edition: May 2023

Printed in the United States of America
1st Printing

Book design by Ashley Tucker

To Marco

For that first mix CD and all the ones that followed,
but especially for turning the volume down

1

Now

I MAKE IT AS FAR AS THE FRONT DESK WITHOUT ANYONE noticing me. It's a striking piece, carved from a large tree trunk—rustic but not shabby, the epitome of Mom's aesthetic—and there's no one behind it. I hurry past, to the office, then shut myself inside and lock the door.

The room is more fishing hut than work space. Pine walls, two ancient desks, a small window trimmed with a flimsy plaid curtain. I doubt it's changed much since the lodge was built in the 1800s. There's nothing to suggest how much time Mom spent here, except for a photo of me as a baby pinned to the timber and a faint whiff of Clinique perfume.

Dropping into one of the worn leather chairs, I switch on the plastic tabletop fan. I'm already sticky, but it's stifling in here, one of the few spots in the building without air-conditioning. I raise my elbows like a scarecrow and swing my hands back and forth. Pit stains are the last thing I need.

While I wait to cool off before changing into heels, I stare at a stack of our brochures. *Brookbanks Resort—Your Muskoka Get-away Awaits*, declares a chipper font above a photo of the beach at sunset, the lodge looming in the background like a country cottage castle. It almost makes me laugh—it's Brookbanks Resort I've failed to get away *from*.

Maybe Jamie will forget I agreed to do this tonight, and I can sneak back to the house, slither into stretchy pants, and douse myself with a bucket of cold white wine.

The door handle rattles.

No such luck.

"Fernie?" Jamie calls. "What's with the lock? You decent in there?"

"I need five minutes," I reply, voice pinched.

"You're not gonna bail, right? You swore you'd do this," he says. But the reminder is unnecessary. I've been dreading it all day. All my life maybe.

"I know, I know. I'm finishing up some paperwork." I clamp my eyes shut at the mistake. "I'm almost done."

"What paperwork? Is it the linen order? We have a system for that."

My mom had a system for everything, and Jamie doesn't want me messing with any of them.

He's worried. It's peak season, but many of the guest rooms are vacant. I've been back for six weeks, and Jamie thinks it's only a matter of time before I shake things up. I'm not sure if he's right. I'm not even sure if I'm staying.

"You can't shut me out of my own office. I have a key."

I curse under my breath. Of course he does.

It's going to be embarrassing if he has to drag me out of here, and I'm pretty sure he'll do it. I haven't made a scene at the resort since my senior year of high school, and I'm not about to start.

Being here sometimes makes me feel like I've regressed, but I'm not a reckless seventeen-year-old anymore.

Taking a deep breath, I stand and smooth my palms over the front of the dress. It's too tight, but the ripped jeans I've been living in aren't appropriate for the dining room. I could almost hear Mom when I changed earlier.

I know you'd rather wear pj's all day, but we have to set the tone, sweet pea.

I open the door.

Jamie's flaxen curls are cropped short and styled into obedience, but he has the same baby face from when we were young and he thought deodorant was optional.

"Is it the linen order?" he asks.

"Absolutely not," I say. "You have a system."

Jamie blinks, not sure if I'm teasing. He's been the resort's general manager for three years, and I can't get my head around it. In pressed pants and a tie, he looks like he's playing dress-up. In my mind, he's still a lake rat in swim trunks and a bandanna.

He doesn't know what to make of me anymore, either—he's torn between trying to please me, his new boss, and trying to prevent me from wreaking havoc. There should be a cosmic law against exes working together.

"You used to be fun," I tell him, and he grins. And there, with his deep smile lines and sky blue eyes, is the Jamie who once sang the entirety of Alanis Morissette's *Jagged Little Pill* stoned and wearing a purple caftan he'd nicked from Mrs. Rose's cabin.

The fact that Jamie loved attention as much as he loved going commando was one of my favorite things about him—no one looked at me when Jamie was around. He was a good boyfriend, but he was also the perfect diversion.

"So did you," he says, and then squints. "Is that your mom's dress?"

I nod. "It doesn't fit." I pulled it from her closet earlier this evening. Canary yellow. One of at least two dozen brightly colored sleeveless shifts. Her evening uniform.

There's a beat of silence, and it's all it takes for me to lose my courage. "Listen, I'm not feeling—"

Jamie cuts me off. "Nuh-uh. You're not doing this to me, Fernie. You've been dodging the Hannovers all week, and they check out tomorrow."

According to Jamie, the Hannovers have stayed at Brookbanks for seven summers, tip like they've got something to prove, and refer a ton of guests. From the way I've caught him frowning into his computer screen, I think the resort needs good word of mouth more desperately than Jamie's let on. Our accountant left another message today asking me to call him.

"They've already finished dessert," Jamie says. "I told them you'd be right out. They want to give you their condolences in person."

I scrape my nails across my right arm a few times before I catch myself. This shouldn't be so hard. In my real life, I manage a trio of indie coffee shops in Toronto's west end called Filtr. I'm overseeing the opening of our fourth and largest location this fall, the first with an on-site roastery. Talking to customers is second nature.

"Okay," I tell him. "I'm sorry. I can do this."

Jamie lets out a breath. "Awesome." He gives me an apologetic look and then adds, "It would be extra awesome if you stopped by a few tables to say hello while you're there. You know, carried on the tradition."

I do know. Mom visited the restaurant every single evening, making sure this person liked the rainbow trout and that person had a restful first night. It was bonkers how many details she could recall about the guests, and they loved her for it. She said being a family-run business didn't mean anything unless you put a face to the Brookbanks Resort name. And for three decades that face was hers. Margaret Brookbanks.

Jamie has been not-so-subtly hinting that I come to the dining room to greet the guests, but I've shrugged him off. Because as soon as I go out there, it's official.

Mom is gone.

And I am here.

Back home at the resort—the last place I planned to end up.

JAMIE AND I MAKE OUR WAY TO THE FRONT DESK. THERE'S STILL no one behind it. Jamie pauses at the same time I do.

"Not again," he mutters.

The desk clerk who's on tonight started a few weeks ago and tends to disappear. Mom would have fired her already.

"Maybe we should cover the desk until she's back," I say. "Just in case anyone comes."

Jamie raises his eyes to the ceiling, considering. Then he narrows them on me. "Nice try, but the Hannovers are more important."

We continue toward the French doors that lead to the restaurant. They're propped open, and the clinking of cutlery and happy hum of conversation drift into the lobby along with the smell of freshly baked sourdough. There are soaring beamed ceilings beyond the entrance and windows that look over the lake in an impressive semicircle. It's a renovation my mom choreographed after she took over from my grandparents. The dining room was her stage. I can't picture it without her walking among the tables.

Taking a quiet breath, I tuck my white-blond bob behind my ears, her voice in my head.

Don't hide behind your hair, pea.

As we're about to pass through the doorway, a couple exits arm in arm. They're in their sixties and swathed almost entirely in beige linen.

"Mr. and Mrs. Hannover," Jamie says, hands spread by his sides. "We were just coming to find you. Let me introduce you to Fern Brookbanks."

The Hannovers give me their kindest smiles, the facial equivalent of a *there, there* pat on the shoulder.

"We were so sorry to hear about your mother's passing," says Mrs. Hannover.

Passing.

It's a strange word to describe what happened.

A dark night. A deer through the windshield. Steel crushed against granite. Ice cubes scattered across the highway.

I've been trying not to think about Mom's last moments. I've been trying not to think of her at all. The daily barrage of grief, shock, and anger can make it hard to put weight on my feet in the morning. I feel a bit wobbly now, but I try not to let it show. It's been more than a month since the accident, and while people want to express their sympathy, there's a limit on how much suffering others can tolerate.

"Hard to imagine this place without Maggie," Mr. Hannover says. "Always had that big smile on her face. We loved catching up with her. We even talked her into having a drink with us last summer, didn't we?" His wife nods enthusiastically, as if I might not believe them. "I told her watching her run around was making me dizzy, and boy, did she laugh."

My mother's death and the future of the resort are two topics

I'm not prepared to discuss, which is the other reason I've avoided the restaurant. The regulars will have something to say about both.

I thank the Hannovers and change the subject to their holiday—the tennis, the beautiful weather, the new beaver dam. The small talk is easy. I'm thirty-two—too old to resent the guests or worry about their judgment. It's her I'm furious with. I thought she'd accepted that my life was in Toronto. What was she thinking by leaving the resort to me? What was she thinking by dying?

"We're terribly sorry for your loss," Mrs. Hannover says again. "You look so much like her."

"I do," I agree. Same small stature. Same pale hair. Same gray eyes.

"Well, I'm sure you want to head up to your room to enjoy your last night. You'll have a great view of the fireworks from your balcony," says Jamie, rescuing me. I give him a grateful smile, and he sneaks me back a wink.

We were a good team when we worked together as kids, too. At first, we used a code word when one of us needed rescuing from an annoying or overly needy guest: *Watermelon.* The elderly widower who wouldn't stop telling me how much I reminded him of his first love: *Watermelon.* The bird-watcher who gave Jamie a detailed description of every species he'd seen in the area: *Watermelon.* But after a summer spending every day together down at the outfitting hut, hauling canoes and kayaks out of the lake, we began communicating silently—a slight widening of the eyes or a curl of the lip.

"Not so bad, was it?" he says once they move toward the elevator bank, but I don't reply.

Jamie extends his arm to the dining room entrance. Many of the people inside will be guests of the resort, but there'll be plenty of locals. With my luck, someone I went to high school with will spot me as soon as I step inside. Blood roars in my eardrums like a transport truck on the freeway.

"I don't think I can do this," I say. "I'm going to go back to the house. I'm exhausted."

It's not a lie. The insomnia began as soon as I got back. Every day, I wake in my childhood bedroom underslept and a bit disoriented. I look at the dense tangle of tree branches out the window, reminding myself where I am and why I'm here. In the beginning, I'd put a pillow over my head and go back to sleep. I'd rise around noon and stumble downstairs, filling the rest of the day with carbohydrates and episodes of *The Good Wife*.

But then Jamie started calling with questions, and Whitney popped by without warning often enough to give me a talk about how much time I was spending in my pajamas—the type of tough love only a best friend can provide—and so I began getting dressed. I began leaving the house, visiting the lodge, wandering down to the family dock for a swim or to drink my morning coffee, the way Mom used to. I've even gone out in a kayak a few times. It feels good to be on the water, like I have a shred of control, even if it's just steering a small boat.

I'm still greeted by a procession of grief, anger, and panic when I open my eyelids, only now it passes quietly instead of clanging like a marching band.

Over the last couple of weeks, Jamie has patiently updated me on everything that's changed in the many years since I've worked here, but what's wilder is all the stuff that hasn't. The sourdough. The guests. The fact that he still calls me Fernie.

We knew each other long before we started dating. The Pringle cottage is a couple bays down the lake. His grandparents knew my grandparents, and his parents still come to the restaurant for fish and chips every Friday. They spend most of the summer in

Muskoka now that they've retired, venturing back to Guelph in September. Jamie rents a place in town, but he bought the vacant lot next to his family's to build a year-round home. He loves the lake more than anything.

"It's Canada Day," Jamie says. "It would mean something to the guests and the staff to see you. It's the start of summer. I'm not asking you to get up on the stage and make a speech before the fireworks begin." He doesn't need to add, *The way your mom did.* "Just go say hello."

I swallow, and Jamie holds my shoulders, looking me in the eyes. "You can do this. You're so close. You're already dressed. You've been in there a million times." He lowers his voice. "We've done it in there, remember? Booth 3."

I let out a huff. "Of course you know what booth it was."

"I could draw you a map of all the spots we desecrated. The outfitting hut alone . . ."

"Stop." I'm laughing now, but it's slightly frantic. Here I am with my ex-boyfriend, talking about the places we've had sex at my recently deceased mother's resort. I've been punked by the universe.

"Fernie, it's no big deal. That's all I'm saying."

I'm about to tell Jamie that he's wrong, that it's a very big deal, but then I see an excuse in the corner of my eye. A very tall man is wheeling a silver suitcase up to the front desk, and there's still no one behind it.

The skyscraper's back is facing us, but you can tell his suit is expensive. Custom made, probably. The black fabric is cut to his frame in the kind of impeccable manner that requires precise measurements and generous room on a credit card. I doubt an off-the-rack number would be long enough for this guy's arms, and the cuff of his sleeve is perfect. So is his slicked-back hair.

Inky and glossy and as meticulously styled as his jacket is tailored. He's overdressed, to be honest. This is a beautiful resort, one of the nicest in eastern Muskoka, and the staff is always well put together, but the guests tend to keep things casual, especially in the summer.

"I'm going to go help him," I tell Jamie. "I need practice with check-ins. Come make sure I do it right."

There's no arguing. We can't just let the fancy man stand there.

As we round the desk, I apologize for making him wait.

"Welcome to Brookbanks Resort," I say, glancing up quickly—even with me in my heels, he's got almost a foot on me.

"Did you have any trouble finding us?" I ask, punching a key to wake up the computer. Tall dude still hasn't said anything. The last stretch of road is unpaved, unlit, and has some wicked turns through the bush. Sometimes city people find it stressful, especially when they arrive after sundown. I'm pegging this guy as a Torontonian, though he could be from Montreal. There's a medical conference starting next week—some of the doctors are arriving early, making a holiday of the long weekend.

"No." He runs a hand down his tie. Says nothing more.

"Good." I type in my passcode. "Are you with the dermatologists?" I navigate to the main menu, and when he doesn't answer, I clear my throat and try again. "Do you have a reservation with us?"

"I do." He says the words slowly, like he's scanning them for errors.

I have no idea what his problem is. Men who wear suits like his usually sound a lot more confident. But then I look up, and I'm met with a very handsome, very chiseled, very tense-looking face. He's about my age, and he's strangely familiar. I'm sure I've seen this face before. It's something about the nose. Maybe he's an actor, although celebrity types don't usually show up in suits and a fresh shave—or at least they didn't used to.

"The name?"

His eyebrows rise at my question, like he's surprised I've asked. Then I notice how dark his eyes are, black as a crow's wing, and my stomach twists. His posture is flawless. My heart races, pounding in the pads of my fingers and balls of my feet. I search for the scar immediately. And there it is: below his lip on the left side of his chin, barely visible unless you know to look for it. I can't believe I still know to look for it.

But I do.

I know this face.

I know his irises aren't actually black—in the sunlight, they're espresso brown.

I know how he got that scar.

Because even though I've tried to forget him, I know exactly who this man is.

2

June 14, Ten Years Ago

WE ONLY HAD FIVE MINUTES TO GET TO THE STATION, AND THE streetcar was stalled. Whitney and I shoved our way from the back of the vehicle through the dense mass of bodies, mumbling half-hearted apologies before we stumbled out onto the sidewalk and took off.

"Hurry up, Whit," I yelled over my shoulder.

Being late was not an option. There was one bus north that day, and while neither of us had said so, Whitney and her oversized suitcase needed to be on it. We'd spent three days together in my teensy apartment, and our friendship might not survive a fourth.

The sun crouched low in the sky, winking between buildings and glittering off glass towers, as we ran along Dundas Street, our sneakers pounding on the gum-pocked pavement. If you looked up, the glare was blinding, but at ground level, Toronto's down-town core was cast in blue-gray morning shadow. The contrast was beautiful. The way the light bounced off the windows re-minded me of home, a sunset shimmering on the lake.

I wanted to stop and point it out to Whitney. But we didn't have a second to spare, and even if we had, I doubted she'd find anything magical about the sparkling skyline. I'd been trying to get her to see Toronto through my eyes for her entire trip, and I hadn't succeeded yet.

We arrived at the coach terminal one minute late, but a long line of travelers stood beside the bus parked at Bay 9, looking various degrees of irritated. The driver was nowhere in sight.

"Thank god," I breathed.

Whitney doubled over, hands on her knees. Strands of her thick chestnut hair had fallen from her ponytail and were stuck to her crimson cheeks. "I. Hate. Running."

When she'd caught her breath, we checked that we had the right departure information and attached ourselves to the back of the queue. The station was essentially an oversized garage—a dark, dank armpit of Toronto. The air tasted of vending machine sandwiches, diesel fumes, and misery.

I checked the time on my phone. It was already after ten. I was going to be late for my shift at the coffee shop.

"You don't have to wait," Whitney said. "I can take it from here."

Whitney and I had been best friends since grade school. She had a round face with hazel doe eyes and a tiny cherry of a nose that under most circumstances made her seem deceptively inno-cent. It was sweet that Whitney was trying to sound brave, but she was clutching her nylon purse to her middle as if it would be snatched away with any less vigilance.

At twenty-two, Whitney had never been alone in Toronto, not even for ten minutes, and while I knew she'd be safe, I wasn't about to ditch her in one of the city's dingiest crannies.

"It's fine. I want to see you off," I told her.

"Just think," she said, bouncing on her toes. "Soon I won't have to come all this way for us to see each other."

It wasn't a long drive—two and a half picturesque hours—but whatever.

I stuck on a smile. "I can't wait."

"I know you like it here." She peered over her shoulder. "But sometimes I don't get it."

A sarcastic reply stood waiting on my tongue.

How seldom Whitney visited me during university was a sore spot. I wasn't sure whether it was because our relationship hadn't found solid footing since our big fight over my "self-destructive behavior" in senior year, or simply because she didn't like the city. But each trip, it was clear she'd rather be in Huntsville. She didn't say no to my suggestions, but she wasn't overly enthusiastic, either. It wasn't like her. Whitney was the ultimate *yes and* person—for her, any possibility for antics and adventure was good news.

"Honestly, I'd be happy eating bread and hanging out in your apartment for the next two days," she'd said when she arrived this week.

Frankly, it pissed me off. My time in Toronto was running out, and there were so many things I still wanted to do. Whitney was supposed to be my wing woman. Instead, I felt like I was dragging her around.

"What's not to get?" I said now, gesturing around the station with mock grandeur as a man horked on the concrete the next bay over.

Whitney cringed, then glanced down at her phone. "Jamie's texting me. He wants me to give you a kiss for him." Her nose wrinkled as she read his messages. "Kiss Fernie goodbye for me. Tongue allowed. Encouraged. Send photo. Winky face."

I shook my head, fighting the upward curve of my mouth.

Jamie was like a human Labradoodle—a happy-go-lucky, pleasure-seeking mop of golden curls. Hearing his name made me feel a little lighter. "My boyfriend said that? I'm shocked."

"He's dying to get you up there. We all are."

I swallowed, then with relief spotted a man in a telltale navy uniform ambling toward the bus.

"Take your time," one of the passengers yelled at him. "It's not like we're behind schedule."

"I'm so excited we'll be in the same place again," Whitney went on.

I nodded, pushing the words out. "Me too."

Four years of living apart from my best friend and my boyfriend: I should have been counting the seconds until we were reunited. I hadn't seen Jamie since his surprise trip on Valentine's Day. During the winter, he worked as a snowboarding instructor in Banff, but he'd been back at the resort since the May long weekend. I'd finished my final year of university—I should have been there with him. I should have packed my bags after my last exam in April. Instead, I talked Mom into letting me stay until the end of June so I could bum around the city until convocation, which was now a week away. I played on her sympathies as a business owner, telling her my boss was having trouble finding a barista to replace me.

The bus rumbled to life, and then the driver began tossing luggage into its underbelly. As passengers shuffled forward and the line dwindled, Whitney and I gave each other a long squeeze.

"Love you, Baby," she said.

Growing up at a *Dirty Dancing*–style resort came with a *Dirty Dancing*–style nickname. "Baby." I hated it. It didn't even make sense—Baby was a guest.

I stood on my tiptoes and pulled her hood up, yanking on the strings to cinch it around her face. "Love you, too," I told her. At least that wasn't a lie.

Once Whitney had found a seat, I blew her a kiss and took my headphones from my canvas tote bag. I pressed play, letting Talking Heads drown out the bus engine and the ticking countdown that grew louder with each passing moment.

Nine more days until I had to go home.

MY HEADPHONES WERE BOTH MY THERAPIST AND MY invisibility cloak. Two Sugars was only a few blocks from the station—not far enough for the music to wash away my guilt or make me forget about the resort and the responsibilities waiting for me there. My past waited for me back home, too. The Huntsville High rumor mill was once powered by Fern Brookbanks gossip. Years had gone by, but I knew people still thought of me as That Girl—the one who'd gone off the rails. With any luck, the coffee shop would be busy enough that my mind would switch to autopilot by the time I pulled my tenth shot of espresso.

I walked east, jostling through the horde of tourists at Yonge and Dundas. I liked its tackiness—the concrete, flashing billboards and the double-decker tour buses—but I loved how there were people everywhere, and not a single one was looking at me. Every day, one hundred thousand people crossed the intersection, and in that madness, I was a perfect nobody.

I told people I was from Huntsville, but it wasn't totally accurate. The resort was far outside town, on the rocky shores of Smoke Lake. Coming to Toronto for university felt like moving to the moon. I wished I could play space explorer forever.

I turned up my music, rolling my shoulders forward then back as the sun found my neck. The temperature was supposed to set a record high. Toronto was at its best in June. The patios and parks spilled over with unbridled early summer giddiness. In June, a hot day was a gift. By August, it would be a burden, and the city would reek of stewed garbage.

I'd dressed for the heat in a pair of frayed jean shorts, and a tank top under a short-sleeved blouse I'd found at Value Village. It was flowy and sheer and had a tiny brown floral pattern I thought was stylish in a nineties way—you could hardly see the yellow stain near the hem.

A row of metal newspaper boxes stood guard outside Two Sugars, and I grabbed an issue of *The Grid*, the free alt-weekly I liked best, before pulling on the door. It was locked. Confused, I yanked on the handle again, then pressed my nose to the glass. The coffee shop was my favorite place in the world, and it was empty except for Luis. The smell of wet paint licked my nose as soon as he opened the door.

"Why are we closed?" I asked, taking my headphones off and stepping inside. I stopped at the sight of a black-and-white painting covering one wall. "What's this?"

"What's *this*?" Luis pointed at my head.

"A trim."

He snorted. "That's not a trim. You cut off all your hair." He smiled. "I like it."

I tugged at one of the short strands at the back—it was barely long enough to hold between my fingers. I'd had it done after my last shift, before Whitney arrived. Considering my hair had been well past my shoulders, it was a big change.

"I don't remember asking your opinion, but thanks," I said. "So what's going on in here?"

"You didn't know about the mural?" Luis folded his arms across his impressive chest. Other staff members had come and gone at Two Sugars, but the two of us had worked together for three years.

"Nope."

"Well, we have a mural now. Or we almost do."

I looked around. The artist appeared to be missing. "And you and I are playing babysitter?" I guessed.

"One of us is. I've been here the last couple of days." He pulled a small key ring out of his pocket. "It's your turn."

I stared at Luis. Spending hours alone with some random stranger, having to make conversation—the idea was almost more repellant than public speaking. "No," I said.

"Yes," Luis replied in singsong. "I'm going to the island. I'm meeting friends at the ferry in half an hour."

I growled out a "Fine" and took the key, then threw my stuff onto a table and wandered closer to the mural. "So where's our Michelangelo?"

"He went to grab something to eat," Luis said. "He should be done by early afternoon, and then you can take off. We're closed until tomorrow."

I could survive a few hours. I had a joint in my bag and plans to smoke it in the alley after I was done. I wanted to walk through my city and back to my place in Little Italy.

"Do you like it?" Luis asked.

I studied the mural. The artist had made a fun-house version of Toronto's skyline and waterfront. Everything was a bit distorted—the CN Tower was tiny, clutched in the claws of a raccoon. Toronto was getting off on itself lately, and this type of trendy city pride was everywhere: on T-shirts; on posters; even on my tote bag, which was designed with a map of Little Italy, its street names forming the neighborhood grid.

"I don't know," I said. "It seems kind of . . . basic?"

"Ouch," a deep voice said behind us.

I turned around slowly.

Dressed in loose blue cotton coveralls was a guy around my age, holding a paper take-out bag. He was extraordinarily tall and held himself even taller. His mussed black hair fell just past his ears. His nose was a touch on the long side, but it suited him.

"This is our Michelangelo," Luis said.

The guy's jaw and cheekbones were angular, almost sharp. I didn't know where to look, there was so much of him, and it was all very . . . nice.

"Your basic Michelangelo," the guy corrected. I dropped my gaze. He was too pretty to look at directly. He wore a pair of tan work boots with neon pink laces.

"I usually go by Will." He stuck out his palm. "Will Baxter."

I stared at his large hand and then met his eyes. They were as dark as an oil spill.

"And you are?" Will asked after a moment, dropping his arm to his side.

I glared at Luis, irritated. Guys this hot were the worst. Cocky, self-absorbed, dull. Plus, he was tall. Hot plus tall meant he'd be completely insufferable. I bet the only thing this guy struggled with was finding pants that fit properly. Luis made a little wave as if to say, *He's fine.*

"Fern."

Will raised his eyebrows, asking for more.

"Brookbanks," I told him, running my fingers behind my ear to tuck my hair in place, only there wasn't enough hair to re-arrange.

"Sorry to hear you think my work's basic, Fern Brookbanks," Will said with exaggerated cheer, "because I believe you're stuck with me for the rest of the day."

I gave him a tight smile.

"Well, kids, I'm gonna split," Luis said. "Will, despite first impressions, Fern won't bite."

"Hey," I said.

"I'll see you Monday." Luis kissed my cheek, then whispered in my ear, "He's a doll. Be nice."

I locked the door behind Luis, feeling Will's eyes on the side of my face.

"What?"

"Tell me why you don't like it."

He took a muffin out of the paper bag, peeling off the parchment. My stomach gurgled. I'd made Mom's pancakes as a special goodbye breakfast for Whitney, but that was hours ago. Will broke the muffin in half and held out a hunk.

"Thanks," I said, shoving it into my mouth. Lemon-cranberry.

We turned to face the wall. Everything but the right-hand corner looked finished.

"The raccoon's fine," I said. When he didn't respond, I peered up at him. He was better looking at close proximity. His bottom lashes were an exaggerated curve, as black as the lake at midnight. They were long and delicate, kissing the skin below his eyes, and the contrast with his splattered, saggy work gear was weirdly thrilling. I studied the mural again. "It's not terrible."

His laugh came out of nowhere, popping like a firework. It was delight made acoustic. "Tell me what you really think."

"It's just not what I would have chosen. It's so different in here than it was six months ago." My boss had decided the space needed "modernizing." The beat-up cherrywood chairs were now molded black plastic. The turquoise walls had been painted white. There were no more Renoir posters.

I made the mistake of looking at Will again. The way he

watched me with fascination made me uneasy. "Not a big fan of change?"

"I liked the way it was before." I pointed to a corner by the window. "We had this old orange velvet armchair there, and all these Nigella Lawson cookbooks." Hardly anyone looked through them, but Nigella was our thing. "There were wooden beads hanging over there." I gestured to the doorway that led to the prep kitchen.

The wall Will was painting once had a large corkboard over the milk and sugar station, where people tacked flyers for piano lessons, missed connections, knitting circles—anything, really. Last year, one of our regulars proposed to his boyfriend by pinning up a sign that read, *I love you, Sean. Will you marry me?* He'd cut vertical strips into the bottom, each with the same answer: *Yes.*

"It used to be cozy in here. It's like a totally different place now," I said. "It's so . . . stark."

"I know what you mean," Will said, brushing muffin from his chest pockets. There was a plain gold signet ring on his pinkie. "Every time I come back to Toronto, it's changed a little. Sometimes more than a little."

"You don't live here?"

"Vancouver," he said. "But I grew up here. And yeah, it's always evolving. I don't mind it, though." He pushed a slice of hair off his face. "Whenever I'm home, I have the chance to get to know the city all over again."

"How romantic," I said, deadpan. But his words hit my bloodstream like an espresso shot.

3

Now

I STARE AT WILL ACROSS THE FRONT DESK, FINGERS HOVERING over the keyboard, throat dry. His eyes are fixed on mine. He still hasn't given me his name, and Jamie is looking between us, his head whipping around like a puppy choosing between chew toys.

Will and I were twenty-two the last time we saw each other, and he's not at all like how I thought he'd turn out. I wonder if he's thinking the same about me. Because he must know who I am. He must know this Brookbanks Resort is *my* Brookbanks Resort.

"I just need your name so I can look up the reservation," Jamie says, nudging me out of the way while Will and I watch each other. His eyes tighten at the corners. He's not sure I've recognized him.

But of course I have, even though this Will Baxter is very different from the Will Baxter I once knew. He's still all long lines and keen edges, though the suit is throwing me. So is the hair, combed back from his forehead and cemented with product. He's still trim, but there's a sturdiness to him. It's the suit and the hair and the body, plus the ten years since I last saw him.

As unexpected as they are, the bespoke clothing and the two-hundred-dollar haircut suit him. That grace he has.

"Will Baxter," he says, eyes locked on me as he slides his credit card and ID onto the counter.

I spent just one day with Will, and it changed my life. I once thought he might be my soulmate. I once thought he and I would be here together under very different circumstances. I once thought a lot of things about Will.

And I have wasted far too much of my adult life wondering what happened to him.

I might have been able to stop my jaw from hitting the burgundy carpeting, but I can't get a handle on my breathing. This goddamn dress of my mother's is so tight, I can see my chest rising and falling. Will also notices. His eyes drop for a second, and when they come back to mine, he sucks in a jagged breath.

"Mr. Baxter, I see you're booked in one of the cabins this year," Jamie says.

I barely hear him.

Will must not, either, because he doesn't answer. Instead, he dips his head.

"Fern." Will's voice is deep, and my name comes out thick, as if it got caught in tar.

I'm not sure what the right move is here. What the safest move is. Pretending I don't remember him offers me the most protection, but I'm not a very good actor. I've never been sure whether it's unreasonable that I can recall the twenty-four hours I spent with Will so clearly or whether it would be absurd if I didn't.

I tear at the skin on my forearm, and Will tracks the scratching. I press my hands flat against the desk, annoyed he has this effect on me.

"You're here." He says it as if he didn't just string together the two most ironic words in the English language.

I'm here? I'm here? I want to scream back at him. I want to ask him where the hell he's been. It was his idea to meet at the resort. I showed up. He's nine years late.

I open my lips, then close them. I open them again, but nothing comes out.

"Are you okay?" Jamie whispers next to my ear, and I shake my head.

Watermelon, I mouth, hoping he remembers.

"Mr. Baxter," Jamie says, rubbing his hands together. "Ms. Brookbanks has to depart for the evening, I'm afraid. But I'd be pleased to get you settled."

Not meeting Will's eyes, I give his shoulder a nod and edge around the desk.

"I see you're staying in Cabin 20," Jamie says.

Shit. Shit. Shit. Shit.

I charge toward the main doors, keeping my head down. Just before I slip outside, I hear Will call my name, and then I break into a run.

RUNNING FROM WILL BAXTER IS EXHAUSTING. I KNOW, BECAUSE I've spent nine years barreling down this trail. It was supposed to lead far away from him, through some kind of magical mist and enchanted forest, to a land of forgetting. I've fled from the feeling of his finger linked with mine, from the hurt. It used to burn hot and sharp, like a lance through the sternum. Over time it faded to a dull ache. But tonight, there is no escape.

I dart down the flagstone steps in front of the lodge. As soon as I land on the path, my high heels sink into the gravel, and I stumble. I shift my weight onto the balls of my feet, but I can only shuffle a few inches at a time. I left my Birkenstocks in the office. Swearing, I pull off the shoes and grit my teeth against the bite of pebbles. I've been living in the city too long. Whitney and I used to scamper around the property in bare feet all summer.

I get three strides farther when I hear footsteps hurrying down the stairs behind me.

"Fern. Wait."

But I don't wait. I pick up my pace, trip, and go soaring forward. The humiliation hits before the stinging in my palms and knees.

"Are you okay?" Will asks above me.

I rue the day he was born. I rue the people who held each other close nine months before that. I do a lot of rue-ing as I lie there. I press my forehead against the ground and dig my fingers into the stones. Maybe I can burrow my way out of this.

"I'm going to help you up, all right?"

Before I can say no, that it is not all right, that nothing about this is all right, Will takes my arms and pulls me to my feet.

I stall, brushing away bits of dirt and rock, and Will curls down to inspect the damage. His head is a few inches from my own—so close, I can smell his cologne, smoke and leather and something sweet, like burnt caramel. I keep my attention squarely on my legs.

"That looks bad," he says, then runs his finger beside a bloody patch that's already starting to swell. I'm too stunned to do anything but watch.

"It's fine," I snap. When I chance a look at him, he's peering back through the dark hedge of his lashes.

"It's you," he says. He doesn't look surprised to see me.

I straighten, and Will does the same, unfolding himself to his full height.

I stare at his tie. He once said he'd never wear one. I wonder what other parts of the plan he didn't follow through on.

"Are you okay?" he says. "Do you want to sit?" He motions to a log bench that looks over the lake, though it's too dark to make out the far shore. The air smells of freshly cut grass, petunias, and pine—the manicured lawns and gardens around the lodge colliding with the nearby bush. My eyes drift to the docks, where a few local firefighters are setting up for tonight's fireworks display, and I swallow.

I shake my head, my mind spinning. There are a thousand things I've wanted to say to Will, and I can't seem to pick a single one of them.

Will rubs his neck. "You do remember me, right?" His words come out like they're tiptoeing across a tightrope. Five cautious steps.

Remember him? The question is so ridiculous, it's almost funny. It was my mom who saved my life, but it was Will who helped me figure out how to make it my own.

Will picks my shoes up off the ground and takes a step closer to pass them to me, his expression guarded, and the movement jolts me. There are guests everywhere, lying on blankets on the lawn, stretched out on loungers by the beach, waiting for the fireworks to begin, but I don't care.

"Oh, I remember you," I say. The lamplight caresses the high planes of his cheeks, and an image of him from that night, candlelight flickering across his face, flashes in my mind. "And what I'd like to know is what you're doing here."

He blinks at my tone, holding the shoes out between us.

"At *my* resort," I add, snatching the heels. "Did you get the date wrong?"

"No. I—"

"Don't try to tell me this is some kind of coincidence," I say.

"You don't know?" He sounds confused. "I'm here to help," he says, lowering his voice.

"What are you talking about?"

"Your mother didn't tell you? She hired me as a business consultant."

My neck pulls back like a slingshot. "My mother? How do you know my mother?" I hiss, and then I close my eyes. For a moment, I forgot that she's gone.

"I met her here last summer," Will says. "I thought she might have told you. I thought that might be why you're here. She asked for my help with strategic planning and ideas for—"

I wave my shoes to stop him. I'm overwhelmed. I can't focus on the unlikelihood of my mom hiring a consultant, or the even weirder twist of that person being Will. Will, who is here. Will, who came here last summer. Will, who knew my mom. Will, who thought I knew he was coming. Will, who despite all this, still never contacted me. This is all too much.

I take a deep breath so I can address the most important fact. "Will," I say, and his name feels strange on my tongue. "My mother's dead."

"What? No. I just spoke to her . . . it wasn't that long ago," he mutters, more to himself than to me.

"It was a car accident. Back in May." I list the facts like pulling off a Band-Aid, cleanly and with as little attention to their meaning as possible. I explain how the restaurant's ice machine broke during the middle of dinner service, how the bartenders were making do with a dispenser on one of the guest room floors. When someone complained about the constant noise, my mom decided to drive into town herself to bring back a trunk full of ice. It was dark, and I doubt she saw the deer until it crashed through her windshield.

It makes me irrationally angry, how she insisted on doing tasks she could have easily assigned to someone else. In the end, her dedication killed her.

Will runs a palm down his face. He's gone a shade paler. "Are you okay? Of course you're not okay," he says, answering his own question. "You really didn't know I was coming. You're here because you've lost your mom."

I hold out my hands, palms up—it's a gesture of bewilderment, not showmanship. "I own this place now. She left it to me."

Will stares down at me, and I look away. The weeks of waking in the middle of the night and tossing and turning for hours are catching up with me, the exhaustion that's deep in my bones seeping to the surface.

"Fern," he says quietly, gently. He twists the ring on his pinkie. I forgot about the ring-twisting. "I'm so sorry."

The apology slams into my chest like the blunt end of an ax. It's not what I want him to be sorry for. My bottom lip trembles.

He reaches for my arm, and I jerk it back. "Don't."

"Fernie?" Jamie calls from the top of the staircase. "You all right?"

"I'm fine," I say, moving aside to make room for a group heading toward the lodge.

Jamie wishes the guests a good evening and remarks on the excellence of the crab cakes before descending the steps two at a time to join us. He isn't as tall as Will, but Jamie has always been extremely comfortable in his body. He wields it like he's a giant.

"You left your key behind, Mr. Baxter," he says, eyes narrowed, passing it to Will. "And your suitcase, but I'll have it delivered to your cabin."

Will puffs up taller as he takes the keycard. "I appreciate that."

"So you two know each other?" Jamie asks, looking between us.

"No," I say at the same time Will answers, "Yes."

Jamie's eyes drop to my legs. "There's a first aid kit back in the office. Let me clean that up."

"Don't worry about it," I say. "Really, Jamie, I'm fine."

I see the precise moment when the name registers with Will. He blinks twice, and shock washes over his face like a tide coming in.

Jamie crouches in front of me, examining the injury. My eyes dart to Will's. A reflex. But he's watching Jamie, his hands clenched at his sides.

"You sure you're good, Fernie?" Jamie asks, then peers up at me. "I don't like the look of this."

I'm standing between Jamie Pringle and Will Baxter, with bare feet and banged-up knees, less than two months after my mother's death. "Uh-huh," I tell him.

"Not buying it. You're coming with me," Jamie says, standing again. "You can't get anything by me, Fernie," he says into my ear, but I'm sure Will can hear.

I shouldn't feel guilty, but I do. I hate that I do.

Will clears his throat. "I'll leave you two to it, then," he says. "I'm sorry, Fern." He gives me a long look. I think he might say something more, but then he turns down the path.

The first firework explodes overhead with a bang and a fizzle, lighting the treetops. But I don't look up. I stare at Will, walking away from me like he did ten years ago.

You and me in one year, Fern Brookbanks. Don't let me down.

That was the last thing he said.

4

June 14, Ten Years Ago

GUYS WERE ALWAYS SO SLUMPY. THEY LEANED IN DOORWAYS and slouched over cafeteria tables. Jamie often used me as a resting post, his elbow propped on my shoulder. Will was much more vertical.

He was outlining the wing of a plane soaring above the skyline while I pretended to read *The Grid*. I had my notebook on the table, open to the list of things I wanted to do, see, eat, and drink before I went home in little more than a week. Between classes, homework, and shifts, I hadn't made the most of living in Canada's largest city. I was hoping to find a couple of cheap ideas in this week's issue to add to my bucket list, but I'd been staring at the long line of Will's back and the steady grip of his hand around the brush. Mostly I was struck by the upright way he held himself. Definitively unslumpy.

"I can feel your judgment," Will said. "It's extremely loud." He looked over his shoulder, hair falling into his eyes, lips slanted up. "Want to put on some music to drown it out?"

So he was funny *and* hot. I glared, but Will's smile only widened. I'd never seen one as beautiful as his.

"Are you always this toothy?" I asked.

"Are you always this friendly?"

"Pretty much."

He chuckled, and I could feel the sound in my belly, warm and sweet. "I won't take offense, then." He nodded to my iPod on the table. "Music?"

"Sure." He'd found my weak spot in record time. I rubbed the newsprint off my fingers onto my shorts and thumbed through my albums with chipped blue nails, taking a guess at what he'd like. "I've got the new Vampire Weekend. Have you heard it?"

"Is that what you were listening to when you came in? I saw you out on the street earlier."

I cleared my throat, surprised. "Oh, no. That was one of Peter's playlists."

"Your boyfriend?"

I snorted. "Peter's my mom's best friend. Playlists are kind of our thing."

Understatement. Peter and I communicated through music. Mom called it our secret language.

According to her, Peter didn't let a lot of people into his life—we had that in common. From how she told it (and she loved telling it), Mom had elbowed her way in long before I was born.

He didn't know what to make of all my talking, and he didn't know how to ask me to shut up, so after a winter of living at the house, he was stuck with me for life. Confinement—it's how I forced him to be my friend.

I was glad she had. Without Peter, it was just Mom and me. He'd bought me my first set of headphones, and every pair since. We sent each other mix CDs in the mail, and I put them on my iPod.

"What's on it?" Will asked, wandering closer. There was a tiny pin fixed to his collar, the word *surrealist* written on it. I held my screen out and he leaned over, his brush suspended in midair, reading out song titles.

"'Stop Your Crying.' 'I'm Only Happy When It Rains.' 'Road to Nowhere.'" He looked down at me, eyes sparkling. "I think he's trying to tell you something."

"Peter likes a theme." I was impressed Will picked up on it. "He said I sounded cranky the last time we spoke, and this is what he sent me."

"What were you cranky about?"

I shrugged.

"Top secret business?"

"None of *your* business."

Will studied me for a second, his smile unsure. "Let's put it on."

I ducked behind the counter and connected my iPod to the speaker system. Fiona Apple filled the coffee shop. I looked up to find Will watching me. My stomach dipped.

"I love this song," he said. "It's called 'Every Single Night,' right?"

"Mm-hmm." So he was funny and hot *and* had good taste in music. Whatever.

Will returned to the mural, and I went back to my paper.

"What's in that notebook?" he asked after a few minutes. "Are you a writer?"

I crossed my arms over my chest, but I didn't answer.

"Poems? Diary entries? Top secret world domination business?"

"You're a smidge nosy, you know that?"

A bright clap of laughter erupted from him. "A *smidge!*" He glanced over his shoulder, and I tried to glower, but I was smiling harder than I had in months. There weren't many people who could make me smile that June.

When Will had finished the plane, I jumped out of my seat, announcing that I needed coffee. "Do you want one?"

"Yeah, please. That'd be great."

"What's your order?"

"A latte. With a double shot?"

"No problem." I was hoping he'd want something with foam.

I poured hot milk over Will's coffee, angling the cup and wiggling the pitcher in one direction across the surface then dragging it back in the other. Spiritualized played on the speakers. If the café had been full, it would have been perfection. I was in my zone behind the bar—no one paid attention to me there; it was almost as good as walking through the city.

"I'm basically done," Will said, wiping his hands. "I'll let this dry for a bit and then do a varnish coat. It won't take long to apply."

I set the mugs down on a table. "This one's yours. Do you take sugar?"

"Three?" Will grinned. "I have a sweet tooth. It's a problem." Will's coveralls were so baggy, it wasn't obvious what he kept underneath them, but I was certain it was no problem.

He took a seat while I pulled back the cloth covering the milk and sugar station.

"You said three like you wanted four," I said, dropping an extra packet of sugar and a stir stick on the table as I sat down. Will looked up from his drink with an odd expression on his face.

I had a latte art code. I gave most of my customers hearts. Fat hearts. Little hearts sitting atop big hearts. Rings of hearts. Hearts made them feel special. But my favorite customers didn't get hearts.

"A fern from Fern," Will said, his voice low.

I made ferns when someone rippled with joy, or if they seemed sad, or when they complimented the music when I was in charge of the stereo. The day Josh proposed to Sean with his poster, I topped his drink with two fern fronds, their stems joined at the center. I made ferns for my favorite people. I hadn't realized I was making one for Will until I'd finished pouring the milk.

I pushed the sugar closer to Will. "Your coffee's getting cold."

He blinked, then picked up all four packets.

"I'M MOVING BACK HOME RIGHT AFTER CONVOCATION," I told Will after he'd taken his first sip. I ran my fingers over the soft black leather cover of my notebook. It was a gift from Mom before I went away for school—it had refillable pages and a snap closure. *A grown-up journal for my grown-up daughter. I'm so proud of how you've turned things around, pea.* "I've got a bunch of stuff I want to do before I leave, so I've been keeping track. Nothing too exciting."

"That depends on what's on your list," Will said. My eyes followed the slow spread of his smile, catching on a tiny scar below his lip.

"It's a bit of a jumble," I said. "A bunch of it is food. There's a restaurant in the financial district making a twenty-dollar chocolate bar. It sounds douchey, and I'm definitely too broke to blow twenty bucks on candy, but like, what does a twenty-dollar chocolate bar taste like?"

"I have no idea."

I opened the book, scanning the list. "There are some neighborhoods: the Distillery District, the Junction. I haven't been to High Park. Can you believe that? I've lived here for four years." I paused. "Which part of the city did you grow up in?"

Will half cringed. "Right around High Park."

"Shut up."

He held his hands up, laughing. "It's stunning, especially when the cherry blossoms are out in the spring. You should really go."

I threw my pen at him. "I missed blossom season."

"I always thought Toronto would be a boring destination unless you had a local showing you around. All the cool stuff is kind of hidden," Will said, turning an empty sugar packet in his fingers. "Where's home?"

"Muskoka—just outside Huntsville." Muskoka was a large lake district north of the city, and prime cottage country.

"Must be gorgeous there."

I stared at the milky brown puddle in my cup. "It is."

"But . . ."

My eyes rose to his.

"There's no *but*," I lied.

Will's gaze flickered over my face, then down to my fingers scratching at my left wrist.

"So overpriced candy, urban parks . . . what else?"

I recited a few of the bigger attractions.

"The CN Tower?" Will asked. "Isn't that kind of . . ." He smirked, eyes dancing. "Basic?"

"Oh, I see," I said. "You're a snob."

I was about to ask Will what he thought was worth seeing, but I stopped myself. I didn't usually get along with people so quickly, but I was enjoying talking to Will. I was really enjoying his smile. A bit too much for someone who had a boyfriend. I pushed my chair out, collecting our cups and utensils and taking them over to the sink.

Jamie had been a fixture of my summers for as long as I could remember. But the summer I was eighteen, I hadn't seen him coming. Stories of my teenage antics were spread on whispering lips through the resort, and I'd come to dread working the front desk and waiting tables at the restaurant, where too many people knew who I was and what had happened. Mom agreed to assign me to the outfitting hut for the season. So it was me and Jamie down at the docks, schlepping boats and sizing guests for life jackets and paddles.

Jamie was three years older than me, and a relentless flirt. He wasn't a skilled flirt, but he was persistent. With his tan and his matted curls, he had this grimy-surfer thing going on that I didn't hate and an unhurried way of speaking that made him seem either wise or dense, depending on the situation. Unlike some of the other Brookbanks employees, Jamie didn't treat me differently because of my last name or any of the stupid stuff I'd done. When I kissed him at a staff bonfire on the August long weekend, I was as surprised as he was. That was four years earlier, and we'd been together since.

"Want to give me a hand varnishing?" Will said as I washed our mugs. "If we do it together, we can get out of here faster." He twisted his pinkie ring.

"You want me to do your job for you?" I wasn't sure working alongside Will was a good idea.

He walked behind the counter and picked up a tea towel, then began drying one of the cups. "With me," Will said, and my insides swooped.

WILL DEMONSTRATED HOW TO APPLY THE CLEAR COATING IN a crosshatch pattern with a wide brush, starting at the top of the wall and working down. "It's kind of hard to mess up," he assured me.

"Why are you living in Vancouver?" I asked as I covered the mural with gloss.

"I moved out there for school. I just graduated from Emily Carr."

"That's an arts university, right?"

"Yeah, and design."

I pointed my brush at his lapel pin. "Surrealist—is that the style of painting you do?"

"No." He pulled out his collar as though he'd forgotten it was there. "I guess it's kind of an inside joke since my work is fairly literal. My girlfriend gave it to me."

The word *girlfriend* was like a finger prodding between the ribs. I flinched. I couldn't help it.

"Literal how?" I asked, trying to loosen the tight squeeze of envy. I had no business being jealous. I had Jamie.

"I'm an illustrator. Comics, mostly. I dabble with portraiture, but—"

"Dabble! I'm pretty sure *dabble* and *smidge* are related."

Will laughed. "Definitely from the same gene pool."

"Okay, so you *dabble with portraiture*," I said in my haughtiest English accent.

"Cute," Will said. "I had a comic strip in a campus newsletter last semester. My dream is to turn it into a graphic novel."

"You have your own comic?"

He raised one shoulder as if it was no big thing. "Fred was the art director of the newsletter. I had an in."

"Fred?"

"My girlfriend."

Of course his girlfriend was the *art* director of an art school newsletter, and had an awesome, non-plant-based name like Fred.

We finished our sections and shifted farther down the wall.

"You said playlists are your thing—you and this friend of your mom's," Will commented after a while.

"Peter. Yeah, we've been listening to music together since I was little."

Mom got snippy whenever we geeked out in front of her. *If I hear the words* distortion *or* tonality *one more time tonight, you two can find someone else to play cards with.* But I could tell she never meant it.

"That's different. I mean, it's cool," he added. "I don't know my parents' friends well. You and your mom must be super tight."

"My mom and I are . . ." I listened to the swish of Will's brushstrokes, trying to figure out what Mom and I were. Our relationship had been strained throughout my teenage years—I was annoyed by how much she worked and how often I had to cook dinner for myself. Then I read her diary, and I became a human wrecking ball. But I'd spent the last four years at university showing her I was responsible—earning a business degree, same as she did. We spoke every Sunday. We watched *The Good Wife* together, our phones on speaker, while I folded laundry and she did her nails. Alicia Florrick was our hero. "I wouldn't say we're super tight, but we're getting there."

I started painting again. Will hadn't paused to look my way, and I wondered if he knew that made it easier for me to talk. "Peter helped raise me. He says he oversaw my musical education. Mom says it was more like indoctrination."

Peter was the head pâtissier at the resort. When I was a kid, I was his resident taster. He kept a white plastic stool in the pastry kitchen so I could stand beside him, dipping my fork into various tarts and pies, music blaring. Whenever Mom came in, she nagged him to turn it down. *Or better yet, Peter, turn that crap off.* Mom hated our music.

"You make him playlists, too?"

"We go back and forth. Our only rule is there has to be a theme."

"Are you putting one together now?"

"I am." I pressed the brush against the wall with undue force. "The Endings playlist."

Will was quiet for a moment, then said, "Some people might think of this time in their life as the beginning."

"Some might," I said.

"But not you."

I blinked at the mural, and then looked over at Will. He turned my way.

"What I want to know," I said, deflecting, "is how you ended up here of all places."

"Oh, that's just nepotism," Will said. "My mom is friends with the owner. When I mentioned I was coming out here for a visit, she suggested I do a piece."

I imagined having a passion, a parent who supported it, and the freedom to follow it through. "That's so amazing. She obviously really believes in you."

He looked at me, and something about it—the way his eyes held on to mine for three long seconds—snagged in my chest. It was the first time I'd seen him without any trace of merriment. He seemed older. Maybe even a bit tired. The urge to tell a joke, to see a smile bloom on his face, was strange in its intensity.

"She says my desire to draw in boxes and paint on walls lays bare my inner rigidity, and that I have a ruinous case of perfectionism that has no place in the heart of an artist."

My jaw hung open. "Your mother said that? Like, to your face?"

"More than once."

Mom and I had been through a lot. But I couldn't imagine her saying something so cold.

"My mother is an artist," Will said, as if that was an explanation. "A sculptor."

I frowned. "Are all artists mean?"

"Some of them," he said quietly, then cleared his throat. "But I like working within a box. I get off on the limitation."

I heated immediately, palms burning as if I'd pulled baked potatoes from the oven.

"What about you?" he asked. "What gets you going?"

"Me?" I turned to the wall, and then Will leaned over and spoke into my ear, making the hair on my arms stand. "Relax, Fern Brookbanks."

Unlikely.

"Likes: coffee, music, walking." I glanced at Will. "The basics."

"The fundamentals," he corrected. "What was your major?"

"Business management?" I sounded unsure. I felt unsure, even though I'd all but donned my cap and gown.

His eyes skated over me. "That's not what I would have guessed."

I wanted to ask him what he would have guessed, but we'd reached the end of the wall.

"Well, that's it," he announced. "I'll clean up and put everything away, then we can take off." He put his hand out for my brush.

"Do you want help?" I offered.

"Nah, that's okay. I already roped you into varnishing."

I nodded, disappointed. I packed up my things and unhooked my iPod, leaving the café silent except for the sound of Will washing his brushes in the back.

I wandered over to the mural, studying the painting while I

waited, my eyes moving the direction we had worked, finally landing on the plane. My breath caught, and I stepped closer. Will had
varnished this section, so I'd missed it. He'd put a tiny fern frond
on the plane's rudder.

"You gave me a fern on a coffee, so I gave you one on a
plane."

I turned at Will's voice. He was drying his hands on a towel.
"You painted a fern on a wall for me."

"A very small portion of the wall. Do you like it?"

It was the best fern I'd ever seen. I wanted to chisel it out of
the plaster and take it home. "Yeah," I murmured. I loved it.

"So I have an idea," Will said, throwing the towel over his
shoulder. "I thought I could show you some of my favorite spots,
if you're free. Nothing basic, I promise."

I was temporarily speechless.

"I'm going back to Vancouver tomorrow," he said when I
didn't reply. "I've got a mural commission starting Monday—
another coffee shop. I'd be into spending the afternoon walking
around the city."

Hours ago, all I wanted was to get high, make my way home,
and starfish across my bed, but the idea of seeing Will's Toronto
was exciting. Spending more time with Will was exciting. And
that was a problem. Jamie was the only guy I should want to
spend time with.

"So?" Will asked. "What do you think?"

I could feel my heartbeat everywhere—in my lips, my throat—
a heavy thud of warning throughout my body. I looked over my
shoulder at the plane and then back at Will. He was fidgeting with
his ring.

"I'd love to," I told him. Because more than anything, I didn't
want to waste one more moment of my time left in the city.

5

Now

I WAKE UP AT 2:02 A.M. IT'S ALWAYS JUST AFTER TWO—MY IN-
somnia arrives with Swiss precision. Sometimes I open the window
and listen to the breeze in the tree boughs and the lake lapping
against rock, willing myself to doze off. Sometimes I put on a
meditation app and attempt to mindfulness my way back to sleep.
Most often, I lie here in my childhood bedroom, trying to figure
out what the hell I'm going to do with my life.

Tonight, I shift onto my side, then my back, then my stomach, but I can't get comfortable, not when my mind is circling on
the fact that Will Baxter is here, and that my mom met him. My
mom *hired* Will.

I know the resort isn't as busy as it should be, but the idea of
my mother ceding an ounce of power to a consultant doesn't
track unless things are far worse than I guessed. Why did Mom
seek Will's help instead of mine? The possibility that she didn't
believe I was capable bothers me.

Eventually, I text Whitney.

You up?

Unfortunately. Everything OK?

It's one of the perks of my best friend having a five-month-old. Owen is the sweetest little guy, but he's a terror when it comes to sleep.

Do you remember Will Baxter?

Whitney never met him, and at first, I didn't tell her much. She and Jamie were close, and I was afraid she wouldn't approve. But I couldn't not talk about Will.

The Will Baxter from a million years ago? The one you were obsessed with?

Ha ha, I write back.

What about him?

He checked in here today.

In seconds, my phone is vibrating.

"Tell me everything," Whitney says in an excited whisper when I answer, and I can't help but laugh. I feel less stressed already.

I fill Whitney in on the little I know.

"What does he look like?"

"Tall. Dark," I say.

"And handsome?" Her ability to sound so gleeful while whispering is a skill.

"Extremely," I grumble. "And he's staying in Cabin 20."

There are two rows of cabins on the lakeshore. My grandparents built our house, a small board-and-batten home with a gabled roof, at the end of the north path. It's tucked into the woods and directly across from Cabin 20.

"This just gets better." Whitney lets out a squeal. "Mystery Guest!"

I groan.

Mystery Guest is the spy game we invented the summer between sixth and seventh grades. It essentially involved us low-key stalking one of the resort guests, collecting as much information about them as possible. We tracked our findings in a spiral-bound notebook, the words TOP SECRET scrawled on its cover in black marker. Because they were so close to the house, the lucky residents of Cabin 20 were often our unwitting subjects. If Whitney shows up on my doorstep in the morning dressed in a trench coat and holding a pair of binoculars, I won't be surprised.

"Anyway," I say, "I'm supposed to be back to work at Filtr next week, but . . ."

"You can't leave yet. You shouldn't leave at all." Whitney isn't subtle about wanting me to move home for good. She went away to school for her dental hygiene diploma and has been back in Huntsville ever since. "Besides, I'm sure they'll survive without you a little longer. No offense."

Normally, I'd protest—we've had versions of this conversation before—but tonight I know she's right. I've been back to my apartment in Toronto once, just to make sure there were no science experiments growing in the fridge and to ask my neighbor to collect my mail. I miss my things. But I have to stick around at least until I find out what's happening at the resort. I'll call the accountant first thing tomorrow, and after that, I need to talk to Will.

"I spoke to Philippe yesterday," I tell Whitney. "He said to take all the time I need."

Philippe was my boyfriend—that is, until I found him bent over the hat designer from the shop next to our original location. I should have known something was up when he started wearing fedoras. Lesson learned: Dating your boss is always a bad idea.

We broke up two years ago, and I've been on a hiatus from men ever since. Scratch that, I added sex back into the equation after five very long months—it's relationships I have no interest in. All that time and energy and compromise, for what? Dirty man socks lying around my apartment followed by the disappointment of things not working out. No thanks.

"I would have told him to take a biscotti and shove it," Whitney says.

"We don't serve biscotti."

"Then whatever gross vegan hemp energy ball you do serve. You should have left that job a long time ago."

I'm not going into this with her again. Philippe aside, I like what I do. I started working at Filtr when there was only one location. Now we're a little west end espresso empire, and I helped get us there. I have an office on the second floor of our original coffee shop, and when they're slammed, I'll pop down and help behind the counter. The crunch of the grinder, pressing the coffee into the portafilter, the whir of the steamer—I find it soothing. Crunch. Press. Whir. Repeat. There's a singular satisfaction in watching the line dwindle. A task conquered, disorder controlled. It's perfect, except for the fact that I share the office with Philippe. And that it's his empire, not mine.

I've wanted my own place for ages. The fantasy goes like this: I renovate the little mom-and-pop convenience store in my neighborhood, the one the owners will never sell. But this is my fantasy, and they do. It's a red-brick building with big windows on the corner of a leafy residential street. I paint the walls the deepest shade of blue and outfit the space with overstuffed furniture from antiques markets. The orange velvet chair goes in the corner by the window. I hang a community bulletin board and find a gorgeous old bookshelf. I fill it with cookbooks. Instead of Nigella Lawson, I collect ones with recipes for pastries and tarts and pies—*The Violet Bakery Cookbook, Maida Heatter's Book of Great Cookies, New World Sourdough, The Complete Canadian Living Baking Book.* They are a nod to Peter. The shelf of Agatha Christies is a nod to Mom. I spend weeks selecting the music for opening day—songs that are all triumph and joy. The first one I play is Nina Simone's "Feeling Good." My coffee shop is cozy and warm and not at all like Filtr's Scandinavian cool. I name it after myself. I call it Fern's.

I had at least another year of saving before I could cover start-up costs and look for a space to rent, but now everything's changed. If I sell the resort, I'd be able to buy a commercial property outright. I could turn Fern's into a reality, minus my fantasy location. But giving up Brookbanks to bankroll my dream doesn't sit easily with me. The resort has been in the family for more than fifty years. It was my mother's life's work. It's home.

Owen starts crying and Whitney swears. "I thought he'd nodded off," she says. "I should go, Baby."

I growl.

"Sorry, sorry. It slipped out. I'll call you tomorrow."

Realizing how one-sided our conversation has been, I ask, "What about you? Are you okay?"

"Yeah? I mean, as okay as you can be when you're a certified dairy cow functioning on little to no sleep."

"I'm sorry. I get the no sleep part, but not the milk thing. You're a hero."

"You know what's weird? I miss Cam. I see him even more than when I was working, but it's all in service of the baby, you know?"

"How about I babysit for you one evening? I can watch Owen and you two can go out."

"Maybe," she says. "I left Owen with my mom for an afternoon, and it didn't go well."

"Just think about it. I'll take him anytime."

"Does that mean you're staying?"

"Nice try. Good night, Whit."

"'Night, Baby."

She hangs up before I can scold her.

I drag myself out of bed and slump down to the kitchen for a glass of water. As I reach for the switch, I notice a warm yellow glow through the trees—a light is on in Cabin 20.

I creep over to the window. Will's curtains aren't drawn and I can see clear into the living room, but only enough to glimpse the fireplace and coffee table. I lean over the sink to get a better look and laugh at myself—this used to be one of the spots Whitney and I would spy from. I have regressed.

When a figure suddenly appears, it takes me by such surprise, I let out a yelp.

Will raises his hand, but I don't mimic the gesture. He knows this is my house, I realize. He knows it's me in the window. We stand there, looking at the shape of each other.

My breaths come fast and shallow. I'm trying to decide whether I should march over and demand answers, but then he moves out of view and his cabin goes dark.

I return to bed, heart pounding as though I sprinted up the stairs.

It's been a long time since the question of what happened to Will Baxter kept me up at night.

Why didn't he meet me nine years ago like we planned? Why leave me waiting, wondering?

I turn the pillow over, pressing my cheek against the cool side, a whole new set of questions swirling.

Why, after all this time, did he come here last summer? How did he end up talking with my mother? Was he hoping to see me?

It's that final thought that has me lying awake until the chickadees begin to chatter outside my window.

I MUST FALL BACK TO SLEEP IN THE EARLY MORNING, BECAUSE I dream of driving down the highway in my mother's car. It's night and I don't see the deer until it's leaping in front of me. A huge, graceful whitetail. I have no time to swerve, yet I'm not hurt. I topple out of the front seat to see if the animal is injured, but it's not a deer lying bloody on the road—it's Will.

I wake with a jolt. It's light out now, and the chickadees have been joined in their dawn bird song by finches, vireos, and a cawing crow.

By the time I've scrubbed, shaved, and shampooed, I'm still rattled. I haven't dreamed about the accident before. Most of my dreams about Mom are the same warped flashback. I walk into the kitchen and find her wearing an apron—the one with the red apples on it. She's mixing pancake batter, which means it must be Sunday. Sundays are Mom's day off, and sometimes we stay in our pajamas until noon. Mom lets me finish stirring the batter while she melts butter in the cast-iron pan. She tries to make a pancake in the shape of a fern, but it looks like a regular pancake. She tells me to set the table, so I lay out the cutlery and a bottle of maple syrup, then take a seat to wait for her to finish. But Mom doesn't stop cooking. She makes pancake after pancake, and I never get to the part of the dream where she sits down and we eat together.

I throw on a robe and trudge downstairs. Mom isn't in the kitchen wearing her apron with the red apples on it.

Before I make coffee, I call Reggie, the resort's longtime accountant. He began leaving messages about a week after the funeral, gentle prods that he was available and that we should meet sooner rather than later. He picks up on the second ring and agrees to meet, even though it's Sunday.

I pop a green disc into the coffee machine. It's one of those pod contraptions, same as the guest rooms have. I watch as the brown liquid comes out, too hot and too weak, thinking about how it's typical of my mother not to get herself a decent coffee maker. She didn't bother redecorating the house, either. She treated this place as little more than a landing pad—it's pretty much the same as when my grandparents lived here with us. Only the sunroom has been given a face-lift. I don't spend any time in it, though. I'm still not at peace with the memories it stirs up.

Despite her disinterest in home decor, Mom's imprint is everywhere, little hints of the person she was beyond her job. The framed black-and-white photos from the trip she took to Europe just before I was born. The bookshelves, stuffed with Louise Penny novels and paperback mysteries and nineteenth-century British classics.

I'm about to take my first, unsatisfying sip of coffee when I hear a knock. I can tell who it is from the rhythm of the *tap, tap, tap*. Peter's had the same knock forever.

I step onto the porch, not worried that I'm still in my robe. I've known Peter my entire life. My grandparents hired him right out of culinary school—let him stay at the house his first year working here. My bedroom was his. Mom was still in high school then.

Nothing about Peter says baker except perhaps for the softness that's crept in over time. Everything else—the thick fingers, the salt-and-pepper beard, his propensity for plaid and aversion to overt displays of emotion—says retired lumberjack, not creator of sugared pansies and master of sourdough.

"Jamie get you into the dining room last night?" he asks by way of greeting. His voice is gentle, the kind that makes you lean in and listen, but right now my attention is set on the three shoeboxes he's holding. One orange, one red, one black. I haven't seen them for years, but I know exactly what's inside. I look up at Peter, unsteady.

"Where did you get those? I thought she threw them out," I say. It's something I've always felt guilty about. The fire was my fault, not hers.

"She gave them to me for safekeeping," he says. "Figured she'd want you to have them."

"I'm not sure about that."

Peter sets the boxes on the rattan love seat. "They belong with you. And you might want to read them again one day. You're older now—older than Maggie was when she wrote them."

I could argue, but I learned a long time ago that Peter is always right. "Have you read them?"

"No. I figured they were private and that there'd be stuff in there I didn't want to know."

I nod. I used to wish I'd never read them.

"I thought about it," he continues. "I thought it might be like hearing her again."

"Why didn't you?"

"Because Maggie would kill me. She wouldn't want me knowing what was going through her mind back then."

"But you were best friends," I say, though I know secrets are a key ingredient in close friendships.

"Sometimes." What does he mean he and Mom were *some-*

times best friends? He's about to say something else, but then he shakes his head.

"I should get going," he says.

Over his shoulder, I see a golf cart pull up to the cabin beside Will's. The resort has a small fleet of carts that deliver luggage and room service. Years ago, Mom had them re-covered in peppy green and white striped tops. There's a rip in this one. It's something I noticed last week—all the golf cart covers should have been replaced a few seasons ago. I watch a young woman in a hunter green Brookbanks polo and khakis take a silver domed tray from the back.

"Did Mom say anything to you about hiring a consultant?" I ask Peter before he leaves.

"She mentioned bringing someone in a while back, yeah. I'd forgotten with everything." Peter's memory is usually infallible, but he's not himself these days. He's so quiet, I'm not sure anyone else would notice, but he's slightly off. Whenever I've visited him in the pastry kitchen, there's been no music playing— only eerie silence. His sarcastic sense of humor—it's like it left with her.

"Maggie said he was overqualified," Peter says. "Think she was pretty pleased about the deal they struck up."

Before he goes, Peter gives my shoulder a pat. I watch him set off back down the walkway, then I turn my gaze to Cabin 20.

I RAP MY KNUCKLES AGAINST WILL'S DOOR, TAKING STEADY breaths to ease my heart rate. Will caught me off guard last night, but today I'm channeling Mom. I will set the tone.

It's after nine, but it's hard to tell if there's any movement inside Will's cabin. Like the others, Number 20 is postcard cute—

wood sided with dark green awnings. I'm standing at the back, where there's a screened porch facing the bush and the gravel path that leads to the lodge and the beach. I press my nose to the screen, but I can't see whether there's a light on inside.

I knock again, wait a few seconds. Nothing. I'm walking down the set of wooden steps when I hear him.

"Fern?" His voice brushes over my name in a rough rasp.

After Peter left this morning, I blasted my You've Got This playlist while I coaxed my bob into submission and formed a plan. Invite Will over for coffee. Ask him about the scope of the work he agreed to do for my mother. Act professionally. Do not bring up nine years ago. Or ten years ago. But as I stare up at him, the plan gets ripped to pieces and scattered to the wind.

Will is wearing sweats and his hair is mussed, like he just pulled on his T-shirt. His face is shadowed with stubble, and he's squinting as if his eyes are adjusting to daylight. Because they are. Will was clearly sleeping.

He runs his fingers through his hair, and I see a flash of the tattoo on his arm. My heart does a Rockette kick. I follow his hand as it moves from his head to his side, where he shoves it deep into a pocket, and my mouth goes dry.

"I'm sorry," I say with a wince. "I thought you'd be up already."

"I didn't get much sleep last night." His expression is indecipherable.

"Oh," I say as if I hadn't been standing in the window across from him at two a.m. "Was it the bed? The mattresses are supposed to be good."

"It wasn't the bed," Will says.

A beat of silence passes between us. A spark flares to life in my chest, a candle in a dark apartment. I quickly snuff it out, then scramble to get back on track.

"We should talk." I gesture over my shoulder. "I'll make coffee. Meet me on my porch when you're ready?"

Will's eyes drift to the home where I grew up. "I'll be there in ten."

"IT'S TERRIBLE, YOU'RE WELCOME," I SAY, HANDING WILL A MUG and sitting across from him on the rattan love seat. His frame fills the tiny wicker chair. He's combed his hair and changed into proper pants and a white shirt, sleeves rolled, top button undone.

He takes a sip and winces.

"Told you."

"No, it's great," Will says. "Subtle, but great. Thank you."

I take a drink of my own. It's awful. "I don't know what this is, but I don't think you can call it coffee. It's like the suggestion of coffee."

"Mmm," he says. "Very water-forward."

I smile despite myself. I don't want to feel too warmly toward Will. Preferably, I wouldn't feel much of anything at all.

"You put sugar in it," Will says, taking another sip.

I took a chance. Some people change how they doctor their coffee, but a four-packet sugar fiend? I made Will's so sweet, it's essentially blackened simple syrup. I can't tell if he's pleased or surprised or simply making a statement. His face is as blank as an untouched canvas.

I let his comment pass. "So how did my mother come to hire you?" *Of all people*, I don't need to add.

Will smooths his hand down the front of his shirt. "A friend of mine got married here last summer. I considered not coming, but . . . I stayed in the lodge for a week, ate at the restaurant every night, and I spoke with your mom a few times. She was all over this place—it was like there were two of her."

I close my eyes for two seconds, rubbing my chest. It hurts. That she's not here, that he can describe her so perfectly.

"I'm sorry," he says quietly.

I nod and take a beat to collect myself. "You were saying?"

Will searches my face before speaking. "My firm specializes in marketing and rebranding, but I have a soft spot for turning around struggling businesses. Helping them modernize, cut costs, reengineer their growth strategies—whatever they need, really."

I don't know what is more unlikely: that the resort might be in real trouble or that Will is the kind of person who talks about *reengineering* growth strategies. His voice is formal, like he's making a practiced pitch.

He takes a sip of coffee, and I try not to stare at his mouth and the scar beneath it.

"When your mother found out what I do, she had a lot of questions. I offered to have coffee with her, and she told me about some of the challenges she was facing. I made a few suggestions. We emailed a couple of times after I left, and then a few months ago she proposed a deal," Will says. "A four-week stay this summer in one of the cabins for my help."

"Four weeks?" My surprise is audible.

"Right. Your mom wanted to keep my work private, and Cabin 20 is closest to the house."

I do the math on this. A monthlong visit isn't cheap, but I'm guessing from the suit Will rolled up in yesterday, his fee would be exponentially higher.

Will must see the confusion on my face, because he adds, "The deal was based on a significant discount for my services."

"But why? If you're so successful, you must not be short on clients. What's in it for you?"

Will shrugs, looking out at his cabin. The lake lies beyond, glittering through the trees. "I like it here."

It can't just be that, can it? Even if I weren't back at the resort, he must have known I'd find out he was working with my mom and staying here for a month.

"How are you holding up?" Will asks, turning back to me, his voice softer. "It must be difficult. You never wanted this."

When I lay awake last night, I told myself that I'm not the same person I was in my early twenties, and that Will almost certainly isn't, either. But when my eyes shift to his, it's like being pulled into a black hole.

"No," I tell him. "I didn't. But here we are." Will Baxter and me, at Brookbanks Resort.

"Here we are," he murmurs.

For a fleeting moment, I picture leaning my head against his shoulder and feeling his voice vibrate against my cheek when he tells me that everything is going to be okay. It's the exact kind of thinking I need to avoid. I will not fall down the Will Baxter vortex again. There's still a faint purple bruise on my heart from last time.

And right now, it feels as fresh as it did nine years ago. I don't know if it's the kindness in Will's voice, or the fact that he's here and my mother's not, or if the weeks of sleeplessness have finally caught up with me, but I feel raw. Ravaged.

"We were supposed to be here a long time ago," I manage to bite out. Will's eyes return to mine, which sting with tears I refuse to shed. "You could have seen all this before last summer."

"I know."

We watch each other, and I hold my mug with two hands to keep it from shaking.

"Why didn't you?"

He looks away, jaw clenched.

"Did you forget?" I ask. It's not the first time I've wondered if I became a distant memory as soon as Will left me.

He lifts his eyes to mine again. "I didn't forget, Fern." My name sounds rough on Will's tongue. When he speaks again, his voice is low and ragged, its corporate sheen abandoned. "You wouldn't have liked who I was back then anyway."

I blink in surprise. Whatever I thought he'd say, that wasn't it.

Will's gaze is dark with an unspoken apology and I'm about to ask him more when my phone buzzes. Jamie's name lights the screen, and I send him to voicemail, but not before Will sees.

Our eyes meet. And then Will's up and out of his seat, running a hand through his hair. "I've taken up enough of your Sunday," he says, the formal tone slammed back into place.

He sets off down the stairs before I have a chance to reply, to ask him one of the many questions swimming through my mind.

You wouldn't have liked who I was back then.

But then Will turns around and says, "I would like to help. Think about it. You know where to find me if you need me."

I watch him walk toward his cabin, hoping I don't need him at all.

6

June 14, Ten Years Ago

WILL WAS IN THE BATHROOM CHANGING OUT OF HIS COVER-alls when my phone lit up with a text from Jamie.

Let's smoke a j tonight and talk ;)

Can't, I replied. I'm fresh out.

:(

Nine more days and I'll be back. I erased the period and added three exclamation points before pressing send.

How was your visit with Whit?

I sighed. Good? I dunno . . . A bit weird. I'll fill you in later.

I hadn't told Jamie how I was dreading moving back, but he knew everything about my falling-out with Whitney and how precarious our friendship still felt. It was as wobbly as a suspension bridge, one of those ones from a children's book with missing slats and fraying rope, hanging across a gorge. At least I could repair it when I went home.

"That looks intense," Will said, emerging from the hallway.

This was the moment to tell him I was texting with my boyfriend. Instead, I slipped the phone into my bag and said, "It's nothing."

I wasn't a cheater, and I never questioned Jamie's loyalty during our four years of long-distance coupledom. We were one unit in the summer, but otherwise it was mostly phone calls and texts and Skype sessions. But on that day, part of me—and not a small part—wanted to pretend like I wasn't going home. That Jamie and Whitney and my mom weren't waiting for me to say goodbye to this life. I wanted to enjoy myself without dragging Muskoka all the way down to Toronto. I'd be there soon enough.

Will's jeans were scrunched into the top of his boots, and he had on a black T-shirt with a lightweight cardigan overtop that he'd left undone. Out of his coveralls, his body had taken shape. He seemed taller somehow. He was lean, but not skinny. Broad shouldered with a long torso. I pictured him so wrapped up in his art that meals were forgotten or poorly planned—a slapdash PB and J over a kitchen sink filled with dirty dishes at midnight, a shawarma wrap scarfed on the sidewalk in the late afternoon.

"Clever," I said, pointing to Will's T-shirt. The word *sketchy* was written across his chest in a fine white cursive.

"I try not to take myself too seriously."

With the neon pink laces and the work boots, the cardigan and the mess of hair, Will's style was hard to define. It definitely wasn't what I saw on the guys in my lecture halls—who I was certain dressed by a sniff test of whatever lay atop the closest floor heap. Or on Jamie, either.

Jamie was board shorts slung low, flip-flops slapping on the plywood floor of the outfitting hut, curls wrestling with a hunter green bandanna. Bare bronzed skin and muscle and sweat. The first time Jamie visited me in Toronto, he leaned against the Pitman Hall residence security counter in dress pants and a navy wool coat, his hair tucked inside its upturned collar, a bouquet of dahlias in his hand. I walked right by him.

"So, Fern Brookbanks," Will said, hitching an army green backpack onto his shoulders. "Are you ready for the world's greatest tour of Toronto?"

Will wouldn't say where he was taking me, only that we needed to hop on the Queen streetcar for a short ride. Fifteen minutes of standing at the stop, and we were still waiting.

"I don't think the world's greatest anything begins with the Toronto Transit Commission," I said, stepping out into the street to see if I could spot a car in the distance. Griping about public transportation was practically a sport in this city. "I think there's one behind that truck."

Will pulled out a tin of lemon hard candies from his backpack, offering them to me.

"No thanks. For the record, I'm twenty-two, not eighty-two."

Will put one in his mouth and I watched his cheeks hollow around it. "For the record, I am eighty-two," he said. "I may look twenty-two, but that's just diet and exercise."

A handful of people waited with us. An elderly couple sat on the sole bench, hands tightly clasped, a trumpet case by his feet and a cane by hers. As the streetcar pulled up, the man helped the woman to her feet. We followed behind, and when they began to slowly climb the stairs, his hand on her lower back, Will offered to hold the case.

"World's greatest love story," Will said in my ear after he'd handed the instrument back, his breath lemony sweet.

The seats were full, so we moved to the end of the vehicle, stumbling as it lurched forward. Will steadied me by the waist, letting his hand fall almost as soon as he touched me.

"World's greatest staph infection," I said, grabbing a metal pole, and he chuckled.

We swayed against each other, and when we got to Yonge Street, the car half emptied. I pointed to a pair of free seats, taking the one by the window. I was a little over five feet tall—there was plenty of legroom I didn't need—but Will soared past six feet, and the geometry problem meant his knee was pressed against mine. There was a small rip in his jeans that I had a bizarre urge to stick a finger into. Disturbed, I combed my hand through my hair, looking up to find Will watching me.

"What are all these about?" I asked, pulling at the front flap of his backpack, which was decorated in pins and patches, a Canadian flag at its center.

"Most of them are from places I've been." He pinched a miniature electric blue guitar between his thumb and index finger. "Seattle." He tugged on a mushroom. "Amsterdam."

Some were food—a taco from L.A., a plate of poutine from Montreal.

"That one was hard to find. My friend Matty ditched me after a couple of hours of searching. No stamina." My brain sizzled.

The largest was an oval brooch, more old-fashioned than the rest, a lemon embroidered on its face. "What's with this one?"

"Fred made it for me. She's really into needlework and textiles—tapestries mostly. And I like anything lemon flavored."

The summer Jamie and I first hooked up, he'd lob these random questions at me to pass the time at the outfitting hut. I'd be sweeping pine needles off the docks, and he'd be lifting a canoe out of the lake and call out, "What's your favorite water-dwelling animal, Fernie?"

Or, "Fernie: ocean, lake, or pool?"

Or, "If you were one of Peter's desserts, Fernie, which one would you be?"

"I don't know," I'd told him. "I love all the desserts."

He mulled it over all afternoon, then pronounced, "You're a lemon tart. You're a bit sour, Fernie. But in a good way—in the way that makes the sweet taste better."

I stared at Will. "Really?"

"Really," he said. "Ice cream, cake, pie—lemon's always the best."

I cleared my throat and touched a little silver box with a rounded top. "And what's this?"

"That's a lobster trap. It's from a family vacation to Prince Edward Island the summer before my parents split."

"Oh," I said. "I'm sorry."

"Don't be. It was actually a great trip," Will said, though his voice had gone sad.

"And where did you get this one?" I tapped the I ♥ NY button. "It's a little *basic*, don't you think?"

"This is my first one, and it's classic." He traced the outer edge. "Another family trip, before things got really bad between my parents. I was probably ten."

Will was quiet for a second, but then he turned his head. "Got any more salt in that bag of yours to rub into my familial wounds?"

I dug around my tote, pulling out a pack of Doublemint. "I have gum?"

Will laughed. "My parents are better apart anyway. I can't imagine they ever made sense as a couple. My dad's this uptight real estate lawyer who doesn't even pretend to care about art. And my mom lives and breathes her work. They fought a lot. Mom lives in Rome now."

I looked at the tiny Colosseum on Will's backpack. "Italy. That's it so far."

He didn't say anything for a long moment. "I used to visit a couple times a year, for holidays and stuff," he said, squinting into the sun before looking back to me. "But now with visiting my dad and my sister here, it's harder to get over there."

"Are you close with your sister?"

"Yeah. Annabel's three years younger than me, so she was eleven when Mom left. We got along before, but after, it was us against our dad. We're tight."

I straightened the Colosseum. "Do you think she'd ever move back?"

"My mom? No way. She says Toronto's the birthplace of mediocrity, and she needs to be somewhere that inspires her. Her art comes first."

"That must have been hard."

He shrugged and looked at his hands. "I sometimes feel like a selfish asshole for moving away and leaving my sister to deal with Dad by herself."

"Hey," I said, nudging him with my elbow until his eyes found mine. In the sun, I could see they weren't black. They were a deep coffee brown with an ebony ring around the perimeter. "I don't think living your life in Vancouver makes you an asshole. But I only met you today, so I'm sure there's a whole bunch of other stuff that does. Just not that."

Will's gaze darted around my face. "You're sweet."

"I haven't really been anywhere," I said after a moment.

He cocked his head. "I find that surprising."

I copied the gesture. "I'll take that as a compliment. I visited my grandparents in British Columbia once. I didn't make it to Vancouver, though. They're in Victoria."

The four of us lived in the house together until I was about seven, when Grandma and Grandpa moved into a retrofitted apartment in the resort's lodge. After school, I'd find them playing cards in the library among a crowd of white-haired guests, and I'd settle down on the couch in front of the fireplace with my homework. On Fridays, Peter and I would fail to beat them in euchre, and Mom would send over fish and chips from the restaurant. When she finished her rounds in the dining room, she'd join us, a tray with three frosty beer glasses and a Sprite balanced on one hand. We'd all cheer at her arrival, and if there was no one else in the library, she'd lock the doors and kick off her heels, rolling her ankles and cracking her stocking-covered toes.

"What did you think of Victoria?" Will asked. "I've been out to Vancouver Island a few times. Drove up to Tofino with a couple friends last summer. For the record, I can't surf for shit."

"I didn't get outside the city, but I liked it. Beacon Hill Park, Butchart Gardens, the harbor. I'm going out to Banff in November for the ski season to work at one of the resorts."

Jamie and I were looking for a short-term furnished rental, but I was nervous. He was a good long-distance boyfriend, but I didn't know about sharing an apartment with him. I'd seen the state of his bunk in the staff cabins, and the way his hair became a blond nest by the second week of summer.

"Why Banff?"

I pulled at the frayed edge of my shorts. "My mom owns a resort up in Muskoka—it's kind of our family business. So Banff is partly a travel opportunity, but it's also good work experience." When I floated the idea to Mom, hoping to buy a few more months out in the world, I expected her to shoot it down. But she thought some time at one of the bigger hotels would be valuable.

"You grew up at a resort?"

"Uh-huh." I looped a thread around my finger, pulling it tight until the tip turned white. "I'm moving back there in nine days."

Will put his hands over mine, then unraveled the thread. Blood filled my finger. My eyes skidded to his, and he let go.

"When you say it's the family business, does that mean you're going to run it one day?"

"That's the idea."

"But you don't want to."

"No, I do." My voice had gone up an octave, and my lungs felt pinched, like there wasn't enough space for them in my rib cage.

Will leaned a little closer, stealing all the oxygen between us, his gaze hooked on mine. "One great thing about meeting someone you'll likely never see again is that you can tell them anything about yourself without any consequences."

I shook my head. "Everything has a consequence." I learned that when I was seventeen.

7

Now

DOWNTOWN HUNTSVILLE IS CHOKED WITH COTTAGERS AND tourists from May until the trees give up the last of their fall color. Luckily, I find a parking spot large enough to maneuver the Cadillac that Whitney's uncle has loaned me. The thing handles like a cruise ship and smells like dusty potpourri, but I need a car— the resort is twenty minutes outside town—and I don't own one.

When Mom died six weeks ago, Whitney brought me back. By the time Peter called to tell me about the accident, she was already on her way south, baby Owen in tow. In all the years I've lived in Toronto, it's the only time she's braved driving there. She packed my suitcase and took me home, white-knuckling the steering wheel until we were an hour north of the city.

I ring the doorbell of a powder blue house, and Reginald Oswald greets me. He's well past retirement age, wearing suspenders, as always, and a wrinkled checked shirt. Reggie's been the resort's accountant since my grandparents bought the place in the late sixties.

"Rosemary's at church, but she said to give you a big hug."

Reggie does not share his wife's commitment to Sunday service. "How are your grandparents faring? I've been meaning to check in with them."

The flight from Victoria was too much for Grandma Izzy, so Grandpa Gerry came on his own for the funeral. He'd seemed so much older. Small and frail and so unlike the bombastic man I'd known growing up.

"They say they're holding up, but I think they're trying to make me feel better."

The last I spoke with Grandma Izzy, she broke down midway through our conversation. "You just sound so much like her," she'd said.

My grandparents lived on the other side of the country, but Mom was on a first-name basis with the staff members at their retirement community. She knew their events calendar better than they did. She befriended their neighbors' adult children who lived nearby so she had someone with eyes on the ground to check in. She gave Grandma and Grandpa regular reports on everything happening at the resort.

"I expect you to do the same for me when I retire," she used to tell me, and I'd roll my eyes. "Mom, we both know that will never happen."

"I'll call them this afternoon," Reggie says as he leads me down the hallway to his office, the smell of a bacon and eggs breakfast lingering in the air.

Reggie extends his hand at one of the guest chairs. "You a coffee drinker? You might need some for this."

Reggie fixes me a cup and then delivers the news. It isn't good.

"I'll be honest with you, Fern," he says, peering out at me over his wire frames. I'm playing with the hole in my jeans, but my fingers still at Reggie's expression. "Maggie was a smart businesswoman, really turned things around when she took over from your grandparents. But with the tourism business being what it has over the last couple of years, finances are break-even. Your mother stopped taking a salary."

I rub at the spot between my eyebrows. This is so much worse than I could have guessed.

Reggie blows his gin-blossomed nose into a polka-dotted hanky and continues. "Hopefully, this year will be stronger than the last two. Do you know how bookings are heading into fall and winter?"

I shake my head. Jamie said room reservations are flat for July and August, but I don't know what the rest of the year looks like. I don't even know our current percent occupancy. The resort has two conference spaces—the dermatologists are using one of them this week, but have we had any other groups since I've been home? I've been back for more than a month. I should know these things. Even if I end up selling the resort, I need to know the numbers.

My alarm must be clear across my face, because Reggie's expression softens. "Don't be hard on yourself," he says. "You've suffered a terrible loss, and those are some big shoes Maggie left you to fill. I'm here to help in any way I can, when you're ready."

When I finally told Mom I didn't want to work at the resort all those years ago, she stopped talking to me about the business altogether. But Brookbanks was her first love, and over time, she let me back in—asking my opinion about the band she was thinking of hiring for the end-of-summer dance, or a dish she wanted to take off the menu. Would the guests revolt if we lost the fish and chips? (Yes.) Knowing Mom kept the resort's problems from me is sobering. I thought we were closer.

I used to resent how much she worked when I was a kid. I hated every dinner I ate alone, every emergency phone call that pulled her away when we were supposed to have a girls' night. I never wanted to tie myself to work the way she did, but I've been putting in fifty-hour weeks at Filtr. I know what it takes to run a business. I know how much Mom cared about this business. *Stressed* wouldn't begin to describe how she must have felt. The worry would have been constant, gnawing at her from the inside out. My guilt is a lead jacket. While I've helped Philippe make Filtr a success, Brookbanks has floundered. For the first time since my mom died, it really hits me—Brookbanks is mine. Actually mine. Not my mother's.

"I'm ready," I tell Reggie. "Do you have time to get me up to speed now?"

I ask him for a pen and paper, and he digs out a fresh yellow legal pad from his desk. He points out areas where we could cut back and some costly updates Mom delayed to help offset the slowdown. I think of the golf cart covers, and the ice machine that broke down the night of the accident. Jamie said it had been on the fritz for a while.

When we finish hours later, my head is spinning and my hand is cramped from taking pages of notes. I'm supposed to meet Mr. and Mrs. Rose for cocktails at their cabin this evening, but I could use a martini now.

It's clear the restaurant's food costs are too high, but otherwise Mom kept expenditures low and staff hours modest. I'll have to dig into scheduling and our supply orders to see if we can tighten any more. But it's obvious what we really need are more bodies through the door. I'm overwhelmed, but underneath there's a spark of excitement.

I've always been competitive. Before I got kicked off my high school soccer team, I lived for the rush of winning. Brookbanks, I realize, is something I want to win at. Mom may not have asked me for help, but I want to prove to her I can do it.

"Did Mom ever mention hiring a consultant?" I ask Reggie before I duck out to the garden to say hello to Rosemary. She returned from church a while ago.

Reggie takes his glasses off, rubbing the lenses on his shirt. "She did. Couldn't believe the deal he gave her, but Maggie could charm the knickers off a nun." It's true. Mom had a vibrant energy and sense of showmanship that drew people to her. She was naturally chatty, but at home, when she didn't have to be "on," she softened a little.

Reggie chuckles to himself. "Why do you ask? Did he get in touch?"

"He showed up yesterday."

"Well, that's a piece of good luck. I hope you don't take offense to me saying you need reinforcements," Reggie says. "I know you've got a business degree, and Maggie said you were running an impressive operation down there in Toronto."

"Really?"

"Don't look so surprised. She was proud of you. Maggie wouldn't have left the resort in your care unless she believed you could do it."

My throat goes tight. I thank Reggie for his help, blinking away the stinging in my eyes, and escape to the backyard.

I find Rosemary tying tomato vines. She's wearing a yellow sundress and a straw hat, and as she takes me around her vegetable patch, explaining her trick for keeping the slugs off the leaf lettuce, I notice I'm more casually dressed than she is for mucking around in the dirt. Torn jeans and Birkenstocks were probably not appropriate for a business meeting, even if it was with someone I've known my whole life.

If I'm going to get more involved in Brookbanks, then I'm going to need something to wear. My mother's bright shift dresses aren't me, and while ripped denim and cotton tees fit Filtr's mini-

malist sensibility, they're not right for working at the resort. As I
walk to the boutiques on Main Street, I realize that's what I want
to do. Work. Not follow Jamie around aimlessly like I have been,
but actually work. It doesn't mean I'm not going to sell, I tell myself. It doesn't mean I'm staying.

I manage to find more than a few things I don't hate—simple
pieces that don't make me feel squirmy about the weight I've collected on my mom's couch. I've never been a clotheshorse. Jeans,
I'm good with. I know I can rock a camisole. Pushing too far
beyond that tends to stretch my already limited fashion patience.
I used to dig for treasures in secondhand stores, but I have no
time for that anymore.

As I'm heading back to the car, I notice there's a slick record
shop that never used to be here and a guitar store that also serves
food. I've always wanted to learn how to play. I pause in front of
the Splattered Apron, a cute kitchenware shop, and duck inside. I
leave thirty-five bucks poorer. Mom may have been content to sip
watered-down sludge every morning, but I'm not.

Once I get back to the house, I pack up the pod coffee maker
and put my new French press on the counter. It feels monumen-
tal. Even if I'm only here for a short time, I don't have to drink
my coffee like Mom did, and I don't have to run the resort like
her, either.

Then I pick up my phone and call Philippe.

I ARRIVE AT CABIN 15 ALREADY BUZZED. IT FELT GOOD TO QUIT.
Philippe didn't think I'd ever do it, even though he knew I wanted
to open my own place. But Philippe has always been arrogant in
the extreme. From the cotton of his T-shirts (exclusively pima,
always white) to the temperature of the oat milk in his flat white

(135 degrees), he's also picky in the extreme. For a long time, that's what I liked about him. That someone so particular was attracted to me was an ego boost, and mine was dented for years after Will.

"You look good, girlie. You've got a bit more color than you did last week," Mrs. Rose says, holding me at arm's length for inspection.

Mr. and Mrs. Rose have hosted Sunday cocktail hour at Cabin 15 since before I was born. First, it was my grandparents who joined them, then my mother, and now me. Sometimes there's a larger crowd, an assortment of longtime Brookbanks visitors and newbies they've befriended at the horseshoes pit, but otherwise, the ritual is the same: ice-cold gin martinis and plain Ruffles chips on the porch at five p.m.

They never had children, and I'm not sure whether that was by design or just how things worked out, but either way, they give off major kooky grandparent vibes. Mrs. Rose's neck is always draped with so many strands of wooden beads, you'd suspect them of causing her hunched back. Mr. Rose was a theater critic "back when the theater was worth critiquing." I don't think either has eaten a vegetable in their lives, save for the pickled onions in their cocktails.

I was bitter about the guests when I was young, how their needs came before my own, but the Roses were as good as family. Before I left for university, they threw a rowdy wine and cheese party that spilled from their cabin into several others, Mrs. Rose slipping me plastic glasses of chardonnay when my mom wasn't looking. Since I've been home, they've insisted on hosting me for cocktails every week. I think they're checking up on me.

"I've been swimming down at the family dock and taking the kayak out in the morning before the lake gets busy," I tell them.

"I did a few hikes. I was becoming inert." Initially I needed to leave the house and get my blood moving, but I'm enjoying my treks around the property and time at the lake. I didn't appreciate how stunning it is here when I was growing up.

"Glad to hear it," Mr. Rose says. He's standing behind the bar cart, stirring an awfully large pitcher of gin. Grandma Izzy had the cart delivered back in the eighties before the Roses arrived for their annual summer vacation. It's brass with large swooping handles and in no way matches the quaint cottage decor. We all know it as Izzy's Cart, even though Mr. Rose doesn't share bartender privileges.

"I'm relieved to see that you're no longer dressing as a street urchin," says Mrs. Rose.

I've put on a pair of capris and a new cream silk blouse—it's sleeveless with a high halter neckline and open in the back. Cocktail hour is something the Roses *dress* for, although I've never seen them in anything remotely shabby. It's always natty suits for Mr. Rose and swaths of loose-fitting silk for Mrs. Rose. Tonight he's in butter yellow and she's in a turquoise caftan with gold embroidery on the bust and sleeves. I've been showing up in shorts and tanks, and neither has said a word about it until now.

"I went shopping in town today," I tell her, taking my place on the wicker love seat, same as the one at the house, while Mrs. Rose settles into a bamboo rocker. On the coffee table, in addition to the regular paper-towel-lined bowl of chips, is a cheese ball—an honest-to-god, rolled-in-parsley-and-walnuts, old-fashioned cheese ball—surrounded by a ring of Ritz crackers.

I gesture at it. "What's the occasion?"

"We've got company, dear," Mrs. Rose says as Mr. Rose fills a fourth martini glass. He garnishes two of the cocktails with pickled onions and mine with a trio of plump green olives.

"We thought we'd invite your friend," Mr. Rose adds.

"My friend?" I look around the porch. There's no one else here.

"I sent him inside to see if he could repair our TV," says Mrs. Rose. "I don't know what we've done—can't seem to get any picture on the thing."

"Hoy, there he is," Mr. Rose calls as Will appears in the doorway, remote in hand. He's dressed in a navy suit with a crisp white shirt, the top button undone, his hair slicked back like it was last night. My lungs compress.

"Hello," he says with an unreadable glance my way. Actually, it's more than a glance. His eyes catch on mine and then they grow darker, but then he blinks and brings the remote to Mrs. Rose. "All fixed. You just have to press the input button a few times." He shows her on the remote.

"How do you know the Roses?"

"We met last summer, and I bumped into them again this afternoon."

"Take a seat, William." Mr. Rose points at the small slice of cushion next to me, then brings Mrs. Rose and me our drinks. They are full to the brim. "Remind me how you take your martini," he says to Will. "Let me guess. Are you a twist man?"

"I am," he says, sitting beside me.

I watch as Mr. Rose takes a paring knife to the citrus rind, and I can suddenly taste the lemon drop candy in my mouth and feel Will's body, hard muscle and damp skin, pressed to me.

"I hope it's okay I'm here," Will says quietly as Mr. Rose settles into his rocker.

"Of course," I say, trying not to think about the smoky-sweet smell of him and his thigh wedged against mine or the fact that goose bumps have risen on my arms.

Will's eyes expand at the size of the drink Mr. Rose passes over, spilling a little on the table. He doesn't notice, and Will dabs it up with a paper napkin while Mr. Rose isn't looking.

After everything that Reggie told me, I'm almost certain I need Will's help, but could I really work with him? I've been turning the idea over in my mind like puzzle pieces dumped from the box.

We clink our glasses together, and I take a big sip. From the corner of my eye, I see Will inspecting me, his gaze lingering on my shoulder.

"You look nice," he says.

I tuck my hair behind my ears, saying a quiet thanks.

"I was given a strict dress code, too," Will says. "No shorts or sandals allowed."

"There's nothing less appetizing than a man's bare foot," Mrs. Rose pipes up.

"So tell us how you two know each other," Mr. Rose says. My stomach flops, and I raise my glass to my lips.

"Fern and I met ten years ago. I painted a mural at the coffee shop where she worked." I feel Will looking at me, but I keep my sights on the cheese ball as he tells the Roses about our day.

What he doesn't know is how our time together altered the city for me. It's like we left behind an imprint on the places we visited, and now twenty-two-year-old Will and Fern wander around downtown Toronto on a permanent loop in my memory.

"How nice that you kept in touch all this time," Mrs. Rose says, and neither of us corrects her.

"A mural, eh? You don't strike me as an artist," says Mr. Rose, and my eyes dart to Will, an odd protective feeling whirring in my chest.

"I'm not one anymore," he says, his voice flat. "I was never very good. Fern can attest to that."

The Roses look at me. I have so many conflicting emotions about the man sitting beside me, but the most confusing is my need to defend the Will I once knew. He feels separate from this Will. This Will is the one who hurt me; that Will is the one whose drawing still hangs in a frame in my bedroom. That Will is the one I stand up for.

"I thought Will would be a famous illustrator one day. He was *very* good."

I ignore Will's gaze, boring into the side of my face. I supply myself with another dose of gin. His thigh presses against mine, a purposeful nudge, and I splutter into my drink, my cheeks heating.

"At my age, I should know people aren't always who they seem on the surface," says Mr. Rose. "Look at Fern. You wouldn't guess it now, but she gave her mother quite a bit of trouble when she was a teenager. A real mutineer. Got brought home by the police once. Maggie was beside herself—all the guests around to see."

I tense, and Will shifts beside me.

"That wasn't even the worst of it," Mrs. Rose says, oblivious to my discomfort. Just as she's about to go on, Will claps his hands loudly and we all look at him.

"I've already heard this one," he says in a tone that makes it clear he doesn't want to hear it again.

I stare at him, and for a second time, he bumps his leg against mine.

"What about you, William? Get up to any mischief when you were a lad?" Mr. Rose asks.

"The regular—parties, beer, maybe a bit of pot," he says. "I was a pretty boring kid."

"You were *not*," I contradict. Apparently, I'm Young Will Baxter's most vocal advocate. I don't appreciate this stoic, self-deprecating version, even though he looks like a sex dream. I spread a cracker with an orangey wedge of cheese ball, hoping the conversation moves on, but nope. There are three sets of eyes on me. "You were . . . unique." A blush settles on my cheeks.

Will studies me for a second, the skin around his eyes crinkling. There's something reassuring about this hint of a grin. I find myself smiling back.

"I think that day with Fern was the most exciting thing that happened to me." Will looks right at me when he says this, and my mouth falls open.

"Well, if traipsing around Toronto is the most riveting experience of your youth, I hope you've gotten up to more trouble as an adult," Mrs. Rose says, breaking the silence.

"Far less, I'm afraid," Will says, taking a sip of his martini, his expression turned impenetrable. He doesn't sound sad exactly. Maybe a bit wistful? I want to know why. I want to know why this Will Baxter is so different from *my* Will Baxter. He's still the most fascinating person I've ever met, only now he's a complete mystery.

Mrs. Rose clucks. "Young people don't know how to have a good time anymore," she says, then launches into a story about Christopher Plummer, a cast party, and a marriage proposal I'm almost positive never happened.

Soon talk turns to Will's vacation. "What are you going to do to keep yourself busy for four whole weeks?" Mr. Rose wants to know.

"I'll be working most of the time. It's easy to do my job remotely." He looks at me as if to ask permission, and I nod. I don't mind if the Roses know why he's here.

"I was going to do a bit of work with Maggie, help her with some ideas for the resort," Will says. Hearing him call my mom Maggie is jarring. "I hadn't heard the news before I arrived."

"What do you mean, you were 'going to'?" Mrs. Rose asks. Nothing gets by this woman. She lasers her eyes on me. "You need all the help you can get, my dear. And that's not a slight against you."

I know she's right. Only I'm not sure I can keep it together for an entire month. Just sitting beside him makes me want to crawl out of my skin. Or onto his lap.

"And what about that young woman you had with you last summer?" Mr. Rose asks as he tops up our glasses. Will has a girlfriend? A familiar squeeze of envy cinches around my ribs. "What was her name?"

"Jessica," Will tells him with a quick look in my direction.

This is good. This means any possibility of crawling onto his lap has been removed from the equation once and for all. This is great, I tell myself, even though it feels almost cruel that, when Will finally came here, it was with another woman. I take a long sip of my cocktail.

"Jessica, that's right. A real looker, that one." I can feel Will watching me as Mr. Rose makes a little whistling sound through his teeth. "We taught them how to play cribbage," he tells me. I smile in reply, but it must look as false as it feels.

"And where is Jessica? Is she joining you later?" Mrs. Rose asks Will.

"No," he says, and I'm sure I feel his elbow press into my arm, just a little. "We broke up."

DUSK HAS FALLEN WHEN THE ROSES KICK US OUT. WILL AND I amble along the gravel walkway, and each cabin we pass has its own soundtrack—the slap of screen doors, the clatter of dinner dishes, a tumble of dice and a cheer of victory. The house and Cabin 20 are the farthest from the lodge, and as we walk, the woods grow denser. The path is lined with ferns and begonias planted in old logs. It's hard to tell, but I think Will's tipsy. I know I am.

"I think my blood is two parts gin," he says, eyes glimmering in a way they haven't since he arrived.

"That's probably a conservative estimate." I feel buoyant. It's the booze, absolutely. But it's more than that. It's quitting my job and the beautiful summer night and the feeling of taking back some control for the first time since Mom died.

I blame the martinis for allowing me to reach out and touch his arm. "Hey, Will?"

He stops walking.

"Thanks for redirecting Mrs. Rose earlier. It's not my favorite story."

"I know it's not." We watch each other, the lamplight casting Will's face in shadow.

"Did you mean what you said—about that day being the most exciting thing that happened to you?"

"I did," he says. "I don't spend much time in that part of the city, but when I'm downtown, I always think of it."

I blink. "You live in Toronto?" I don't know why I hadn't guessed that before.

"I do," he says slowly.

"For how long?" I ask, my pulse quickening.

Will's eyes dart to the trees. He doesn't want to answer.

"Just tell me."

"A long time."

I stare him down. That's not good enough.

"Almost ten years," he says quietly.

I nod once, but it's mostly for the purpose of making sure my head is still attached to my neck. I didn't think the great ghosting of Fern Brookbanks could get any worse.

"Wow."

"Fern," he says, and I wave my hands, hurt and disappointment rising up my throat.

"Don't."

"Fern."

"Listen, I gotta go. I'm drunk. And you're"—I study him—"too tall."

I leave Will there, on the path, standing among the pines and poplars.

THAT NIGHT, THE DREAM STARTS THE SAME WAY. I CAN SMELL the pancakes before I go downstairs, but when I get to the kitchen, Will is at the stove instead of my mother. He's wearing a dark blue suit, his back turned to me. His hair is past his ears, like it was when he was twenty-two, and when he looks over his shoulder, his face breaks into the most gorgeous smile I've ever seen. I pull him to the table and peel his jacket off slowly. His grin turns wolfish, his eyes hungry. I reduce my speed as I unbutton his shirt, watching him starve, then I press my teeth to the skin over his heart while the pancakes burn.

8

June 14, Ten Years Ago

WILL AND I STOOD IN THE NARROW MOUTH OF A LANE, RAIN-
bow brick walls stretching before us. Graffiti Alley was the city's
most famous display of legally sanctioned street art.

"Have you ever been here?" he asked.

"No." I'd heard about it, but I didn't know the exact location.
"It's basically Frosh Week 101: Don't leave your drink unattended; don't pet the raccoons; don't traipse through alleys, even
beautiful graffiti-covered ones."

"You think it's beautiful?"

I nodded as I looked at the bright orange lettering next to us.
I reached into my tote and pulled out my Ziggy Stardust coin
purse, jiggling it in the air. "I know what would make it even more
beautiful."

Will grinned. "Oh yeah?"

We walked deeper into the lane to where we were wedged
between two buildings. Even in the shade, it was hot. Everything
around us was coated in spray paint—walls, grates, garage doors,

dumpsters. There was a rickety wooden bench that looked as though it were fashioned out of oversized Popsicle sticks covered in swirls of blue and yellow. It was also covered in a crust of dried bird droppings, so we tucked into a corner beside a dumpster, and I lit the joint, inhaling deeply before passing it to Will. He took a long pull, eyes half-closed, hand wrapped over the top of the joint, and I thought it was probably the sexiest thing I'd witnessed.

"So what's so great about Toronto?" he asked when he came up for air.

"What do you mean?" I took a hit before passing it back.

"I get the impression you're not exactly pleased to be leaving."

I leaned my head against the wall and stared up at the runway of clear sky above the alley. I could already feel the pot moseying through my bloodstream, a loosening lull. I was an easy high. I snuck a peek at Will as he inhaled, then I gazed back at the sky, thinking about his question. There was so much I liked about living here, but there was one big reason.

"Back home, everyone knows everything about me," I said, tilting my head toward Will. "In the city, I can disappear."

Will's eyes flickered over me, and my skin went tight. "I find that hard to believe."

I took one last puff and stubbed the joint out on the wall. "There's a freedom that comes with being in the city. I'm no one here."

"And that's a good thing?"

We started walking slowly, the sun in our eyes.

"Yeah. At home, I'm Fern Brookbanks."

Will smirked. "Aren't you Fern Brookbanks here, too?"

"I am, but it doesn't mean anything. Back home, I'm Margaret Brookbanks's daughter." Resort brat. Screwup. Reformed business grad. "I'm making it sound like I'm important, and I'm not. It's more like who I am is already determined—small communities are kind of like that, and the resort is its own tiny empire."

"Got it. You're Princess Fern."

"Ha." I cupped my hand around my forehead, blocking out the glare. "I went through a bit of a . . ." I faltered. I hadn't talked about what happened when I was in high school with anyone other than Jamie in years, not even Whitney.

When I'd read Mom's diary, I'd called her the worst names imaginable. I threw the book across the room at her. I lashed out in the most irresponsible ways for months until I finally ended up in the hospital. An image of Mom sitting beside my cot, her face red from crying, sprang into my mind. I squeezed my eyes shut, willing it away. Things were much better now.

"You all right?" Will asked.

"Yeah. Just lost my train of thought."

"You were saying you went through something."

"I went through a bit of a rebellious phase when I was younger, and none of that stayed secret. There's no privacy up there. I know living at a resort seems like it would be amazing, and sometimes it was. But you try being flagged down to unclog a toilet or give directions to the tennis courts every time you step outside your front door. There are guests everywhere."

I was on a roll now, my hands conducting my list of grievances. "When you're the owner's daughter, you're also staff, whether you like it or not. I've worked there every summer since I was fourteen, plus shifts during the school year. I was cooking dinner for myself by age ten because my mom was hardly ever home. I mean, I guess technically the resort is home, but she worked so much, she was never at the house."

I heard the tone of my voice and grabbed the hem of Will's sweater. "I'm sorry. I'm being a whiny teenager right now. I thought I was over my angsty stage."

"Angst away," Will said. "I think that's the most you've spoken all day." He spun so he was facing me and started walking backward, opening his arms. "Paint me a picture of tortured teenage Fern."

I shoved his shoulder. "It wasn't all bad. The lake is stunning. If you're outdoorsy, there's tons of stuff to do—canoes, kayaks, hiking trails. The lodge was built more than a hundred years ago, so the whole place feels like it's from another era, which is pretty cool."

"I'd love to see it," Will said. "I've never been anywhere like that. I've gone to friends' cottages, but when my family traveled, it was usually outside of Ontario."

I made a face. I used to find it annoying when Mom complained that people didn't appreciate our own province. But then I moved to Toronto and met so many people like Will, who had the opportunity to travel but went farther afield without exploring home.

The alley had opened to a small parking lot in full sun. Heat wafted off the pavement. Will dropped his backpack on the ground and shrugged off his cardigan.

"I didn't really get the whole outdoors thing until I moved out West. The level of natural beauty in British Columbia is so absurd," he said, folding his sweater and putting it into his backpack. I wiped sweat from the back of my neck, unable to look away. "The first time I took my bike to Stanley Park, I rode around the seawall literally laughing out loud. I couldn't get over all the different shades of green. I'm still not used to it."

I murmured something to show I was paying attention, but

the thing I was paying attention to was Will's body. He had been completely covered, and now there was skin. Skin that stretched over lean muscle and ran under the sleeve of his T-shirt. There were moles and veins and elbows and creases.

Will closed his backpack and slung it over one shoulder. It caught on the hem of his shirt, flashing a small triangle of flesh at his hip.

The joint had been a bad idea. I should have known that. Pot made me feel like liquefied candle wax, hot and runny. My fingers had already started tingling.

Before Jamie, I'd had sex two times with two different guys. Neither experience had been good. I told Jamie I wanted to take things slow, so we waited until our second summer together, and then spent May to August with our hands all over each other, sneaking quickies between shifts—fooling around in his bunk, darting behind trees, racing up to my bedroom. More than once, we hung a BACK IN FIVE MINUTES sign on the outfitting hut door. Sex with Jamie was fun and silly, and after we figured each other out, it felt so much better than I thought possible.

Leaving for university in September after four months of nonstop screwing was like being denied fresh water after living beside an Alpine spring. Phone sex was his suggestion. The first time, I lay on my bed, staring at the crack in my apartment ceiling, trying not to laugh. Not surprisingly, Jamie took to dirty talk with gusto. I kept apologizing and he kept telling me to relax. Eventually I did, but not enough to come. "I've got an idea," Jamie said once he'd finished.

Even though joints were as common as cigarettes on any given night out in Toronto, I'd been wary. I was a new Fern— one who made smart choices. But Jamie assured me a little weed wouldn't cause me to lose control and hooked me up with a buddy who dealt downtown. The next time we tried, I got high first. Pot made it so I could say words like *lick* and *wet* and mean them, but it also turned my insides to warm honey. Phone sex became our thing.

Will ran his hand through his hair, and I followed the movement as if it were happening in slow motion. There was a smudge of paint on the inside of his right arm, and beside that a line of black ink. Desire hit me in a rush. Jamie made me feel good, but I'd never felt such a singular bolt of want.

Will gave me a funny look. "What's up?"

I swallowed. My tongue had turned velvet. "There's a smudge of paint on your arm."

He twisted his elbow, revealing more of the tattoo. "So there is. It must have come off my coveralls." The tingle was spreading, transforming into a low pulse. Will glanced at me, catching my stare.

"Is that a tree?" I asked, pointing to his tattoo. (It was obviously a tree.)

"Yeah." He hiked up his sleeve. A spindly evergreen grew from elbow to armpit on the underside of his arm. "I got it a couple years ago. I guess it's kind of a cliché."

"How so?"

Will gave me a lazy smile. Will, I realized, was high. "Well, I went to Emily Carr."

"I've heard."

"Emily Carr is an arts school," he said. "And she was also one of this country's most important painters, may she rest."

I laughed. "Tell me more, Dalí."

"The lone tree was a common motif in Carr's work, so it's almost like getting a tattoo of the school logo. But there's something so majestic about firs. It's what I love most about Vancouver—how nature and the city collide."

I leaned in to get a closer look. Most of the tattoos I'd seen were the kind picked out of a binder, but Will's was unique. It was obviously a custom piece—the shading was so delicate.

"Well, it's a very nice cliché," I said, peering up at Will to find him peering down at me. We stared at each other for what was probably a second, but it felt like minutes, until a siren's wail startled us.

"I guess that means you prefer my illustrations to my murals," Will said, tugging his sleeve down.

"You drew that?" I dug a bottle of water from my tote bag, draining half, then offered the rest to Will. He tipped his head back and closed his eyes to the sun, his throat moving as he swallowed. A drop of water ran from the corner of his mouth. I was stalking its path down his chin like a leopard when I felt my phone vibrate.

I frowned at the screen. Jamie didn't call unless we'd planned to "talk" ahead of time.

"Sorry, I'm going to take this," I told Will, moving a few steps away.

"Hey," I said to Jamie. "Is everything okay?"

A chuckle filled the other end of the line.

"Of course it is. I'm about to take a couple kids on a canoe tour of Smoke." Jamie dropped his voice. "I missed you, Fernie. I wanted to hear your voice for a sec. It's been a while."

My stomach sank. "I know. It was tricky with Whitney here," I said, though we both knew it had been longer than that. We'd spoken a handful of times since school finished—calls that were little more than sex. I couldn't let Jamie know how miserable I was about coming home, which made me even more miserable. No matter how I spun it, the underlying message would always be: *Hey, babe, I don't want to come home, even if it means spending the summer with you. No offense! It's just that the idea of working at the resort for the rest of my life makes me want to tear the skin off my arms. Don't take it personally, but it's a little awkward that you love my family business more than I do.*

I knew what I really wanted would be a stick of dynamite in our relationship. I hated keeping things from Jamie, so I'd started avoiding him instead.

"Whit told me you seemed off," Jamie said.

That stung. I thought I'd done a very good job of seeming on. "She did?"

"In a text. You said your visit was weird?"

I watched Will. He was typing something on his phone.

"Yeah, it was weird. I feel like she doesn't get me sometimes, you know? She thinks I'm going to come home, and everything will be like it was when we were twelve, but we're different people now." Whitney never wanted to talk about what happened in high school. She pretended that we never had that massive fight, that we hadn't begun drifting apart years before that when she started dating Cam. "I feel like she doesn't trust me." I saw the way she eyed my drink when I ordered a second at the bar last night, but she didn't have to worry. I rarely had more than two these days.

"You're overthinking it, Fernie. Give that brain of yours a rest. Once you get back here, you'll see—there's nothing to worry about. You and Whit are going to be buds your whole lives."

I sighed. "I hope so."

Will put his phone away and wandered over to a school of fish painted on the side of a three-story building.

"I've gotta go," Jamie said. "Love you."

"Love you, too."

I watched Will from a safe distance. His back was turned to me, his hands resting on his head.

Four years had passed without me being interested in anyone

but Jamie. I'd flirted a little. I'd danced with guys, but I drew the line at letting them buy me a drink. And I'd withstood constant teasing about being in a long-distance relationship with someone I'd known since childhood.

"You are never going to be hotter," Ayla lectured me once. We'd met in our first-year macroeconomics class, and she was my closest friend in the city. "You are wasting your prime years." Then she met Jamie. He won her over within thirty minutes after he suggested a karaoke bar as the evening's entertainment. When he pulled out his Alanis (a banging "You Oughta Know"), she was a goner. The night ended with Ayla dragging us back to her apartment and the two of them singing Nelly Furtado songs neither could remember the lyrics to.

Jamie was twined around every part of my life. I thought I wanted him to stay that way forever.

"Everything all right?" Will asked when I walked over.

"Fine. It was just a friend."

I looked at Will's profile for a long time. I was stoned, I had zero shame, and I had a theory. I let my eyes run across the hard line of his cheek and jaw. I perused his arms and down his torso. When I got back up to his neck, it was pink. This tingly thing I felt for Will, it was purely physical. I was sure of it.

"What's Fred like?" I asked.

Will's nose scrunched. "Fred?"

"Yeah." I moved toward the alley. There was more ground to cover. "Sensitive topic?"

"No," Will said, following. "Of course not. Fred . . ." He paused. "Fred's specific. There's no one like her." He laughed. "She makes sure of it. If everyone was going through the front door, Fred would be searching for a side entrance. She comes at everything her own way."

I tipped my head down so I could roll my eyes.

Will told me all about Fred. Fred had a tapestry hanging in a gallery in Gastown. The tapestry was called *Curse* and wove together the pain, power, and fecundity of menstruation. Fred had committed to an all-red wardrobe while working on the tapestry senior year. Fred's ideas were bottomless. For example, Fred came up with the theme of "failure" for their newsletter's graduation issue and helped track down Emily Carr alumni to share their biggest flops.

Fred sounds like she takes herself pretty seriously, I thought. "She sounds fun," I said. "How long have you been together?"

"About five months."

That's it? The words almost left my lips.

"What?" Will said.

"Nothing."

"No, come on. You've got a look on your face."

"I don't."

"You do." He pointed to my mouth, and we both stopped walking. "You have a smidge of a look."

"Well, now I do. But only because you said *smidge*."

"You weren't judging the length of my relationship?"

I put my hand on my chest. "Nope, not at all."

I didn't love that I was jealous of Fred, but so what if I was? Will was stupid hot. That was it. There wasn't anything else going on here.

Will arched down to meet my gaze, his eyes shimmering. "Liar."

9

Now

"WHAT DO YOU MEAN, YOU HAVEN'T GOOGLED HIM?" WHITNEY waves a diaper in the air.

I've convinced her to let me babysit Owen while she and Cam have a date night. It's only dinner at the Brookbanks restaurant, and the plan is for them to leave the baby with me at the house while they enjoy some alone time, but I still haven't managed to get them out the door.

They've set up Owen's travel crib, explained the ins and outs of bottle feeding, given me a detailed description of his diaper rash, and handed me a printout of Owen FAQs. She's tried to make it funny—with headings like, *Oh shit, he pooped! Now what?*—but it still borders on obnoxious. It's also completely unlike Whitney.

I look at her, kneeling over Owen, who's wriggling on the couch sans diaper. She's wearing a magenta wrap dress that has a discreet panel in the front for breastfeeding. Her boobs are huge. There's a thin band of sweat around her hairline—the strands by her temple are short, wispy bits that she's been complaining about.

Apparently you lose hair after having a baby and that's what grows back. Parenthood is changing her in ways I hadn't noticed, probably in ways she hasn't, either.

"You know how I feel about creeping on people online," I say, rummaging in the diaper bag for wipes. I haven't diapered a baby before, but how hard can it be? "Let me do that, Whit. You're going to be late for your reservation."

"Quit changing the subject," Whitney says, looking at the package in my hand. "You don't need wipes when it's just a little pee."

She finishes wrapping Owen's bottom and gets off the floor, picking him up with the swift competence of someone who's done it hundreds of times, which she has—Whitney is a mom. I knew it before, but not the way I know it now, in this moment. We haven't lived in the same place since high school. There's so much we've missed along the way to becoming adults.

"So you've never looked him up?" Whitney says. "Not even back then?"

"Not really." This is completely false.

"You're going to hand over the future of the resort to him, and you haven't so much as searched to see if his business is legit?" She looks to Cam for backup, but he shrugs one blocky shoulder. He's a few inches taller than Whitney and has arms that belong in a firefighter calendar.

The two of them have been inseparable since we were fifteen. Cam had been a twerp in elementary school, but the summer between ninth and tenth grades was kind to him, and it was impossible not to notice Whitney noticing him when school started up in the fall. Cam had his yearslong crush right where he wanted, and I remember how he asked her to the winter formal as if it was a dare, his chin lifted in challenge. Whitney couldn't resist a dare.

Now he's a counselor at our old high school, and he's such a steady, kindhearted person that I bet he's great at his job. I know Whitney's good at hers. She's the most passionate dental hygienist anywhere, without question.

"I didn't agree to anything, and I may have done a quick search years ago. But that's it."

I made the mistake of googling Will yesterday, but I haven't seen him in the flesh since Sunday cocktails with the Roses. That was three days ago, and I've been dodging him ever since. I'm a little surprised he hasn't just packed his things and left.

I've spent most of my time with Jamie, getting up to speed. I even made it into the dining room. I could feel eyes on me as soon as I entered, and I wanted to vaporize, but I did it. It's become apparent how much Jamie has protected me from while I've made my way through the murky haze of grief.

Now when I'm awake in the middle of the night, I tiptoe to my bedroom window and look at the soft glow coming from Cabin 20. I'm not the only insomniac around here. I stare at that square of light through the trees and wonder if I could survive even an hour working alongside Will. Because the more I learn about the resort, the more I can't deny we need his help.

Whitney passes the baby to Cam, who immediately starts shifting his weight from side to side, making funny faces as he sways. Ever since Owen started laughing, his parents have become obsessed with getting giggles from him. He's a gorgeous baby, with Cam's dark brown skin and Whitney's wide eyes.

Whitney roots around her purse and pulls out her phone, tapping the screen.

"This him?" She holds it up to my face. It's a headshot of Will—his hair is smoothed back and he's wearing a jacket and tie. I've studied every pixel of the image already. The thick lashes, the black-brown eyes, the bow of his top lip, the strong line of his jaw, and the long one of his nose. He is ridiculously attractive.

"I'll take it from the way your pupils swelled that it is," Whitney says.

She points the photo at Cam, who gives it a quick glance and then does a double take, pressing his glasses almost right to the screen.

"Shit," he says. "Nice work, Baby."

"Cam, for the love of god, do not call me that," I say. "And what do you mean, *nice work?*"

"You hooked up with him, right?"

"No," Whitney and I reply in stereo.

Cam frowns. "Wait, you're not sleeping with him? Why do we care about this guy again?"

"Because he made Baby fall in love with him, and then he left her brokenhearted. Keep up, Camden."

"Oh, this is the guy you dumped Jamie for?" Cam asks.

"I didn't dump Jamie," I snap. I hate that these two think the breakup was my doing. The four of us hung out during the summer when Jamie and I dated, but Cam and Jamie kept in touch. They're close friends now.

"Technically," he says. "But you forced his hand."

I glower at Cam as Whitney begins reading from the website.

" 'William Baxter is a partner at Baxter-Lee.' Blah, blah, boring, boring. 'He specializes in strategic branding and marketing and was named one of 2019's "Most Exciting New Visionaries" by *Canadian Business*. William holds a Bachelor of Fine Arts from Emily Carr University and an MBA from the Rotman School of Management.' "

Whitney's eyes pop as she scrolls. This is what I was afraid of.

"I think Will might be some kind of socialite," she says. "There are photos of him at parties and on red carpets."

She returns to the screen with the same determined look she had when we used to play Mystery Guest.

"Give me that," I say, grabbing the phone. I intend to turn it off and pass it to Cam for safekeeping, but my eyes get stuck on the photo that fills the screen. I've seen this one, too. It's of Will, dressed in a tux, his arm wrapped around a woman who's wearing an emerald green gown. She's horribly pretty. She has hair as dark as his, but hers falls in soft, hot-tool-aided waves past her shoulders. He broods at the camera; she beams at it with white-white, straight-straight teeth and the kind of plush pink lips the word *pillowy* was invented to describe.

"She's in a lot of them," Whitney says. "Jessica Rashad. One of the captions said she's an art collector and philanthropist. Doesn't that just mean she's rich?" Her eyes go even bigger, brightening like fog lights. "Let's look her up!"

"Nope. You are officially cut off," I say, trying to act like it doesn't bother me that Will's ex is as hot as a Jonas Brothers wife. "It's time for you two to hand me that baby and get out of here."

I give the phone to Cam to be safe and extract Owen from his arms. My friends look at each other, faces screwed up with concern.

"Seriously, we'll be fine." I tap Owen on the nose and he gives me a gummy grin. I raise my eyebrows at Whitney, a silent *I told you so*. "And don't rush back. Have a cocktail. Order dessert," I say, though I give them an hour before they return.

They apply a smattering of kisses to Owen's head and then, finally, say goodbye. I watch them leave from the porch, holding up the baby's chubby arm, waving as they go.

It takes all of fifteen minutes before Owen starts to scream.

I HAVE DONE EVERYTHING. I CHANGED OWEN'S DIRTY DIAPER. Tried giving him a bottle. Bounced him on my knee. I made funny faces. I sang an electric rendition of "There's a Hole in My

Bucket." But the kid won't stop wailing. I'm worried he's going to make himself sick. And I'm no longer wearing pants, having spilled milk all over both Owen and me.

"Owen, honey. Please, please, please stop crying," I beg as I walk him around the living room on the verge of sobbing myself.

I'm not usually a crier, but after Mom died, it was like someone installed a leaky faucet behind my eyelids.

Something fundamental shifted between us when I told Mom I didn't want to go into the family business. I felt guilty, but I also felt free. Mom couldn't understand why I'd want to live paycheck to paycheck in Toronto when I could come home and earn a real salary. We had our weekly call every Sunday, but we often spent it arguing. By the time I became a manager at Filtr six years ago, I thought she'd resigned herself to my living in the city. We'd stopped fighting. She visited to take me to lunch and was impressed by how busy our flagship location was.

When Philippe and I started dating, I could tell she was suspicious. "He seems very pleased with himself," she'd said. It was an apt description, but I figured he had a lot to be pleased about: a successful business, visible abdominal muscles, a fantastic condo in a converted church. She told me to be careful.

It was a Sunday when I found him with the hat designer. He and I had spent the afternoon in the office, reviewing renovation plans for our third location, and while I often stayed at his place, he said he needed Sunday evenings to himself for "restorative care." That worked for me. I had my own routine. First groceries, then my call with Mom. I had just stepped onto the streetcar when I realized I'd forgotten my phone. To say I was surprised to find Philippe folding someone over my desk is an understatement. I was still in shock when Mom called, and I spilled the whole story—the most I'd ever divulged to her about my love life.

She showed up at my apartment the next day with a small

suitcase I didn't know she owned and a loaf of Peter's sourdough. She stayed three nights, the longest time we'd spent together in years outside of Christmas. She didn't ask questions. Didn't press me on whether I had an inkling he'd been cheating. I suspected she was working up to telling me to come home, to come work at Brookbanks. But she didn't do that, either. We watched a lot of Netflix and ate a lot of bread. When she hugged me goodbye, I didn't want her to go. And when I told her I was going to miss her, I felt something shift again, an easing of tension. We were closer in that moment than we had been in the one before it.

She died two years later.

It feels like I lost her just as we'd begun to find each other. I've mourned my memories of Mom. The way she would sneak into my room and kiss me good night after returning from the lodge, thinking I was asleep when all the while I'd been waiting for her. The crisp fall mornings when things got a tiny bit slower and she'd wake me early to sit with her by the water while she drank her coffee. The way she introduced me as My Fern. Her pancakes. She was adamant about making them with buttermilk, though we never had any in the house. She'd mix lemon juice into milk so it soured instead. But I've also mourned the future we'll never have, the relationship we were only starting to make solid.

I got so sick of crying—the stinging eyes, the stuffy nose, the feeling that I'd never be able to stop—that I tried cutting myself off a couple weeks after the funeral. I've slipped a few times, but now, trying to soothe an inconsolable five-month-old, I fall off the wagon. Hard.

The knock is almost imperceptible through the cacophony that is Owen. I stop shushing, and there it is again. Whitney and Cam must have cut their evening short. I'm so relieved, I don't care if I've completely failed as a babysitter.

But it's not Whitney and Cam I see when I open the door. It's Will.

I couldn't say what it is about him that muddles my brain. The blue jeans and faded gray T-shirt. The sheer length of him. The fact that he's here at all. But if I had to pick, it might be the hair. It's shorter than it was back then, but seeing it like this, messy and unstyled, lying in a black stripe across his forehead, makes me feel like I'm twenty-two again.

"I'm here for the ritualistic infant sacrifice. Eight p.m., right?" Will says while I blink at him, Owen wiggling hotly in the crook of my arm.

I picture how we must look to Will: both puffy-eyed and tearstained. The baby is naked except for his diaper. My nose is running. I'm not wearing a bra or pants, and my gray tank top is speckled with my best friend's breast milk.

"You heard the crying?" I ask, trying to sound as if I were, in fact, wearing pants and not in the midst of spectacularly losing my shit. I'm grateful Will keeps his eyes on my face.

"I think they can hear the crying in Alaska."

"I'm sorry." I raise my voice over Owen's vocal pyrotechnics. "I'll close the windows."

"Actually," Will says, "I was coming to see if I could help."

"With the baby?" From the disbelief in my voice, I might as well have asked, *With the infant sacrifice?*

"Yeah. I know a thing or two."

The smart thing to do in this situation is lie, to tell Will I've got things under control, then politely ask him to leave.

"So," Will says, "can I come in?"

But the reality is that Owen has been out of his mind for at least twenty minutes, and I'm desperate. I hold the door open with my hip.

As soon as Will's inside, I know I've made a mistake. He stands across from me in the hallway, and there is just so much of him so close to me. He's brought his burnt sugar smell in with him, and when he leans down to Owen, I see the spray of freckles across the tops of his cheeks. I've imagined alternate endings of the day we spent together so many times, it's shameful, but nothing has taken me back there so quickly as having Will Baxter in my home. Humiliation and desire hit me in equal measure.

Will puts his hand on my elbow.

"Why don't you let me take . . ." He pauses.

"Owen."

He squeezes Owen's foot. "Why don't you let me take Owen, and you can get dressed?" He looks up at me, and the mischief in his eyes almost makes me gasp. It's the first glimpse I've had of the old Will. "Unless you two have some kind of pants-free policy going on here."

"I spilled the milk," I whisper. "On both of us."

"I won't tell," he says. I shift Owen into his arms, and he lays him on his shoulder in one easy movement.

"The living room is to the left," I say. There's no way I'm leading him there. My underwear has MONDAY written across the backside under a picture of Little Miss Grumpy. Plus, it's Wednesday.

Upstairs, I splash cold water on my face, thankful I'm not wearing makeup and that my cheeks don't have mascara tracks on them. I run a brush through my hair, swipe on deodorant, and throw on a bra, a clean tank top, and a pair of denim shorts. I give myself a once-over in the mirror.

When I come downstairs, Owen's cradled in Will's arms, looking up at him quietly while Will sings. I watch from the landing. Owen is now dressed in a turquoise sleeper, and Will, I realize, is serenading him with "Closing Time," the song that ended every single elementary school dance I attended. When he's done, he lifts the baby to his face, and Owen, the little menace, laughs.

"The undeniable power of Semisonic—works on grade-seven girls and babies," I say, moving closer, and Will turns around. He takes me in, clocking my outfit.

"What?"

Will shakes his head. "I kissed Catherine Reyes dancing to this song."

I laugh despite myself. "I kissed Justin Tremblay." I give Owen a rub on his head. "How did you tame this dragon? Nothing I did worked." I glance up at Will, and there's so much warmth in his eyes, I take a step back. And then it dawns on me. "Oh. Do you have one?"

"A kid? No." He sounds startled.

"You don't want them?"

"No." He pauses. "I don't know. What about you?"

"I've got five," I deadpan. "Owen's the youngest."

I'm rewarded with a miniature smile for that. Will peers down at the baby. "I saw you waving goodbye to a couple who I'm guessing are his parents."

"My best friend, Whitney, and her husband." I scan Will's face for a sign that he recalls the name, but I get nothing. "It's the first time I've babysat. Clearly."

Owen lets out a well-timed squawk and shoves a fist into his mouth.

"Did you manage to feed him?" Will asks, twisting his upper body around to soothe Owen. "I think he's hungry."

"I tried, but he didn't stop crying. I couldn't really get him to drink. We can give it another go."

I warm up the milk in the kitchen, and when I return, Will and Owen are snuggled in the armchair, a cloth bib around Owen's neck. I hadn't thought of a bib earlier. Will reaches for the bottle.

"I can do it," he says. "Unless you want to."

"Be my guest." I fold myself onto the sofa.

"Hungry guy," Will says as Owen begins glugging away happily. I watch, astonished. Will looks up at me, and there's no way he doesn't see my shock, but he offers no explanation for his expert baby handling.

Owen starts to squirm and Will sits him up, patting him gently on the back until he makes an outrageously loud Homer Simpson burp, then slumps in Will's hands.

When the bottle is drained, Will burps the baby again, wipes his chin, and takes him to the travel crib in the corner of the room, setting him down gently. Owen doesn't make a peep.

"Is there another room we can sit in?" Will whispers, surprising me. I assumed he'd leave. "Unless you'd prefer for me to go?"

"Stay," I tell him. "If he wakes, I'll need backup."

I LEAD WILL INTO THE KITCHEN. THE SHOEBOXES OF MOM'S diaries are still on the table, exactly where they have sat, unopened, since Peter gave them to me. I take a bottle of white wine out of the fridge, holding it up to him in question. He nods and taps a finger against Whitney's babysitting FAQs, which lie on the counter.

"What's this?"

"Proof my friend doesn't trust me with her infant son?" I pour the wine. "No idea why she'd feel that way."

Will reads from the sheet of paper. "Owen's favorite lullabies are 'Edelweiss' and 'What a Wonderful World.'" He glances at me. "Advanced."

"I'm convinced the doctors gave Whitney a personality transplant when the baby came out of her."

He studies the page, the lines on his forehead deepening. "Parenthood can really fuck with you." It's a forceful statement coming from someone who's reportedly not a parent.

"This is nice," he says as we pass through the sunroom that Mom used as her office. I don't like coming in here, but there's no way to get to the back without going through it. "It's so modern," he says as I slide open the glass door to the deck.

"Yeah," I say quietly. "This part was rebuilt."

Will's gaze finds mine, and I can see him connecting dots. I don't want to think about that night, or all the extra shifts I took so I could help cover the repair costs.

Recognition ripples in Will's eyes, but all he says is, "Oh." I tilt my head, gesturing for him to step outside.

The deck faces the bush so there's no lake view, but I've always liked how private it feels, how you can't see any of the guest cabins. I leave the door open so we can hear Owen and settle into one of the chairs.

"You really seem to know your way around a diaper bag," I say. "You sure you don't have a baby at home?"

Will freezes, holding his glass halfway to his mouth. He stares into his wine, and then slowly sets his glass down.

"I have a niece. My sister has a daughter," he says after a second. His voice is clipped, like it costs him something to share this information.

"Did she have her recently?"

"No."

Will drops his gaze to his wine, his jaw tight. I can almost see the wall he's erected.

I want to shake him. I want to yell, *Who are you and what have you done with my Will?* I want to sharpen my claws and tear every brick from that wall. "Care to elaborate?"

Will takes a drink, then meets my eyes. "My sister was young when she became a mom. I helped out."

"Proud uncle?"

"Something like that."

"I don't know how my mom did it all by herself." It's an afterthought, one I didn't really intend to vocalize.

"Single moms are superhuman," Will says. "Yours seemed like a very determined woman."

"She was a force," I say.

We fall quiet. Will sits back in his chair, legs stretched in front of him, gazing at the trees.

"It's nice here," he says. "This whole place is gorgeous, but it's peaceful back here."

"Yeah, I used to come out here a lot when I was growing up," I say. "And go down to the family dock."

"To hide from all the guests?"

"Something like that," I say, looking into the bush.

"You must be considering selling," he says.

"Must I?"

"You weren't interested in running a resort—I assume selling is on the table."

I pull a gust of air into my lungs and let it out slowly. "It's on the table."

"It's not an easy decision to make."

"No, it's not," I agree. "It feels impossible."

He watches me closely. "Does Jamie have something to do with that?"

I'm not touching that one right now. "I guess there's not much point in having a consultant if I'm going to off-load the place, is there?" I say.

Will slants his head. "How serious are you about listing it?"

I take a drink. "The million-dollar question."

"I don't mean to pressure you."

"Minus the fact that you need to know whether I want to work with you."

"True." He crosses one ankle over the other. "But I'm not asking as your potential consultant, I'm asking as your . . ." He drifts off.

I raise my eyebrows, waiting to see how he could possibly end that sentence. There's no label that describes what he is to me.

"I'm just asking," he finishes. But then he pins me with a hard stare. "And I guess I'm surprised that it's even a question. That you wouldn't just sell."

"Because of the plan?" I say, voice hoarse. It's been years since I looked at the list Will and I made. If I shut my eyes, I can still picture his handwriting. FERN'S ONE-YEAR PLAN. I have the four items on it memorized.

"Because you didn't want to end up here."

My fingers wriggle with the urge to scratch. "For a long time, my plan has been to open a coffee shop in the city."

"One without a mural of Toronto on its wall, I imagine." Will's lips twitch. "Too basic for you."

My insides fizz with pleasure. "I might let you paint a fern on the wall," I say. "A small one."

"That's the only way I do them," he says. "I'm very fond of small ferns."

I go still, though beneath my skin I'm fully carbonated. That *f* sounded capitalized. We look at each other for a full minute. Or maybe it's five seconds. However long, it's dangerous.

"Do you still do murals? For fun, I mean."

"No," Will says quietly. He gazes into the darkness. "I haven't picked up a brush in a very long time."

"What about a pencil?"

He shakes his head.

"You should," I tell him. "It's wasteful not to use talent like yours."

His eyes snap to mine and hang on tight. "Careful," he says. "That sounded like a compliment."

"It wasn't—I was pointing out how you're squandering a gift."

He makes a humming noise, low in his throat. It feels like having my back scratched.

"Anyway," I say, bringing us back to our original topic. "Brookbanks was my mom's entire life—it's not easy to say goodbye to that. I have no idea what to do."

Will sets his glass down, still watching me, and twists his ring. I stare at his hands, falling through time. I can almost feel his pinkie wrapped in mine. "If you really don't know, I could work on two scenarios. One for selling, another if you decide to run this place yourself."

"That sounds like a lot more work."

"Looking at both options might help you make a decision."

I move my head from side to side.

"You're not sure you want to work with me, are you?" he asks. "I'm good at what I do, but that's not the issue, is it?"

His question tugs at something inside me that I don't want to explore.

I can't hold on to my hurt so tightly that I'm unable to do what's best for the resort. I'm a good manager, but I've never overhauled a business. I might be able to figure it out with time, but Brookbanks needs help yesterday. "Actually," I tell Will, "I've been thinking I'd like to accept your help."

The smile that takes over Will's face could guide a ship home. He looks a decade younger. He looks like the Will I remember.

"Are we interrupting?" Whitney sticks her head out the back door.

"Hey!" I jump out of my seat. "You're back. How was it?"

"Great," she says, eyes trained on Will, who's getting to his feet. "But enough about that." She flicks her wrist.

Whitney is highly excitable, and when she's ready to play, her big eyes go even wider and her lips smack together as if she's struggling to contain herself. I call it her Evil Villain Face. And right now, she is wearing her Evil Villain Face.

"I see you've broken your man hiatus," she says.

I glance at Will, whose eyebrows are a good inch higher from where he last left them.

"There's a hiatus?"

Before I can confirm, deny, or implode from mortification, Cam steps onto the deck.

"Owen's fast asleep," he says, but no one pays him any attention because Whitney is sticking her hand out, saying, "You must be Will. It's so nice to meet you."

He clasps her palm, clearly taken aback.

"We googled you earlier," Whitney says. Traitor.

Will's eyes flare at this, and he shoots me a smug look, another flash of the younger Will.

"Just to check your credentials," Cam says, offering his hand. I'll thank him later. "I'm Camden, and this troublemaker is my wife, Whitney."

"Nice to meet you both," Will says. "I also met Owen earlier. He's a beautiful baby."

"We didn't realize Fern was having a boy over this evening," Whitney says. "Not sure we left enough pizza money to feed two people." She's making a joke, but the underlying question is obvious: *What exactly are you doing here, Will Baxter?*

I'm about to explain how Will helped with Owen, but he speaks first. "I saw Fern and Owen waving goodbye earlier, and I stopped in to meet the baby. We got to talking and . . ." Will gestures to the wine and the porch. "It's such a nice evening."

"Do you two want a glass?" I ask.

Whitney glances between us, a look of pure agony on her face. I know the calculation she's trying to make: Stay and get a read on Will, or leave and let us continue whatever it is they interrupted. An excruciating choice.

"We'd love to, but we should get Owen home," she says. Her words are so saturated with disappointment, it's comical.

Will stays in the back while I see them off, Whitney carrying the sleeping baby in her arms and Cam lugging the diaper bag and travel crib.

"Whitney seems fun," Will says when I return to the deck.

"She's a maniac."

"I should head out, too," he says. I almost tell him to stay, to have another drink. "Thank you for the wine," Will says.

"I owe you an entire bottle for helping me out tonight. I'm not sure what I would have done if you hadn't shown up."

"Any time." He pauses and his eyes zip around my face like a searchlight. "You were serious earlier, right? About us working together?"

"I was." Though the idea of spending more time with Will makes me feel light-headed. "I have a real estate agent coming next week. Could you come to the meeting?"

"I can do that," he says. "But can you and I meet before then? There's a lot I'd like to go over. Tomorrow would be great, if you're able?"

We agree to meet here in the afternoon, and I lead Will to the front door, holding it open.

"Good night, Fern," he says. "I hope you sleep well."

AFTER WILL LEAVES, I STAND AT THE KITCHEN TABLE IN FRONT of the stack of shoeboxes. I think about Will and the past, and how different things look after so much time, and I carry the boxes to my room. The bedsprings squeak when I set them down.

There are more than a dozen journals, starting from when my mom was eight until just before I was born. I read them all during the summer I was seventeen. But I never finished the last one. I got up to the point where Mom found out she was pregnant before I confronted her.

I stop breathing when I find it, its fabric cover patterned with cheerful sunflowers, its pages only half-full. My mother's handwriting is so familiar, slanting to the right with elongated *y*'s, *j*'s, *g*'s, and *f*'s. The first entry is dated May 6, 1990. Mom would have been twenty-two—it was right after she graduated from the University of Ottawa.

One hundred and twenty-seven sleeps until Europe! she wrote at the top. A lot of the entries begin this way, with a countdown to her big trip.

Peter brought me a calendar today and said I need to start crossing off the days until I leave. I've only been home for a week, but I think he's sick of hearing me talk about traveling so much. So now I go into the pastry kitchen every morning and x off the date.

Have I mentioned that the music Peter's playing is even more depressing than the mixtape he mailed me last winter? His poor staff! Tomorrow I'm going to sneak an Anne Murray cassette into the stereo when he's not looking.

I smile to myself—Peter still has that old tape deck. I flip through the pages, looking for his name. He's in here a lot.

Tonight, after I get ready for bed, I curl up with the diary, laughing out loud at Mom's description of the Roses and my grandparents.

It's the last day of the long weekend, and it's finally starting to feel like summer. Lots of the regulars got here yesterday. The Roses brought an entire case of gin. Almost all the seasonal workers have started (the new lifeguard is the cutest by far), and the staff cabins are full. There'll be fireworks off the docks tonight. I'll have to watch Dad. Last Victoria Day he had one too many of Mr. Rose's martinis and almost lost his nose lighting a Roman Candle.

Mom writes about how badly she wanted to get involved in the business in a "meaningful way." She references Peter visiting her at school in Ottawa for her birthday a few times. Nothing happened between them, but it's plain to me now that deeper feelings were at play.

As my eyes grow heavy, I put the diary down and shut off the light. My mind drifts to Will, replaying our evening together, fixing on the smile that transformed his face when I told him I wanted to work together.

For the second time in my life, Will Baxter is going to help me make a plan.

10

June 14, Ten Years Ago

"I HAVE A CONFESSION TO MAKE," I SAID WHEN WE REACHED THE end of the alley.

Will had stopped a few times to point out graffiti he found *honest* or *vivid* or *raw*, but mostly we talked and meandered. He told me about *Roommates*, his comic based on "living in squalor with three other guys in a two-bedroom apartment," and how murals began as a hobby, but he quickly figured out there was enough demand to help pay rent. While he spoke, I tried not to let my eyes get stuck on his tattoo or his hands or the bulk of his shoulder for an indecent length of time.

"I wasn't really paying attention to the art," I said in an exaggerated whisper.

"I also have a confession to make." He sounded serious.

He leaned toward my ear, and the shock of his breath on my neck sent goose bumps down my arms. "I'm starving."

"Oh. Do you want to take off?" I smiled to show that this would not be a disappointing turn of events whatsoever.

"Actually, I was thinking we could grab a bite before the next stop. I mean, unless you had somewhere else to be."

"The rest of my plans for today were walking around," I said. "And hanging out in my apartment. So I'm all yours." I squinted at my choice of words.

His smile widened. "Perfect." He pulled his phone out of his pocket. "Do you mind if I call my sister? She and my dad had a big fight yesterday. I think I should probably check in."

"Of course not. I'll just . . ." I hooked my thumb over my shoulder.

He waved his hand, motioning for me to stay put as he held his phone to his ear.

"Hey, Bells," he said, watching me. I glanced around, listening to Will ask his sister how she was doing, where she was, if she was coming home tonight. I could hear the answer to the last one: an emphatic *no*.

"I did tell him, believe me," Will said after a few seconds, rubbing the heel of his hand against his brow. "We got into it after you left. I spent the night at Matty's. But you and I are still doing breakfast tomorrow, right?" he asked after a minute.

Once he'd settled on a time and a place with his sister, Will laughed, then caught my eye. "Her name's Fern."

I narrowed my gaze when he slid his phone back into his jeans. "You told your sister about me?"

"Mm-hmm. She said to tell you the Annabel Baxter tour of Toronto is ninety-eight percent less pretentious."

"Is that a fact?"

"Allegedly."

"Is she okay?"

"She will be. She's still cooling off. My dad was way out of line, but she really lost it, and the whole thing escalated. It was more vicious than usual. I feel like something's going on."

I touched his arm. "Listen, Art School. I know this is your tour, but this is my city, too. I'm picking lunch."

We were close to a popular Vietnamese sandwich spot that had opened a couple years ago, and I was thrilled Will hadn't heard of it. Loud music and air-conditioning blasted us when I opened the door. It was well past the midday rush, so the line that often snaked onto the street was only three people deep. I checked to make sure Will wasn't a vegetarian (a good chance, I figured) and that he ate pork, then sent him to snag the only empty table.

I ordered two types of pork banh mi sandwiches (belly and pulled) and a massive cardboard container of kimchi fries, topped with mayo and green onions and more pulled pork, as well as fancy lemon sodas.

"It's so good," Will said, taking his first bite of his sandwich.

We ate in gluttonous silence until Will set his soda down. "I heard you on the phone earlier. Who's Whitney?"

I hesitated.

"Do you want me to pretend I didn't?" Will sucked a dab of mayo off his thumb, and I was momentarily silenced.

"Maybe?" I said as he wiped his hands with a napkin.

I couldn't pinpoint why I felt so comfortable around Will, but I knew it wasn't the pot. I needed to talk to someone—I'd been drowning under the weight of my secrecy. But I didn't want to unload about Whitney in the middle of a crowded restaurant, either. "Shall we continue with the tour?"

We spilled out onto the sidewalk, and Will fished his tin of lemon drops from his backpack, holding them out for me. This time I took one.

We sucked on our candies as Will led us through Chinatown to his next destination. He kept positioning himself so that he was on the street side of the sidewalk.

"You don't have to do that," I told him. "It's weird."

"It's good manners," he said.

"In 1954." I yanked his arm and pulled him so that I was beside the curb.

"Whitney is my best friend," I said after a while. "She has been since the fifth grade." I told Will our origin story, how I slugged Cam in the stomach for spreading a rumor that Whitney stuffed her bra. The tale had Will grinning widely—the way Cam, who was twice my size, doubled over in tears, how Peter came to pick me up from school and told the vice principal Cam got what he deserved and that I would not be apologizing.

"They're dating now," I told Will.

"No." His laugh slid down my throat like chocolate sauce.

"Since tenth grade. It turned out Cam had a huge crush on her. Anyway, we've been best friends since. I'm an only child, but Whitney is basically my sister." We dodged around a sidewalk rack of ten-dollar T-shirts. "She was here visiting me for a few days. The whole trip was kind of awkward."

"You didn't insult her artwork, did you?"

I let out an amused huff, then gasped as a bike messenger zoomed past, giving my tote a smack. Suddenly, Will's arm banded around my middle, pulling me to his side.

"Are you okay?"

I looked down at his hand tight on my waist, and he immediately dropped it, a flush spreading from his neck to his cheeks like grenadine into a Shirley Temple.

"Assuming you didn't call Whitney basic, why was her visit so awkward?" he asked after we'd started walking again, slow enough that people pushed by us.

"I think I wanted it to be something it wasn't," I said. "I thought I could make her fall in love with Toronto, but she never will."

"Does that matter? You're not going to be a city person soon."

My head jerked back. "I'll always be a city person. It's not one or the other—rural or urban."

Will raised his hands. "Yeah, you're right. But why is it so important to you that Whitney likes it here?"

I scratched the inside of my wrist. "I guess I thought if she saw Toronto the way that I do, then maybe she'd understand . . ."

Will looked at me and then at my scratching.

"It's a stress reaction," I said, schooling my fingers. Ripping at my own flesh was a revolting habit, but Will didn't look grossed out.

He shuffled me to the side of a large building. I had the vague sense of groups of people milling around, but my focus had narrowed to Will, who stood in front of me, watching and waiting. "She'd understand what, Fern?"

I didn't want to tell Will the full, horrible story. But I could tell him this part. I let it out in a rush. "I don't want to move back home. I haven't told anyone, but I don't want to work at my family's resort. Everyone expects that I'll run it one day, but I definitely don't want to do that, either. I didn't even want to go to business school—it was my mom's idea."

Will listened silently. I waited for judgment to mar his expression, but it didn't, so I kept going. "I think I felt like if Whitney got why I loved living here, then maybe I could have told her about the other stuff. But she hates Toronto. She wouldn't understand why I'd want to stay. I've sort of been lying to her, to everyone."

"Hasn't it been hard, keeping all this to yourself?" Will's eyes darted around my face like he was looking for something.

I nodded. "You think I'm pathetic, right?"

"No." His gaze locked on mine, and for a second, I thought he might say something else. For a second, I thought he might kiss me. But then he glanced around and announced, "We're here."

"THE AGO? REALLY?" I ASKED, LOOKING AT THE BUILDING WE stood beside—the Art Gallery of Ontario. I felt lighter having confessed to Will. "It's a little—"

"Don't say it," he interrupted. "I can hear what's happening inside your head right now. You're as transparent as a window."

I raised my voice. "It's a little *basic*, don't you think?"

His laugh was bright and merry and bursting like a balloon on a pin. A pitch-perfect chord hummed through me.

"It's one of my favorite places in the entire city. It was renovated a few years ago. Frank Gehry did the design—it's an architectural masterpiece inside and out." Will moved his hands through the air as he spoke, motioning to the curved glass facade that soared above the street and stretched the length of the block. "And then there's the art, of course."

"Of course." I clamped my lips together to keep a laugh behind them.

"Now what?"

"I was just thinking I should see if your sister's free. Maybe I can still get in on her tour."

"Come on. There's an exhibit on that I'm pretty sure you'll like."

"Really?" Most of my courses were required for my major: business law, calculus, game theory—and I took as many music electives as possible—music and film, global guitar, a history of music in cities. I couldn't imagine what art Will would think I'd like—I didn't know what art *I* thought I'd like. But then I caught a glimpse of a large poster hanging in the window.

"Patti Smith?" I looked at Will, confused.

"There's a showcase of her photography on. I thought you might be into that."

"I'm extremely into that."

Will paid for our tickets and we went straight to Patti's show. I had expected larger-than-life images of grit and grime. I'd expected punk. But the exhibit was so subdued, austere. The walls were whitewashed, and the photos were small black-and-white Polaroids of inanimate objects. A stone cherub, Walt Whitman's tomb, a pope's prison bedroom, a fork and spoon. A handful of Patti's personal items were displayed under glass.

"It's not very rock and roll, is it?" I whispered to Will once we'd worked our way through.

"I dunno. Death is a recurring theme in her work," Will said, gesturing to a photograph of a withering flower. "What? You're making a weird face."

"Nothing," I hissed. *"Death is a recurring theme.* Go on." I liked Will's arty talk.

"As I was saying, there's a lot of death going on. Death's pretty rock and roll."

I leaned closer to him. "Am I an asshole if I say I prefer her music?"

Will cackled, and the sound raced up my spine. A man with a fanny pack strapped around his waist and a DSLR camera slung over his neck glared at us.

"He's not very rock and roll," Will said into my ear.

"Disagree," I said, pointing to the man's feet. He was wearing cannabis-leaf-patterned socks. "But this is a Patti Smith exhibit. It's silly that we can't laugh or speak at a normal volume."

"We can," Will said in his regular speaking voice, and the man scowled again. "But should we move on?"

"Sure. You've been here a bunch of times, right? Do you have a favorite piece?"

"I don't have a favorite piece," he said. "But I do have a favorite part."

Will led me to a massive glass-and-wood atrium that spanned the entire length of the building. One side was floor-to-ceiling windows, looking out onto the city. It was called the Galleria Italia, and there were giant curving beams that made it seem like we were in the upside-down hull of a ship, except there was so much light. Massive tree trunk sculptures grew throughout the hall, and as we made our way through, I decided it wasn't like being in an upside-down ship.

"It's like being in the woods," I told Will. Even though it was clearly Toronto on the other side of the windows, it reminded me of home. It was both—city and bush. "This is your favorite part?"

"Yeah. I like how the space is so overwhelming, it makes you feel insignificant and alive at the same time. It basically forces you to take a deep breath. It's the same way I feel when I look at the mountains out West."

I thought it was the loveliest thing I'd ever heard. "Seriously?"

"Yeah, what? Why?" He rubbed the back of his ripening neck.

I shook my head. "Nothing."

After we left the Galleria, we found our way to the permanent collection of Canadian art.

"There's your girl," I said, pointing to a display of Emily Carr paintings. Will looked at me, impressed.

"Hey, I may not have gone to art school, but I can spot an Emily Carr." We moved toward one of a single massive evergreen. "Someone once told me Emily Carr painted a shit ton of lonely trees," I said.

"A snotty art school grad, I bet."

I vaguely recognized a handful of the pieces in the Group of Seven area. They were some of the most celebrated paintings of the nation's wilderness, all done by a troupe of seven men. It was wall-to-wall lakes and snow and mountains and oh so many trees. But others felt familiar because they looked like home.

"I guess Emily wasn't allowed in the Group," I said.

"Oh, definitely not," Will replied. "She was painting at the same time. Lawren Harris even told her she was one of them." He gestured to one of Harris's icy peaks. "But she wasn't, really. No women were."

I fell silent as we walked around. There was a canvas of a lake on one of the last days of winter—sky gray, trees bare, snow melting into smudges of brown. I could smell the wet pine needles, the promise of muddy earth, and spring buds forming on branches. I blinked up at the lights, my throat tightening.

I could feel Will's eyes swing to me. He'd been watching me like this as soon as we stepped inside the AGO. It reminded me of how I'd been with Whitney during her visit. He was checking to see what I thought.

We came to a Tom Thomson—a storm-dark lake in the background, a rocky shore and saplings in the fore. Looking at it was like standing on the banks by the family dock. The trees were bare in this painting, too, but it wasn't winter. Late fall or early spring— shoulder season, when the resort wasn't busy. When Mom and I would head down to the water in the morning and she'd drink her coffee slowly. When she came home earlier in the evening. When life didn't seem to revolve entirely around Brookbanks and its guests.

The stinging started in my nose. I looked up at the lights again, but a tear escaped, then another.

Will stood beside me. "Are you okay?"

I nodded. It took me a little while to speak. "It's beautiful up there, you know?"

"I'd like to know."

"I miss it sometimes." I missed my mom, too. So much. The older I got, the more I seemed to miss her.

"You sound surprised."

"I guess I am." I looked at him then, and he turned from the painting. "I'm sorry. Sometimes pot makes me . . . tender."

"Tender's okay."

I took a shaky breath. "I'm not sure about that."

"Did you know," Will said after a moment, "that Tom Thomson wasn't actually part of the Group of Seven? He died in Algonquin Park just before it was founded. Some say he was murdered. Very mysterious."

I sniffed. "I think I did know that, yeah."

Will leaned closer. "Did you know trees were a recurring theme in Thomson's work?"

I sputtered out a laugh.

"I learned that in art school," he said.

I looked up at him, wiping my cheeks. "Oh, I'm sorry. Did you say you went to art school?"

He smiled. "Yeah, I think I might have mentioned that earlier?"

"Emily Carr, was it?"

"Emily Carr," he said. "Come on, let's get out of here. I think I know what you need."

June 2, 1990

I spent my morning in the pastry kitchen with Peter, filling profiter-oles and telling him about the improvements I'm going to make if Mom and Dad let me take over as general manager. I was worried things would be different when I came back this summer, that Peter wouldn't have time for me now that he's head pâtissier. I suppose I've always worried that he'll get sick of me. But he's the same old Peter. Only this summer he's experimenting with sourdough starters, and he gets to control what music gets played in the kitchen. If I never hear Sonic Youth again in my life, I'd be perfectly happy. He's also growing a beard, which makes him look even more handsome, not that he cares about that type of thing. And not that I care anymore, either. I got over my crush on Peter years ago—he'll never think of me that way.

He doesn't like Eric, but Peter never likes the lifeguards. He says all the sun must have fried his brain cells. That's okay. Peter wouldn't be Peter if he approved of the guys I date. Anyway, I know Eric's smart—engineering degrees are no cakewalk. And you should see him in a bathing suit.

11

Now

I SLIDE THE KAYAK OFF THE EDGE OF THE FAMILY DOCK INTO the water, then ease myself into the boat like I do every morning before I head over to the lodge. It's a flat-water kayak, no skirt or top covering my legs, and as I head south, I stare down at my golden-brown shins. I was a teenager the last time they were this tanned.

It's gray today and the lake is almost empty. As I pass the Pringle cottage, I hoist my paddle in the air to wave to Jamie's mom, who's on the deck. There's a small excavator working on the slope of the next lot, disturbing the quiet, clearing rocks to make way for Jamie's dream home. He used to imagine it when we were dating—the two of us living there together, working at the resort. Smoke Lake was always his happy place.

This summer, it seems to be mine, too. My post-coffee paddles have become a ritual. Some days I inspect a reedy bit of marsh where a great blue heron has made its nest in a tree. I always look for moose—they've been spotted here before—but I never see one. Other days I stay close to shore, snooping on the cottages and saying hello to anyone already awake on the dock. These little voyages give me a break from everything that's happening back at Brookbanks, a break from Will, though I never manage to get him out of my head completely.

It's been a week since we agreed to team up, and we've also fallen into a rhythm. Our days are split in two. In the mornings, I'm at the lodge while Will works in his cabin. From midafternoon on, we're together at the house. I can tell when he's had videoconferences, because he shows up in white dress shirts, and the days when his schedule is lighter, because he's at the house as soon as he sees me walking up the path. Today is different. Today we're showing a real estate agent around the property.

I find Will in the lobby, and for a moment I watch from a distance, struck by how familiar the sight of him has become. He's inspecting a row of photos that capture three generations of Brookbanks as well as the decades before our time.

There's one of Clark Gable during a famed stay in the forties and a classic of my grandparents when they bought the place. Grandma Izzy's dress is tie-dyed, and Grandpa Gerry is sporting a fringed vest and an epic beard. You'd never know he came from money, though how else would two twentysomething dreamers buy a sprawling, if somewhat run-down, resort? It was always something of a lark for them.

There are others, too. My mother as a flossy-haired toddler, playing in a galvanized bucket of water by the shore. Mom and I in matching tartan dresses in front of a gigantic tinsel-covered Scotch pine in the lobby.

The photo Will is looking at is from the end-of-summer dance. I'm about five years old and wearing a ruffled white dress with a pale blue satin bow around the waist. I hold Mom's hands and gaze up at her with an adoring expression, and she wears a cocktail dress the same shade of blue as my bow. We're in the middle of the dining room's dance floor; the photographer has captured us in some kind of silly waltz. I used to love dancing with her, how it meant having her undivided attention. It was a rare thing, even at that young age.

"Should I be offended that the real estate agent gets the suit treatment?" I say. Will's always clean-shaven and well dressed, but a jacket and tie rarely make an appearance.

He looks down at his outfit. "Is it too much? My coveralls were in the wash."

Working alongside Will requires that I not think about the past. There have been no more *basic* references, no discussions of small- or big-*f* ferns. We don't talk about that day. I thought we had an unspoken agreement not to.

He taps the photo of Mom and me. "You were an exceptionally cute kid."

I don't have time to reply because bells begin tolling from his phone. I already recognize the ringtone—whoever it belongs to has called several times when we've been together.

"I have to take this," Will says. "Excuse me."

He talks to his business partner in front of me—colleagues, too—but he always takes these calls elsewhere. If we're on the back deck, he'll step inside. If we're in the kitchen, he'll go to the front porch. Now he exits the main doors to speak to whoever's on the other end.

It's not just the calls. At thirty-two, Will Baxter is a very private person, and I am an undercover agent. I collect every scrap of intel I can, sneaking covert looks while he types, and recording it all in my mental spy journal. Although if this were a game of Mystery Guest, I wouldn't have much to report. Not only do we not discuss *that* day, but we hardly talk about anything other than the resort. I know he owns a house in Midtown close to his office. I know he has a gym membership and that he meets his trainer on his lunch hour. I know his office has a shower. After he tells me this, I imagine him sweaty and glistening and then soapy and glistening, and I give myself a stern lecture.

Then there are the things I've learned just from being around him. His workday beverage of choice is sparkling water with two lemon wedges. He fiddles with his ring when he's lost in thought. He has a particular tone of voice for business calls that's pleasant and also very . . . firm. When I hear it, it makes me feel things I should not, and I give myself more talking-tos.

None of it is enough. Will is a lockbox with no key, and the more time I spend with him, the more I want to jimmy him open. Sometimes I see a glimmer of the old Will, but he disappears as quickly as he came. I'm desperate to hear his laugh.

I have more important things to think about, but when I lie awake at two a.m., I workshop zippy one-liners to sidesplitting perfection. I wonder what happened to make Will so reserved and why he gave up on his art and who he's speaking to when the bells chime on his phone. Sometimes I peek out the window in the middle of the night, and I find that his light is almost always on. But I don't ask him why he's not sleeping, and he doesn't mention it, either.

Will returns to the lobby, running a hand down his tie. It's another tell I've picked up on. He's stressed.

"Everything okay?" I ask, noticing the hint of a blush under his collar.

He grunts. "Fine."

"Got it." I can take a hint.

The hard line of Will's mouth softens, and he looks like he's going to say something else, but I spot a woman in a red skirt suit striding through the lobby. I recognize Mira Khan from her head-shot, FOR SALE signs, and prolific Instagram updates.

I take Mira around the resort, Will accompanying us mostly in silence. There's something about her that reminds me of Mom. It might be the speed at which she walks or the way I feel like she's assessing me from behind her sunglasses, or maybe it's that I can't stop seeing Mom everywhere. It's gotten worse since I started reading her diary. Whatever it is, I'm anxious to impress upon Mira how capable I am. I tell her about how I see altering the decor and adding new amenities.

"One of the things Will and I have been talking about is how to generate revenue from parts of the property that aren't cur-rently monetized," I say when we get to the library.

Mom replaced the colonial furniture when my grandparents moved out West, and now tan leather armchairs are arranged in groups of two, giving one the impression of being in a ski lodge rather than a Victorian study. There's a stone fireplace framed by tall windows that look over the lake. The walls are lined with dark wood shelves, thick and raw-edged, that are filled with books, some of which were here when my grandparents took over. Others Mom collected over the years. Some have been left behind by guests. Once, Mom spied a copy of the *Kama Sutra* tucked between *Summer Sisters* and *The Stone Angel* and was horri-fied by how long it may have been there. Peter thought it was hi-larious and told her to put the paperback on a high shelf. "Give the guests some bang for their buck, Maggie." Mom whacked him on the chest with the book, but I found it in her bedside table a few months later, and read it cover to cover while she was working.

I tell Mira about my idea to add an espresso bar and a communal table so people can work at their laptops. "We'd get more people in here and add value."

I wait for her to respond with enthusiasm, but she only gives me a polite smile.

I keep my thoughts to myself for the rest of the walk-through.

Are you okay? Will mouths to me as we escort Mira to her Mercedes.

I nod, but I feel deflated.

"It's a beautiful property, Fern," Mira says. "Totally adorable. I'll have to do further research to come up with a suggested list price. We're looking at seven figures, at least, for an operation of this size with such a substantial amount of waterfront footage." She gives us a ballpark estimate, and I manage not to gasp.

I glance at Will, but he doesn't look fazed.

"I'll send you an email in a few days with what I'm thinking. Obviously big-ticket resorts and hotels like this have a limited number of prospective buyers—there are the luxury chains and maybe a handful of independents. Developers are a strong possibility, too."

"Developers?" I repeat.

"Yes," Mira says. "You're a little far from town, but the cabins and lodge could be razed for a condominium development. Town houses, low-rise apartments, that sort of thing, if zoning isn't an issue. It could be quite adorable."

"No." I don't even think before I say it. Selling the resort is one thing. Flattening it is another. "No developers."

Mira frowns, purses her lips, and nods. "Understood." She lifts her chin to address Will, which is annoying—I introduced him as my consultant, but I'm the potential client. "I'm sure I don't have to tell you how important it is to keep the price as reasonable as possible so we can remain competitive."

"Of course," Will says.

Mira makes a dubious *mmmkay* sound. "Well, let's make sure everyone is aware of that, yes?"

It's clear that I'm the everyone and that I'm missing something.

As soon as her car pulls out of the lot, Will says, "I'll fill you in when we're somewhere private."

I open my mouth to protest, but Will cuts me off. "Trust me, this isn't a conversation you want anyone listening in on."

To underscore his point, a woman in tennis whites interrupts us, asking where the courts are.

"House?" I ask Will once I've pointed her in the right direction.

"Actually," he says, "I have a better idea."

I WALK DOWN THE HILL TO THE WATER. WILL HAD A FEW CALLS to make after our appointment with Mira, but now here he is, standing next to the outfitting hut in swim trunks and T-shirt, a paddle in each hand. My stomach dips as soon as I see him, which is funny because it's been at my ankles ever since he asked me to meet him at the docks. He didn't give a reason, but I changed into a bathing suit and shorts. I had a feeling.

"I was wondering if the offer still stands," Will says as I walk toward him. There's already a canoe in the water.

I don't know whether to laugh or push him in the lake. First the coveralls comment and now this.

"What do you think?" he says.

"I think you're nine years late for your lesson."

"I know," he says, wincing. "I'm sorry." He nods his head at the canoe. "I was hoping you'd teach me anyway. You said you'd make sure I don't embarrass myself."

"You remember that?"

Will's eyes search my face. Out here, the espresso brown is more like a glass of Coke held up to the light. "I remember everything." He says it slowly, holding my gaze, and my stomach dives into the water.

I take the short paddle, willing my hands to remain steady. "Fine." I square my shoulders. "Get in the boat."

It's overcast, and for a July afternoon, there's hardly anyone out on the water. I like gloomy days for this very reason. We paddle for a while, not talking, just gliding across the water, past the cottages that dot the banks—classic log cabins with red-painted window frames, ostentatious summer homes with oversized boathouses. Will sits in the front, and I watch the muscles move across his back. I lose minutes staring at the evergreen tattooed on his arm.

It's surreal, being out here with him, a moment I thought about for an entire year after we met. While I walked to work, as I fixed lattes, before I went to bed, I'd imagine giving Will Baxter the world's greatest tour of Smoke Lake.

"So," Will says, glancing over his shoulder, "how do I look?" He flashes me an Old Will smile, and suddenly I'm confused about what's happening. He's different today.

"Too tall for a canoe," I tell him.

I point out a sandy ribbon of crown land and we pull the boat up on the shore. We sit on the small strip of beach, our toes in the water, just like I thought we would nine years ago.

"We haven't gone into detail about what a sale might involve yet, and at this point it's all speculative," Will says, pulling me back to the present. "But essentially, there's a limited pool of buyers for an operation this large. And while the business isn't as strong as we'd like, the price for the property and buildings alone will be hefty."

"Mira said I'd need to keep it competitive."

"Right. To do that, a lot of businesses in similar situations would make sure they're running things as lean as possible." He pauses. "It usually involves doing an audit of the entire staff and . . . laying people off."

My stomach roils. "How many?" I whisper after a minute.

"I'm not sure," Will says. "It could be a few roles here and there, or we might want to look at a more substantial cut. I can figure that out with more time."

Will studies my face. "We'll get another agent's opinion, but here's the thing: If you decide to sell, you can do it without switching so much as a light bulb, but no buyer is going to come in without making changes, significant ones, likely including cuts. Chains will do things their own way. They'll standardize everything, bring in their own people to fill some of the senior roles."

I think of Jamie and how chuffed he is with our locally made shampoos and soaps, and the comment Peter made recently about how few hotels employ on-site bakers anymore. Everything comes in premade and frozen.

"I don't want to alarm you, but I don't want to sugarcoat it, either," Will says.

I stare out over the water, trying to quell my nausea.

Mom is going to be heartbroken. The thought comes and goes in one brief, painful second, and I have to shut my eyes.

"Fern?"

"I started reading my mom's diary, the one from the summer before I was born." My voice wavers, and I pause. I don't know why I'm telling him this. Will's arm comes around my shoulder. It's nothing more than a comforting embrace, but being touched by him is such a relief, like opening a pressure valve in my heart. He smells so good, and it takes every particle of restraint I possess not to rest my head on his shoulder and curl into him.

"She always knew," I say when I can speak steadily. "She always knew she wanted to run the resort. Selling would have killed her."

"Can I make an observation?" Will asks after a minute.

"Sure." I twist so I can look at him. His arm falls and his hand comes to rest on the sand between us.

"You light up when you talk about the resort and the possibilities for the future. You're passionate about this place and your ideas are solid. And, I hope you don't mind, but I sat in on one of your staff meetings."

"You what?"

After Jamie told me that my presence was "freaking people out," I held two meetings to introduce myself properly, applaud everyone for holding things together following Mom's death, and take questions—many of which I couldn't answer, including whether or not I was selling the business. I wanted to puke the entire time. Mom loved being the center of attention, but I'm still uncomfortable when eyes are on me. I'm terrified people will be able to tell that I'm making half of it up as I go along.

"I wanted to see you in action." He leans toward me. "You were awesome. Confident, as transparent as possible, strong but empathetic. It's hard to get in front of a large group and tell them you don't have all the answers—a lot of leaders won't do that."

I'm surprised by his praise. I was sure everyone could see my hands tremble, hear the wobble in my voice. I could sense their skepticism. The executive chef glowered at me the whole time, arms folded in front of his chest. "I don't think I won them over."

"Would you have been won over if you were in their position? You grew up at the resort, but to most of them, you've swooped in from nowhere."

"I just didn't ever picture myself here," I murmur. Even to my own ears, the argument is starting to sound thin, a favorite shirt worn till it's threadbare—comfortable but probably ready for the trash. "I'm actually starting to enjoy being back. Parts of it feel right." It's scary to admit it, but it's true. Outside of staff meetings, I mostly like the work. I love being near Whitney. I hardly miss the city. "Shocking, right?"

Given everything Will knows about me, I expect him to agree. "I wouldn't say that. Sometimes plans change."

The statement feels loaded. We watch a boat putter by, a man casting a fishing line off the end. After a moment, Will adds, "We're not the same people we were at twenty-two. It's okay to want different things."

I look down at our fingers, inches away from each other in the sand, worried that I want some of the same things I did then.

"So tell me about this man hiatus of yours," Will says, and my gaze flicks up to his. Apparently my thoughts are being broadcast on a frequency only Will can hear.

"There's not much to tell," I say with caution. Love lives are firmly in the category of things we don't talk about. "Bad breakup, vow of celibacy, et cetera."

"Vow of celibacy, huh? How's that going?"

"I lasted five months." I don't get the laugh I crave. Instead, Will goes still.

"So you are seeing someone. Jamie?"

I dig my toes into the sand and press my chin to my knees. "He and I broke up a long, long time ago."

"He's still in love with you."

My eyes snap to Will's. "No, he's not."

"Trust me. I've seen the way he looks at you."

"Trust me. You're wrong. Jamie loves the resort," I say, trying to convince myself as much as Will. "Anyway, the hiatus has more to do with taking a pause from relationships."

"Ah," he says. "How much of a pause have you taken?"

"About two years."

"Two years," he repeats. "Was it serious—the relationship before the hiatus?"

I chew on my cheek. I have to think about this. Philippe and I exchanged *I love you*s. Met each other's families. I thought of his pug as my own—I still take care of Mocha when Philippe's out of town. But I never pictured us as a couple forever.

"We were together for a year and a half and worked together for a long time before that."

"So why the breakup?"

I let out a breath.

I didn't use to think I had a type, though Whitney maintains that I have two: The person who is perfectly fine, but not even close to perfect for me (almost everyone I've dated). And dickheads (Philippe).

I've never been ready for the sharing of keys and consolidating of furniture, but it wasn't until Philippe that I started thinking Whitney might be right, that maybe a part of me was picking the wrong people on purpose. I guess there's nothing like seeing your boyfriend with his pants around his ankles behind another woman to make you question your choices.

"Sorry," Will says. "I didn't mean to pry."

"No?" I ask with a little laugh. It's so strange, talking like this to him again, but I find myself wanting to share. It was always like that with Will. "It's okay. I guess it's a bit embarrassing. He cheated. I found them together. We broke up."

"Why would that be embarrassing?" Will asks, his voice cold enough that I peer over at him. He's staring out at the lake, jaw tight.

I shrug. I don't want to tell him what a knock to my pride

Philippe's infidelity was. I reach for a subject change. "So what's your story?"

Will's forehead wrinkles.

"This isn't exactly how you imagined yourself." I think of what I wrote on his plan.

"No, it's not," he agrees. I suspect this will be all he says on the subject, but he adds, "It's not a short story."

"I've got time."

He leans forward, twisting his ring.

"You do that a lot," I say.

Will assesses me from the corner of his eye.

"Who gave it to you?"

"My grandmother," he says after a moment. "It was my grandfather's."

"You were close."

"With my grandmother, yeah. You remember?" A hint of a smile graces his lips, and I want to hook my thumbs on the corners of his mouth and pull the edges up higher.

"Of course," I say quietly. "I remember everything."

He hums and looks at the water. "My grandfather died when I was four. I don't remember much about him, but my grandmother was around a lot. She was a tough lady. Dottie. You would have liked her, I think."

I find this oddly pleasing. "Oh yeah?"

"Yeah. She was a real straight shooter. Very independent. My sister and I used to sleep over at her house almost every weekend when we were little. We had our own bedrooms there. She taught me how to use a screwdriver and change the oil in a car. When my mother left, she gave me this ring and a long talk about responsibility and looking out for my sister." He looks over to me. I nod. I remember that part, too. I think about tracing my finger over the scar on his chin, but I stay still.

"She was funny, but her sense of humor was bone-dry. I could never tell if she was being serious or not. When I got older, I realized she was almost always joking. She died about a year ago."

"I'm sorry."

"She was ninety-three. She had a good run."

"It still sucks—good run or not."

"It did suck. It sucked a lot."

A light rain begins to fall. It's only a misty drizzle, but we fold ourselves into the canoe and paddle back at a brisk clip, which is just as well because the drops come down with more vigor as we approach the resort.

We lift the boat out of the water and carry it to its rack. By the time we bring the paddles and life jackets to the storage shed, we're both soaked. I finish hanging the jackets, and when I turn around, Will is watching me a few steps away.

Rain falls outside the door behind him, drumming on the metal roof. His shirt is sopping, hugging the ridges of his chest. We stare at each other for three long breaths and then he takes a step forward, his eyes dropping to my mouth.

"Don't," I tell him.

"Don't what?" he asks, voice rough.

I suck in a breath. "Don't look at me like that." I don't know how to handle this Will, the one who is studying my face like a treasure map.

"Like what?"

"Like you give a shit about me," I say, pressing my nails into my palms.

He takes another step. "What if I do give a shit?"

"Well, you're not allowed to." I take a step back.

"Why not?"

I've been pushing down the hurt all afternoon, but it pops to the surface like a buoy. "Because you left me waiting for you on that dock nine years ago."

"I didn't want to," he says quietly.

"Then why did you? You knew I would be here. You knew how I felt about you." My voice sounds strangled.

He swallows. "Yeah, I knew."

I can feel my bottom lip quake, and I bite down on it. Hard. I have to leave. I move past Will, but he catches my arm and turns me around. He ducks down, his eyes moving between mine.

"I was worried that I was different from how you remembered, and that you'd be disappointed."

"But you did disappoint me," I whisper. "You made me think it was all in my head."

"It wasn't," he says. "Believe me, it wasn't your head that was the problem." I want to ask what he means, but he catches a tear on my cheek and tucks my hair behind my ears before pulling me toward him.

I wrap my fist in the hem of his shirt, tugging him closer. I want to run my fingers over his shoulders and press my tongue to his scar and do all the things I wanted to do when I didn't hate Will Baxter.

He leans down and holds my face between his hands. His nose brushes mine. I slip my hands under his damp shirt, flattening them against his stomach, and he closes his eyes. His skin is hot, his flesh hard. I press against him.

Will traces a path down the bridge of my nose to its tip with his finger. "Perfect."

As he brings his lips to mine, he whispers my name, and it snaps me out of whatever haze of nostalgia I got lost in.

"I'm sorry," I say, stepping back. "I shouldn't have done that. We can't do that."

"Okay." He's breathing as heavily as I am.

"I'm in over my head," I say, my voice hitching. "I need your help. I need us to be okay, to be able to work together."

He stares at me. "I would never do anything to jeopardize your business, no matter what happened between us," he says. "I want you to know that. You can trust me."

I shake my head. Trusting Will would be like trusting a mirage. "I can't. I don't know who you are. And you don't know me." Then I walk out of the shed and into the rain.

THE KNOCK COMES WELL AFTER TWO A.M. IT'S A SOFT THUD. NOT Peter's *tap, tap, tap,* or the frantic rapping of a guest who's spotted a pair of yellow eyes in the bush.

I'm already awake. I gave up sleeping a few minutes ago.

No one is at the door when I get downstairs, but there's a thin, square parcel on the welcome mat. It's wrapped in bright striped paper and there's an envelope on top with my name on it. I recognize Will's penmanship immediately. It hasn't changed.

I take the gift to the kitchen table and open the card. Inside, there's a sketch of a woman holding a paddle in the air like a sword, and a short note.

You do know me. And I know you, too.

I rip off the paper and stare at the album cover, smiling into the dark.

12

June 14, Ten Years Ago

WILL TOOK ME TO SONIC BOOM. IT WAS ONE OF THE BIGGEST record stores in the city, and I'd been there many times, but I wasn't going to tell him that. He was right—it was exactly what I needed after my minor meltdown at the gallery. I'd been homesick before, but the paintings stirred a deeper kind of longing.

I felt better flipping through the vinyl, showing Will which albums I'd get if I could afford them. Not that I owned a record player—there was no room in my apartment.

"If you could buy one today, which would you choose?" he asked.

"Only one?"

He nodded.

I stared at the rafters, thinking, then led him to another section to dig for my prize. I plucked out an LP of Patti Smith's *Horses*, displaying it to him between both my hands. "In commemoration."

"I've got an idea," Will said.

But he didn't elaborate.

We spent what was left of the afternoon strolling around Kensington Market, a small neighborhood of vintage stores, trinket shops, and food vendors that remained steadfastly ramshackle despite the influx of specialty butchers and boutiques. We panned for gold in every knickknack store. I went straight for the sunglasses rack, looking for cheap frames to suit my new haircut, while Will did his own hunting, though he wouldn't say what he was searching for.

"What about these?" I called over to him at our last stop. He was eyeing something near the register. The glasses I wore were oversized with plastic arms and yellow-brown lenses. They were also $7.99.

"You look like a film star from the sixties."

I checked myself out in the mirror again. "Sold."

By the time evening fell, the air had turned humid, and the sky was covered in a thick bed of gray clouds. We needed drinks, we agreed.

"This is an excellent gin and tonic," I said after we'd sat down at a tiny metal table on the tiny front patio of a tiny bar. It was what my mom always drank on the first warm day of the year.

"I didn't realize there were degrees of excellence in a gin and tonic."

"Oh, there are. I've had some truly heinous G and T's in this city. Flat tonic. Dried-up limes. Crappy gin."

Will laughed. "I'm very excited we've arrived at the portion of the evening where your preppy side has decided to make an appearance."

"Taste it. It's so good." I pushed the glass across the table.

He took a sip. And then another, longer one. "That's refreshing," he said. "But it's strange."

"What is?"

"For some reason, I have a very strong urge to play squash and learn how to sail."

"Ha. Ha."

He smiled. "But it is good. Way better than my beer, actually." Will had ordered some kind of craft ale. "I'll be right back."

I watched him head into the bar, then took out my phone. There was a text from Whitney.

> Thanks for having me! Cam and I want to take you and Jamie out to celebrate as soon as you're back. COUNTDOWN IS ON!!!

There was also one from Jamie, saying he was throwing a bonfire at the staff cabins later that night.

Don't overdo it, I texted back. He would definitely overdo it.

There would be too much beer and too many joints. No-name chips and hot dogs cooked on sticks over the coals—more lost to the fire than to hungry mouths. Someone would inevitably bring out an acoustic guitar, which was usually my cue to leave, but I'd hang around if Jamie played. He had a three-song repertoire (strictly Neil Young), and if he wasn't hamming it up, he had a beautiful voice. The night I first kissed him, in front of a dozen other staffers by the campfire, he'd sung "Heart of Gold." When he wrapped his fingers around mine, they were sticky with marshmallow. Still, I held on tightly for the rest of the night.

Will returned with two gin and tonics and origami'd himself into his chair. "Since I drank half of yours," he said.

"Much appreciated." I reached for the tumbler, my foot bumping his under the table. "Sorry. I have massive feet."

Will's eyebrows rose. "Really?"

"Yeah, I'm a very short person with disproportionately large feet."

"That's not a thing."

"It is so." I kicked up one of my size nine Converse high-tops. "See."

"I don't know. They seem okay." He tilted his head. "Maybe stand up so I can see everything all together."

I jumped out of my seat, hands on my hips.

He eyed me up and down and then started laughing. "Actually, you're right. They're gigantic. It's a wonder you don't trip over them more."

"Thank you," I said. "I'm sure you have very normal-sized feet." I glanced down at his boots, which were gargantuan. When I looked back up, Will was smirking.

I slunk into my chair, red-faced.

"You were saying?" Will said.

I threw my lime at his chest. "Don't be cocky."

My eyes popped at the same time Will's did, then we both exploded with laughter. I'd just caught my breath when Will gave my foot a kick under the table, and we cracked up all over again.

The sky was darkening by the time we finished our second round. I ran my finger around the rim of my glass. I didn't want to say goodbye, but I could almost see the credits rolling on our day.

"I had fun." I didn't know what else to say.

"So did I," Will said. "Which reminds me." He dug around in his jeans pocket and set two miniature plastic baggies down on the table. Inside each was a shiny red streetcar pin. "One for you and one for me," he said. "In commemoration."

I fastened mine to the corner of my tote bag as Will fixed his to his backpack. I met his eyes when he was finished. "I love it. Thank you."

As we took our final sips, I had the sudden, terrifying notion that Will was quite possibly the best person I'd ever met. He was more than met the eye—more than a beautiful face.

Peter once made a flourless chocolate torte. It looked perfect—dark and glossy, its surface sprinkled with crystallized sugar. But when I'd taken a bite, I realized it wasn't sugar on top, it was flaked salt, and Peter had added chili to the cocoa. It was the most incredible thing I'd ever tasted, as decadent as it was unexpected. Will was like that.

"A friend of mine has a show tonight," he said. I looked up at him from my drink. "At Sneaky Dee's," he continued. "I've never ordered a gin and tonic there—I'm sure they're shit. But would you want to come?"

"I've been to Sneaky Dee's before," I said slowly. It was a Toronto institution—bar downstairs, small concert venue up-stairs, graffiti on all available surfaces, the most famous nachos in the city.

Will played with his ring. "I don't think there's an undergrad in this entire city who hasn't."

"This wouldn't be part of the official Will Baxter tour?" I sat perfectly still, but blood bubbled under the surface of my skin.

"Tour's over. I'm off duty. I wouldn't drink on the job."

"Of course not. I didn't mean to insult your professional-ism."

"They're on at nine. We could grab a bite there first?"

I rested my chin in my hand, observing him longer than I should have. "You're really leaving tomorrow, huh?"

"Yeah. I really am."

"And then you're never coming back?"

He tipped his head to the side, not sure where I was going with this. "I'll come back, but maybe not until the holidays." And I'd be long gone.

"So what you're saying is that this is a once-in-a-lifetime opportunity?"

Will's lips curved. "Precisely," he said. "Take it or leave it."

"I FEEL KIND OF GROSS," I SAID WHEN WE'D ALMOST REACHED the bar. We'd been spelunking our way through the city all day, and I was covered in a distinct layer of urban grime. I needed a shower. "My place is nearby. I was thinking I'd go wash up, get changed, and meet you there in a little bit?" I could make it to my apartment and back before the band's set.

"What? Come on. I thought we were going to have nachos first. Plus, once you get home, there's no way you're going to want to come out again."

"I smell like old bong water."

Will leaned down, bringing his face an inch from my neck, and inhaled deeply. "You smell like sunshine," he said into my ear.

My head snapped toward his as if it had been yanked by a string, and our noses almost bashed together.

"Sorry, that got weird," he said, pulling back with a nervous laugh.

"Yeah." I cleared my throat. "Anyway, I'm not exactly dressed for going out." I was close to suggesting that Will come with me, but the idea of showering with him in the next room seemed like an exceptionally bad one.

"You look great," he said. "You don't need to change. It's Sneaky Dee's—no one will be dressed up."

"You're just worried I'm going to ditch you, and you'll be

stuck listening to some weird Nirvana cover band all by yourself." Will had neglected to mention it was a *ska* cover band until about a block ago.

"Petrified," Will said. "Don't make me go alone."

I could see the iconic skulls on the Sneaky Dee's sign ahead. "Fine. But you owe me."

Once we'd arrived, Will scored one of the wooden booths while I made a quick getaway to the basement bathroom. I ransacked my tote, hoping a tube of mascara or a comb had magically appeared inside it, but all I came up with was gum and a tin of Smith's Rosebud Salve. I wasn't the kind of girl to carry around a kit of makeover supplies. I hadn't even bothered with makeup in the morning. I scrubbed at my armpits with a soapy square of wet paper towel, splashed water on my face, and smoothed a thick, shiny coat of gloss on my lips. I would have kissed the floor for a stick of deodorant.

There was a guy sitting next to Will when I got back upstairs. Even from across the room I could see he was meticulously tended. He had olive skin and a dark beard that was trimmed like a topiary, tidy and perfectly edged.

"Fern, this is Eli," Will said.

"A pleasure to meet you." Eli stood, taking my hand between both of his. He wore red jeans, a black skinny tie, and a white button-down I was certain had seen an iron earlier in the evening. I bet the rest of him had seen a gym before that.

"Same," I said, taking a seat on the side of the booth opposite them. "How do you two know each other?"

"We went to grade school together, then high school," Eli said. "But it's been a while. Can't believe I finally got this guy out to a show."

I threw Will a look, which he declined to catch. I assumed

he'd seen the band perform before and that we weren't in for a night of *terrible* ska Nirvana covers.

"We were in the area, and Fern is a bit of a music nerd, so we thought we'd check it out," Will said.

"That's cool. I think we put on a pretty decent show," said Eli. He flagged down a server so we could put in our orders, then turned to me. "Do you live in Toronto, Fern, or are you in from Vancouver, too?"

"Oh, no. I'm from here. My place is a couple streets over."

He tipped his head at Will. "How's the long-distance thing working out? I live in Liberty Village, if you're finding it too much of a drag." He winked.

"Oh, no," I said, pointing between Will and me. "We're not a thing. At all."

Will laughed. "Should I be offended by how repulsed you sound right now?"

"I definitely would be," Eli said. "She looks like she's eaten bad shellfish."

Our server dropped off a pitcher of beer and three glasses, and I poured, then took a big gulp of mine.

As Eli and Will chatted, it hit me that we were in uncharted territory. My day with Will had been spontaneous and unusual, but we'd unwittingly given ourselves a road map, a rule book, and an end point. Now, not only had we gone off course, but we'd opened our odd partnership up to spectators.

Someone kicked me under the table, and I looked up from my beer.

Are you okay? Will mouthed as Eli refilled our drinks.

I nodded.

Our server placed a platter on the center of the table. It was heaped with a disgusting, magnificent mound of nachos. There had to be two pounds of toppings aside from cheese and salsa—ground beef, refried beans, veggies, guacamole, sour cream. We moaned in approval.

"So what was this one like as a kid?" I asked Eli as I dislodged a chip.

"Wild Bill? He was pretty much the same," Eli said.

Wild Bill? I mouthed to Will, and he rolled his eyes. I thought I could see his neck pinking.

"Skinny. Drawing all the time. He was a bit emo."

I raised my eyebrows. "Really?"

Eli glanced at Will, who gave him the tiniest shake of the head. Eli turned back to me, ignoring my question. "And he had zero athletic capabilities."

"I did the sports," Will said. "I always kicked a ball around during recess."

"And that sport is called?" Eli gave me another wink.

Will scratched his forehead. "Badminton?"

"Badminton," Eli said. "Yes. A classic schoolyard game."

When we had almost decimated the nachos, Eli took a twenty out of his wallet. "I should probably head up soon. Our drummer gets grumpy if we're not all present and accounted for at least fifteen minutes before our set."

"What are you guys called?" I asked.

Will's eyes widened across the table. Underneath, he bumped my foot.

"The Mighty Mighty Kurt Tones," Eli said, straight-faced.

I shoved a soggy chip into my mouth. I needed a subject change or else I was going to laugh out loud. "You guys want to know how to make these nachos even better?"

"Yeah," they replied in unison.

I explained my theory, which involved divvying up the toppings and cooking the nachos in layers so the chips stayed crisper. Will and Eli stared at me blankly.

"You disagree?" I shoved a flaccid chip into my gob. It was still excellent.

Eli spoke first. "Fern?" He put one hand to his chest. "I know we've just met, but I believe you're my soulmate. Will you marry me?"

I laughed.

"A date, then."

I shook my head.

"Hear me out. We live on the same side of the city. You're incredibly hot, and I'm moderately gifted in bed." He pointed at Will. "I have a good job, my own place, and I'm a sick sax player. We have one mutual friend, who will vouch for me. There's really no reason not to."

"It's not you, honestly," I said. I looked at Will for backup, but he was staring at Eli.

"What's it going to take? I'll make a reservation somewhere nice."

I shook my head again. My hands had started sweating. I knew where this was going.

"Fern, you're killing me. How about a coffee?"

I swallowed. "I'm sorry," I said quietly. "I have a boyfriend."

As soon as the words had left my mouth, Will's head twisted toward me.

"That sounds like a line," Eli said, then turned to Will. "Is she really off the market?"

Will's eyes locked on mine, and my stomach pinched.

"I really am," I said, still looking at Will. "His name is Jamie, and we've been together for four years."

June 14, 1990

Peter's helping me with my gardening project. Dad said I could plant ferns and begonias along the path to the cabins if I took care of them. We took a golf cart out today so I could show Peter where I want everything to go. I told him Eric and I agreed to be exclusive, and he almost drove us into a tree. He says Eric is conceited, shallow, and has nothing interesting to say. He says he's not good enough for me. But considering Peter has said something similar about every one of my boyfriends since I was seventeen, it's not exactly a surprise. I used to think it was because he's five years older and sees me as a little sister. These days, I'm not sure.

Earlier this year, when Peter stayed the weekend with me in Ottawa, there was this moment. It was the night of my twenty-second birthday, and after everyone left, he started picking up empty plastic cups and told me to go to bed while he finished cleaning. I gave him a hug, and when I pulled back, he kept his arms around me. I swear he was going to kiss me. If I'm being honest, I was disappointed he didn't. I thought I must have been imagining things. But now I don't know.

13

Now

WILL AND I ARE WORKING ON THE BACK DECK, A WOOD-
pecker's hollow knock reverberating in the trees. He sits with his
legs stretched in front of him, a sliver of skin peeking out below
the hem of his pants. I don't know why I find his ankles so
compelling. I'm like a Regency era viscount hoping for a flash of
flesh.

It's well past six when his phone sounds—it's the ringtone
with the bells, and he rises to take the call.

A week has gone by since we took the canoe out on Smoke
Lake. Since we almost kissed. Neither of us has mentioned it, but
when I thanked him for the Patti Smith record, I could feel the air
pull taut between us. Otherwise, it's like I dreamed that moment.
Except sometimes I catch him watching me, hear him whisper
Perfect, and it takes me ages to refocus.

I'm texting with Jamie about the August dance and talent
show. It was a tradition even before any Brookbanks owned the
resort, an annual end-of-summer send-off with dinner and live mu-

sic. Mr. and Mrs. Rose have performed "The Surrey with the Fringe on Top" from *Oklahoma!* every year since my mom recovered the golf carts in the striped covers. There used to be a staff kick line, but Mom did away with it in the nineties. It's a major production, and I think it's too much for us to take on this year. Jamie and I have been debating for fifteen minutes. When Will steps inside with his phone and closes the sliding door behind him, I press the call button.

"You hate speaking on the phone," Jamie says instead of a hello. He drops his voice. "Did you smoke a little something, Fernie?"

"Very funny. I thought it would be easier to talk you out of this."

I've given Will full access to our books, and he has almost as many questions for Jamie as he does for me. I can tell Jamie is suspicious. He's pressed me for details about how I know Will, and all I've said is that we met once a long time ago. But he hasn't been defensive about having a consultant poke around. The dance is the one thing Jamie's stubborn about.

"You're not talking me out of it," he says now.

"The idea of throwing such a big event with everything else that's going on—I don't think it's a good idea." It's hard to imagine the dance without Mom there—I'm not sure I'm ready for that. *We'll do it next summer*, I think, catching myself before I say so.

"Fern." He says my name like a sigh, and I know whatever comes next will be serious. I don't think he's called me Fern (no *ie*) more than three times in my life. "We all loved Maggie, but it feels like the resort is still in mourning. I don't want to suggest that it's time to move on, but we need a celebration—the staff as well as the guests."

I close my eyes. In the background, Will's raised voice rumbles through the glass door. He's not yelling, but he sounds frustrated.

"You're probably right," I say to Jamie.

"I am. Plus, I've already booked the band."

I huff out a laugh.

"I'll take care of everything," Jamie says. "I've got you."

When Will returns ten minutes later, he's holding two cans of the lemon Perrier I've started stocking for him, the sleeves of his white shirt rolled to his elbows. I don't know why I find his forearms so compelling, either.

I look up from my laptop. The restaurant's executive chef has sent me a condescending email mansplaining the many reasons I should stay out of menu planning.

"Sorry about that," Will says, handing me a mineral water.

"About what?"

"I'm sure you could hear me."

"It's private. None of my business." I go back to my computer, trying to figure out the most professional way to tell the chef to screw off.

Will's quiet for a few minutes. "If I were to stay another two weeks, would that be okay with you?" My eyes spring to his. "The second real estate agent isn't coming until next week, and after that, I can review both scenarios with you: selling or staying on."

Will is supposed to leave next Sunday, something I've been quietly dreading.

"Stay as long as you want," I say, my tone neutral. "I'll make sure we can keep Cabin 20 open for you."

I fire off an email to our head of reservations. If Will stays for two more weeks, he'll be here for the dance. It might not be so bad, if he were there with me. I stare at the screen, but my mind has drifted back in time to us hot and sweaty and pressed together on a different dance floor.

"When you go over everything, are you going to tell me what you'd do if you were in my place?" I ask, collecting myself.

Will hasn't said if he thinks I should sell or not. I appreciate it, but I'm also dying to know his take. I've told him about my coffee shop fantasy and the little corner store I've wandered into so many times, the owners suspect me of shoplifting.

"I'll lay everything out for you, but this is your decision. And even if you wanted me to," Will says, seeing that I'm about to disagree, "I don't know what's best for you. Only you know that."

I narrow my eyes. "Will Baxter, you too-tall coward."

He lets out a laugh, big and booming and sunny as an egg yolk. I haven't heard that laugh in ten years. A blaze of victory radiates from my chest.

Will leans forward, his elbows resting on his thighs. "Have dinner with me."

"Dinner?" We've had beers after work a couple times, but dinner would mean crossing the keeping-things-professional line we've drawn. "With food?"

Will smiles, the corners of his eyes crinkling. "Food is usually involved."

I blink at him.

"Tonight," he says. "At my place."

The breathy laugh that leaves my mouth is ostentatiously nervous. "Technically it's my place. I don't know if you've heard, but I own this joint."

"I may have heard something like that." He holds my eyes. "Is that a yes?"

"I don't think you've asked me a question." It's supposed to come off as sassy, but I sound like a mouse negotiating with a lion.

He grins, and anticipation tightens my skin. "Fern, would you like to come over for dinner?"

"Yes," I say. I really would.

WILL ASKED FOR THIRTY MINUTES TO GET HIMSELF ORGANIZED. In that time, I have:

- Stood in front of my bedroom mirror, trying to determine whether I should wear something nicer than shorts and a tank top or if that would seem like I was trying to impress him. (Which I am. Maybe.)
- Tried on a blue silk dress I bought last week.
- Considered whether blue silk was too far out of my black, white, and gray fashion comfort zone.
- Debated changing out of granny panties.
- Dry-shaved my legs.
- Put on an itsy-bitsy pair of underwear.
- Taken off the sexy underwear and put the granny panties back on. (Just friends. Just friends. Not even friends! Colleagues!)
- Decided I was neurotic, bordering on gross, for putting on dirty underwear and changed into clean, unsexy briefs.
- Sweated through my dress and changed back into shorts and a tank top. Note to self: Colored silk is the enemy.
- Questioned whether to bring red or white wine.
- Downed a glass of white. I'll bring the red.
- Stared at myself in the mirror again and put on a sleeveless

black jersey dress that's plain in a *What, this old thing?* way but clingy in a *These hips don't lie* way.

By the time I knock on Cabin 20's screen door, I have worked myself into such a tizzy, I'm annoyed with both myself for being nervous and Will for being the cause of my dithering.

But when he steps onto the porch, his hair sticking up erratically like he's been running his hands through it, I forget all that. Because Will Baxter is wearing an apron. A black apron with vertical white stripes. I didn't know an apron could be sexy, but this apron is the lost Hemsworth brother of aprons.

"You're wearing an apron," is how I greet him.

"I'm wearing an apron," is how he replies. "I don't like to mess up my clothes."

"You do have very nice clothes," I say, still standing on the step.

He looks down at what he's wearing—a black T-shirt and a pair of faded denim cutoffs that come down to his knees.

"Usually," I amend. "Not that you don't look nice. You look nice." I may have forgotten about my nerves, but clearly, they have not forgotten about me.

Will's cabin is the same as the Roses', minus the bar cart. Screened back porch, a deck off the front that looks over the lake. A small eating area and kitchen with views of the water. The cast-iron fireplace is ancient but charming and the pine floors are well trodden. The walls used to be wood, too, but Mom had them insulated and drywalled so the cabins could be used year-round.

I follow Will into the kitchen and set the wine on the counter. There are veggies on a cutting board, two hamburger patties that look homemade, and a tinfoil packet of something ready for the barbecue.

"Burgers from scratch?" I ask, impressed.

"It's a very complex recipe," he says. "Meat, salt, pepper."

"Can I help with anything?"

"I think I've got it under control. Burgers, salad, potatoes. Sound all right?"

"Sounds perfect," I say, digging a corkscrew out of the utensil drawer. All the cabins are stocked with the basics. "I'll make my-self useful." I grab glasses from an upper cabinet and pour the wine while Will finishes chopping a cucumber and peppers for the salad. I watch, one hip leaning against the counter. His knife skills are dynamite. Mom would have liked that. He holds up a red onion, and I nod.

"You're one of those awful people who's good at everything, aren't you?" I ask as he slices it into thin, even rings. Half go in the salad, and the rest go on a plate with the other burger top-pings.

"Not at all, I'm terrible at . . ." He looks up at the ceiling, lips twisted to the side and one eye closed. He makes a humming sound.

"Humility?" I supply.

"No. I excel at humility."

I like Will like this. Loose and a little silly. Aside from the day of the almost-kiss, he's been so zipped up. I wonder what changed.

We move everything outside to the front deck, where the sun is starting its descent over the lake, casting everything in a saffron glow. Dragonflies twirl through the sky, hunting for their evening snack. I set the picnic table, placing cutlery and folded paper tow-els for napkins on the same side so we can share the view.

"This is nice," I say, looking at the water as we sit down to eat. Will's still in his apron, but I don't comment. I'm hoping he for-gets to take it off for the rest of the evening. Watching Will Baxter wear an apron is my new hobby.

"You sound surprised."

It's the first time I've sat on one of the decks, having a meal like a guest would. There are cedars between the cabins for privacy, but you can glimpse the neighboring cottages with their cheerful green awnings. The murmur of other dinnertimes carries down the shore. It's comforting.

"I guess I am. I mean, I knew it was gorgeous out here. I spent enough time cleaning cabins when I was a kid to get a good look at them. But I thought it might feel a bit exposed." I gesture to the row of cottages. "It doesn't, though. I don't mind the other people. It's kind of . . . cozy?"

"I think that's why a lot of people come to a place like this—you can be surrounded by nature but not isolated. There's a feeling of community."

I take a bite of my burger. It's good, maybe the best I've had. I'm not sure how, considering how simple it is: lettuce, tomato, onion, cheddar, meat. Even the salad is extra tasty, the dressing homemade.

"Where did you learn to cook like this?" I ask through my last mouthful.

"I'm not sure barbecuing counts as cooking."

"Don't be modest—it doesn't suit you," I say, wiping my hands. "Besides, I saw you with a knife earlier. You know what you're doing."

"I taught myself to cook, but I took a knife skills class a few years ago."

"I don't want to stereotype," I say, taking my gaze away from the sparkling water to look at his profile. "But guys like you don't usually cook. They go to restaurants and order delivery."

"Do they?" he says. "Tell me more about guys like me."

"I only mean you've got a big, fancy job. I'm sure there are long hours and client dinners."

"Fancy?"

"I saw the pictures online. Parties and fundraisers." Super-attractive ex-girlfriend.

"Ah." He slides his legs out from under the table and stands in one graceful movement, picking up our plates. I've reached the extent of New Will's low tolerance for personal information.

I rise, but he motions for me to stay seated. "I've got it," he says, stacking the salad bowl on the plates and taking the dirty dishes inside.

When he comes back out, he's not wearing the apron any-more. He takes a seat across from me and puts his arms on the table, slanting forward. He fixes his eyes on mine.

"I don't work long hours," Will says with the same tone he uses for business calls, like this is important information. It's true that Will is usually done between five and six, but he's also awake in the middle of the night. I assume he's working.

"Okay."

He studies me, serious, almost stern. A muscle ticks in his jaw. "And I cook most nights."

I feel like I've walked into a brick wall I somehow didn't see coming. I knew he and Jessica broke up, but I didn't think to ask if he was seeing anyone else.

"But not just for yourself." I try to keep the disappointment from my voice, but it comes out loud and clear, wearing a high-lighter orange construction vest.

"No."

I'll be mad at myself later for being so transparent, but I can't sit across from him for another second. I hoist myself off the bench. But Will's up fast, his hands reaching for mine. "Stay."

I look at him across the table and shake my head. I don't want to speak. I don't want either of us to hear my voice waver.

"Please," he says. "You asked for my story the day we went out in the canoe." *The day we almost kissed.* The words go unsaid but they're right there with us, shouting from a billboard. Will's hands fit around mine, his thumb tracing the pulse in my wrist. "I want to share it with you, if you'll listen."

I'M CERTAIN WHAT WILL IS GOING TO TELL ME WILL HURT, BUT I sit back down, blood sloshing around in my eardrums. He keeps his hands over mine, and he doesn't pull them away when he starts to speak.

"I wasn't totally honest with you," he says, and the sloshing turns into a roar. "But it's not what you think. The night I came over to help with Owen, you asked if I have children. I told you I don't, and that's true, but it's not the whole truth. I live with my sister and her daughter."

Despite my silence, it must be obvious that I'm not going to bolt, because Will takes his hands away.

"Annabel was young when my niece was born. I learned how to cook around then. They're the reason why I don't work late. Family dinners are kind of a thing in our house." He pauses. "My ex hated when I called it 'our house.' I own it, but they've always lived there with me."

"So that's why you know so much about babies," I say.

He nods. "And that's why I have my fancy job."

"I'm not sure I'm following."

"You remember I went to school in Vancouver?"

"Emily Carr," I say, quick as a reflex.

He smiles. "Emily Carr. I came back when Annabel was pregnant. It was complicated with our dad. He was about to get remarried, and Linda, his wife, wanted Annabel and the baby to stay with them, but I couldn't see that ending well for anyone. Dad and

Annabel were barely speaking. They had a huge fight when he found out she was expecting and wanted to keep the baby."

"And you couldn't stand being that far away."

"Right."

"What about the father?"

"David. He's not a bad guy, but he was young, too. They'd only been dating for a few months, and they were nowhere near ready to make a commitment to each other. Our grandmother was starting to need care of her own. I thought, at the very least, I could help Annabel out with a place to live."

I refill our wine, and Will takes a sip.

"My friend Matty was working at his dad's consulting agency in Toronto. He set me up with a graphic design job and a good salary. Helped me out with first and last month's rent. I had this idea that my sister and I would be roommates, and that I could lend a hand with babysitting after my niece was born." He plays with the stem of his glass. "I had no clue what I'd signed on for."

"How old is your niece?"

Will eyes me closely. "Nine."

"Nine," I repeat back. Will wasn't just a babysitter or proud uncle. "You helped raise her."

"Yeah."

Will tells me how Matty's dad offered to sponsor his MBA and how he earned it through night classes. He and the girls lived in an apartment until he saved enough for a down payment. I listen, and I can almost feel my mind bending to accommodate the new information.

"The early years were rough." Will rubs his neck as if he's deciding whether to say more. "I went from doing whatever the hell I wanted to having a nine-to-five and a baby at home. It kind of messed with me."

"What do you mean?"

He presses a finger against a knot on the tabletop like he's pushing something down into the woodwork. He doesn't look at me when he speaks. "We were so sleep-deprived, I was barely functional."

I don't think that's the full story, but I'm afraid if I press, he'll snap shut. "What about your art?"

"It's just not something I do anymore. There's no time."

"But you loved it," I say, and his gaze rises to mine. "You were so good."

Something flashes in his expression. "Yeah, well. I was lucky to find something that's allowed me to support my family." He hesitates. "Is that weird? That I call them my family?"

"Why would it be weird? Your sister and niece are *literally* family."

His shoulders relax. "That's how I feel, too. But it's been an issue . . . for women."

I don't react to the mention of other women, not outwardly. Inside, my dinner curdles. But then Will's eyebrows rise a little, like he wants to know whether it would be an issue for *this* woman, and my mouth goes dry.

He runs his hand through his hair when I stay quiet, further shuffling the haphazard sections. "Anyway," he says, "I like my work. My partner, Matty, he's the real brains. I'm mostly there to charm the clients."

"Hence the fancy parties," I say, though I don't believe this for a second. I've seen Will in action. I've googled him extensively. He's always been more than a pretty face. But I also remember how he used to talk about art—it's hard to buy that his job gives him the same satisfaction.

"Hence the fancy parties," Will agrees. "It's not what I pictured myself doing when I was twenty-two, but who the hell knows anything in their early twenties anyway?"

"You knew a few things," I say. "You helped me figure out I didn't have to end up here."

Will watches me. "But maybe that's changed for you," he says after a few seconds. "Maybe this is where you were supposed to end up after all."

I've wondered that, too. If I took the long route to find my way back home. I look out over the water. "Maybe."

WE'RE AT THE KITCHEN SINK WHEN THE TEXT COMES. WILL wouldn't let me wash the dishes after dinner, but I grabbed a tea towel, and he reluctantly began passing me clean plates to dry. He's wearing yellow rubber gloves, and they're almost as hot as the apron.

My phone lights up on the counter. It's from Philippe, and it's just one word.

Fate.

I frown at the screen, not sure what he's referencing.

"Everything okay?" Will asks, and then Philippe's second message arrives.

It's a photo of the outside of a building taken at night. It's slightly blurred so I have to examine it to recognize the redbrick corner store and see the sign in the window. I pinch the screen to zoom in.

"Oh my god."

"Fern? What's going on?"

I hold out my phone to Will, and he takes off the dish gloves. "It's for sale."

He studies the screen. "This is your coffee shop."

"Yeah." We stand side by side, looking at the photo together.

"This is it. I can't believe it's actually for sale." I thought the elderly couple who owned it had drunk the elixir of life and would hang on to the place forever.

Another text from Philippe pops up on the screen.

No time like the present, BB. Come back home.

Will double blinks and then clears his throat. "'BB'?"

"Short for Brookbanks."

I look at the photo again. Philippe's right. This *is* fate. This is the moment to make my dream happen. I have access to money. I have years of planning. I have a stack of baking cookbooks in my apartment closet and a storage unit of vintage furniture. I could put the orange velvet chair in the corner by the window. I could open Fern's.

"I used to want this so badly," I murmur, surprising myself. When did that change?

"You still talk to your ex?"

"Hmm?" I glance at Will, distracted. His eyes are darker than usual.

"I don't, really. We've exchanged a few messages."

Will frowns. "He asked you to come home."

"As in back to Toronto. He knows how much I want this."

"Do you?" he asks.

"I don't know. I don't know what I want anymore." I stare at the photo, my head beginning to throb. "I should go."

I thank Will for dinner, and he walks me back to the house. He says something when we pass the trail to the family dock, but I don't catch it because inside I'm unraveling. I'm not sure about anything right now—Will, the resort, my coffee shop.

I ignore the focused way he studies me when he says good

night. I close the front door behind me and seconds later there's a knock.

Will's in the doorway, his hands on either side of the frame. "I think that's bullshit," he says.

My hackles rise. He's never spoken to me like that before. "Excuse me?"

"I think you know exactly what you want. I think you want to stay here and run this place and you're afraid."

"You don't know anything about me," I snap, and Will's head jerks. The movement is subtle, but it's so satisfying. I want him to feel the way I did nine years ago.

"Don't say that," Will starts. "I know you're scared that—"

I cut him off. "You think you can show up here after all this time, spend a few weeks with me, and think you know me. You don't know a single thing about who I am and what it feels like to be back here."

His fingers whiten around the doorframe. Good.

"That's not true, and you know it," Will says, his eyes focused on mine. "You want to be mad at me? Fine. You want to scream at me? Do it. I deserve it." He leans in closer. "But don't tell me I don't know you."

I open my mouth, but nothing comes out.

Will's lip quirks and he goes on. "I know you love it here. It's plain across your face—the way you looked at the lake this evening. But it's also clear from how hard you're working. You wouldn't consider selling to a developer, and I don't think you want anyone else running the show here, either." He pauses. "I know you don't want to become your mother." His eyes drop to where my nails are scraping against my wrist. "I know you scratch when you're stressed. You chew on your cheek when you're making a decision, and play with your hair when you're nervous. You hum Talking Heads when you're concentrating. You love your friends. And you love it here." Every word is an arrow of truth piercing the center of a target.

"Screw you," I spit out, my chest rising and falling like I've been running on a track. "Who are you to tell me anything about my life? Just because you gave up on your dream doesn't mean I should give up on mine." I regret the statement as soon as it leaves my lips, but I'm too angry to take it back.

We stare at each other. I curl my hands into fists to keep from reaching for him—to push him away or pull him to me, I'm not sure.

"I don't think you should give up on anything, Fern," Will says. "I just think you won't admit what you want to hold on to."

And then he turns around and leaves.

14

June 14, Ten Years Ago

I THOUGHT WILL HAD DITCHED ME. HE'D EXCUSED HIMSELF TO the bathroom as soon as Eli went upstairs to get ready for his set. He was gone for so long, I leaned across the table to see if he'd taken his backpack with him. But there it was, across from me on the bench.

I ordered two Jäger shots while I waited, then applied lip gloss with an unsteady hand, wiping the excess on my thigh.

I'd been lying to Will all day about Jamie. Now we both knew it.

I held my breath when he returned. His hair was damp and pushed off his forehead as though he'd washed his face in the sink. He sat, not meeting my eyes, and stared down at the shot glasses, lips pressed together. I considered apologizing, but I wasn't sure what I should apologize for. It shouldn't have mattered that I had a boyfriend. I wasn't up-front about it, but it wasn't like I was leading Will on. He had a girlfriend.

"Listen," I started, although I had no idea what words would follow.

But Will lifted the glass closest to him and brought it toward his mouth. His eyes found mine and held them until I raised my shot. "Cheers," he said, and we tipped the black liquor down our throats.

Will slammed his glass down, then stood. I was certain he was about to say goodbye, but he walked to my side of the booth and held out his hand. "Let's go dance, Fern."

I wouldn't have guessed a Nirvana ska cover band would have much of a following, but the Mighty Mighty Kurt Tones had packed the people in. The upstairs venue was a long, narrow space, with a bar running along one wall near the back and a tight stage at the front. I'd never seen it so crowded.

Without speaking, Will led me to a stack of chairs in a corner. He took the tin of lemon drops from his backpack and stashed our bags under the chairs. He pressed one candy into my palm and popped another into his own mouth before threading his fingers through mine and leading me through the crowd. He'd said five words to me since he'd returned from the bathroom, and I couldn't tell if he was mad at me, mad at himself, or some combination of the two. It pissed me off.

I eyed the band as we made our way to the front. Every member was as dapper as Eli. They were squished on the stage in plaid pants and bowlers and checkered suspenders. Some of the audience was similarly dressed. Suit jackets. Fishnets. Fingerless gloves. I brushed past a woman in a kilt and crop top, then told Will to give me a minute and pushed my way back to our things. He didn't want me to go home and change, fine. But I wasn't going to feel like a frump. I unbuttoned my blouse and scrunched it into my bag, leaving me in my tank top.

Will didn't say anything when I found him, but I could feel his eyes straying from my neck to my arms to my chest. My top was tight, white, and not opaque. My bra was black. One of the straps had slipped off my shoulder, and I didn't care to pull it back up. With my short hair, there was nothing to hide behind. But I'd had four drinks and a shot of Jäger, and for the first time in years, I didn't feel much like hiding.

The lead singer stepped up to the mic, her hair rolled like a retro pinup girl, her waist cinched in a full-skirted polka-dot dress. As she introduced the band, I tiptoed up to Will's ear.

"You should have warned me about their name before I met Eli." I kept my eyes trained on his profile.

"Why would you need a warning?" he asked, his gaze not leaving the stage.

I didn't answer him. He knew I'd almost lost it when the words *Mighty Mighty Kurt Tones* left Eli's lips. "And you haven't even seen them play," I said.

I leaned closer, putting my hand on his arm to steady myself. Will knowing about Jamie made me feel as if a safety net had been unfurled below whatever balancing act we were performing. "You've taken a certified music snob to what could be the world's worst concert. Pretty bold move, Will Baxter."

He turned his neck, bringing his nose inches from mine. His gaze dropped to my mouth and lingered there. The net vanished. He met my eyes, then opened his mouth to say something as the bass began the first bars of "Smells Like Teen Spirit."

His mouth closed and we stared at each other as the drums kicked in, and then suddenly there was a burst of trumpet, sax, and trombone. We looked at the stage, and then back to each other, and then the room suddenly became a frenzy of leaping elbows and arms and knees.

"Holy shit, they're good," I yelled.

Will's smile was fluorescent. He grabbed my hand and lifted it above my head, twirling me around.

"I don't really dance," I said, trying to pull my arm back. It was mostly true. My friends sometimes forced me out when they wanted to shake off shitty dates or disappointing grades, but it was always under duress.

"You dance," Will shouted. He put his other hand on my waist. "We're dancing."

Will's moves were extraordinarily good. Even with my stiff hips and the number of times I stamped on his toes, I thought we probably looked like we knew what we were doing. Not that anyone was paying attention. We were smooshed onto the dance floor, and with every song, the room got warmer, more humid. Will's hair fell in his face, slick with sweat, and my shirt was soaked.

It didn't take much for our bodies to come together. A shove from someone sent me stumbling into Will. I glanced up at him to apologize, but he took my wrists and hung them around his neck. His body was hard and warm against mine.

"For the record, I can't dance for shit," I said the fifth time I trampled his foot.

He ran his hands down my back and along my sides, resting them on my hips. "You're perfect."

We danced like that, lined up together, eyes locked, his fingers pressing into me, until the Kurt Tones paused to fix a broken drum pedal.

We stopped moving and watched each other. Will swallowed, and his gaze dropped to my mouth again, and I knew that if he were single and I were single, his lips would have dropped there, too.

"Drink?" I said.

"Okay."

We wriggled our way to the bar, and he ordered two gin and tonics, and I tried not to look at the way Will's shirt stuck to his chest while the bartender fixed our drinks. He set them on the counter in front of us, a shriveled lime on each of their rims, and we grinned at each other. I took the straw out of mine and chugged it like it was water. It was half ice and so weak, it may as well have been.

"Let's stay near the back," I said when the music started up again. I was beginning to feel dizzy—fighting the heat and the noise and the ache in the arches of my feet. "It's so hot in here."

We stood at the edge of the crowd. Will kept looking between me and the band.

"You okay?"

I wiped my neck and nodded. But my thoughts swirled like a tornado, thoughts of Will and Jamie. Of Will's body moving against me. Will's arm brushed mine, and I automatically reached for his hand, pulling back when my fingers glided over his wrist. What was I doing? I wasn't used to drinking this much anymore—it had been years since I'd allowed myself to be anything more than slightly tipsy. I needed air. I looked around the room, judging the distance to the exit. When Will touched the small of my back, I jumped.

"You sure you're okay?"

"I have to get out of here."

He nodded. "Wait by the door. I'll get our stuff."

Will disappeared into the crowd. I edged over to the wall, pressing my forehead against the sticky surface. I stayed there, with my eyes closed, taking deep breaths, until someone touched my shoulder.

"Here," Will said. "Drink this. Then we'll get out of here."

I opened my eyes to find him holding a glass of water. He leaned over me, blocking out the room. I took a few long sips and handed the glass back to Will, and he finished the rest.

"Come on," he said, tucking my arm in his and helping me down the stairs.

We pushed out onto the front patio and then stopped. It was

pouring. Water spouted from the corners of the bar awning and pooled in gutters. Light reflected off the wet sidewalks, the air heavy and metallic. The street was almost empty, except for a few people huddled under a streetcar stop. It wasn't just rain. It was a torrential summer downpour. I stepped right into it.

I heard Will call my name, but I ignored him because I was already feeling better, the droplets cool against my skin. I raised my arms, closed my eyes, and lifted my chin to the storm. A minute later, a car raced through a puddle, drenching my shins, and I leapt back, shrieking.

Will stood beside me, water running down his face.

"All right," I said, tugging on his arm. "Let's go."

"Where are we going?"

And even though he already knew the answer, I told him anyway. "Back to my place."

July 5, 1990

Peter's been such a crab lately. I thought a double date for the Canada Day fireworks would cheer him up. He's always been nice to Liz. I thought everything would be fine and he'd change his mind about Eric if he spent more time with him. We sat on the hill in front of the lodge to wait for the sky to get dark. Liz and I were talking about our trip, and out of nowhere, Peter started grilling Eric. He wanted to know about his plans for the future and his entire dating history. I had to yell at him to cut it out.

When I went to the kitchen the next morning to tell Peter to back off, he was already in a bad mood. He called me superficial for liking Eric. He's never spoken to me like that before, like he couldn't stand me. I told him to take it back, but he turned up his music and ignored me. "I don't even hate The Cure that much," I yelled at him. He just glared at me and turned the volume up again. That was two days ago, and we still aren't speaking.

15

Now

I DON'T KNOW WHY I BOTHERED WITH PAJAMAS. OR LYING down, for that matter. I'm not going to sleep. Will left hours ago, but I'm still keyed up, my right foot tapping against the left like I've downed six shots of espresso. The moon must be bright—it's well past two, but I can see the lacy web of branches outside my window.

What I said to Will tonight was awful. I wanted to inflict pain. I could feel it in my teeth, the urge to bite down, to leave a mark. I didn't think I could explode like that anymore. My rage was like a tangible thing, something I could ball up and throw at him. It took me right back to being seventeen and screaming at my mother.

I haven't finished reading the diary entries that set me off, not that my mom was to blame. I couldn't handle the truth, even if I'd known it all along.

But I don't want to be angry. I don't want to lash out the way I did tonight. I'm ashamed of how I spoke to Will. He just started to open up to me, and I used it against him.

I shove off the sheets and walk to the window, although I don't need to check. Will's light is always on.

I don't give myself time to change my mind. I charge from my room, down the stairs, and out of the house, my skin pebbling as I run along the short path in my bare feet and up the steps of Cabin 20.

I'm smacking my palm on the screen door before I can question the logic of running here with my fuzzy bed hair and the oversized T-shirt I wear to sleep in. It says POT HEAD above an image of a coffeepot, and when I first saw it on the rack, I hated it, but then I decided I couldn't live without it.

Will appears in his underwear, pulling on a shirt. I catch a glimpse of skin and swirls of black, but it's hard to make out much of anything with the light shining behind him.

"Fern, what's going on?" He walks across the porch in three strides, but I don't give him a chance to open it before I start speaking.

"I was an asshole earlier," I tell him through the screen. "I'm so grateful that you're here, helping with the resort. I should have told you that before. And I think it's amazing that you have a job you like and a family who you love and that you know how to cook. You make a truly excellent hamburger, Will, and I want that salad dressing recipe." I let out a breath to put a stop to my rambling. "I didn't mean what I said about giving up your dream. I'm so sorry."

His face is in shadow so I can't see his expression. "All right," he says, his voice low. "Is that why you came here?"

"Yes? No." Will opens the screen door for me to come in, but I can't make my feet move. "I came here to apologize but also because I wanted to tell you that you were right. I know what I want."

Will pulls me through the doorway and onto the porch. He

puts his hands on my shoulders and leans down. Without thinking about what a terrible idea it is, I kiss him.

It's clumsy and quick, less a kiss and more of a leap toward
his lips, my mouth landing somewhere near the corner of his. I
pull away almost as soon as I make contact because Will does not
kiss me back. His arms do not encircle my waist.

Shit. I hadn't meant to do that. I meant to tell him I think I
want to stay at the resort. Now he's blinking at me, eyes wide.
Turns out insulting someone's life choices and then attacking
them with your mouth in the middle of the night is not an effec-
tive wooing strategy.

"I'm sorry," I sputter. "I should go."

I spin around, but Will catches my arm.

"Tell me what you want, Fern," he says behind me.

I shake my head, and he turns me to face him.

"Why not?"

"Because you already know," I say, barely audible. He knew it
then, and he knows it now. He doesn't need me to say it out loud.

"I want to be sure." His voice is a low rumble. "What do you
want, Fern?"

I take a breath and then whisper, "You."

The word has barely left my mouth when everything happens
at once. His arms band around me, pulling me up and off the
ground. My legs wrap his waist, my arms his neck. Our mouths
come together so fast that our teeth collide, and I start to laugh,
but it's extinguished by the urgent press of our lips.

Will walks us into the cabin, his mouth on mine, citrusy and
warm, shutting the door behind. I don't have time to register
anything except the dim glow of the living room lamp, because in
an instant Will has me pinned against the door. I take his face
between my hands, pressing my lips to his scar before I find his

mouth again. He rocks against me and I rock back, my thighs tight around him, moving my hips as much as I can, but it's not enough. An unfamiliar growl vibrates in my throat.

"I've thought about you for so long," Will says as he kisses down my neck, and I pull at his shirt, trying to get it off from under my legs. It takes me a second to realize he's whispering into my skin, telling the space below my ear how much he wants this, telling the underside of my jaw how beautiful I am.

Delirious and frenzied, I reach my hand between us, but he wraps his fingers around my wrist, bringing it above my head. He does the same with the other, so both my arms are held high.

"Don't move them," he says, looking me in the eyes. "Okay?"

I nod, but he doesn't move. "Yes," I tell him.

He unwraps my legs from his waist and sets me down so that I'm leaning against the door while he runs his hands up and down the sides of my hips.

"I've got a very long list of things I want to do to you, to do with you," he says, his voice rough.

"Better make a plan, then," I whisper.

A small smile sneaks across his lips. "I could do that." He takes my earlobe between his teeth, one hand reaching up to hold my wrists in place. "I could go from top to bottom," he says, tracing his nose down my neck. "Would you like that?" He presses his tongue along the underside of my arm toward my elbow, pushing his hips against mine to keep me still when I squirm.

"Yes," I tell him. "That works." He leans over me, and my forehead presses into his chest. The contrast of soft fabric and hard muscle and the smoky-sweet smell of him is overwhelming. And then I feel the hot damp of his tongue as he takes my pinkie finger into his mouth.

"Oh my god," I murmur, and I feel him smile around my

finger, his teeth brushing against the knuckle. He moves his tongue to my ring finger and does the same, sucking it into his mouth. I tilt my hips forward, rubbing against his bare thigh, but he slants himself back and out of reach. A more composed person might be embarrassed by the moan that I make. But I am not composed. I feel like I am being unwritten with every movement of Will's mouth, with each finger he envelops with it.

I'm shaking by the time he applies his lips to the opposite wrist, kissing my pulse, and then running his tongue back down my arm, sucking and biting until he's found my neck, back to where he started. He pulls my shirt up, bringing it past the tops of my legs, past my underwear, exposing my stomach. "I'm going to need this off," he says, but he doesn't keep pulling.

"Okay," I tell him, and in one swift movement, my shirt is gone. I hear him curse under his breath and he pauses for a long second, then reaches with both hands to tuck my hair behind my ears before crushing his mouth to mine, running his tongue over my bottom lip and then moving it back to my neck.

"Gotta stick to the plan," he says into my collarbone, cupping my breast and moving his mouth down my chest as he rolls the nipple between his fingers, gently, then a little harder. I cross my ankles together, squeezing my thighs, and the movement is so blatant that Will stops and looks between us.

"Or maybe you want a second option to consider?" He grins at me. "I could start at the bottom and work my way up. See if you like that better?" He runs a hand from my knee up to my hip, sliding his fingers under the cotton of my underwear.

"Good idea," I breathe. "I choose option two."

There's a flash of mischief in Will's eyes. "You sure?" He twists the fabric in his hand, pulling it tight between my legs.

I sigh out an "uh-huh" and then he drops to his knees with

his hands on my waist. My legs are shaking in anticipation, and I hold his shoulders to keep myself upright. Behind him, I get a glimpse of papers strewn about the floor and a set of pencils on the coffee table. But then Will wraps a hand around my left ankle and brings my bare foot to his mouth, his eyes on me. I try to pull it away. He traces his index finger along the bottom of my foot, and I squeal, twisting and attempting to stay upright.

"Option one," I cry.

"Too late," Will says, but he puts my foot on the ground. "I've already put option two into motion."

He grips both of my hips tightly. Even kneeling, he comes up almost to my chest, and he dips his head to trace up the inside of my leg with his tongue. I dig my fingers into his hair, pulling it back from his forehead so I can see him better.

"So soft," I murmur, and he nips the flesh of my inner thigh in response. He moves his thumb over my underwear to where every sensation is pooling tightly inside me, and I let out a sound that starts as a laugh but ends as a groan. He slips his thumb under the fabric, moving in little circles, and he brings his lips to my other thigh, lightly biting. My body can't make sense of the rapid transitions between pleasure and denial, between tickling and teeth.

"What are you even doing to me?" I mumble.

Will looks up at me from beneath the black line of his lashes, the golden lamplight kissing the tops of his cheekbones. He keeps moving his thumb, faster now, then shifts his hand so he can bring a finger over the spot where I'm wettest. I close my eyes, because Will is watching me with such hunger, I won't be able to maintain any semblance of control. I feel him slip a finger slowly inside, then after a few seconds, he adds another, setting a rhythm that brings me right to the edge, and just when I'm about to fall over, he slows down.

"No, no, no. Keep going. Keep going." I open my eyes, and Will's are fixed on me.

"I want to make you want this as much as I do," he says. "I want you to feel as desperate as I have all this time."

I tighten my grip in his hair, tugging in frustration, and Will closes his eyes. I make a new compartment in my brain and label it WHAT WILL LIKES. I tug a little harder and watch as he brings his hand under the waistband of his underwear, moving it back and forth a few times. I want to do that, I think, and I begin to lower myself to the floor, but Will stops me, holding my hips.

"I'm very dedicated to finishing my work, Fern," he says, and slides my underwear down, helping me step out of them. He eases my legs apart and then grabs my ass in his hands, bringing his mouth to where his thumb was.

My legs go weak, and I give his hair a sharp pull.

He moves his hands to steady me by the waist.

I feel the vibrations through me when he speaks. "Trust me."

He puts one leg on his shoulder, and when I'm close, I tell him don't stop, don't stop, don't stop, and this time he listens.

After I've gone still, he loosens his hold and I stumble. He stands, puts his hands on either side of my face, his fingers in my hair, his eyes darting between mine. Checking.

I want to tell him how good that felt, but I seem to have lost the ability to turn vowels and consonants into actual words, let alone string a bunch of them together in a sentence. Instead, I stand on my tiptoes and close the distance between our lips, kissing him hungrily. I reach down between us, running my hand over the hard length of him. I want more, more, more.

"I want more of you," I say. I'm not sure it makes any sense, but Will is nodding.

"You can have it all."

I feel like someone has handed me the keys to the most in-credible theme park and told me to play. I want to do everything at once. I want to be under him, on top of him. I want to fall to my knees. I want to push him to the couch. I feel frantic. My hands are trembling. I start with the basics. I grab the hem of his shirt and move it up over his stomach. Will helps me take it off, and when it's gone, I let out my most reverent "Holy shit."

The man is covered in ink. Not so much that there isn't a square inch of unadorned skin, but there have to be at least half a dozen tattoos over the planes of his chest, the ridges of his abdominals. The contrast between his fair skin and the designs, all done in black and gray, is striking.

"Have you always had these?" I trace the pencil that sits atop the jut of his right hip bone. It's held by long fingers. There's a meandering line that swirls out from its sharpened tip and disap-pears into the waistband of Will's boxer briefs.

"Since birth," he deadpans, sucking in his breath as I move my finger to his rib cage.

"I mean back then." If I had known he was hiding all this under his clothes ten years ago, I don't know if I would have had so much restraint.

"Some of them."

The name *Sofia* sits at the top of his right side, almost under his arm. I hate it immediately. I don't ask who she is. There's a lemon on his ribs that I adore and a comic strip across one side of his stomach. The lettering is instantly recognizable.

"You drew all of these, didn't you?" I say, peering up at him. He murmurs in the affirmative.

"Fern, I'll give you the guided tour later, okay?" he says, voice strained.

"I don't think so." I bend, bringing my mouth to the lemon.

"You had your turn, and now I want mine." I move my hand inside his underwear, wrapping it around him. "I want the world's greatest tour of Will Baxter."

Will tilts his head back, and I move my tongue along the ridge of his pelvis. He sucks in a sharp breath and clasps my wrist. "Bedroom."

I disagree. I have my own ideas that involve Will coming apart in my palm right now, so I keep going. Will puts his hands on his head, and just as his stomach muscles tighten in a way that tells me I'm about to get what I want, he hoists me right off the ground, and I have no choice but to hold on to his neck.

"But you were so close," I say in protest, and he sucks on the skin below my ear and says, "You have no idea how much self-control I can exert when it comes to you."

I bite his shoulder as he walks us into the room. "I'm very dedicated to getting what I want."

We tumble onto the bed on our sides, and I reach for the waistband of Will's underwear, but before I've lowered it an inch, he puts his hand on my cheek and says my name. My eyes find his. "Slow down, okay? I've waited a long time for this."

I nod, but his words and his gaze—the way he's looking at me, open and steady—stir up something I didn't feel moments ago. I'm lying on a bed, naked, with Will Baxter. I don't know where to put my hands. I don't know where to look.

Will lifts my chin so I'm staring at him. "Are you okay?"

I tell him the truth. "I think I'm nervous."

He smiles. "Me too. Do you want to stop?"

I shake my head. "Definitely not."

Will moves my hair aside, then kisses my neck. We make out for a long time, and Will keeps his touch to my shoulders and waist and hips, until I'm not nervous. I'm impatient. I move myself against him, taking his hand to my breast. I push his underwear down over his hips, and he doesn't stop me.

"I want you inside me," I tell him.

He begins to pull away, and I wrap my leg over his to hold him close. "Now."

"Condom," he says, and I blink. Right. He brings a strip back from the bathroom, and I watch him roll one on, then I pull him onto the bed.

"It's best for me like this," I say, turning so that he's spooning me. He reaches his arm around me, and I press back against him, but he doesn't take it for the invitation that it is. He pinches my nipple and kisses my shoulder, and then says, "I'll do whatever you want"—and then he shifts so that he's on top of me—"but I'd really like to look at you the first time. Okay?"

I swallow, my throat tight, then whisper, "Yes."

Will holds my gaze as he pushes inside me, taking his time, until we fit together fully. We stare at each other, unblinking. My heart feels like it's going to burst with an emotion I can't quite name. I don't realize there's a tear running from the corner of my eye until Will kisses it away.

I apologize. "That's never happened to me before. I'll be fine."

"You're sure?"

I nod. "I'm okay."

Will presses his lips to mine, sweetly, and then begins to move in a slow rhythm. "We can do better than okay."

THE SUN HASN'T YET RISEN WHEN I'M WOKEN BY A LOON'S mournful tremolo. There's only the soft predawn light and the bird's strange, beautiful song. It takes a few seconds for my eyes to adjust enough to see where I am, to remember that I'm not at the house. Last night comes back in a flash of sweat-slicked skin and tattoos. My face pressed against a pillow, Will curved over me, whispering in my ear. That was the second time.

I remember gathering the courage to ask him to hold me as we fell asleep, wanting the comfort of his body pressed to mine. It's not something I usually request of my bedmates, to fit themselves around me, and I wasn't sure I could ask it of Will. In the end, I didn't need to. He tucked himself around my back, holding me to him. I drifted off with his lips pressed to my shoulder.

Rolling over, I find Will stretched out on his back, sheets bunched around his waist, his hair a black bramble.

I decide to take the opportunity to look at his tattoos more closely before I slip out. I don't want a guest witnessing me sneaking back to the house in my pajamas. More than that, I don't know how to be with Will in the light of day.

"I guess we didn't get around to the tour last night," Will rasps, startling my study of the name *Sofia* on top of his ribs.

"I decided to take a self-guided one."

He tucks a hand behind his head and pulls me up so I'm resting in the crook between his chest and arm. It catches me off guard, and I stiffen. Casual sex and morning-after cuddling don't usually go together, and this was the dictionary definition of a late-night hookup.

Will squeezes me. "Hey, where did you go?"

"Sorry. I was thinking."

"What are you thinking about so hard?" His fingers twist around a strand of my hair.

"I think," I say, running my hand over his stomach, "you have a lot of tattoos."

He tousles my hair, and everything inside me unwinds a little. "Are you always this observant in the morning?"

"I don't really boot up properly until I've had coffee." I clear my throat. "I should probably get back to the house before I have to walk-of-shame it in front of guests. I don't think that's the kind of wildlife they're hoping to see here."

He moves his hand down my bare back, cupping the arch of my hip. "But I had big plans this morning." I suck in a breath as his fingers skim lower.

"Tempting, but—"

"Fern," he says softly. "Don't leave yet. I'll go over to the house later and get you a change of clothes, okay?"

"Okay." I turn my head and bury my smile in his chest. I know this isn't going anywhere. Will has a life in Toronto, and I . . . well, I think I'm going to have one here. For now, though, I can stay a little longer.

"So why all the tattoos?" I run my finger down the fir tree on his arm.

"Women love them."

"Women like Sofia?"

He chuckles and runs his hand through my hair. "Oh yeah, Sofia definitely loves them." I twist my neck to find him smiling down at me. "Sofia's my niece." Will must see the relief as plainly as I feel it, because his smile deepens.

"Oh," I say. "I don't think you told me her name before." He tucks me back in the crook and snakes his fingers through my hair again.

"No? That wasn't intentional, but now I'm glad I didn't. You're cute when you're jealous."

I make a *pfff* sound. "You're impossible." I run my hand over the name. "Do you miss her?"

Will lets out a breath with a *whoosh*. "It's the longest I've been away," he says slowly, like he's choosing his words from a forty-page menu. "But my sister was adamant it would be a good break for all of us."

"And has it been? A good break, I mean?"

He tilts his head down so he can see my face. "Are you kidding?"

I shake my head.

"I've been working, yeah, but it's felt like a complete vacation. I haven't had this much alone time in ages. It's been amazing. A total break from reality."

A break from reality. The words bash around in my skull.

I point at the four-panel comic on his stomach; the first shows a scruffy guy surrounded by moving boxes. "Is this your comic?"

"The first strip of *Roommates*, yeah."

"Do you ever think about starting it up again?"

"The comic, no."

"But what about drawing? Even if it's just for fun?"

He's quiet for a long beat. "I've been sketching a little since I've been here."

I think of the cartoon in the card he gave me and the pencils I saw scattered about the living room last night. "You've had more time to yourself."

"Yeah, it's that. But it's also . . . I don't know. I guess I've been reminded about that side of myself."

I look up at him and am startled by the weight in his expression.

"I'm glad," I murmur, then brush my hand over the tattoo below his collarbone. Two tiny words. *Only thoughts.*

"What does this mean?"

Will goes completely still. "It's a reminder," he says.

"For what?"

He blinks twice. "Nothing important."

"Usually people don't get tattoos of things that aren't important."

"I guess that's true," he says. But he doesn't elaborate.

I look up at him, frowning, and he rubs his thumb over the lines between my eyebrows, trying to smooth them out.

"Let's talk about something else," he says. His other hand skims over the flesh of my bottom. "Better yet—let's not talk at all."

FOR THE SECOND TIME TODAY, I WAKE UP IN WILL'S BED, BUT he's no longer in it. I hear the gurgle of brewing coffee, and I'm about to take one of his pristine white button-ups from its hanger, but I pull a soft navy blue T-shirt from the dresser instead. The logo on the chest is a little red heart with cartoon eyes, and I know that means it's expensive, but I like his T-shirts. They remind me of twenty-two-year-old Will. The hem falls midway to my knees.

I walk through the living room. There's no sign of the paper and pencils I saw last night, and I find Will looking out the kitchen window, palms flat on the counter. He's put on underwear, but that's it. I stop before he hears my footsteps, taking a moment to appreciate the topography of bone, muscle, and smooth skin that is Will Baxter's back.

"Good morning," I say. "Again."

Will turns around, his eyes sliding down to where the shirt brushes against my legs.

"I like . . ." He raises his eyebrows, and nods in my general direction. "This."

"This?" I slant my head.

"Yeah. You here. In my clothes."

There's a shadow of stubble on his cheeks that I haven't seen since the first morning he was here, and I want to run my hand over it. But I pull a couple of mugs down from the cupboard, heart hammering under my ribs. Morning-after caffeination is not usually something I stick around for. "And I like . . . coffee."

"I hope I didn't wake you up when I got out of bed. I didn't want to move you off me." His eyes glimmer at this. "But I have a call at ten."

"That's okay. I should have left earlier." I fill the mugs, passing one to Will.

He pulls a carton of half-and-half from the fridge and pours it into his cup along with three heaping spoons of sugar. I take a sip of my own, black, sighing at how good it is.

"Wait a sec." I pause. "Where'd you get the coffee maker?"

Will grimaces. "I bought it in town my third day here. Those pod machines are terrible."

"God, I know." I've got to replace them. "That reminds me. I have a bunch of resort stuff I want to talk to you about later. What does your schedule look like?" The last thing I want is to jeopardize our working relationship. If I decide to stay, I'll need Will's help more than ever. But I'm not going to get into all that before his meeting.

"We have a pitch today. It's at two and will probably drag on for a bit."

I feel a pang of guilt for coming here so late. "Who's the client?"

Will's forehead creases. He puts his mug on the counter and takes a step closer. "Do you really want to talk about my work right now?" he says, brushing a strand of hair behind my ear. "Because I would rather talk about last night."

"Oh," I say. "Last night was . . ."

Will puts his hands on my hips and pulls me toward him, kissing my neck under my jaw, and then he says into my skin, "Last night was what, Fern?" He nips at my earlobe.

"Last night was . . . nice." *A break from reality.* Will's description crawls through my mind.

"It wasn't nice." He cups his hands around my face. "It was amazing. This morning was pretty amazing, too."

I should tell Will that, as amazing as it was, I can't see him like this again. It's one thing to have a crush, but naked sleepovers will only lead to ruin. I don't think my heart can handle being Will's break from reality for the rest of his time here.

But then he kisses down my neck, his stubble tickling my skin. "I think we should try it again, don't you?"

I nod. "Come over as soon as you're done."

16

June 14, Ten Years Ago

IT WAS ALMOST MIDNIGHT WHEN WILL AND I MADE IT TO THE mansard-roofed Victorian where I lived. It would have been a grand home at one time, but its guts were now hacked into a warren of apartments. The smell of fried onions accompanied us down the gloomy, narrow hallway to the back of the building. I hoped Will wasn't paying attention to the yellowing paint and the stained orange carpeting.

He leaned against the wall, hair plastered to his cheeks, while I struggled with the lock.

"My hands are slippery," I mumbled.

We were drenched. The rain was so heavy that running would have been pointless. Instead, we walked quickly as lightning flashed in the northwest and the old trees that lined my street swayed in the wind, their branches thwacking the power lines.

Will followed me inside, and together we surveyed the tiny room that contained the whole of my life in Toronto. A double bed was pushed against one wall, the "kitchen" on the opposite.

You could stand between the two and touch the counter with one arm and the end of my bed with the other. There was just enough room for a pair of vinyl-covered dining chairs and a little wooden table.

"Small would be an understatement, as you can see." I wasn't a tidy person by nature, but I'd learned to keep it neat. I made my bed every morning, washed the dishes after I ate. There wasn't much to decorate, but I'd painted the walls a pale shade of mint and hung a couple of prints I found at a secondhand shop—a forest under an inky night sky and a donut ad that looked antique but certainly was not.

Will slipped off his backpack, his eyes traveling to a Grizzly Bear concert poster hanging above my bed. "It has a lot of personality," he said. "It seems very you. The window is amazing."

It was. It looked onto the backyard and had deep sills and a leaded glass pane across the top. It was what I liked best about the apartment—the hallway was ominous, but inside, the original hardwood floors and thick baseboard trim were still intact.

"There's a claw-foot tub in the bathroom, too," I said. "But the water pressure sucks." Why was I talking about water pressure? Bringing Will back to my apartment had not been premeditated. Dancing was one thing—a step too far, probably. All I knew when I invited him here was that I didn't want to let him go. But now what?

I scratched my wrist. "Well, I should probably get changed. I'd lend you something, but I doubt even my biggest shirt would fit you."

"I think it would be a smidge small." Will gave me an off-kilter half smile. "But that's okay. My coveralls are in my bag."

I pulled dry clothes out of my dresser, tossed Will a towel, and shut myself in the bathroom, taking twice the amount of

time I needed to change. I brushed my teeth, slicked on deodorant, and twisted my body around in the mirror. I'd put on a pair
of baggy gray sweats and another white tank top and a white bra.
No silly business here. I waited until I couldn't hear Will shuffling
around on the other side of the door.

He was standing by the table, holding a framed photograph
while rain pelted the window. His hair had been rubbed into
chaos, and his sleeves were rolled past his wrists, hiding his tattoo
once again. The walls appeared to have shrunk in around him.
My apartment was not big enough to accommodate a Will.

"Is this your mom?" he asked.

The lights flickered.

I moved beside him, looking at the picture. "Yeah, and that's
Peter with us." It was taken the night of my high school graduation. I'm wedged between the two of them on the lodge deck, the
lake a blue blur in the background. Peter hadn't wanted to be in
the shot. I remember Mom whispering something in his ear and
having the strange sense I was witnessing something private. Peter's face remained placid, but he'd nodded and stood beside me,
wrapping an arm around my shoulders.

"You look just like her."

"I know. It used to bother me." Mom had worn her hair short
since I could remember. After I cut mine, the likeness was un-
canny. I didn't mind the resemblance anymore. I wasn't sure when
that changed.

"She's beautiful," Will said. My eyes swung to the side of his
face, but he continued to study the photo.

"Your hair used to be so long."

"Yeah, this is pretty new." I twiddled a strand near my forehead.

Will put the frame down. "Was it always just you and your
mom?"

"I don't have a dad, if that's what you mean."

I took a step to the right so I could fill glasses with water. The kitchen was only a few feet of counter, a sink, an ancient gas stove, and a small fridge. I passed Will a tumbler and sat on the edge of the bed, kicking out a chair for him to sit in.

"My grandparents lived at the resort until I was twelve, but Peter was always around. He's the pastry chef there. His days start early, so he'd be done with work by the time I got home from school. We used to have these tea parties when I was little. He'd make crustless cucumber sandwiches and we'd listen to Talking Heads and the Ramones." I smiled. "One of my earliest memories of Toronto is having afternoon tea at the Royal York hotel with Peter." He'd been trying to convince Mom to do a fancy tea at the resort—he lost that argument.

Will inspected the room again, his eyes landing on the closet. It was little more than a single-door cubby and so stuffed it wouldn't close properly. "I guess you couldn't start packing with your friend here?"

I flopped back on the bed. Whitney's visit had given me an excellent excuse not to think about boxing up my stuff. "I can't believe I'm going to have to live with my mom again."

"Why do you have to?" I heard Will say.

I blinked up at the crack that ran through the ceiling. I could draw the fissure with my eyes closed. "Well, unless I want to bunk in the staff cabins, and I definitely do not, there really isn't another option. The resort is kind of remote and I don't have a car."

"Right," Will said. "But what I meant was, why do you have to go home at all?"

A crack of thunder saved me from answering. I jerked upright, sending a crushing pressure to my skull.

"We need some music." I opened my laptop on the table next to Will, and the Brookbanks website stared back at us. Mom had called as Whitney and I were heading out the door this morning. She wanted our opinion on the new room reservation tool.

"Is this it?" Will leaned forward. The photographer had gone out in a boat to get the shot of the lodge sitting atop its grassy hill, the beach below. It looked like an oversized ski chalet, a three-story stone-and-wood château with a gabled roof.

"That's it." I clicked off the page and over to my iTunes, scrolling through my albums.

"What about them?" Will asked. When I turned to see what he meant, his face was so close, I could see an almost invisible smattering of freckles on his cheeks. I followed his gaze to the poster on my wall.

"Grizzly Bear? Sure." I clicked on their most recent album. "I saw them at Massey Hall last year. Peter bought me tickets. That's when I got the poster."

I sat back on my bed as the first track began. "In my ideal world I'd have the space and the money for a record player."

"And a brand-new *Horses* LP."

"Exactly. But I'm very happy with my streetcar pin."

Will tapped his fingers on the table. Our conversation felt stilted for the first time.

"If *you* could have anything right now, what would it be?" I asked to fill the dead air.

Will blinked in surprise, and a blush slunk up from under his collar. "I'd probably have something to eat."

"You're hungry? After all those nachos?"

"I'm hungry after almost everything."

"Noted."

I might have been able to open the fridge with my foot if I were as tall as Will, but as it was, I needed to get up to stare at its empty shelves. I hadn't had a chance to restock after Whitney's visit.

"I've got pickles?" I looked over my shoulder and noticed the paper bag on the counter. "Oh, actually. I have something much, much better."

Peter had sent two loaves of sourdough down with Whitney, and there was still part of one left. "It's not super fresh, but it'll toast up great." I held it out to Will in one hand and waved my other around it as if it were a prop in a magic trick. "Prepare to be amazed."

"I'm not sure I've seen someone this excited about bread before."

I stopped moving. "This is not just bread. This is Peter's sourdough—and it's going to change your life."

"Is that so?"

The lights flickered again, and we both looked up, then back at each other.

"I guarantee it. After tonight, you'll never be the same, Will Baxter."

As I was getting our snack ready, a gust of wind toppled the garbage bins in the yard. The rain came harder against the glass, and my light dimmed, flashed once, then went out.

"Shit."

"Do you think it's only your place?"

I shuffled over to the window to check the streetlights, which had also gone dark.

"Nope."

"You've got a bit of a serial killer thing going on right now," Will said, his face glowing in the blue of my laptop screen. I was still holding the bread knife.

"Ah, you've figured it all out," I said, raising it in the air. "I tricked you into thinking I was an innocent country lass." I frowned, dropping the knife to my side. "The toaster is out of commission." I chewed on my cheek, thinking. "I'll just use a pan." The stove was older than me and the back right-hand burner was broken, but because it was gas, I could cook in a power outage.

"Do you have a lighter?" Will asked as I was frying the bread. "I can do your candles."

"In my bedside table." I was so caught up thinking about the equation of romantic lighting plus Will plus small room that it wasn't until he was opening my drawer that I remembered what was inside. "No, wait. Don't do that. It's in my bag. In the Ziggy Stardust pouch."

Now my pulse galloped, and with every snick of the lighter, my skin felt snugger. Will lit all five of my candles, each nestled safely in a glass jar, delivering one to the bathroom and one to the counter next to me. Another went to the table, a fourth to my dresser, and the last beside my bed. When he'd finished, the room quivered with gold.

"Your laptop only has twelve percent battery. Should I shut it down in case the power's out for a while?" Will asked, interrupting my increasingly attentive bread frying.

"I guess you better."

With that, the music halted.

It was just the two of us now. And one plate of toasted sourdough.

I set it on the table along with a small ramekin of flaked salt and butter and took the chair beside Will.

"Put a little salt on top," I said, demonstrating. I waited for Will to do the same before I took a bite, watching as his eyes widened. The sound he made, his mouth still full, was something along the lines of *Fuuuuh*.

"Peter made this?"

"Yeah. It's what we serve at the Brookbanks restaurant."

"Now I have another reason to get up to your resort. I'm go-

ing to shake that man's hand and eat seven loaves of sourdough."
He took a bite and said while chewing, "The lake looked nice,
too—maybe I'll take a canoe out while I'm there."

"Oh yeah? I'm having a hard time picturing you in the bush.
Will Baxter in a canoe?" I shook my head, smiling.

He gave me a scowl. "I'd look great in the bush. Sensational
in a canoe. You'll just have to show me how to hold a paddle."

"How about this: I'll take you out in a canoe, teach you how
to do a J-stroke, and make sure you don't embarrass yourself. But
in return, you have to show me your drawings." If we were going
to play make-believe, I might as well shape the fantasy how I
liked.

"You want to see my work?"

"Yeah." I sucked butter off my fingers. "So bring your portfo-
lio when you come."

Will pushed his cheek out with his tongue, regarding me. "I
could show you now."

I paused, index finger still in my mouth.

"I have a sketchbook with me," he said. "I always carry one
around. It's mostly ideas for *Roommates*. There are a few portraits."
He shrugged. "If you want."

"Really? You don't mind?"

He scratched the back of his neck. "I don't love watching
people look at my stuff, but I trust you not to say something terrible." He gave me a serious look. "Even if you think it's basic."

"I would never."

But as Will rummaged through his bag, I began to worry. I
was terrible at faking it.

"Here." He handed me a battered green Moleskine, then sat,
elbows resting on knees, chin perched on one hand.

I started at the beginning and went slowly, studying the figures on the unlined pages. The same four characters were drawn many times over, sometimes rendered in fine black ink and sharp, confident lines and other times in scratchy pencil.

"You are good," I said, glancing up at him, but he didn't respond, just watched as I turned the pages.

One of the characters was dozy-eyed, slumped, and always carried a sandwich in his hand. Another wore a man bun. The one who was obviously Will was a beanpole with an exaggerated nose. One page was full of notes. He wrote in tidy capital letters.

"Ideas for strips," Will said when I got to it.

Scattered throughout were realistic sketches of trees and bridges and everyday objects—a bowl of lemons, Will's backpack dropped in a corner. There were a few portraits. My favorite was of a girl swimming, her hands splashing up water, a toothy smile on her face.

"This is incredible," I told Will.

"Thanks." He cleared his throat. "That's my sister. It's not always easy to find people to sit for me, so mostly I use photos. That was from our family vacation to Prince Edward Island when we were kids."

"You can do me if you want." I closed my eyes. "I mean, if you wanted to draw me, you could."

Will didn't say anything, so I opened one lid. "Was that weird? I just thought you might want the practice." I picked up another slice of sourdough, examining the holes with new fascination.

"Actually, I'd like that."

I peered up from the bread. "Really? So how do we do this? Do you want me to put a chair over there?" I motioned to the other side of the room, near the door.

Will took the piece of bread from my hands and set it on the plate. He looked around the space, his eyes settling on the bed. "No. You go there."

IT STARTED WITH ME AT THE HEAD OF MY BED AND WILL ON A chair by the foot. He turned to a fresh page, staring at it for a full minute and then at me, first my face and then the rest. His hand moved across the page in quick, short strokes. He kept tilting forward, squinting at me in the darkness.

"Do you want me to move closer?" I said after his third tilt and squint.

He looked up, pausing. "Yeah, that'd be great."

I shimmied forward. "Can we talk, or will that mess with your process?"

"We can talk."

"How long do you usually stay when you come back to Toronto?" I hoped I wasn't being completely obvious.

Will gave me a lickety-split smile before he went back to drawing. "Depends. This trip was a bit over a week. Usually it's just a few days."

Not very long, then. Not enough time to visit me up north. "Oh. Why the longer stay?"

"My dad's getting remarried. There was an engagement party last weekend, and I hadn't met his fiancée, so there was a lot of getting-to-know-you stuff."

"Did it go okay?" I'd never had to navigate the ins and outs of parental love lives. If I didn't know better, I might have believed Mom willed me into being.

"I guess. She seemed genuinely into my dad. But I wanted to be like, *This guy, really? You know he washes prewashed salad, right?*"

I laughed, and he thought for a moment.

"It was weird to see him with someone other than my mom. Annabel has met her a bunch of times and likes her, and my sister is a tough critic. I hope . . ." He stared down at the sketch.

"Are you all right?"

He nodded once, then looked up at me. "It bothers me. That I left, like our mom did. Dad is so hard on Annabel, but maybe when Linda moves in, things will get better." He rubbed his eye. "Anyway, I unloaded on him last night, not that it will make a difference. It was good to have a distraction today, to not have to go home and deal with him." Will went back to drawing.

"If you want to crash here tonight, you can," I blurted out.

The pencil stopped.

"If you want."

He looked up at me.

"You can."

We watched each other, and then Will resumed sketching. Neither of us spoke for several minutes until he said, "So what's he like—the boyfriend?"

"Jamie?" I stared at Will, trying to intuit why he was asking, but all I absorbed was the length of his eyelashes.

"Yeah. Jamie."

"He's great," I said slowly. I hadn't described Jamie to another person in such a long time, and I didn't love the task of explaining him to Will. "He's very chill. Funny. He's the kind of person everyone likes—he's the caramel pudding of humans."

"You've lost me," Will said.

I looked at the *surrealist* pin on his collar. "It's kind of an inside thing—what type of dessert we'd be. He's caramel pudding—sweet and smooth and crowd-pleasing."

Will glanced at me. I could have sworn he was smirking. "And what about you, Fern Brookbanks? What kind of dessert would you be?"

"Me?" I swallowed. "Jamie thinks I'm a lemon tart."

I watched Will's chest rise and fall. He tipped his head toward his book. "And what do you think *I'd* be?"

I could taste Peter's salted chocolate torte, that hint of chili. "I dunno . . . a chocolate log?"

"Chocolate log?"

"Yeah. You know, with the chocolate wafers and whipped cream?" I should have thought before I'd opened my mouth.

"Uh-huh," Will said. "What else?"

I knew he didn't mean what else about the log. I took a deep breath.

"I've known Jamie for a long time, but he was always just an older lake kid."

Will glanced at me. "How much older?"

"Three years. His family has a cottage near the resort. Anyway, I was kind of a mess at the end of high school, and Jamie and I were working together. He was the only person who didn't judge me." Will looked up from his drawing. "That was the beginning."

"Four years ago?"

"Right. We work together at the resort every summer. Jamie stays in the staff cabins instead of his family's cottage because he likes it there so much." I picked at the blue polish on my index finger. "I do not relate."

"That's not the sense I got."

"Are you serious?" Had I not explained to him how I didn't want to go back to the resort?

"Yeah. At the gallery today . . . and the way you spoke about it. I don't know. I got the impression you love it up there."

I blinked at him. In so many ways, I did. I loved watching a storm move across the lake. I loved hanging out in the pastry kitchen with Peter, and playing cribbage with the Roses, and taking a kayak out on a still day. "Maybe."

I stared down at my hands. Things had been better with Mom

since I moved in here before the start of my second year of university. I never appreciated her Type-A-ness, but the day she and Peter helped me unpack, she attacked scrubbing and organizing the apartment as if it were a military operation. In one afternoon, the burnt cheese was scoured from the stove; the bathroom tile grout was revealed as white, not gray; and each of my pots, pans, and utensils had been washed and assigned a home. I was grateful and tired when we were done, but instead of them going back to their hotel room, Mom suggested the three of us celebrate. We sat outside at a little restaurant on the end of my street and ordered pizza and red wine and reminisced about the summer. It felt like we were a normal family having a night out, and I guess we were. When Mom dropped me off at my dorm the year prior, I couldn't shove her out the door fast enough. But I clung to her as we hugged goodbye that night, wishing she could stay a little while longer.

"If I didn't go home . . ." I shook my head. "It's not an option."

"And what about Jamie? You haven't told him?"

"No. I can't see that going over well. I think Peter is the only person I could talk to." I thought about the playlist he'd made me. "He probably already suspects anyway. He knows me better than anyone."

"You love him?"

I glanced at Will, surprised.

"Peter? Yeah. He's the closest thing I have to a dad."

"I meant Jamie."

I didn't intend to leave a gaping pause, but he'd caught me off guard. "Of course. I wouldn't be with him if I didn't."

He nodded.

"Are you in love with Fred?"

"No," he said without hesitation. After a second he added, "I thought I might have been. But I've realized I'm not."

I wanted to know how he figured that out and when, and why they were still together if that was the case. But asking those questions seemed dangerous. Instead, we both went quiet, and I watched the candlelight flicker against Will's cheeks, getting lost in its hollows.

The rain fell harder, hitting the window sideways. Eventually, Will's hand stilled.

"I'm worried you're going to hate it," he said.

"Honestly, me too."

He shifted to the edge of the bed. I scooted beside him. I left a few inches of space between us, but I could feel the heat of his body, smell the rain in his hair and the paint on his clothes.

I leaned over the page, and there I was, captured in fine strokes of graphite, in shadow and light. The illustration was careful and detailed, the focus clearly on me, the bed and room blurring out around me. My chin rested on my knees, arms wrapped around my shins, feet bare. There was a slight upward slant to my lips, my eyes widened in a kind of secretive delight.

"You have this look when you're excited about something—I was trying to get that." He ducked his head so he could read the expression on my face. "Your nose was hard, too."

"My nose?" I brushed my fingers over it.

"How did I do? Do you hate it?"

I shook my head. "No. It's . . ." I wanted to explain how it felt as if no one had really seen me before that moment, but all I came up with was, "It's me."

August 3, 1990

My period is late. My period is never late. I was supposed to get it six days ago.

But I can't be pregnant. I've been careful. I'm on the pill.

I have a plan. Managing the resort by twenty-three. Married by twenty-six. Two children before I'm thirty.

I'm not supposed to have kids for at least another five years!

Europe. Work. Marriage. Babies. That's the order things are supposed to go in.

I'm not pregnant. I'm not. I can't be.

Except my boobs hurt. A lot.

17

Now

I DIVE OFF THE END OF THE FAMILY DOCK, SLICING THROUGH the water until I'm forced to surface. I put on my suit as soon as I got back from Will's cabin and took the kayak out. But it didn't help me take the edge off having spent the night with him, the prospect of spending another night together.

Long before I was born, my grandparents and mom would come here to spend time by the water. The shoreline is private, tucked into a small bay—you can't see the cabins or the resort's beach. There are two metal chairs, their red paint peeling, and a short, equally worn dock. A gnarled cedar grows out over the water; the base of its trunk lies parallel to the surface. Whitney and I used to strut down it like it was a catwalk. When we were eleven, she talked me into dressing up in Mom's formalwear and taking a stereo with us to get the full effect, but she fell in the lake wearing a silk tea dress. Mom had us collecting errant tennis balls around the courts for the rest of the summer.

I preferred swimming at the family dock, away from everyone, but Whitney liked the beach for scouting Mystery Guest targets when we were younger and cute boys later on. This was Mom's favorite spot, where she came to enjoy her coffee and a sliver of solitude.

My brain is like an overstimulated magpie, struggling to decide which shiny object to land on.

The resort.

Will.

The resort.

The thing Will does with his thumb.

I'm not much of a swimmer. I love being in the water, though I'm mostly a lounge-on-a-pool-noodle kind of fish. But today I paddle back and forth until my mind shuts up.

Wrapping myself in a towel when my lungs and arms give up on me, I sit in the same chair I always have, the one on the left. I watch the waves from a boat's wake crash against the rocks and scrub at the shore, and for a second, it's like Mom is right there beside me, holding a steaming mug.

This was our place—the only one that ever really felt like hers and mine alone. We'd come in the mornings, and Mom would leave her BlackBerry at the house. In the middle of summer, she wouldn't have time to linger, and as soon as she finished, she'd be up and out of her seat. But in the fall, we'd bring streusel-topped muffins Peter had baked and stay here until I needed to get ready for school. In spring, we'd trudge through the melting snow and huddle under blankets.

I love it here, she would sigh. *Aren't we lucky?*

I can hear her voice so clearly.

I wish so hard I could hear it again. The diaries are the closest thing I have. It's been more difficult reading the final one this time. I didn't think that was possible. Mom was young when she became pregnant. I've always known that—but reading her journal as an adult is so different because now she *sounds* young.

A monarch butterfly flitters by, then lands on the purple petal of a wild iris growing at the water's edge. Even when I was in the throes of my teenage rebellion, Mom would make me come here with her. I'd sit with my arms crossed over my chest, not speaking, until she was done with her coffee, and then I'd slump back up the trail to the house.

I can't remember the last time we sat here. I don't think we got to the lake together once in the past twelve months. The more responsibility I took on at Filtr, the harder it was to find time to come home, though I stayed for a full week the Thanksgiving after Philippe and I broke up. On my last morning, I told Mom about my decision to swear off men. I said I'd be happier on my own, like she was.

She leaned over to take my hand, fixing me with her gray eyes. *I know you're not ready right now, honey, but I think one day you'll find your heart's too big for just you.* I nodded, though I didn't believe her. It was chilly outside, the sky bright blue, the leaves red and gold. Mom tipped her chin to the sun, sitting there with her eyes closed, a smile across her mouth, until I told her the time—she needed to get over to the lodge. She shook her head. *Let's stay a little longer, pea.*

I stare at the empty chair beside me, and I know. My heart's too big to let go.

People change. Dreams change, too.

When I get back to the house, I sit on the end of my bed in my damp bathing suit, towel around my waist. I pick up the diary from the nightstand and run my fingers over Mom's writing. I want to tell her I'm going to stay. I want to ask her for advice. I want her to tell me how proud she is. I want my mom.

After I've wiped away tears with the edge of the towel, my gaze lands on a name on the page, and I pick up my phone and press the call button.

"Fern?" Peter's deep voice sounds in my ear.

"Hey, Peter. I wanted to tell you first. I've made a decision about the resort."

"IT HASN'T CHANGED AT ALL," JAMIE SAYS AS HE LOOKS AROUND the living room. "I haven't been in here since we were dating."

I'm not surprised. As much as my mother lived and breathed Brookbanks, she kept her relationships with the staff professional. Peter was an exception.

I always thought Mom's reserve was purely about establishing boss-employee boundaries. Now that I'm reading her diary with adult eyes, I'm certain that's not the whole story.

But I'm not my mother.

After I got off the phone with Peter, I asked Jamie to come by the house.

He's wearing a hunter green tie with white pine cones printed on it. It's something I noticed only a few days ago—he always wears a tie with at least a splash of Brookbanks green. I wonder how much time he spends online, hunting for green ties. I wonder when he morphed into the Jamie he is now, organized and tidy.

Maybe it was when he lived in Banff. He stayed there for a few years, working his way up at one of the resorts before moving to Ottawa to manage a hotel downtown near Parliament Hill. It was Jamie's parents who told my mom how much he enjoyed his summers at Brookbanks and suggested she give him a call.

Her text message arrived out of the blue a few years ago.

We still like Jamie Pringle, right?

I hadn't heard his name in years. We didn't really stay in touch after our breakup.

We do, I wrote back. I hadn't said much to Mom when we'd split, and I knew this was her roundabout way of asking.

Thinking about hiring him for the manager job.

He'd be great, I texted.

Aside from my mom, no one loved the resort as much as Jamie.

"I really appreciate all the support you've given me the last few weeks," I tell him once we're seated at the kitchen table. My voice sounds stiff. I don't know why I'm nervous.

"What the hell, Fernie? Are you firing me?"

"What? No."

He lets out a gust of air and then drops his head to the table. "I really thought you were going to fire me," he says, voice muffled.

"Why would I do that?"

He looks up at me with a lopsided grin. "Because you're still in love with me, and you can't stand to be in the same room without wanting to tear my clothes off?"

"Am I that transparent?"

"The drooling gave you away. You drool when you're turned on."

I laugh. "I brought you here because I wanted to tell you that I'm not going to sell the resort. I'm going to stay on as owner."

Jamie slaps his hand on the table. "Now, that is excellent news."

"But there are going to be changes."

Jamie has some understanding of Will's consulting work, but I explain more about what we've been doing. "You know Brookbanks and the guests," I say. "I'd love your input."

"Of course, Fernie. I would be honored to help." *Honored.* He's serious, too.

"You really thought I'd fire you because we dated?"

He eyes me. "I was worried you might. We have a history, and I thought you could want a clean slate."

"I have a history with a lot of people here. At least half a dozen people on staff changed my diaper. A couple of the guests, too. There's no such thing as a clean slate for me."

"But how many of them have you slept with?"

I blink. An image from last night slinks through my mind. Will beneath me, his swollen lips around my nipple, looking up at me with darkened eyes.

"Wait a sec, who else have you slept with, Fernie?"

"No one," I say, cheeks burning. "We can't talk about our sex lives if we're going to work together."

"Okay." He flashes me a grin. "Though we'll have to if we start sleeping together."

I kick him under the table.

Two hours later, I'm curled up on the couch while Jamie warbles out a shockingly good version of "Ironic." He insisted that we celebrate, insisted we needed to do that with the good stuff, and insisted on it being his treat. He called the lodge to have a bottle of "our finest, cheapest sparkling wine" sent over.

"Your Alanis is unreal," I cry, clapping my hands when he's done.

"I know." He flops down on the sofa, putting his socked feet up beside me, and sips his beer. The bubbly didn't last long.

I sigh. "I can't believe they're going to let us run this place."

Jamie bumps my leg with his foot. "I'm happy you're back. I missed you."

"I missed you, too," I say, because it's true. I lost a close friend when I lost Jamie.

"All right, Fernie. You're up."

"What do you mean, *up*?"

"The floor is yours."

"Nope, sorry. You know I don't do karaoke." Public displays of tone deafness are firmly on the list of embarrassing things I do not take part in. Also: kitschy holiday sweaters, bachelorette party games, sparkly eyeshadow. But Jamie razzes me until I relent.

I'm almost through "Insensitive" (Mom was a major Jann Arden fan) when Jamie turns toward the doorway. In it stands Will. He's wearing the full Will Baxter: jacket, tie, combed-back hair, and an unreadable expression.

"I was hoping you wouldn't notice me," he says. "Please, continue."

I shake my head, mortified. "How was your meeting?"

"Fine. It ran long." Will looks at Jamie and the empty bottle of cava on the table. "I got here as soon as I could."

"Fernie and I were celebrating her good news," Jamie says, standing.

Will flinches at the word *Fernie* and runs a hand down his tie. "What news is that?"

"I've decided to stay," I tell him.

Will glances at Jamie and back to me. "Congratulations," he says, his voice hoarse. "Sorry I interrupted the festivities."

"You didn't," I say.

"You definitely did," Jamie says. "But I was just leaving. Show me out, Fernie?"

Will's eyes slit, and Jamie winks at him.

"That guy?" Jamie whispers once we're at the front door.

"I can't believe you, trying to bait him like that," I hiss.

"Come on. I get some leeway to hassle him. Four years together buys me that, doesn't it?"

"You don't still . . ." I start, narrowing my eyes.

"Have feelings for you?" Jamie tugs a strand of my hair. "I'll always love you, Fernie. But don't worry. I can be professional."

I'll always love Jamie, too. "I don't want it to be weird with us. I want to be friends."

"Same," he says. "And as your friend, I don't like him for you. He's too uptight, too serious, and there's something shifty about him. It's like he's hiding something. What do you see in him? Does he play an instrument?"

"Goodbye, Jamie."

He kisses me on the cheek. "And he's way too tall."

When I get back to the living room, Will is on the couch, his hands between his knees, staring at the floor.

"You're looking a little broody," I say, sitting beside him. "What's going on?"

"I was thinking about how much I used to hate that guy, and I'd never even met him."

"Really? If we're being honest, I wasn't a big fan of your girlfriend, either."

Will's lip quirks. "I could tell. You aren't the most subtle person, Fern Brookbanks."

I wince.

Will pulls me so that I'm sitting on his lap, my thighs around his. He runs a hand underneath the skirt of my dress, tracing it up my leg. I close my eyes and bury my fingers in his hair, groaning. For so long, Will has been my *what if* guy. What if we had both been single when we met?

He kisses the spot below my ear as he pushes my underwear

to the side. "I thought you were the coolest girl I'd ever met. I was considering breaking up with my girlfriend. Sending her a text."

"What?" My eyes pop open, but he doesn't stop what he's doing.

"But then I found out about you and Jamie." Will's watching me intently, and then he does the thing with his thumb.

"Oh my god."

"I still hate that guy," he says. "I hate that you told him about the resort before me."

Will's fingers are making it very hard to be verbal. But after a few seconds, I manage to ask, "You're jealous?"

He presses his teeth to my neck. "So fucking jealous."

It shouldn't thrill me, but it does. I stand just to slip my panties off, then I reach for the button on Will's pants. He pulls a foil packet from his pocket, and when I lower myself onto him, we both go still.

I murmur when I feel him pulse inside me. I start to circle my hips, looking for friction, but he holds them still and brings his lips to my ear.

"Want to know something else?" he grits out.

I nod. Adverbs have abandoned me.

"I didn't need your help varnishing the mural," he whispers, his thumb going back to work between us. "It would have been much faster if I'd done it myself. I could have finished in half the time, but I wanted to hang out with you."

I murmur again because I've lost all the words in my vocabulary.

"And I thought very long and hard about what you kept in your bedside table drawer."

I'm too focused on the need between my legs and the hunger in Will's eyes to have even a shred of embarrassment.

It's fast, almost feverish. Will watches my face the whole time.

He must be able to tell how much I like the things that come out of his mouth, because when I'm close, he puts his lips to my ear and tells me to come, and I do.

I lean my forehead against his, catching my breath. I want to lie down in bed and replay my day with Will with the knowledge that he was jealous. And then I want to sleep.

TELLING WHITNEY I'M STAYING IS PERHAPS THE MOST REWARD-ing experience of my adult life. She begged me to bring Will to dinner at their place in Huntsville. She's just stashed Owen in the Jolly Jumper that hangs between her living room and kitchen when I give her the news. She screams and bursts into tears, smashing me against her.

I look at Will over her shoulder, and mouth, *Wow*. He and Cam are laughing, and the Jolly Jumper is squeaking with each of Owen's leaps, and Whitney is saying, "I'm just so happy." It's loud and lovely and I think, *This is what a good life sounds like.*

Cam makes spaghetti bolognese, and when Owen gets fussy, Will walks him around the main floor of the house, singing in his ear. He's dressed in jeans and a white shirt, sleeves rolled past his forearms, and both Whitney and Cam ogle him like he's a gift from the babysitting gods. At one point, Whitney asks him to move in with them.

Over dinner, Whitney launches into the story of how we became friends. Cam chimes in, "I still have a dent where Fern socked me." Will squeezes my thigh under the table and gives me a secret smile. He's heard this one before.

When the baby has gone to bed, Whitney steers me into the kitchen under the guise of helping her serve dessert. She wants to know what's happening between Will and me, and I tell her the truth. I have no idea. All I know is that he's decided to stay until the day after the dance. We ordered dinner from the restaurant after our quickie on the couch yesterday, and then he spent the night in my bed. I thought about asking him to leave before we fell asleep, but I couldn't get the words out. I wanted him to stay.

Other than Whitney's prolonged inquiry into Will's oral health regime, the whole evening goes off without any awkwardness.

But then the bells toll on Will's phone.

Whitney is trying to talk us into having another drink and sleeping in their guest room instead of me driving the twenty minutes back to the resort, but as soon as Will's phone sounds, he excuses himself and heads into the kitchen.

He's gone long enough that Cam and Whitney give each other pointed looks.

"I'll go see if everything's okay," I say.

When I walk into the kitchen, Will glances up from his phone. His neck is red and he looks as though he's about to issue a stern warning. "I gotta go," he says to the person on the other end.

"Are you all right?" I ask when he hangs up.

Will blinks twice. "Do you mind if we take off?"

I tell him I don't, but my stomach lurches. We say good night to Whitney and Cam. Will thanks them for the invitation and the meal, but he's tense and distracted. His smile doesn't reach his eyes.

What's wrong? Whitney mouths when Will isn't looking, and I shake my head.

The drive back to the resort is quiet except for the crackling of country music on the radio. I keep glancing away from the road at Will, but he's looking out his window, twisting his ring.

"Has something happened?" I say when I pull the Cadillac into the Brookbanks parking lot.

Will's frown deepens. "It's family stuff."

A puzzle piece falls into place. A bell ringtone for Annabel.

"It's your sister you were talking to?"

Will doesn't answer.

I consider letting it slide. Talking about his homelife does not equal the escape from reality he's clearly seeking. But I reach across the console and put my hand on his knee. "What's going on?"

"Annabel has started looking for her own place, for her and Sofia. She wants to move out," Will says after a moment.

"Oh." I hesitate. "And that's bad?"

"It's . . ." He looks out the window, then at me. "It's not something I want to trouble you with."

"It wouldn't be trouble. I don't mind," I try.

"I mind," he says. "Let's keep them out of this, okay?"

I ask Will to stay over at the house, but he says he can't tonight. He wants to call Annabel back.

I toss and I turn and eventually I fall asleep, only to wake with a gasp from a dream I don't remember. It's 2:08 a.m. I pull the small desk chair up to my bedroom window and stare at the golden square of light coming from Will's cabin. I find it comforting, knowing that he's there.

But I want him here, in my bed. I want him to talk to me. I'm afraid of how much I want where Will is concerned.

18

June 15, Ten Years Ago

I WAS HUNCHED OVER WILL'S SKETCHBOOK, MY NOSE INCHES from the page, staring at the drawing. It must have been well past midnight. Will stood beside me, stretching.

For years I'd escaped notice. I sat in the back row of lecture halls. I partied, but not too hard. I had only a few close friends. I waited to make a dramatic hair transformation until after classes had ended. I dated someone whose boisterousness let me fade into the background.

I didn't want attention.

Deep down, I suspected something was wrong with me—that I had unearthed a core of rot at seventeen, and I was worried if someone looked too closely, they'd see it, too. I diligently covered my mistakes with economics classes and good grades and shifts at Two Sugars and Sunday phone calls with Mom. I was never late to any of them. Aside from the occasional joint, I was the picture of responsibility. And when I felt the cold trickle of my future running down my neck, I put on my headphones and I went for a walk. I disappeared into the veins of the city.

But for some unfathomable reason, I let Will sit across from me and scrutinize. I let him see.

And, yes, I liked how he made me look—the mysterious curve of my mouth and the arch of my neck—but it was more than that. There was no question the person Will had seen was beautiful—he hadn't found a rotten core.

"Can I have it?" I asked.

A small smile answered me first. "It's all yours."

I watched him stretch a little longer. "The way you move," I said, not sure how to describe it. "You're kinda graceful? And your posture—it's very good."

Will opened his eyes. "My posture's excellent."

He smirked, then sat on the chair, absently ruffling his damp hair, sending it in all sorts of fascinating directions. "My grandma's got a thing about posture." He smiled. "And table manners, handwashing, walking on the outside of the sidewalk when one is escorting a young lady."

I laughed. "Aha. It's all coming together. Did you spend a lot of time with your grandma growing up?"

He nodded and rubbed at the spot on his chin where his scar was. He seemed to hesitate before he spoke again. "My sister and I lived with her for a few months after Mom left."

"Your dad was having a hard time?" I guessed.

"We all were. But"—his eyes searched my face—"I guess I had the hardest time."

I blinked. "You?" Will seemed so together.

"Me."

I thought of the comment Eli made at the bar, about Will being emo.

And then I could see it clearly. "You were mad at her," I said. I knew all about being angry at a parent.

Will looked away for a long moment. "I was fucking furious."

I could feel my heart racing, like it was trying to break through my ribs and reach out to his. *I know you*, each thump said. *You're like me.* I wanted to leap off the bed and throw my arms around his neck. "What did you do?"

"I picked a lot of fights. It was dumb, but it was the only thing that could shut my brain off."

I stared at the scar on his chin. "Is that how you got it?"

He nodded. "I got jumped by a few older kids walking home from school after mouthing off one too many times. It was only two stitches, but it was enough to send my grandma flying into action. I guess my dad didn't know how to deal. Annabel and I stayed with her until the end of the school year, and for the summer. I got a lot of lectures about responsibility and choosing what kind of person I wanted to be."

"And that worked?" None of my mother's talks were enough to put a stop to my antics when I was a teen.

"I didn't know who I wanted to be, exactly, but I knew who I didn't."

"And who was that?"

Will twisted the ring on his finger. I could barely hear him when he said, "My mother."

"Your mother?" I repeated, surprised. "In what way?"

"In every way. Selfish. Critical—"

I cut him off before he went on. "You're not like that."

"I can be. We're a lot alike," he said. "I left like she did. I look like her. Think like her."

I thought of how calmly Will had spoken to his sister earlier today. How he seemed to know when to ask questions and when to stay quiet. How he let me fall apart at the art gallery and then cheered me up after. "For what it's worth, I don't think you're any of those things."

We watched each other. The air felt thick. "It's worth a lot," he said in a low voice.

I moved to the edge of the bed and leaned toward him, lightly pressing my index finger to his scar.

"The way you drew me . . . it's like you saw something I wasn't sure was there. I don't think a selfish person could capture someone like that—could see other people the way you do."

Will's gaze moved down my face and then he reached out, touching his finger to my chin, same as I had done. He slanted his head.

"What?"

"Nothing." He raised his hands. "It's nothing. It's not my place."

"What do you mean, it's nothing? What do you mean, it's not your place?" I felt feral. Whatever it was, I wanted it to be Will's place.

"I just think . . ." He lowered his palms. "You don't want to go home and work at the resort, so don't. You want to be here. You should stay."

I ran my nails over the inside of my wrist. "Everyone is expecting me to go back. My mom would kill me. Sometimes she will literally say stuff like, *The day you become the resort's manager will be my proudest moment.* I can't do that to her."

Will's hand covered mine, putting a stop to the scratching. I looked down at his fingers.

We stared at the red welts on the inside of my wrist. "You don't really seem like the kind of person who goes along with what other people want."

I chewed on the inside of my mouth.

"Am I missing something?"

I nodded slowly.

He ducked to meet my eyes. "Do you want to tell me about it?"

I looked at Will and nodded again. I wanted Will to know me. I wanted to tell him everything.

August 13, 1990

Eric's gone. He left a note in his bunk. Just eighteen words. I counted. "Maggie, I'm sorry but I can't be a dad. I wish you all the happiness in the world." He didn't even sign it. I knew he was shocked about the pregnancy. I knew he was surprised I wanted to keep the baby. But I thought he'd be in this with me. I thought he loved me. How can I be a mother if I can't even pick a boyfriend? Peter was right about him. It's been more than a month since Peter and I have spoken, and I miss him. I need him. He'd know exactly what I should say to Mom and Dad. I never thought our fight would last this long.

19

Now

WILL SHOWS UP WITH A BAG OF GROCERIES THE MORNING after dinner at Whitney and Cam's. His hair is wet, and I'm still wearing my POT HEAD pajamas.

"I haven't had a chance to make you breakfast yet," he says as I let him in. "My omelet is excellent."

"I'm sure it is."

He sets the bag on the counter and asks if I have an apron, and I dig out Mom's—the one with the red apples on it. I'm sure he won't wear it. But Will ties it around his waist and kisses me on the cheek, and I'm so charmed, I reach around his back and un-knot the strings.

Will gives me a questioning smile, and I pull my shirt over my head so my intentions are as clear as the fact that I'm only wearing underwear.

He backs me up to the kitchen table and lifts me onto it, pushing my knees apart and stepping between them.

"Lie back," he tells me, cupping my neck to set me down

gently as I do. He slips my panties down my legs, and then brings his lips to my navel, tracing it with his tongue. He leads a wet trail to my hip bone, and when I put my fingers in his hair, he kneels. Will pauses only to tell me that he missed me last night, and I last only a few seconds after that.

As I shower, Will makes omelets with spinach and caramelized onions and we spend most of the day in bed until it's time to get ready for cocktails with the Roses. We stay for long enough to seem polite, and then race back. I turn to head up the path toward the house, but Will tugs on my arm, leading me to his cabin.

"Closer," he says, biting my earlobe.

It's the best Sunday I've ever had, and I fall asleep with a smile on my lips. But the next day, the week from hell begins.

Following lunch service on Monday, I gather everyone in the dining room to announce my decision to stay on as owner. I keep my hands clasped behind my back so no one can see how badly they're shaking. One of the housekeepers asks what qualifies me to run Brookbanks aside from my last name. Eyes widen at his bold choice of words, but I can tell from the way people lean forward in their chairs that they're wondering the same thing. I say something about my degree, my hospitality experience, and how I helped oversee Filtr's expansion, but I can't hear myself speak over the blood rushing in my ears.

Then the air conditioners start dying. The maintenance team is able to fix most of them, but one family decides to leave early because we can't get a new unit in their cabin soon enough. A scathing one-star review appears online, calling us out for the AC issues, and describing resort management as "inept" and the cabins as "out-of-date." "You couldn't have paid me to stay there another night," it reads.

The next evening, Jamie sends me a link to a newspaper article headlined, TORONTO HOTELIER REVAMPS ROADSIDE MOTEL, about the renovation of one of Muskoka's derelict motels. According to the article, The Daisy will be a "retro playground for urbanites looking for a cooler side of cottage country." The rooms will have all the modern amenities and a seventies decor vibe courtesy of an up-and-coming interior designer. There's going to be a saltwater pool, lobster rolls delivered by servers on roller skates, and an emphasis on "funky, hard-to-find wines." It's major competition, a shiny new hipster-approved hot spot that will make our battle to stand out even more difficult.

I think things are turning around on Thursday when Will goes over his big-picture strategy. He dials in four Baxter-Lee colleagues and walks Jamie and me through a three-year plan and marketing campaign timed to a grand reopening next May. There's a flashy presentation and charts and a new employee structure that doesn't involve every manager reporting to me.

I walk out of the meeting confident and excited and am quickly pulled aside by my head of reservations, who gives me her notice. She's going to manage The Daisy.

It doesn't help that it's hot, the air so still you can see clear to the bottom of the lake. It's the kind of hazy August heat that drives people inside by early afternoon, and moisture collects in your every cranny if you dare walk out the door. The kind of heat where every third sentence out of your mouth is, *It's so hot.*

Will and I go swimming at the family dock in the evenings to cool off. The lake is like soup, and dead bugs speckle its flat surface, but it's so hot, we don't care if we're lying in a watery grave. We float, arms and legs spread, a pair of stars drifting across a liquid sky. Back on dry land, Will cooks dinner, and I pretend I don't love the game of house we're playing. I pretend it doesn't bother me that he excuses himself when the bells chime on his phone. I think about what Jamie said—about Will hiding something—and I pretend I don't believe he's right.

"HAVE YOU EATEN YET TODAY?"

I look up from the small pile of job applications on my desk to see Peter standing in the doorway of the office.

"Breakfast," I tell him.

When I came downstairs this morning, Will had coffee made. Grapefruit juice on the table. Bread in the toaster. I've been getting these little glimpses of what I imagine he's like at home. Not that he talks about his life at home.

"Sit for five minutes," he'd instructed, setting a plate of scrambled eggs, tomato, avocado, and toast in front of me. That was seven hours ago.

"I need a taster," Peter says, motioning for me to get off my butt with a tilt of his head. Everything Peter does is sparse. He speaks minimally. Moves quietly. He doesn't get angry. His lips rarely deviate from their straight line. All his extravagance is poured into his work. The lemon-lavender pound cake, the pistachio-orange olive oil cake with cardamom drizzle, the salted caramel pecan pie.

I stare at the applications for the reservations manager job. They've been coming in drips, and most candidates are vastly underqualified. A trucker looking to make a career change. A Pilates instructor slash tarot card reader.

"Come on. It'll all be there when you're done," he says, and adds under his breath, "Just like Maggie."

"I heard that," I say, pushing out of my chair and giving Peter my best death stare, though secretly, I'm pleased.

As I follow him down the carpeted hall, through the swinging doors, and into the staff passageways of the lodge, I get a sudden sinking feeling. I grab Peter's arm so he stops walking.

"You're not quitting, are you?"

"'Course not," he says.

I put my hand on my chest and exhale, my eyes closed. When I open them, I think the corners of Peter's mouth have arched up infinitesimally, but it's hard to tell with the beard.

"I told your mother once that she'd have to drag me out of here if she ever wanted to get rid of me. This is me telling you the same thing." He waits to make sure I've absorbed what he's said, and then he keeps moving in the direction of the pastry kitchen.

The yeasty smell of bread finds its way to us before we enter Peter's stainless-steel sanctuary. It's not sourdough—I know that scent so well, it's almost a physical object I can feel the contours of. Inside, boules, baguettes, brioche, and oil-slicked bread knots cover the work counter. I've seen the kitchen like this before, when Peter was developing a new dessert menu or during one of his experimental phases—frozen custard was my favorite. But it was always sweets he played around with.

"Time for a change, I think," he says, ripping off a piece of a plain-looking roll from a cluster of four and handing it to me.

"Why?"

He takes a piece himself and puts it into his mouth, chewing before he answers.

"Maggie picked the sourdough. Thought you'd want to have something that was yours. Something to suit your vision." He doesn't say *vision* like it has air quotes around it. Peter knows I want to make the dining room and the food less formal. Lose the white linens. Scale back the menu.

My throat tightens. "I love the sourdough."

"I did, too," he says quietly.

He points at the piece of roll I'm holding, and I pop it into my mouth. It's warm and soft and surprisingly buttery for something that seems so ordinary.

"Wow," I say, but Peter doesn't react. He hands me a slice of olive loaf. We chew together in silence, no music to lift the mood, one hunk of bread after another, avoiding eye contact. With each bite, I feel like I'm saying goodbye. I wipe a tear away with the heel of my hand, and Peter acts as if he doesn't notice.

"It's the roll," I say when we're done.

"I thought so, too," Peter says. "With whipped butter."

I sigh. "I can't believe we're going to lose the sourdough."

"I'll make it for you whenever you want. The starter is my only child. I'm not going to give it up." His hand freezes midway to his mouth. "Sorry," he says. "I didn't mean . . ."

It takes me a second to catch on to why he's apologizing. "It's fine, Peter. I came to terms with all that a long time ago," I say, then add after a moment, "I've been reading Mom's diary. I know you knew him. Eric, I mean."

He goes to the fridge and pulls out a wedge of cheddar and some leftover cooked ham. He slices them, spreads butter on a piece of roll, and sets it all on a plate that he pushes in front of me.

"I didn't know him well, and I didn't like what I did know of him," Peter says. "He was a good-looking guy. Real charmer. Thought pretty highly of himself. I figured maybe I was jealous."

I stop chewing.

"You thinking of looking him up again?" he asks, and I shake my head.

"That ship has sailed."

He nods, then after a beat says, "Your mom said she loved you enough for ten dads."

"That sounds like her." I think of how much time I've spent with Peter in here, watching him work. "But I had you, too."

"Not quite the same as your own father."

"Better," I tell him. "Much better."

Neither of us says anything for a minute, and the quiet of the kitchen is louder than any of Peter's music. "Are you doing okay? I know you must miss her."

He watches me from the corner of his eye. "Maggie was my best friend. I miss her like hell."

"Did you ever . . ." I pause. "I've been wondering if the two of you ever . . ." I sneak a glance at him, and he turns to face me. "If you were ever more than friends?" It's a question I've had since I started rereading the diary.

Peter doesn't say anything. I don't breathe. "Maggie should be here for this," he says, looking at the ceiling. He shakes his head and then meets my eyes. "There were times when we were close like that."

I stare at Peter, holding a piece of cheese.

"I fell in love with Maggie the first day I met her." His eyes gleam. "She gave me a tour of the resort, talking a mile a minute, and I thought I'd never be lonely if she was around. And I wasn't."

"Mom never told me," I whisper.

"Maggie'd say she was private; I'd say she was secretive. She wasn't always like that." Peter smiles a little. "I waited a long time for my chance with her. After you were born, I told her how I felt. But she wouldn't let me take her on a date until you got older."

"When?" I gasp. My head is spinning.

"Once you and Whitney became friends, going for sleepovers and running around here together. I think she felt like she could relax a little."

That was so long ago. I was ten.

"I wanted to get married—she knew that. I thought she was ready, but then you"—he pauses, choosing his words—"hit a rough patch as a teenager, and she blamed herself. She said there was no way she could be a good wife when she couldn't manage to be a good mother. I know you think she picked this place over you time and time again, and maybe she could have worked a little less, but running the resort was the one thing she felt she was doing well."

I stare down at the plate of food, guilt turning the bread in my throat leaden. Peter and my mom as a couple? The worst part is that I can picture it. How perfect they would have been together.

I start to apologize, but Peter shakes his head. "It wasn't about you, Fern, not really. It was more complicated than that. We argued a lot over the years, but we always found our way back to each other."

A memory. Dinner with Mom and Peter in Toronto. Feeling tired from hauling boxes and assembling Ikea furniture. Hugging Mom good night. It's hard to say goodbye this time. Walking down the sidewalk and turning around for one last wave. Peter's arm around Mom. Mom looking up at him, smiling.

"Do you remember when you and Mom helped me move into my first apartment?"

Peter's smile parts his lips. "That place barely fit the three of us in it at once. Maggie made me hang your mirror three times before it was perfectly centered over the dresser."

"You and Mom stayed at a hotel for the night."

"Stayed a couple more after we got you settled. We didn't tell you that."

I can't believe I didn't suspect anything. "When she died, were you together then?"

"As together as we ever were." Peter sees the shock on my face and pats my shoulder. "Our relationship wasn't traditional. We were best friends, and sometimes we were . . . partners. I always wanted more than Maggie could give, but I figure I'm lucky I got as much of her as I did."

It might be the saddest, sweetest thing I've heard.

Before I go, Peter packs me two paper bags of leftover bread.

"When do you think you'll start playing music again?" I ask as I'm leaving.

He looks over at the old broken tape deck by his workstation. "Once I'm ready for a day when your mother doesn't walk through that door and tell me to turn it down."

"I'll make a playlist for then," I tell him. "Something Mom would really hate."

WHEN I MAKE IT BACK TO THE HOUSE LATE THAT EVENING, MY heart is heavy. But then I see Will at the stove, wearing a white shirt and Mom's apron. I love Will in my kitchen, wearing that apron. I love how he never says a word about how much I'm working. I love that when he served me sourdough toast this morning, he kissed my nose and said, *Not as good as you made it.* I told him it's best when it's stale and cooked in a pan during a blackout.

Will smiles at me over his shoulder when he realizes I'm watching. "It's just a stir-fry. Hope that's okay."

"Perfect," I say, moving next to him. He spears a sugar snap pea from the pan and feeds it to me.

"I promise I'll cook for you one day," I say as I chew.

"Yeah? Aside from that dinner with Whitney and Cam, it's been a long time since somebody made a meal for me. Annabel knows how to boil water, put a frozen pizza in the oven, and use the microwave—that's about it."

This is one of the few times Will has volunteered information about his sister. I know she's a makeup artist and works on some of the bigger productions that shoot in Toronto. I know she can't cook. But Will has us sealed in a bubble—keeping his vacation separate from his homelife.

"What about Jessica—she didn't wine and dine you?" We haven't talked about Will's ex, and I'm not sure if she's allowed in the bubble.

"She knew her way around a menu."

I stay quiet, and after a moment, Will goes on.

"We didn't exactly leave things on the best of terms," he says, looking into the pan. "She said I wasted her time and that I'm incapable of commitment. She felt I was too involved with Sofia."

"And you think . . . ?"

"She wasn't wrong. I knew early on it wouldn't work out long-term."

"Because . . ." I prompt when he doesn't elaborate.

Will exhales. "It made her uncomfortable—even them living with me was strange to her. But in truth, my niece and my sister are a big barrier to a relationship."

"For who—you or your girlfriends?"

"Both, I guess. Between home and work, there hasn't been a lot of room for other people."

I feel like Will is waving an enormous red flag in front of my face. "Is this your way of telling me that you don't do relationships?" I try to say this casually.

"It's my way of telling you that I don't do them well. Jessica wasn't the first woman I've disappointed. I'm not the greatest boyfriend. Jessica wanted more of me than I had to share."

"More of you?" I scoff, my heart pounding. "Who'd want that?"

Will pins me with his dark eyes. "Not you, huh? Hiatus and all that."

I think about telling him the truth—that I'll take as much as he can give—but then I remember Peter saying almost the exact same thing about my mom. He spent decades with someone who couldn't give herself to him fully. I always loved when Mom said I was like Peter, but in this way, I can't be.

"Sorry you had to wait so late to eat," I say instead. It's almost nine.

"I don't mind. I usually eat early with the girls." He gives me a quick grin while he plates the food. "I feel very sophisticated right now."

"You look very sophisticated."

He glances down at the apron. "You love it."

"It's weird how much I love it," I say.

But the words in my head say something different. The words in my head say, *It's weird how much I love you.* Surely those words have it wrong.

20

June 15, Ten Years Ago

WILL AND I SAT ON THE END OF MY BED IN MY APARTMENT, facing each other. It was almost three a.m. "I mentioned I went through a rebellious phase in high school," I said, and Will nodded. "It was bad. It started after I found these old diaries of my mom's—one was written the summer she got pregnant with me."

I tilted my head to the ceiling, the back of my nose tingling. It was stupid that this still upset me so much.

"I used to think Peter was my dad." I shut my eyes briefly. "I mean, I knew he wasn't, but deep down I guess I hoped he was. Until I read the diary, I pretended. I wished so hard." I could feel Will's eyes on me, and I swiped a tear from my cheek. "My mom didn't talk about him—my biological father. I knew he'd worked at the resort for a summer, but that was about it." I glanced at Will, embarrassed. "I know it would have been messed up for them to keep something like that from me, but it wasn't rational, you know? Whitney and I were really into *CSI* for a while, and I had this whole fantasy that DNA analysis would show he was my real dad. We can be so similar, Peter and me."

I spent almost as much time with him as I did with Mom and my grandparents. It was Peter who came to my soccer games when Mom couldn't. Peter who was around the day after school when I got my first period. Peter who taught me how to drive, who taught me the art of the perfect mix CD. Whenever I was sarcastic, Mom complained I'd been spending too much time with Peter. "Even when I got older, I held on to the hope that Mom and Peter would sit me down and tell me the truth."

I felt Will's hand close over mine. I'd been scratching again.

"Anyway, Peter's not my dad. It's some guy named Eric who'd been a lifeguard at the resort. It was all there in the diary. How he and Mom dated, how they were in love, how he left when he found out she was pregnant. I was so mad." I blew out a shaky breath, and Will squeezed my hand.

"Long story short, I made my mom reach out to Eric. He had a wife and kids, and he didn't want them knowing about me. He didn't want to meet me, either. Refused to even speak with me on the phone. I didn't take it well. I drank. A lot. I blacked out a bunch. I made some bad decisions with guys," I added quickly. "I cut classes, got kicked off the soccer team, and I, uh, stole a tractor."

"You what?" Will asked.

"Stole a tractor." I told him the entire tale—about the party and the dare that led to me buck naked and "driving" a tractor on Trevor Currie's farm. Trevor said his parents wouldn't be home for hours. He must have started the thing. There's no way I could have done it on my own. I don't remember much except sobering up in the police cruiser beneath a flannel jacket. Will listened, his gaze fixed to the side of my face. He didn't flinch once.

"That was the breaking point for Whitney. We got into a big fight. She told me she couldn't be my friend if I kept putting myself at risk—and I said that was fine, because she'd been a shitty friend since she'd started dating Cam. She stopped speaking to me, but I kept partying. One night, I invited a few random people over while Mom was working. There's a sunroom off the back of the house—we were drinking in there. Eventually I passed out in the bathroom—they think I hit my head on the sink because the smoke didn't wake me up." I had a concussion and a goose egg on my forehead when I woke in the hospital.

"The smoke?"

I looked down at Will's hand over mine, then up at him. His eyes were wide. "There was a small fire. I don't know if it was one of my cigarette butts that started it or someone else's. Someone called the lodge when they saw the smoke. My mom went straight into the house to find me—and Peter in after her. They broke open the bathroom door." I closed my eyes again. "The fire destroyed the sunroom, but we were all so lucky to make it out alive."

I remember waking up in the hospital with the most intense headache and burning in my throat. Mom was sitting beside the bed, a bandage covering the burn on her right arm, her face puffy and crimson. It looked like she'd swum in chlorine with her eyes open for hours. I'd never seen her look so ravaged.

I let out a deep breath, and Will put his arm around my shoulder, pulling me against his side. We stayed like that for several minutes, not talking.

"My mom saved my life—I owe her everything," I said. "That's why I didn't argue when she suggested I apply to business school and hop on the Brookbanks career track." Will leaned back to look at me. "I basically blew up my life, and my mom helped me pick up the pieces. It wasn't like I had a better idea. You're an artist, but I have no clue what I'd do if I wasn't going to work at the resort. I don't have a ten-year plan."

Will cradled my face in his palms and said, very slowly, "Ten-year plans are bullshit."

I laughed. After all that, it wasn't the reaction I'd expected.

"I mean it," he said, dropping his hands. "As if anyone knows where they'll be or who they'll be in ten years."

"I guess, but I also want some kind of a plan. I envy you. You've got your life all figured out. I have no clue."

Will thought about this for a moment. "But you know you don't want to move back home?"

"Yeah. I know that," I agreed, reluctantly.

"And you know you don't want to run the resort?"

"Yeah," I said, watching the candlelight sway in his eyes.

"Your mom may have saved your life, but it's still *your* life, Fern."

We stared at each other for a long time.

"So you know where you don't see yourself," Will finally said.

He picked up his sketchbook and pencil and opened to a blank page near the back of the book. I watched him write FERN'S ONE-YEAR PLAN at the top. And then:

1. *I WON'T BE WORKING AT BROOKBANKS RESORT.*

2. *I WILL NOT BE LIVING IN MUSKOKA.*

"A one-year plan?" I asked.

"One year seems more realistic than ten, don't you think? And you said you wanted a plan." He pointed to the page. "Let's make one."

I looked at the paper again. He wrote in capital letters, a distinct kind of printing that was like its own font. There was something about seeing the words in black and white that felt radical, like by writing them down, an alternate future had become possible.

"Huh," I said. "That's actually pretty smart. But you have to do one, too." I reached for the book. "What would be on yours?" I asked, writing WILL'S ONE-YEAR PLAN on the opposite page.

"That's easy." He leaned back onto his hands. "I'll be broke."

I scoffed. "Your plan is to be broke?"

"Kind of. I'm serious about my art. I'm not going to take some boring office job and wear a tie so I can have a nice apartment. Art isn't a hobby for me. It's all or nothing. With the murals and maybe a part-time gig, I think I'll be able to make rent and spend the rest of my time working on *Roommates*."

"So . . ." I wrote:

1. *I WON'T BE WORKING IN AN OFFICE (NO TIES ALLOWED).*

2. *KIND OF BROKE.*

3. *I WON'T TREAT ART LIKE A HOBBY.*

I showed Will the page.

"That works," he said. "The ultimate would be if *Roommates* were running in a paper."

"Got it." I added *Roommates* to the list.

"Perfect," Will said. "What else should go on yours?"

I stared down at the page. "The only other thing I know for sure is that I want to be in Toronto." Will took the pencil and added it to the list. "Beyond that, I don't really know," I said.

"That's okay." Will held the pencil between his teeth, making a humming noise. "What about: *In one year, adjust the plan as necessary.*"

"Sure," I said. I collapsed back on the bed, staring at the crack in the ceiling as Will finished writing. He set the book on the table.

"I can't imagine why you're tired," he said, then blew out all the candles except for the one in the jar beside my bed and sprawled out next to me on his back.

"Is this okay?" he whispered.

"Yeah," I said through another yawn. "It's fine."

My throat was dry from talking, but there was one thing I wanted to know. "Earlier today, when I told you I went to business school, you said you wouldn't have guessed that. What would you have guessed?"

"I don't know. An English major maybe. I thought you might have been writing poetry in that journal."

"I'm not that interesting."

"You're *more* interesting."

The words lay between us, sweet and ripe.

I looked down at our hands resting beside each other on the bed, then back to him. I inched my fingers closer until they touched his.

"I wish I cared about something the way you care about art," I said after a moment.

"You will," he said, wrapping his pinkie around mine. "You just need time to find it."

Every nerve ending in my body sprinted toward my little finger. I was sure Will could hear the drum of my heart.

"I don't want my mom to hate me," I whispered.

He squeezed my pinkie. "She won't. Trust me, okay?"

"Okay." I blinked up at the ceiling, trying to keep my eyes open. "I trust you."

We stayed like that until my eyelids grew heavy and the candle snuffed itself out.

August 18, 1990

Peter came by the house yesterday. I told Mom I had a stomach bug and have been staying in bed. Peter said I didn't look sick. He knew Eric left—everyone knows. He asked if he'd hurt me, and I told him not in the way he meant, and then I started to cry. Peter lay down and hugged me close. He told me he missed me and my nonstop talking and the Anne Murray's Greatest Hits cassette I sneak into his tape deck. He said he thought he might have been jealous. Then he brought my hand to his lips and kissed my knuckles, so softly, and said he had to tell me something. I'm sure my heart stopped. Because I knew what he was going to say, and I couldn't let him. Not now. Before he could speak, I blurted out that I was pregnant. I told him everything I've been thinking about—how I'd have to raise the baby on my own and cancel the trip and put off managing the resort, but that I want to do it. He was quiet the whole time. After I finished, he said, "Okay, Maggie." Then he kissed my forehead and rubbed my back until I fell asleep.

21

Now

JAMIE AND I ARE HUDDLED IN FRONT OF A COMPUTER IN THE office when Will knocks on the doorframe.

I look at him and then notice the time. "Shit. I'm so sorry."

Whitney and Cam were supposed to arrive an hour ago for dinner.

It's Will's last week here, and I've been working twelve-hour days. I don't have a choice. I've been telling myself that it's only a phase, that if I'd opened my own place, there would be similarly horrendous periods and that busy is better than slow. But our sommelier, Zoe, gave her notice this morning—she's going to run the wine program at The Daisy—and it's become that much harder not to feel discouraged.

"It's fine," Will says. "Whitney and Cam are on cocktail number two, and Whitney's mom called to say Owen is fast asleep. They're in new-parent heaven."

Will achieved what I had not and convinced them to stay at the resort for the night, their first away from the baby.

"I just wanted to make sure everything was okay. You haven't answered our texts."

I glance around the office. I have no idea where I've put my phone.

"Too busy making out," Jamie quips, and I belt him in the chest.

"He's joking," I say, scowling at Jamie. "Obviously."

Will does not seem to find this funny.

"Go," Jamie says while I search the desk drawers for my phone. "I think we've done all that we can for now anyway." I'm trying to stay on top of the bookings while he finalizes all the details for the dance.

"You sure?"

"Yes," he says, plucking my phone out from under a stack of papers. "Get out of here."

I fill Will in on my day while we walk, waving to the Roses as we pass Cabin 15. Will has a standing invitation for martinis. When we showed up on Sunday, he ushered me to the love seat with his hand on my lower back, and Mrs. Rose clapped hers together, crying, "Isn't this a happy turn of events?" I am happy— Will and I spend every moment we can together, and it feels so easy and right. But summer doesn't last forever.

Before we round the corner to Cabin 20, I see multicolored streamers and balloons through the trees. There's a painted sign that reads WELCOME HOME, BABY! hanging over the door. Whitney and Cam are standing on the porch, grinning like kids who raided the candy drawer.

"You monsters."

"Will has been warned to use the nickname at his own peril," Whitney says, pulling me into a hug. "I know I've said it before, but you coming back here is probably the best thing that's happened to me, the birth of my child included."

I laugh, feeling the stress of this week begin to ebb. "You need more friends."

"I have plenty," she says. "And they haven't put me through what you have. But they're just not as good."

Will directs us out to the front deck, where he's set the picnic table with linens and candlesticks he's borrowed from the house and a massive vase of wildflowers, a free-for-all of purple asters, goldenrod, and black-eyed Susans. My favorite.

He steps into the cabin and returns with a gin and tonic for me in one hand and a cheese board in the other.

"The freshest lime in Muskoka," Will says, handing me the drink.

"You wouldn't believe the number of questions I've had to answer this past week," Whitney says over dinner. Will made mushroom risotto. "Pasta or risotto? Mushrooms or tomatoes? Favorite kinds of cheese?"

I glance at Will.

"It's not every day you decide to change your entire life," he says, and he sounds full of admiration. I'm not sure I've ever felt this adored. I don't realize that I'm staring at him and that the meandering stream of chatter has stopped until Cam clears his throat.

We savor Peter's dark chocolate cake in silence. Will says he asked for the recipe, but Peter offered to bake it himself—I've rarely seen him warm to a person so quickly. Yesterday, he gave me a lemon poppy seed loaf to share with "my friend." We invited Peter tonight, but he said he was still perfecting the bread rolls for the dance.

From nowhere, Whitney disrupts the quiet with, "So, Will, when are you leaving?"

His eyes flick to mine. "Sunday," he says. I do my best not to look like hearing this makes me want to rip off my skin. Will and

I haven't talked about his leaving or what it means for us. I didn't think an *us* was possible. But watching him with my friends tonight, seeing how much care he's put into the dinner, maybe it is. Maybe this isn't just a break from reality for him. Maybe this could be the kind of relationship that's worth the effort. Maybe this is the start of an *us*.

"The day after the dance," Whitney says. I narrow my eyes, wondering what she's playing at. I've already told her this.

"Right. I'm looking forward to it," Will says.

"And after that?"

Will looks at me again.

"Whit," I warn. I don't want Will to endure an interrogation from my best friend. That's not what he signed up for.

"What?"

I shake my head at her in a plea to halt whatever scheme she thinks she's running. But she does not.

"What's the plan?" she asks. "Because I really wasn't a fan of how things went the last time."

I shoot Cam a look but he gives me the tiniest shrug.

Whitney points her fork at Will. "Are you going to drop off the face of the earth again? Because I don't want to have to scrape my friend off the floor like I did last time."

"Whitney," I say, my face hot. I can't even look in Will's direction. "Stop."

She glances at me, and then Will says, "I think this is a conversation for Fern and me to have in private."

"Agreed," I say.

Whitney takes a bite of cake. She chews, glaring at Will, until she finishes her slice.

"I like you," she says to him when she's licked the last of the ganache off her fork. "You're too pretty and too tall, but you're good with babies and you seem smart. And frankly, that was the best risotto I've ever had. But if you fuck my friend over again, I will drive to Toronto, and I will kill you."

Will stares at her for a second, and then nods. "Sounds like we have a plan."

"YOU'RE AVOIDING ME, AREN'T YOU?" WHITNEY ASKS WHEN I pick up my phone on Friday.

I have been avoiding her. She meant well, but I'm still annoyed about the other night.

"I know I went rogue at dinner. I'm sorry. I haven't had that much to drink since before I was pregnant."

"It's fine, Whit," I say. She knows she overstepped. I apologized to Will after she and Cam had left, and he said that he didn't really mind Whitney's inquisition, that he was more concerned by how her questions bothered me.

Two seconds of silence. "So why aren't you answering your texts?" she asks.

"Because I'm in a hell of my own making?"

"That bad, huh?"

"The dance is tomorrow, so Jamie is busy with last-minute stuff while I'm interviewing job candidates who call me Fran and think customer service is one of the underlying problems of capitalism."

I take a bite of the cheese croissant Peter dropped off earlier, then wipe the flakes from my chest. He keeps swinging by with food. I think he wants to make sure I'm okay after his revelation about him and Mom. Mostly I'm sad they didn't get a happier ending. I'm sad she never told me about Peter herself. I wish we could have had more time together, the three of us. My family.

"What's going on?" I could use a distraction.

"Much bigger problems over here, let me tell you," she says. "I have no idea what to wear tomorrow. My body is all wonky after having a baby. Nothing's in the same spot it used to be. Can you look at the photos I sent?"

I scroll through the pictures. "You know I'm not good at this stuff. Maybe the pink romper?" I suggest.

"Yeah, maybe. Maybe with heels. What about you? Did you find anything in town?"

"No. I meant to, but I haven't been able to find the time. I'm going to raid Mom's closet tonight." I'm sure she kept every party outfit she ever wore. "I think there are dresses from the nineties in there."

Whitney gasps. "Remember the purple one with the big bow in the front?"

It had ruffles at the neck and the most over-the-top sash. The fabric was so stiff, it could stand up on its own. We were probably fourteen the summer she wore it to the dance.

"We called her Grimace all night," I say. "God, we were assholes."

"Yeah," she agrees. "But she loved us anyway."

She did.

"So . . ." Whitney says after a few moments of silence. "Two more nights with Will here."

"Mm-hmm."

"And after that?"

"After that, he goes back to Toronto."

"But obviously you're going to keep seeing each other."

I don't know if that's obvious. I don't want Sunday to be the end, but I haven't come out and said it.

"We'll stay in touch." I think.

Whitney scoffs. "Stay in touch? That man is into you. Not

into you in the *Hey, let's bang when you come to the city* kind of way. He's into you in the *I'm picturing what our kids will look like* way. Trust me, he's in deep."

I chew on a nail. "I wonder if it's just that he's here, with his first taste of freedom in a long time. He's in vacation mode. Once he goes back to his actual life, he might realize I don't fit in it."

"I really don't think that's what's going on here," Whitney says. "He made risotto."

I laugh. "And a cheese board. I just don't know if I can put myself out there again, especially right now."

Whitney stays quiet for a moment. "Even before the hiatus, you closed yourself off. And maybe that has to do with your mom. And maybe it has a bit to do with he who shall not be named"—which is how Whitney refers to Eric—"and maybe what happened with Will back then didn't help."

I sigh.

I've been trying not to think about what happened nine years ago—how big my feelings were and how suddenly they got crushed. I've been trying not to think about how much bigger those feelings have become.

"Come on," Whitney says. "You can tell some guy you like him."

"Yeah," I murmur. If only that were it.

22

June 15, Ten Years Ago

WILL WAS ALREADY UP WHEN I OPENED MY EYES. HE SAT AT MY table, writing in his book, a dark slash of hair over one eye. Seeing him in my apartment was strange all over. But it felt like he belonged there, scribbling by my window.

The bed groaned as I tucked an arm under my head. Will's gaze shifted to mine. We eyed each other in silence, the morning sun slipping through the glass, capturing bits of dust in its rays and painting squares of light on the hardwood.

"Hi." My voice cracked with the day's first word. The fridge was making a steady whir. The power must have come back on while we slept. "What are you doing over there?"

"Just thinking."

"I can't spell my name without coffee." I crawled off the bed. "I'll make some. It's not as good as at the café, but it is strong." I pulled the box of paper filters from the cupboard.

"Actually, I've got to head out," Will said, standing. "It's almost ten. I'm going to be late for breakfast with my sister, and then I've got to grab my stuff before getting out to the airport."

"Oh." I cleared my throat, trying not to wear my disappointment like a diamond tiara. "Of course."

"It was such a late night—I didn't want to wake you."

"Yeah, no. I appreciate that," I said, my chest tightening. "So?"

"So . . ." He gestured to a piece of paper on the table. He'd torn his drawing of me from his sketchbook. "That's for you."

I swallowed. "Thanks."

"And I had an idea," he said, twisting his ring. "I'm going to be back next June for my dad's wedding. I thought we could check in on each other—see how we're making out with our plans."

He picked up his notebook, holding it open to the lists. He'd written, *JUNE 14, BROOKBANKS RESORT, 3 P.M.* on the bottom of each page.

"You're serious? You want to come visit me at Brookbanks? For real?"

"If only to eat more sourdough." He gave me a hesitant smile. "I want to see where Fern Brookbanks grew up. You can show me how to hold a paddle. Make sure I don't embarrass myself out on the water."

"We both know you will."

His smile widened. "So is that a yes? You'll meet me up there in a year?"

"Yeah, I can do that." My heart had ramped up to double time. "Maybe in a year . . ." I drifted off. I couldn't finish that sentence. I'm not sure I knew how to.

A door slammed out in the hallway. Will blinked, then ripped my plan out of his book, passing it to me.

I looked down at the page. "It's a pretty big place," I said. "We should pick a spot."

"What do you suggest?"

"How about we meet down at the docks near the beach? I'll

need to know how Will Baxter really looks in a canoe as soon as possible."

"Sensational, I'm telling you." He grinned. "The docks it is."

Will tucked his sketchbook into his bag. I eyed the little red streetcar pin fixed to the flap, then grabbed my phone.

"What's your number so we can stay in touch?" I said as he tied his boots. "And if you give me your address, I'll make you a CD. A West Coast theme. Or trees? There probably aren't enough tracks for that, but nature in general could work . . ."

Will stood back up, a pained look on his face. "I think it might be best if we don't."

I frowned. "What do you mean?"

He rubbed the back of his neck. "I don't think we should text each other or become friends on Facebook. You probably shouldn't send me a mix CD. I just think since . . ." He looked over at the bed and the indents our bodies had left behind, then back at me. "Why didn't you tell me about Jamie?"

My legs wobbled.

I could have lied and said Jamie simply hadn't come up. It was less complicated than the truth. Only I didn't want to lie to Will.

"At first, it didn't really matter that I had a boyfriend. But later, I kind of wanted to pretend that the rest of the world didn't exist for a day, and that included Jamie. Not that I would have done anything," I added quickly. "I would never cheat."

Will nodded, but I had no idea what he was thinking.

"Do you think I'm horrible?" I asked quietly.

"No. I think you're pretty fucking awesome, Fern Brook-banks." He squeezed my hand once and let it go. "But I think it would be a bad idea for you and me to continue whatever this is."

"Because of Jamie?"

He nodded.

"A year is a really long time," I said, staring down at his pink laces.

Will ducked to my eye level. "It's nothing. You won't even miss me."

I pressed my lips together, wishing that were true. I reached around Will for the door, holding it open with my hip. I wasn't going to be able to keep it together much longer. I had thought what I felt for Will was physical attraction, but it was more than that—it was so much worse.

Will slipped his backpack onto his shoulders and stepped into the hallway.

"Will?" I said, waiting for him to face me. "I am going to miss you—more than a smidge."

Over the next twelve months, I'd remember the smile that took over Will's face. I'd close my eyes and picture that very moment. The bend of his lips, the surprise in his eyes, the faint lines at their corners. It was electric.

"You and me in one year, Fern Brookbanks," he said. "Don't let me down."

And then Will Baxter turned around and walked out of my life.

August 21, 1990

I went to the pastry kitchen yesterday to find Peter, but one of the guys told me he'd taken the day off. I was worried he was upset about what I'd told him, but then he showed up at the front desk, took me to the library, and shut the door. He pulled out a bunch of prenatal pamphlets from his backpack—he'd gone to see his doctor for information about traveling during pregnancy. He was talking so fast about trimesters and ultrasounds, faster than I've ever heard him talk before. He used the word uterus at least twice.

He must have realized I was having trouble keeping up, because he took a deep breath and said, "You don't need to cancel your trip." I told him a vacation was the last thing I needed to worry about, and he shook his head. He said my whole life was about to change, but that I didn't need to give up Europe. He made me take the pamphlets, and then he told me he'd been thinking about what I'd said about having to raise a baby on my own. He told me that I wasn't alone, that he was here, that my parents were here, that there was a whole resort full of people who'd want to help.

I didn't know how much I needed to hear that. I sat there holding a bunch of pamphlets, crying, and he asked if I was OK. I threw my arms around him and told him he was the best friend anyone could possibly have.

23

Now

JAMIE SENDS ME HOME IN THE LATE AFTERNOON. I CHUCK OUT a "You are literally not the boss of me!" but it has the impact of a cotton ball.

The cool wind is the first thing I notice when I step outside, followed by the faint smell of rain on rock somewhere in the distance. Finally, a break in the heat.

I think about what Whitney said when we spoke on the phone earlier today while I walk back to the house, keeping my arms crossed against the chill.

I think about my mom and Peter and words unspoken. But I can be brave. I can let Will know how I feel.

He's still working, so I send him a text, saying that I'm home early and to come over when he's ready, and then I climb up to the guest bedroom. There's a queen bed, a suitcase stand, and a carafe for water on a tray—but the room's main function is kept behind the bifold closet doors.

I slide them open and run my fingers over the rainbow of

skirts and sleeves and memories—all of Mom's cocktail dresses and holiday outfits, and many of mine, too. There's the purple taffeta number and the long-sleeved black gown. There's the pale blue A-line hanging next to a tiny white dress with a matching pale blue satin bow. So much of our lives are woven into these threads.

Mom's green velvet shift and pink sequined bolero: Peter and me playing fancy tea party, and Mom coming home to find us eating crustless sandwiches and listening to Smashing Pumpkins.

The matching tartan dresses: the Christmas dinner when Grandma and Grandpa announced they were moving out West.

A strapless silver gown: telling Mom she was too old to wear something that showed so much skin, even if it was New Year's Eve.

I pull the silver dress out. It's floor-length with a slit up the leg. It *is* pretty sexy—too sexy for the summer dance, and my god, it's tight. I try on about a dozen more, growing hot and itchy as I do, but most are either too small or too froufrou. I do not do ruffles. Or pink floral. Or rhinestone-bedazzled sleeves. I throw open the window and a gust of crisp air blows through the room, slamming the door shut.

Sweating, I pull out an armful of clothing so I can get to the back of the closet, and wedged between a toile tea dress and a navy and white striped frock is a short orangey-red number with a scoop neck and thin straps. I've never seen it before. Red isn't really my color, nor was it my mother's, but when I slip it over my head, the fabric is light and floaty. It's fitted but not tight.

I head to the full-length mirror in my bedroom. The dress looks incredible. It's kind of nineties but not in a costumey way. The color somehow works. Smiling at my reflection, I know this is what I want to wear when I tell Will how I feel, when I tell him

I want to be a part of his life—his real one—even if I don't know how that works. If he feels the same, we'll figure it out. We'll make a plan.

So that settles it. I'll tell Will tomorrow. I'll tell him while we dance.

I hang everything up and run my hands over the fabric one last time.

"Thanks, Mom," I whisper, and slide the doors shut.

THERE'S ONE ENTRY LEFT IN THE JOURNAL—I'VE BEEN SAVING IT until I have some alone time. I grab the diary from my bedside table and take it out to the back deck. It's shielded from the wind here, but I'm bundled in a sweater and cozy pants.

"Hey." Will pokes his head out the door as I find my place.

"Hey," I say as the rest of his body follows. White shirt. No tie. A casual meeting day. "I didn't think I'd see you so soon."

"I cut out early." He clocks the book in my hands. "Am I interrupting? I could come back later."

"Don't do that." I put the journal down and stand, wrapping my arms around his waist. "You always smell so good," I say into his shirt. "You smell better than other men."

"I'm going to pretend you don't know what other men smell like," he says, pulling back and tipping my chin up with a smile. He kisses me, and it's slow and lush and as sweet as a lemon drop. "I'm going to pretend there's never been anyone but you and me."

I laugh. "We both know that's wildly inaccurate."

"But wouldn't it be nice if it were true?" he says, tracing the line of my jaw with his nose.

"I don't know . . . we might not be as proficient without all that experience."

"Or maybe it'd be even better," he says, "if I had ten years to figure out exactly what you like."

"I think you're doing just fine. But if you want a little more practice . . ." I take his hand and lead him to the couch inside, wiggling out of my sweats, and pulling him down over me. I want to feel the full weight of him pressing me into the cushions.

After, we survey the scattered pillows, the shirt flung over the lamp.

"Might need to try that again," Will says, sitting up and hoisting me on his lap. "To make sure I got it right."

"Good idea. I'll order dinner from the restaurant so you can focus all your energy on studying tonight. Your final exam will be next . . ." The word *week* is about to slide from my lips. Will's smile falls, and a heaviness settles between us.

"Tonight, can we pretend like you aren't leaving on Sunday?" I ask. "Like it's any other night?"

Something flickers in Will's eyes, but it's quickly extinguished. He moves his hands to my lower back, pulling me tight against his chest. "If that's what you want."

"Just for tonight."

We have the restaurant send over fish and chips and coleslaw, and we eat in our underwear on the living room sofa watching *Frasier* reruns. As we're finishing dinner, a crack of thunder rattles the windows. I dart out to the deck to save Mom's diary, putting it back on my nightstand. We get dressed and sit on the front porch, sheltered from the storm, watching lightning branch across the black sky.

Will and I head up to bed. Being with him feels as impossible and inevitable as his leaving. But I don't want to think about that part right now. I curl into him when it's over, pleasantly noodle-limbed, following the lines of his tree tattoo with my finger, writing *Fern* over his heart after he dozes off.

It's the first night since we started sharing a bed that I haven't been able to fall asleep. I flick on the lamp, and when Will doesn't move, I reach for the diary and flip to the final entry.

September 8, 1990

Two sleeps until Europe!

I'm going. A couple of days after I'd told Mom and Dad the news, Peter came over with more prenatal pamphlets to help me convince them it was okay to travel. I think they've finally stopped freaking out, or they're doing a better job hiding it. I'm almost out of the first trimester, and hopefully the vomiting will stop any day now.

I'm excited for the trip. I'm looking forward to being a twenty-two-year-old with no responsibilities for a little longer. I'm going for six weeks. Italy, France, and England.

Peter has volunteered to drive me to the airport. He hasn't mentioned what he wanted to tell me the day I announced I was pregnant. I'm not sure he ever will. But I've started hoping he does. I can't imagine a life without Peter. I think that means something. Something we've been moving toward since the day I gave him a tour of the resort five years ago.

Liz was shocked when I told her the news and a little upset about the change in plans, but she's decided to travel on her own for the full year.

I'll admit I'm somewhat jealous, but whenever I'm feeling down these days, I rub my belly and talk to my baby girl. I'm certain she's a girl. I call her my sweet little pea. I tell her how much I love her. I tell her

I'll love her enough for ten dads. And I tell her stories about all the people who will make up her big, wonderful family here. About her grandparents. And the Roses. And Peter. I tell her how she'll never feel alone when she's at home. I tell her I can't wait to meet her, but that I don't need to meet her to know I will never love another person as much as I love my daughter.

I put the diary down on the bed beside me. I do my best to sob quietly, but when I take a shuddering breath, Will stirs.

"Hey," he murmurs. "What's wrong?"

But speaking is impossible when I'm crying this hard.

"Shh. It's all right," he mumbles, still half-asleep.

I shake my head.

"It was just a dream."

"No," I croak. "It was real. My mom."

It's all I need to say. He kisses my cheeks and wipes the tears, then turns me so my back is snug to his front. He brings his leg over mine, tucking me closer. I grip the arm that's banded around my chest. "She loved me. So much."

"Of course she did," he whispers into my neck, pressing a kiss there. "She was your mom."

"But she didn't know," I say, shaking with more tears.

He holds me until I stop. "Didn't know what, Fern?"

I take a deep breath. "She didn't know that I loved her, too."

Will hugs me tight. "She knew," he says. He kisses my shoulder.

I nod, but I can't help feeling that if I'd been a better daughter, she would have told me about Peter. If she knew how much I loved her, she would have confided in me about the resort's struggles.

"Fern, can I tell you something?" Will says, his lips against my skin.

I roll over to face him.

"I told your mom I met you," he says.

"What?"

"I told her how we met. I told her how much you loved it here, and that I had to see it myself."

"You did?"

"I did. We spoke on the phone shortly before the accident." He brushes my hair off my forehead. "She said I had no idea how happy that made her."

His words wrap around me like a down-filled duvet. *I love you,* I almost say. But then I remember the red dress and dancing with Will. We have tomorrow. We can have more than this summer. It's the last thing I think before I fall asleep.

When I wake up, Will is gone.

24

June 14, Nine Years Ago

I GOT TO THE DOCKS EARLY. I TOLD MOM I WAS MEETING A friend, but I'd been deliberately vague on every other detail. It was my first trip home since Christmas, and she was suspicious. I'd graduated from university a year earlier, and my friend circle was small—more of a triangle, really. Whitney and Cam were up north, and Ayla was my good friend in the city. Aside from my coworkers at Two Sugars, I wasn't close to anyone else.

It had been twelve months since I'd seen Will. After he'd left my apartment, I spent the morning in bed, staring at the spot where he'd lain the night before, his words on repeat in my head.

It's still your *life.*

It wasn't exactly new information, but it felt like I was seeing myself in a different light. Will's light. His conviction that I needed to be honest with Mom and his own passion for art cast one thousand watts on how passive I'd been about my future. I was letting life happen to me.

I had repeated his words to myself in the bathroom mirror

later that afternoon. It was Sunday, and when it was time for my call with Mom, I held the list Will had written, staring at the four items on the plan. I explained to Mom that I had something to tell her, that I wasn't sure how to say it, but I didn't want to work at the resort that summer. Or any summer. Or ever.

"I don't understand," she said. "You're coming home in a week. The Roses are throwing a party. I have you booked on the front desk through July. I was going to show you how to do the scheduling. I ordered you a new uniform." She spoke quickly without pausing for air. "I got the good coffee beans and bought a fancy grinder I still can't figure out. I was going to surprise you on your first morning back. You always say my coffee is too weak." I heard her suck in a breath. When she started speaking again, her voice trembled. "I was looking forward to our mornings at the lake. I thought this was going to be me and you, pea."

I closed my eyes. I apologized and said I was grateful for everything she'd done for me. I told her I didn't want her life. I wanted a life of my own, whatever that was.

She went quiet for a few moments, then she said, "Okay, Fern." Her tone was flat. "You go figure your life out, but I'm not going to pay for it."

I started saying that I didn't have any savings, but the line had gone dead.

Shaking, I put my phone down. I hated hurting Mom. But I was also buzzing with adrenaline. I had done it. I wasn't going home in a week. I wasn't going to work at Brookbanks.

I could hardly believe it. I had to call my boss and beg for more shifts. I had to tell Jamie and Whitney. But the person I most wanted to talk to was Will. Only I couldn't.

Not once did I contact Will, although the first time I got high after he left, alone in my apartment, I typed "Will Baxter" into a

Google search bar. I found an article in the *Vancouver Sun* about a student art exhibit that featured a photo of Will looking just as I'd remembered. I dug up his private Facebook page—the profile pic was a cartoon self-portrait—but I didn't friend him. I searched for *Roommates*, hoping his comic had a digital trail, but came up empty.

I spent twelve months desperate for his company, his wide smile, his explosive laugh. His certainty. I imagined what our day would have been like if we'd both been single. I imagined the night going very differently. I imagined pressing my lips to his scar.

I spent twelve months thinking about what it would be like to see him again. I'd take him out on the canoe. We'd paddle up the lake to the quiet strip of sandy shoreline and sit with our toes in the water, and we'd talk. We would talk for hours.

There was so much I wanted to tell Will—how I had stayed in my apartment in Toronto and how I was broke but much happier than I had been when we met. I wanted to tell him I was working full-time at Two Sugars and that people loved his mural. I smiled whenever I saw the tiny fern on the plane's rudder. I wanted to tell him about the inkling of an idea I had to open my own coffee shop one day. I wanted to tell him I'd gone to High Park to see the cherry blossoms in the spring. I wanted to tell him I was single.

I decided not to go to Banff with Jamie. I convinced myself it was because I couldn't afford the airfare and didn't want to give up my apartment. It was a Tuesday in early July when he broke up with me. I had just gotten home from a double shift when my buzzer rang. I knew why he'd come as soon as I saw him. We sat on the front steps of the building, and Jamie told me that loving me felt like holding water. "I'm trying to hang on too tight, Fernie," he said. "I think we both need to face the next adventure on our own." I knew he was doing what I should have already, but I ached for weeks.

Whitney said she understood why I didn't want to come home, but then she asked why I hadn't mentioned anything while she was visiting, and I could tell I'd hurt her, too.

Ayla, my closest friend in Toronto, was doing an internship in Calgary until September, and I wasn't tight enough with the Two Sugars crowd for more than the occasional after-work drink. I was lonely.

Countless times, I stared up at the crack in my cciling wondering if I'd made a huge mistake by not going home. There were even more times I almost sent Will a Facebook request. I wanted so badly to talk to him. I had feelings for him, I could admit that. But above all, I needed his friendship.

June fourteenth was one of those glorious afternoons where lake and sky form blue parentheses around the green hillside of the opposite shore. The resort beach was crowded with families, the water dotted with canoes and kayaks and paddleboards. It wasn't as hot as the day Will and I had spent together, but there was the same feeling in the air—the thrumming excitement of a summer just begun.

The pair of teenage boys working in the outfitting hut clearly had yet to experience the wrath of Margaret Brookbanks, because the docks were covered in pine needles. I ducked inside, said a quick hello, and grabbed a broom to keep myself busy.

I was surprised when Will was late. He struck me as having a responsible streak—the way he'd checked in on his sister, his idea for a one-year plan, even his insistence we not stay in touch. I was certain he'd be there. I squinted up at the lodge, and when I saw no sign of him, I sat down at the end of the dock. I'd dressed to take him out in a canoe—a pair of cotton shorts and a green bathing suit I'd bought because the color reminded me of the trees in Emily Carr's paintings. I'd packed a straw bag with supplies—a couple of sandwiches, two bottles of lemon San Pellegrino I'd brought with me from Toronto, a tube of sunscreen, and a bucket hat for Will.

I waited until I started to worry my own nose might peel, and I put the hat on.

I waited until the sun had sunk low in the sky.

I waited for Will Baxter for hours.

And then, finally, I felt the prick of being watched. I looked over my shoulder and found a pair of gray eyes identical to my own. The disappointment hit me in one swift blow.

Mom made her way across the dock.

"Want to tell me about him?" she asked as she slipped off her gold sandals and sat down beside me, her perfume tickling my nose. She was dressed for the evening in a turquoise shift and chunky gold jewelry.

I didn't reply.

There was no denying an unease had descended between us after I told her I wasn't coming home.

She and Peter had come for convocation and taken me to dinner after the ceremony, but the evening ended with Mom and me fighting. I hadn't visited her at the resort until the end of summer. When I'd woken up late my first morning home, I'd been confused. Mom hadn't roused me to go to the lake with our coffees—she'd already left for the lodge. She hadn't woken me the next day, either.

Christmas had been a minor disaster. She talked a lot about a whole lot of nothing, but she could barely meet my eyes. Sometimes I caught her studying me like I was a stranger, like she was rewiring her entire idea of who I was.

She was snippy with Peter and worked Christmas Day, which had always been a sacred day off. Peter and I cooked Christmas dinner together. We had the new Haim album up loud, and I was rage-peeling potatoes, fuming about how Mom hadn't once asked about the coffee shop. Peter told me I had to be patient—that she needed more time to adjust to my decision.

"All she cares about is this place," I complained. It felt like my lifelong hypothesis had been proven. Now that I wasn't going to be a part of Brookbanks, Mom had zero time for me, and she'd never had much to begin with.

Peter handed me another Yukon Gold. "When your mom was your age, it was her dream to take over the resort from your grandparents. She's thrown everything she has at making it a success, showing she could do it on her own," he said. "But for the last four years, Fern, all she's been dreaming about is working next to you."

I'd stared at the potato in my hand, stunned. I'd promised Peter I'd give her some slack, but when she'd shown up late for turkey, I'd cut my trip short and hadn't returned until now.

Mom and I sat beside each other on the dock, watching two tweens attempt to steer a paddleboat. She took the hat off my head.

"You could start with his name," she said.

I considered denying that I was meeting a guy, telling Mom my friend's name was Beth or Jane, but a tear tumbled down my cheek. I swiped it away with the heel of my hand.

"His name is Will."

She absorbed this for a moment. "And he was going to meet you all the way up here, at home?" Her voice was laced with skepticism.

"He was supposed to."

"Is it serious between the two of you?"

"I thought it could be." I rubbed my cheek again. "I made him a mix CD."

I'd spent hours perfecting it. I'd wanted it to be summery and meaningful but not in an *I'm totally in love with you* way. I didn't know if he was still with Fred or someone else or if he felt the same way I did. I included some of the songs we'd listened to at the coffee shop and some that reminded me of the day we spent together and others that reminded me of him. The only theme, really, was Will.

Music may have been the language Peter and I shared, but Mom knew what making a CD for someone meant to me. She placed a pink-manicured hand on my thigh and gave my leg a little jostle. "It's his loss then, Fern," she said firmly.

"Maybe," I said, tilting my chin to the sky to fend off another swell of tears.

Mom pressed her palms to my cheeks, turning my face so she could look me in the eyes.

"No, pea," she said, unblinking. "It's his loss. He has no idea what he's missing."

I took an unsteady breath. "You think so?"

She wrapped her arms around me and pulled me against her chest, the same way she did when I was little.

"Oh, honey," she said into my hair. "I know."

25

Now

THERE'S NO NOTE. NO TEXT MESSAGE. NO VOICEMAIL. THERE'S nothing to explain Will's absence.

At first I think he must have had an early meeting and didn't want to wake me, but when I pull on a pair of sweats and walk over to Cabin 20 in the drizzle, there's no light on inside. I don't want to knock in case he's on a call, so I creep around to the front deck to peer inside the kitchen, but the curtains are drawn.

As I head back to the house, I tell myself he's probably gone for a jog or a walk to get some fresh air. I take a hot shower, but he's not downstairs like I'm expecting when I come out. I make coffee, thinking he'll walk through the door at any moment. But after I've had two cups, dread seeps its way into my limbs like a cold fog.

I send him a text.

Where did you go?

I wait for the three little dots foreshadowing his reply, but they don't come. I get dressed and still there's nothing.

I walk to the lodge and tendrils of smoke curl out of cabin chimneys, the smell hanging low in the mist. The late summer heat has turned into the cool damp of early fall. My mind is whirling, but my legs are leaden. Something has to be wrong. A work crisis maybe. Will wouldn't just leave. He wouldn't disappear on me. Not again.

I sit in my chair in the office, no memory of passing through the lobby to get here. I check my email, but there's nothing from him. I stare at the computer. I'm still sitting there, eyes unfocused, when Jamie unlocks the door an hour later. He's fuming about something to do with the florist and a shipment delay but stops mid-sentence.

"Are you sick?" He bends down in front of me, putting a hand on my forehead. "You're clammy but you don't feel like you have a fever."

I blink. "Hungover."

"Shit, Fernie. This is a big day. Want me to get you a Gatorade?"

"Big day?"

"The dance," he says. "How much did you drink last night?" The dance.

"I'm going to go find that bottle of Gatorade," I say, pushing out of my chair, ignoring his offer. I need a few minutes alone to collect myself. "Then you can put me to work."

I duck outside to get some air. My eyes wander down to the docks, and I shiver.

You and me in one year, Fern Brookbanks. Don't let me down.

The day passes slowly with no trace of Will. Jamie won't let me into the dining room to help with setup. I leave Will four voicemails and several more texts asking where he is and if everything is okay. All the while, I can't seem to warm up. A chill has settled in my bones. By late afternoon, when I walk to the house to change, I'm so anxious and worried, I'm vibrating. Something has to be wrong.

I shower, blow out my hair, and put on my makeup. When I slip into the red dress, I look in the mirror, hoping he'll be there. I want him to be okay. I want us to be okay. I want more than okay. The reality of what I want with Will crashes into me with such a force that I have to sit down.

A FLOOD OF GUESTS HEADS TOWARD THE LODGE, AND I FOLLOW, rubbing my hands over the prickled flesh of my arms. I'm not paying attention as I enter the lobby and I almost bump into the glittering back of Mrs. Rose.

"Fern, dear, what's the matter? You're wearing the same scowl you did as a teenager."

I apologize and tell her how lovely she looks, then rearrange my face so I'll look suitably impressed when I enter the dining room.

But I don't need to fake it, because the transformation is so dramatic, I gasp. Everything is pink. Pink linens, pink dahlias, pink balloons. Tables have been arranged to circle the dance floor and there are probably a hundred strands of twinkle lights hanging in the rafters. Candles flicker in glass jars all over the room. The band is already onstage, playing "Be My Baby."

Usually the dancing doesn't get started until sometime around dessert, but as soon as Mrs. Rose puts her purse down, she and Mr. Rose are shimmying their way to the floor.

"You like?" Jamie says, startling me. I spin around and see that he's found a hunter green tie with a pink floral print to go with his tan suit.

"It's incredible, Jamie. I think you may have outdone Mom."

"Nah," he says, but he's pleased.

"I'm serious. Thank you so much for all . . ." I stop. The band has changed songs and is now playing "Love Man." I narrow my eyes. "What kind of band did you book, Jamie?"

"They mostly do Motown covers," he says. "But I may or may not have requested a set list heavy on songs from *Dirty Dancing*."

I shake my head. "You're the worst."

"I'm just happy you're here"—he waggles his eyebrows— "Baby."

I laugh, forgetting Will for a brief, wonderful moment. There was a time when everything about this night—the end-of-summer dance, a band hired specifically to tease me, a room full of guests—would have been my greatest nightmare. I spot Whitney and Cam being ushered to their table, and a flock of children boogieing with the Roses. In one corner, Peter watches the servers deliver baskets of bread rolls. Right now, I just feel . . . at home.

The band takes a break for the talent portion of the evening— Mr. and Mrs. Rose's "The Surrey with the Fringe on Top" gets a standing ovation. It's one of the liveliest end-of-summer parties I've seen. I make my way from table to table, my eyes constantly flicking to the doorway. But Will never walks through it. By the time dessert is served and the band begins its third set, the glow I felt earlier this evening has faded into nothingness, and I have to hold back tears. Why isn't Will walking through that door?

I wish Mom were here. I want nothing more than to bury myself against her, inhaling the sweetness of her perfume and the salt of her skin, the way I did when I was little.

I look for Jamie to tell him I'm leaving—I'm going back to the house to call Will. Again.

"Can I have this dance?" I hear Peter say behind me. He's in a charcoal suit, the same one he wore to the funeral, probably the only one he owns.

"You don't dance."

"You don't, either," he says. "But let's make an exception." He holds out his large paw, and I follow him onto the floor.

We move slowly among the other couples, and after a minute, Peter clears his throat and says, "You're a lot like her, you know?"

I frown. "I am?"

"Not just how you look, though I thought I'd seen a ghost earlier this evening, you wearing that dress."

"You recognized it?"

Peter grunts in the affirmative. "Canada Day, I think. It was probably around 1992."

I rest my head against Peter's chest and take a deep breath, breathing in his Old Spice cologne and along with it a lifetime of moments with him and my mom. The holiday dinners and card games and birthday brunches Peter cooked for her.

"You've got her grit. Coming back here, stepping into her shoes—that's no small thing."

I consider this for a moment. "I've always thought I was more like you."

"Maggie once said you had my soft heart and her strong head. I thought she was trying to make me feel like part of the family. But maybe you do have a little of both of us," Peter says. "Either way, she'd be so proud of you."

"Yeah," I whisper, my throat tight.

We sway in a tiny circle, not speaking.

After a minute, I pull back to look up at him. "Do you think this would all be easier if you'd been married?" I ask. "If you'd gotten what you wanted before she died?" It's something I've wondered.

"It wasn't marriage I wanted, Fern." His feet still. "It was Maggie. It wasn't always easy, but we were always friends. We were always there for each other."

I hug Peter tighter, and as his words sink in, the truth hits me with a sudden crushing clarity.

"I've got to go," I say, and then I rush out to the lobby. I ask the desk clerk if I can look something up in the computer, and even though I know what I'm going to find, the shock of seeing it spelled out in front of me is dizzying.

I rush out of the lodge, imagining all the foul words I'll use once I finally get Will on the phone. But then I hear Whitney.

"Fern, wait up!"

She's jogging to reach me, her heels clutched in one hand, her boobs in the other.

"Thank god I wore the jumpsuit," she pants. "Much better for chasing down fleeing besties."

"I'm not fleeing."

"You literally fled the dance as if escaping the scene of a crime. What's going on?"

I fill Whitney in, and her hazel eyes bulge so wide, I'm worried she may burst a few blood vessels.

"Will checked out this morning," I finish. The note in the file said he'd send for his things. He must have been in quite a hurry.

"He what?" she screeches. "He just vanished? Again? Oh, I will kill this man. Is that where you're going?"

My eye catches on a branch of red maple leaves fluttering in the wind, the first blush of fall. So that's it—summer is over, and Will is gone.

I shake my head. "I'm going to the house. I need to speak with him. You go back to the dance, enjoy yourself."

Whitney looks over her shoulder at the lodge. Cam is waiting on the front steps. "Are you sure? Cam can pick me up tomorrow. I have a lot of Will trash talk in the tank. I can go all night."

"No. Really, Whit. I want to be alone, okay?"

"Okay," she says with obvious reluctance. "But if you change your mind about needing company, let me know."

I call Will as soon as I get back to the house, pacing the kitchen floor. I get his voicemail for the nineteenth time. But I won't let him ignore me. I call again. And again. My anger rises with every ring. My mom got an eighteen-word note when she was abandoned by Eric. I want more.

Finally, Will picks up.

"Fern." He says my name on a frustrated sigh, and it's like being doused in ice water.

"You left," is all I manage.

There's a muffled sound on the other end of the line, and I hear Will apologize to someone. Then the line crackles with the sound of wind whipping into the microphone.

"This isn't a good time," he says to me, voice as sterile as an unopened bandage.

"What do you mean?" I cry.

"I really can't talk about this right now," Will says. "I've got to get back."

"No," I say. "I've been worried all day, wondering where you went and whether you're all right. You need to tell me what the hell is going on. You checked out? What's happening? Where are you?"

Will lets out another sigh. "I'm at the hospital, Fern." It sounds like a chastisement. "Sofia is sick."

My stomach seizes with a mix of fear and relief. I knew something was wrong. I immediately switch into problem-solving mode. "Which hospital? How is she? I'll drive down and meet you." If I pack now, I can be in the city before midnight. I'll call Jamie once I'm on the road. Does the car need gas? "Can I bring you anything?" I ask, opening the fridge. Will won't have eaten. I could pack up the leftover quiche he made for dinner two nights ago.

"Fern, no."

I stop moving.

"Don't come down here."

"What? Why?" I say, confused. "I can help."

"I don't want your help. I'm sorry, but you and I . . . It was a mistake. We were a mistake. It's my fault. I should have known that from the beginning." He sounds vacant. It's like there's a stranger talking to me on the other end of the line, not the person who held me in his arms last night, whispering soothing words into my ear.

"I don't believe you," I tell him, my voice breaking.

I think of the Patti Smith album and the card he gave me. *You do know me. And I know you, too.* I look behind me at the stove, remembering him preparing the quiche in my mom's apron.

"Will, I love you."

There is nothing but silence on the other end of the phone.

I think of swimming together one evening last week. It was so hot, we didn't bother toweling off after. We sat at the edge of the family dock, dripping, our feet in the water. Will pressed his lips to my shoulder. "I don't think I've been happier than I am right now," he'd said.

"And I think you love me, too," I say now, my heart thrashing wildly in my chest.

"Fern, I can't," he says, and for a second, he sounds like Will again. But then his voice goes hard. "It's time we both stopped living in a fantasy and move on with our lives."

I begin to argue, but he's hung up.

I hold the fridge door open, staring at the plate of leftover quiche, unable to comprehend what just happened. I told Will I love him, and he didn't say it back. I told him I love him, and he ended things. I slam the fridge closed. I am not crying.

My hands shake as I fill a glass with water. I take a sip, but my throat is so tight, I can barely force the liquid down. I stand at the sink, looking out the window at Will's cabin, rage turning my blood hot. I think of Will's tailored suits and pristine white shirts hanging in an orderly row in the closet.

I bring the matches with me.

Please be unlocked, I wish as I climb the steps to Cabin 20. I'm wearing the red dress and no shoes, and if someone sees me, they'll think I'm mad.

I'm not mad.

I'm furious.

When I twist the doorknob, it obeys, and I charge inside and head straight for the bedroom. I throw open the closet and Will's clothing stares back at me. I grab as many jackets and shirts and slacks as I can, tamping down on the desire to press my nose into the fabric and get a hit of Will. I carry the load into the living room, and my foot slips on something. When I twist to see what's gotten in my way, I freeze.

Sheets of paper lie on the floor and a large sketchbook sits on the coffee table, a pencil tucked into its rings. I don't register when the clothes fall from my arms, only that I'm picking one of the pages off the floor, staring down at a drawing of me floating in water, arms outstretched, eyes closed. There's a smudge over my nose, like it's been erased at least once. There are three other drawings on the floor, unfinished variations of the same image.

I take the sketchbook off the table and flip the cover open.

Will mentioned that he'd begun drawing again, but I had no idea he'd done so much. It feels wrong, like I'm reading his diary. But I was about to set flame to thousands of dollars of suiting. What's one more bad deed?

I flip past sketches of scraggly trees on rocky shorelines, of a canoe pulled onto a beach, of the Roses playing cards. Of me. In one of the illustrations, my hair is short, the way it was when we first met. I lean against a graffiti-covered wall, my face tilted up to the sky. I press my hand against the sharp pain in my chest. When I turn the page, a shiver runs through my body.

No, no, no, I think as I study the drawing.

The bag beside me on the dock. The hat on my head.

"No." I say it out loud, as if I can make it true. But the more I stare at the page, the more I know.

I sag onto the pile of clothing, the book in my hand, and when the tears fall down my cheek, I don't hold them back. I stay there until a breeze blows through the back door, carrying with it the far-off sound of the band playing "(I've Had) the Time of My Life."

26

Now

MY APARTMENT IS ALMOST EMPTY. OVER THE PAST FEW DAYS, I'VE packed everything into bubble wrap and newspaper, replaying my time in Toronto. My university years, my first shift at Two Sugars, and all the long walks, bad dates, and sloppy nights out along the way. It's just me, the movers, a tray of dark roasts, and about a dozen boxes left now. It's strange seeing my little home this way, stripped of all the trimmings that made it mine.

I've lived here for five years, longer than anywhere other than the resort. I remember how excited I was when I found it, how spacious the one-bedroom layout seemed, how grown up the stainless-steel kitchen appliances made me feel. It's the main floor of a skinny semidetached, and as I look at it now, it feels cramped despite the missing furniture. The view out the kitchen window is of a solid brick wall. There's no outdoor space. Even though I could smell my neighbor's cooking and hear his nocturnal activities and dog's claws clacking above me, this place felt like my own. It felt like me.

My phone vibrates with a message. I drop the cloth I'm using to wipe out the fridge and take off my rubber gloves. For a fraction of a second while I get the phone from the back pocket of my jeans, I think it might be Will, and I hold my breath until I see that it's an email to the Brookbanks events reservation account.

It's been a week since the dance, and I haven't heard a single thing from him. I know today won't be any different. After I picked myself up off his cabin floor, I went back to the house, taking his drawing with me. I composed furious text messages in my head. I typed out a few, but it didn't seem right sending them. He gave me so little in the end. He lied to me all summer. Despite all the questions I have, I decided Will didn't deserve any of my emotions, even the wild, wrathful ones. I wrote a brief message saying I hoped Sofia was okay and to go through Jamie for the rest of the consultancy work. I asked him never to contact me again.

But every time my phone buzzes, a traitorous part of my brain hopes it's him and wishes I hadn't slammed the door between us shut so firmly. Not that I have a script for what I'd say if we were speaking. The foundation of hurt and confusion never falters. A gnawing ache has settled in my belly. I thought I knew what it was like to miss Will Baxter, but the emptiness I felt years ago was a crevice compared to this canyon.

The message is a general inquiry about a company holiday party, so I bookmark it to reply to after I get this place clean, hand over the keys, and head back to the resort in the rusty Cadillac. All week, I've been dreaming of the Webers burger I'm going to eat on my way home.

I promised Jamie I'd keep up with bookings while I was gone and justified the less-than-ideal timing of my trip by meeting with a few potential sommeliers in the city. I think he knew I needed space to clear my head. I'm going to take a few days off once we're staffed up to buy a car, box some of Mom's things, and start redecorating the house so that it feels like me.

"Forget to pack this one, eh?" calls one of the movers. I follow his voice into the bedroom, where Will's ten-year-old portrait of me hangs in the otherwise blank space. My one-year plan is tucked behind the drawing. When I lost the streetcar pin years ago, I tore apart my apartment, emptied all my purses, dumped my dresser drawers out on the bed, but I never found it. I put the list inside the frame that day.

"I think I have an empty picture box somewhere," says the young, bleary-eyed redhead, who reeks of the joint he smoked before getting started. I think his name is Landon or possibly Landry. "Want me to wrap it up?"

"No, that's okay. I don't know if I'm taking it or not," I tell him. Maybe I'll bring it with me. Or maybe I'll dump it in the garbage bin on my way out the door. Fifty-fifty chance.

Landon or possibly Landry shrugs.

I take it off the picture hook and leave it on the kitchen counter for now.

The movers work at an incredible speed for two stoned twenty-somethings. I hired a team from Huntsville, and they aren't used to narrow downtown Toronto side streets. They've pulled half onto the sidewalk but are still blocking part of the road, and between the angry honking, passive-aggressive bicycle bells, and sneers from pedestrians trying to navigate around the giant truck, they seem frazzled and anxious to get the hell out of here. Peter is meeting them at the house since they'll have a head start on me. I direct them out of their makeshift parking space and then start on the stove.

I'm scrubbing the oven when the doorbell rings. I look

around. I don't see anything the movers have forgotten. I poke my head out the front window, but it's not Landon, Landry & Co. on the steps; it's a woman in a voluminous white shirtdress, her dark brown hair falling straight to her shoulders. The man who lives in the unit above mine is a smoking-hot linguistics PhD who teaches French on the side. I assume she's buzzed the wrong apartment.

"Can I help you?" I call out, and she jumps before turning my way. She's stunning. The oversized burgundy leather bag she's carrying probably costs a month's rent. I can see how precisely winged her liquid eyeliner is from five feet away.

She studies me and asks, not altogether kindly, "Are you Fern?"

"I am," I say, wary. Strangers don't just show up on your doorstep in this city.

She looks over her shoulder like she's not supposed to be here and then back at me. "I'm Annabel. Can I talk to you for a minute?"

ANNABEL AND I STAND ACROSS FROM EACH OTHER AT THE kitchen island. It's as though all of Will's extremes have been softened in his younger sister. Her hair and eyes are a touch lighter, the color of pennies rather than cola. Her face is more rounded, her nose less dramatic. She doesn't have the Will Baxter posture, but she's every bit as put-together.

"You don't really look like his type," she says, unfazed by her barren surroundings.

I glance down at my grimy T-shirt, ripped jeans, and running shoes. My hair's pushed back with a headband. No makeup. Sweat sheen. Coffee breath. I'm not anyone's type at the moment.

"Well, I guess I wasn't."

"I didn't mean that as an insult." Her gaze drops to Will's illustration on the counter. "I'm just surprised, that's all."

That doesn't sound much better. "I don't want to be rude, but why are you here? How did you find me?"

She hitches her purse strap higher on her shoulder. "I googled you. Found out where you worked and told your old boss I was a college friend."

Fucking Philippe.

"And you did this because?" I ask. "Is Sofia okay?"

"She's on the mend. How much did my brother tell you?"

"Only that she was in the hospital."

She nods, as if she's not surprised. "It was meningitis. They kept her there until she was out of danger. I called Will early Saturday morning freaking out. Sofia was shivering and vomiting. I couldn't get ahold of our family doctor. Will told me to go to the ER immediately, and I did, thank god. It was awful." Annabel's eyes well, and she waves a hand in front of her face. "I won't go into detail, but she's going to be fine. I don't want to imagine how fast Will must have driven to get back to the city so quickly, but he met me at the children's hospital and stayed with us. Your friend called yesterday."

"My friend?"

"The angry one. I didn't really catch her name. I could hear her chewing out Will through the phone. She was going on and on, and he was sitting there saying 'I know' over and over. I don't think he even noticed I'd taken the phone from him until I was yelling at her."

"Whitney." She didn't tell me she'd called Will, although I'm not shocked.

"That's it," Annabel says. "Apologize to her for me. I may

have called her some not-so-nice things before she explained that my brother had taken off on his girlfriend and that you were in the city if he wanted to make things right."

"I wasn't his girlfriend," I say. It feels important to make the clarification.

"No? It sounded pretty serious from what Whitney told me and from the little Will said."

I want to know exactly what Will said, word for word. I want to know his tone of voice, what he was wearing, and where they had the conversation. "You still haven't explained why you're here," I say instead.

"My brother doesn't really screw up—don't tell him I said that. But according to Whitney and from what I've managed to get out of him, he screwed up with you." Annabel straightens herself to a Will-like stance. "I'm here to defend his honor or whatever."

"Will knows you're here?" I ask, hating how hopeful I sound.

"No, he'd be pissed. He told me you didn't want to be contacted and that I needed to"—she makes air quotes with her fingers—" 'respect that.' But please hear me out. I didn't come all the way to the west end for fun."

I let out a heavy sigh. "All right."

"I've had a long, shitty week, and Will hasn't been as helpful as he thinks—he's just a big, mopey disaster. Anyway, his recent fuckup aside, my brother is extremely loyal to the people he loves. I think when he offered to work with your mom, he was—"

I wave my hands to cut her off, assuming she has misspoken. "Excuse me?"

Annabel slants her head. "Earlier this year? After he stayed at the resort for that wedding? He offered to work with your mom?" She must see the shock on my face. "He didn't tell you that."

"He said it was my mom's idea." I put a hand on the counter, feeling light-headed.

"Well, I'll leave that mess for him to explain. But I think it was his way of making things right with you, at least at first. It took me a while to put it all together. That you're the girl, the one from that day ten years ago."

I nod.

"Will couldn't stop talking about you the morning after he met you—how he showed you around the city, how you were different from everyone else. I'd never heard him speak about someone like that before."

It takes a second for my memory to kick in. "He was meeting you that morning for breakfast," I say. "Before his flight back to Vancouver."

Annabel presses her lips together. "I'll never forget it," she says. "I threw up halfway through our waffles. It's when I told Will I was pregnant."

"He didn't tell me that," I whisper. He didn't tell me a lot of things.

"Our dad found the pregnancy test in the garbage a few days before. He assumed I wouldn't have the baby, and honestly, I thought that, too. But then he started saying how I couldn't take care of myself, never mind a child, and I snapped. When I told Will, he offered to stay in the city and come to the clinic with me, but I'd already made up my mind to prove Dad wrong. I was going to have the baby and become the best mom ever." Annabel shakes her head. "Stubbornness and pride run in the Baxter family, FYI." She glances at the drawing on the counter.

"Will gave up a lot for me. I didn't realize how much he was giving up at the time; neither of us did. But I've learned a lot since I was nineteen." Annabel's eyes move to where my fingers grip the edge of the counter and then she peers around the space. "Is there somewhere we can sit? There's more."

ANNABEL AND I GO OUT TO THE FRONT STEPS. IT'S HUMID IN THE city, the sun smudged out by fat clouds. A spotted white cat is sprawled on the walkway. Colonel Mustard belongs to the next-door neighbor.

Annabel sets her purse between her sandaled feet and fidgets with the shoulder strap. "Does he talk very much about our mother?" she asks.

I shake my head. I know she still lives in Italy and that Will hasn't visited her for a couple of years. Other than what he told me ten years ago, he hasn't said much more.

"I'm not surprised," Annabel says. "He doesn't like to. She's a very gifted artist. And gorgeous and smart and over-the-top charming when she wants to be. But she was kind of an absent parent. Even before she left, she was never totally there. It wasn't all her fault—I know that now. Her depression could be debilitating. During a bad spell, she'd be in bed for days. And when she was well, she was hyperfocused on her work, like she needed to use every drop of her creativity in case it ran out." Annabel gives me a look to make sure I'm following, and something about the steadiness of her gaze reminds me so much of Will, my chest squeezes. But then she notices Colonel Mustard.

"I'm sorry. Does that cat have a mustache?"

"Yep." I click my tongue and the Colonel turns his head, the black patch of fur under his nose on full display.

Annabel squeals and the cat, spotting a mark, stretches, then sashays over, wrapping himself around her ankles.

"We never had pets," she says, stroking his fur. "Will is allergic to almost anything with four legs. Itchy eyes, asthma, the whole thing."

It pokes at me like a pebble in a shoe. I didn't know Will has asthma. The list of things I didn't know about Will grows with almost every word from Annabel's lips.

"Anyway," she says as the Colonel settles by her feet, "when our mother was working, she could shut out everything. Her studio was above the garage, and I remember stomping up the stairs like an elephant. I'd stand right in front of her and have to try four or five times to get her attention before she'd notice I was there. After I became a parent, I wondered if she moved so far away because she felt guilty for not spending enough time with us. Like, if she put an ocean between us, she wouldn't have to attempt some kind of balance. She couldn't fail."

It reminds me of something Peter said about Mom—how one of the reasons she worked so much was because it was the one area of her life where she felt successful.

"Will idolized her when we were growing up," Annabel continues. "Everyone always said how alike they were. He was so proud of that. The two artists. He looks like Mom, too. And he seemed to understand her. When she was suffering, he'd sit beside her in bed, sketching. It used to scare me when she was like that, but Will would just be with her in the quiet."

I can picture it clearly, a young Will trying to comfort his mom with nothing more than his solid presence. I think of how he was when we first met—the way he let me speak when I was ready, how he lay across from me in the dark, assuring me everything would be okay.

"Are you all right?" Annabel asks, looking down at my arm. I've been scratching.

"Yeah," I lie, putting my hands around my shins to hold them in place. The more Annabel tells me about Will, the wider the canyon inside me splits. He's a river, pushing and eroding, and my banks are sand, not granite.

Annabel makes a dubious hum, but she goes on. "When our mom left, Will took it the hardest. We lived with my grandma that summer, and I remember one day, he was drawing out in the backyard. I wanted his help putting a basket on my bike, and I had to call his name a bunch of times to get him to hear me. I said something about him being like Mom, and he got so mad. He told me he'd never be like her. Sometimes I think he's made it his life's mission to prove it."

I stay quiet, watching Annabel's profile.

"The thing is," Annabel says, "Will *is* a lot like our mother. Not in the ways that count—he's the least self-centered person I know, and his heart is too large for his chest. But he's creative and passionate, and when he decides he wants to do something, his commitment is unbreakable." She pulls in a deep breath. "When Sofia was born, he had a hard time. It was different from our mom's depression, and it's not my place to tell you what he went through, but I think it only confirmed his belief that deep down he's the same as her. He stopped drawing altogether. He got an MBA while working full-time. To him, being a responsible adult meant being like our dad—having a steady job, a big paycheck, owning a home—and so that's what he did. But he gave up this huge part of himself, and I don't think he's been truly happy." She looks at me expectantly. "That's where you come in."

"I don't see how," I murmur.

Annabel gives me a look of sheer pity. "No? He said you were smart."

I blink in surprise, and she smiles. "God, you're both so serious." She turns so she can face me. "I haven't heard my brother sound more alive than he has this summer. When he told me he was sketching again, I was so relieved. I thought he was finally starting to take his life back."

I think of the drawing I found at his cabin, and I wonder if Annabel knows what I know.

"He was so mad at himself that he wasn't home when Sofia got sick, and I'm sure he sees it as evidence that he isn't allowed to have all the things." Annabel stares into the clouds. "And that I'm not ready to live on my own with Sofia. But he's wrong about both. Just like he was wrong to break up with you." She looks back down at me, piercing me with her copper eyes. "Although maybe you shouldn't have dumped all your feelings on him when his niece was in the hospital."

My mouth hangs open, but Annabel goes on.

"And he's not going to come to you and apologize, if that's what you're hoping. You asked him not to speak to you, and he won't." She reaches into her dress pocket and pulls out a torn corner of paper and hands it to me. There's an address written on it. "That's where we live. Sofia's well enough to stay at her dad's tonight, and I'm going out with my girlfriends, so he'll be there alone."

"I don't know," I say, shaking my head. I haven't begun to process everything Annabel's told me, and I already feel depleted. "I'm not sure I can."

Annabel gives me a hard stare. "I'm going out on a limb here. I have no idea whether you're good enough for my brother, but he's never sounded happier than when he was with you. I know him better than anyone—better than you. I know he made a mistake, and he knows it, too. He's been a complete wreck. So I'm hoping you are good enough. I'm hoping you show up." She studies me for a moment before standing and slinging her bag over her shoulder. "Even if it's just to end things properly."

27

Now

I STARE AT WILL'S SUMMERHILL TOWN HOUSE FROM INSIDE THE Cadillac. Number 11 is a wide orange brick semidetached, three stories high, with smart black trim and floppy white hydrangeas lining the porch. It's well past eight, late enough that I'm sure Annabel will be out.

After she'd left this morning, I told myself I wouldn't come here. I've got my own shit to deal with; I can't handle Will's, too. I needed to resume the hiatus. I shoved the piece of paper with their address deep inside a trash bag, planning to drive back to the resort as soon as I'd finished cleaning. Fifteen minutes later, I dug it out.

When I got in the car, instead of heading for the highway, I checked into a hotel, showered, then sat at the desk to write a list of reasons why I should erase Will Baxter from my contacts and my life.

But as I stared at the blank page, I couldn't stop thinking about Will at fourteen, angry and resentful and missing his mom.

And Will at twenty-two, feeling guilty about living in Vancouver, worrying about his sister. Ten years ago, Will helped me see myself clearly, and I decided to take ownership of my future. When he walked out of my apartment that morning, I knew my life was about to change. I had no idea his would, too.

I was worried I was different.

That's the reason Will gave me for not meeting me nine years ago. When I found the drawing in his cabin, I thought he'd been lying to me. But as I reflected on what Annabel told me, I began to wonder whether he wasn't lying—if maybe he couldn't tell me the full truth.

Twice, Will has crashed into my world like a meteorite, and both times, I've been left hollowed out. Cratered. But I'd never thought about how the collision might have thrown him off his axis.

I sat at the hotel desk, and I thought about Will at thirty-two, successful and guarded and patient, slowly finding his way back to art, dipping his toe into a relationship, claiming a slice of happiness for himself. I could hear his voice cutting through the dark the night I knocked on his cabin door in my pajamas.

What do you want, Fern?

I looked at that notepad for an hour, and instead of writing all the reasons I should let Will go, I made a completely different list.

And now here I am, outside Will Baxter's house. Scared and in love and ready to fight for what I want. For what I think Will wants, too.

I just wish I didn't feel like puking.

I grab the drawing from the passenger seat. My fingers shake as I press the bell, and I take a deep breath. But when Will opens the door, the speech I've prepared dies in my throat.

He looks nothing like himself. For one thing, stubble covers his face and neck. It's been left unattended so long, it's verging on scruffy beard territory. Dark circles hang beneath his eyes, and his hair is unkempt. He's wearing a baggy pair of sweats and a stained T-shirt. As soon as he registers me standing in front of him, he snaps upright with the jolt of an electric shock.

I open my mouth, and what comes out is an astonished "You look terrible."

"Fern." He says my name like no one else, like it means so much more than a name. But then he blinks, seeming to remember himself. When he speaks again, his voice has cooled by several degrees. "What are you doing here?"

There's so much I want to say, but I start with the hardest, simplest thing.

"I missed you."

The pink creeping up from the neck of his shirt is the only sign he's affected.

I straighten my shoulders, trying not to let his demeanor throw me. I've seen this before—the blank stare, the empty voice—the way he can detach, strip out all emotion, stay safe. Will is on lockdown. "And I'm here so you can ask for my forgiveness."

He shakes his head, but before he can speak, I hand him the drawing.

"And explain yourself."

I've examined it every day since I found it in his cabin, looking for a clue that might tell a different story other than the one I know is true.

He slides the page from my fingers and studies the sketch as though he hasn't seen it before, running his hand over his cheek.

The drawing is of me, sitting at the end of the dock in a bathing suit and shorts. I'm gazing out over the water, looking bored or maybe sad, wearing the hat I'd packed for Will. Beside me is the bag that contained sunscreen and sandwiches and lemon sodas. There was a mix CD in there, too. It had a white label on its case with SONGS FOR WILL written in green marker.

When his eyes return to mine, they are wells of black remorse. "Fern," he says again.

"You were there." My voice cracks.

He nods. "Yeah. I was there."

I swallow back the lump in my throat. "Now is when you invite me inside," I tell him.

He looks like he's about to disagree, but he nods again and holds the door open.

WILL'S HOME IS SPECTACULAR. THE MAIN FLOOR IS OPEN CONcept, and from the entrance I can see past the living room and kitchen to the enormous windows at the rear. The floors are warm honey-colored wood, the furniture looks comfy, and the white walls are covered in art, though I can tell none of it is by Will.

He sets the drawing on the stone counter and takes two bottles of fizzy water from the fridge. He leads me to the poppy-colored couch at the back of the house. It's obviously the rec area—there are framed family photos on the wall and a giant flatscreen. It would be cozy except the ceiling above opens to cathedral height. There are skylights.

I sit at one end of the sofa, and Will brushes past me to take a seat at the other.

"Annabel came to see me," I tell him, and he makes a low groan in the back of his throat. "She said Sofia's going to be fine."

"Yeah," he says, twisting his pinkie ring.

"She also said you were, and I quote, 'a big, mopey disaster,' which I can see was an accurate description."

Will gives me a sideways glance. "I wasn't expecting company." His voice sounds like sandpaper on metal.

I take a quaking breath. I don't think I've ever been this nervous in my life. "Do you want to tell me why you look like roadkill?"

"It's been a rough week."

"I know it has."

"I haven't slept much."

"Clearly." I pause. "You've been worried about your niece?"

"It's been that, yeah."

"And?"

Will leans back on the sofa, his head tilted toward me, but he doesn't speak.

"It sounded like there might be an *and*. Is there?" The tremor in my voice betrays me.

"I think you already know there is," he says, and it chisels away at the wall of fear I'm scaling in order to be here.

"I think I do, too," I tell him. "But I want to be sure."

Will looks up at the skylights. He opens his mouth, and then closes it again, jaw clenching.

"Because you left without saying a word, and then didn't return any of my messages, and then said we needed to stop living in a fantasy?"

He shakes his head slightly, and then his gaze locks on mine. "No," he says, and my heart splits into a million ragged pieces. I force myself to stay seated instead of running out the door. I wait, hands pressed between my thighs, until he speaks again.

"I shouldn't have done those things, and I'm sorry, Fern. I am," he says slowly. "I was stressed and not thinking straight. But that's not why I can't sleep or eat or get that image of you sitting alone on the dock nine years ago out of my head."

"Then why?" I whisper.

"Fern, you must know . . ." His chest rises and falls with a long exhalation.

I stare at him, eyes wide.

His voice is quiet. "I've never wanted anything for myself the way I want you. I'm completely in love with you."

A loud breath rushes from my throat, my relief instant.

"But I don't know if I can do this," he says as I shift closer. "I don't—"

I put my fingers over his mouth. "You can do anything."

Will's gaze softens.

"I'm going to give you some advice that someone once gave me. He was a pretentious art school grad, but he knew what he was talking about," I say, and a faint smile blossoms beneath my fingers. "I know how much your family means to you, and I would never question that. But it's *your* life, Will."

He's silent.

"So I guess what I need to know is whether you want me in it."

Will takes my hand from his mouth and wraps his arms around me. We stay that way, breathing and holding each other, for a full minute.

"Is that a yes?" I ask, my face against his chest. I feel a quiet laugh rumble in his chest. "Because there's a lot of stuff we need to talk about, but none of it really matters otherwise."

He leans back, his fingers in my hair, his gaze darting between my eyes. "I'm sorry," he says. I start to pull back, but he doesn't let me go. "Wait. I told you before that I'm bad at prioritizing relationships along with everything else. I thought I could figure it out this time." He runs his thumbs across my cheeks. "I almost told you the truth about being there nine years ago, but the more time we spent together this summer, the harder it got. I'm sorry I didn't."

"What is the truth?" I can barely get the words past my lips.

"I thought about seeing you every day for a year. I got halfway down the hill to the lake, and then, finally, I did. You looked so beautiful. I wanted to sit down on that dock with you."

"Why didn't you?" I whisper.

"It wasn't you, please understand that. Sofia was four or five months old, and it was a dark time for me. I was a wreck." He leans back, running his hands over his face. "And I guess I was embarrassed. After everything I put down on that list, there I was—working a nine-to-five in an office—doing exactly what I said I wouldn't a year earlier. Back then, I hated my job. I knew you'd see it right away. You'd be able to tell that I'd changed, that I wasn't happy. You would have called me on it."

"Maybe," I say. "Or maybe I would have been impressed by what you'd taken on. You could have at least said hello."

"That's the thing. I couldn't just say hello. You were sitting there in that green bathing suit, and I remembered exactly how it had been between us. We would have talked. I would have told you I'd given up my art, and you would have been surprised. I wouldn't be able to pretend that everything was okay. I didn't want to see myself through your eyes. I thought if I said hello, I wouldn't want to say goodbye. Maybe I wouldn't want to go back to my sister and my niece. Or my job. Maybe I'd be selfish. I couldn't risk it."

"I wish you would have. I wish you would have let me in back then." I put my palms on his cheeks. "You are one of the least selfish people I've met, but it's not selfish to want something for yourself. It's human."

Will lets out a long breath. "Being with you, being at the lake, away from all this—it's like I remembered who I used to be, what I used to want. I don't know that I still want those things. I don't really know who I am, Fern." He pauses, and I don't move, I don't blink, I don't fill my lungs, until he speaks again. "But I know I want you in my life."

I skim my fingers over his jaw, tracing them to his scar. I meet his eyes, and he looks so tired. More than that. He's exhausted. I remember what Annabel said this morning about dumping my feelings on Will at a bad time.

"I've got a hotel room," I tell him. "Why don't we call it a night, and I can come back tomorrow? You really do look terrible."

Will's face crumples a little. "I don't want you to go."

I don't want to say the rest of what I have to say when he can barely keep his eyes open. I chew the inside of my cheek. "How about we just veg for a bit?" I can pretend like this is any other night.

Will agrees, and we settle in on the sofa, a *Frasier* rerun playing on the flat-screen. Eventually, I coax him to lie down with his head in my lap, and when he falls asleep, I switch off the TV and sit in the last gasp of evening light, studying the photos that hang above the couch. There are three. Annabel holding a toddler Sofia in a garden, their noses pressed together. Sofia on what looks like her first day of school, backpack and goofy grin firmly in place. And the one that makes my heart swell: a young Will with shaggy dark hair, staring down at a little pink baby in his arms.

When Annabel unlocks the front door, Will is still sleeping.

"Jesus fuck," she cries, surprised to find us on the sofa in the dark.

"Sorry," I whisper. "I didn't want to move him."

She creeps over. "Finally, he sleeps."

I brush Will's hair from his forehead.

"I'm glad you found me," I tell her.

She smiles. "I hope I am, too."

When my left butt cheek falls asleep, I nudge Will. He looks at me, startled, and begins to speak. I shoosh him. "Let's get you to bed."

We climb two flights of stairs to his room, and Will collapses onto the mattress.

"Stay," he says, reaching for my hand.

"Okay," I tell him, pulling the sheet up. "I'm not going anywhere."

I WAKE BEFORE WILL DOES. THE HOUSE IS SILENT. EITHER ANNA-bel isn't up yet, or she's already out.

Will's room takes up the entire top floor of the house, with sloped ceilings, an enormous sparkling bathroom, and a sliding glass door that leads to a deck. There's no artwork up here. It's serene. Everything is white and the palest shade of blue—it feels like being in the clouds.

I change out of the T-shirt I took from Will's drawer last night and get dressed quietly so I don't disturb him, then make my way down far too many stairs to the kitchen so I can figure out his spiffy coffee maker and get him something to eat. I find a carton of raspberries in his double-door fridge, but then I see the milk and eggs. I hunt out flour, baking powder, and butter. I know Mom's recipe by heart.

Will is sitting up in bed when I return, sheets kicked off around his ankles. He's still wearing the dirty shirt, but the purple blots under his eyes have faded. I want to pull him into the shower and wash his wonderful Will smell back.

"You're here," he says, his voice scratchy.

"I'm here." I put the coffee on his nightstand and pass him the plate of pancakes. "I promised I'd cook for you one day. I covered them in an ungodly amount of maple syrup."

He smiles, crinkles fanning out around his eyes. *There he is*, I think.

"So good," he says after his first bite.

"Eat up. You're going to need your energy."

His eyebrows rise.

"Not for that," I say, rummaging in my purse for the folded piece of hotel stationery. I sit beside Will, leaning back on the white linen headboard while he eats. Once he's finished, I hand him the paper.

"What's this?" he says, opening it. I stay quiet as he reads, amusement tickling the corners of his lips when he gets to the end.

"It's what I want," I say, then pause, reconsidering. "Actually, it's more than that. It's what I need."

Will's grin straightens out, and he reads it again. There aren't many words on the page, but he takes his time.

"Is this all?"

"That's it."

"Do you want to give me any further context?"

"It's how you win me back—a five-part plan."

I lean over his shoulder, and we look at the list together.

Apologize profusely.

Be honest—no more secrets.

Let me help.

Wear an apron. Always. I mean it.

Draw me a picture.

"The first one is pretty obvious," I say.

Will leans against the headboard, and reaches for my hand, twining our pinkies. He watches me, his expression serious. "I don't think there's an apology big enough for how sorry I am, Fern. I've spent years regretting leaving you alone on that dock, and I hate how I treated you last week—the things I said on the phone. I'm sorry for rushing away like that and making you worry. I can't believe you're here after everything. I am sorry, but I'm also so grateful you showed up at my door yesterday."

I exhale. "That was a good apology. The next one is even more important."

" 'Be honest—no more secrets,' " Will reads.

I nod. "Such as the fact that you offered to help my mom with the resort."

Will winces. "Annabel told you?"

"She did. I like her, by the way."

"That doesn't surprise me." He takes a second to think. "I could tell you didn't trust me when I first arrived, and I wanted you to say yes to working together so badly. I was worried if you knew it was my idea, you'd be even more suspicious. I had coffee with your mother, and when she explained how challenging business had been, I found myself volunteering to help. I think she thought I was being polite, but we emailed a couple of times, and I offered again. And no, I wouldn't have done that if she wasn't your mom, or if it wasn't your resort. And yeah, in my dream scenario, you would have shown up while I was there this summer, very eager to have a lot of sex in canoes."

I laugh. "You can't have sex in a canoe." Jamie and I didn't even attempt that back in the day.

"The imagination of my twentysomething self begs to differ," Will says with a smirk, and I laugh again.

"Anything else you want to come clean on?"

Will runs his hand through his hair. "I guess this is as good a time as any to tell you that I take medication for anxiety."

"Okay," I say slowly. "That's not really what I meant, but I'm glad you told me."

He swallows. "I think you should know it can be bad. The first time I spiraled was after my mom left. My mind was so frenzied, but I didn't understand what was going on at the time. And then when Sofia was born . . ." He shakes his head. "It was awful—really dark stuff would go through my head. Terrible thoughts. Images, too. I didn't know what was happening, and I couldn't get rid of them—" He cuts himself off. I think of the two words tattooed beneath his collarbone—*only thoughts*—and squeeze his pinkie.

"You can tell me when you're ready. I won't judge, but you don't have to rush."

He nods. "I was afraid of being alone with the baby, and Annabel figured out something was off. I got help. Started medication. I even went to group therapy."

I shift so that I'm sitting cross-legged, facing him. "I'm sorry you went through that."

"It could happen again, if I have kids," he says. I can tell it's a warning. "And I still worry. I'm a worrier."

"Okay." I pause. "None of it is anywhere close to a deal breaker for me, if that's what you're thinking. But I need you to tell me what's going on in your life. When something is making you anxious or upsetting you, I want to know. If we do this . . ."

A door closes somewhere in the house, and a girl's voice drifts up from a lower level. We listen to Annabel and Sofia moving around for a moment.

"When you left like that," I tell him, "it was like all the fears I had about us had been confirmed."

"What fears?"

"I thought you had been, I don't know, playing make-believe with me? I don't want to be with someone who keeps parts of their life separate from me. I don't want to be an escape. I want to be the reality."

Will leans toward me until his nose brushes mine. "Fern," he says. "You're not an escape. You're everything."

"Really?" I whisper, pulling back slightly. "Because you wouldn't tell me about the phone calls until I forced it out of you. You wouldn't let me in."

He nods. "I know. But as much as someone thinks they're okay with my sister and my niece, and the fact that I do pickup and drop-off and cook dinner almost every night—it's become an issue more than once. I just never cared until now. I didn't want to pull you into all our family drama. I wanted to be selfish. I wanted you to myself."

"I can understand that," I tell him. "But you can't lock me away from the two most important people in your life. No more secret phone calls." I point to the third item on the list—*let me help*—as Annabel's muffled yell floats up to us. "I want to be part of the drama. I want to be part of all of it."

Will smiles. "There's a lot of drama." And then he falls serious. "Annabel has been threatening to move out for a while, but I didn't think she meant it. She told me after I got to the resort that she was working with a real estate agent, so sometimes that's what our calls were about. Some of them were her hassling me to tell you how I felt. Some of them were questions about using the stove. But we've been arguing."

"Because you want them to stay?"

"Yeah. I know that in some ways it could be good for me if they rented a place of their own. I know Annabel thinks so. She feels bad that they've been here so long, but I'm used to having them around. I *like* having them around." He gives me an apologetic look. "I know it's not what most women want to hear, that I want to live with my sister and my niece."

"I'm not most women." I jostle his leg. "And you're not most men."

He makes a skeptical little growl. "I come with a lot more mess."

I hate hearing Will talk about himself this way. I feel protective of the Will I met ten years ago, but I also want to stand up for the man I know now. I crawl onto his lap and take his face in my hands. "Let me tell you something about me: I am extremely picky about people. Most of them, I don't particularly like. I have very high standards for the ones I let into my life these days. And you, Will Baxter, are my favorite of all of them."

He looks surprised. "I am?"

"You are. I love you best of all."

Will's eyes widen and then his lips are on mine, urgent and hungry, like this is the last time we'll do this. I put my arms around his neck and slow it down, melting into the kiss. He tastes like coffee and maple syrup and coming home after a long day. *I'm not going anywhere*, I tell him with my tongue and my mouth.

"You love me," Will says in a hush, running his thumb over my bottom lip.

"I do," I tell him. "Especially the messy parts. You're too perfect otherwise, Will. It's annoying, really."

He smiles, then kisses my jaw. "Fern." He kisses my cheek, and whispers into my ear, "I love you, too." He presses his lips to my nose. "So much."

"Good," I tell him. "Because that will make items four and five easier."

"You like the apron?"

I put my forehead against his. "I adore the apron."

He laughs.

"And I want you to keep drawing."

Will hums.

"Or painting or Mod-Podging teacups with photos of Chihuahuas—don't give up art again. That list we wrote ten years ago was wrong—it can be a hobby." I give him a kiss. "Just start with one picture."

He lets out a long sigh. "Okay," he says. "Since it's on the list, I'll do it for you."

"And you. You can have something that's for you."

Will pulls me against him, and I rest my head on his chest, listening to the sound of his heart and feeling the vibration of his voice on my cheek when he says *I love you* again.

But then footsteps sound on the stairs.

A girl's voice calls from outside the room, "Uncle Will, can I have one of these pancakes? *Annabel* said I had to ask."

"Try again, Sof," Will replies.

"Fine. *Mama* said I had to ask."

"Better," Will says. "And go for it. I'll be down in a few minutes. There's someone I want you to meet." I pull back and he raises his eyebrows.

"Okay," Sofia says. Her footsteps fly back down the stairs as she calls, "*Annabel,* I told you it'd be fine."

"She's what you might call precocious," Will says.

"Oh yeah?"

"And she's a total chaos demon, I'm warning you now."

"Perfect," I say. "I like chaos."

He tucks a strand of hair behind my ear. "Are you sure you want all of this?"

"I'm sure," I tell him. "I want everything."

28

Now

I SPEND ALMOST A FULL WEEK WITH WILL AND THE GIRLS IN THE
city. I make pancakes for Sofia in the morning and drive her to
summer camp so Will can catch up on sleep and Annabel can get
to work early. In the afternoons, Will and I take meandering walks
through Toronto. We walk and we talk, and we come up with a
plan for trying to make things work long-distance. Will is going to
visit me on weekends as often as possible, we'll talk in the evenings
after dinner, and he pledges to send me a photo whenever he
wears an apron.

I give Peter my mom's last diary as soon as I get back to the
resort. I tell him I don't think she would mind if he knew what
she'd been thinking all those years ago, and it might be a pleasant
surprise. For me, reading Mom's journal wasn't quite like hearing
her again—the Margaret Brookbanks I knew was different from
the young woman who wrote in its pages. But I think for Peter, it
might be. He knew that young woman—chatty and optimistic
and impatient. He loved that Maggie like he loved the version of
Mom I knew.

I stay busy. I join Whitney and Cam's monthly game night and spend time with Jamie, hunched over the kitchen table, reviewing blueprints for his dream home. I visit Peter in the pastry kitchen almost every morning, and one sunny day in late October, I hear music before I enter. Peter is playing Anne Murray. I befriend the owners of the record store in town. I buy a guitar and watch lessons on YouTube. I imagine becoming both brave and decent enough to make a surprise performance at the dance and talent show next August. And I work my ass off.

But in the middle of the night, alone in the house, a familiar ache returns to my belly. I creep to the window and look out at Cabin 20, but a light never shines through the dark. Will is never there.

As the months pass and the snow falls and the moon casts a pale glow over the frozen bush, the ache turns sharp with awareness. I don't want to miss Will anymore.

On New Year's Eve, we sway on the dance floor. The DJ is playing the song I requested. It's Elvis and it's corny, but it's also exactly right for the moment I ask Will if he'd consider living here one day. The room sparkles with candles and Christmas lights and the oversized disco ball Jamie talked me into hanging, but nothing is as bright as the smile on Will's face.

It takes time for him to rearrange his work to make that possible, but in May, a year following Mom's death, Will moves into the house with me. The sunroom is now his office. My home is now his. When I go downstairs in the morning, the coffee is strong and the music is playing, and Will is in the kitchen.

Much to his relief, Annabel agrees to stay at his place in Toronto. He still worries, and she calls or texts both of us almost daily with cooking questions, but Will commutes to the city for work at least one day a week, so he sees the girls regularly. I decorate the guest bedroom in dark purple for Sofia—she's spending a couple weeks with us later this summer. The closet is still stuffed with Mom's party frocks. Sofia says she's too old for dress-up, but I saw the way she eyed the pink sequined bolero. I bet I can talk her into at least one tea party with Peter and me.

I hire a new executive chef and rename the restaurant Maggie's. Of all the changes I make to the resort, this is the one I love best. Sometimes, when I want to feel close to Mom, I go to the dining room. But when I miss her most, I find myself wandering down to the family dock. I sit in the chair on the left and look out at the lake and update her on everything that's happening. Sometimes, I can almost hear her say, *We're so lucky.*

Even though the resort is poised for a good year, some days are too long and too hard and just plain suck. But now Will is there when I come home. While he cooks dinner, he reminds me of all the things I've accomplished and how much I love what I do, and I stare at him wearing Mom's apple-print apron, not quite sure someone so wonderful can be real.

I'm sleeping better than I have in a long time, but there are times when I wake just after two a.m. and find that Will's not beside me. I tiptoe downstairs and pull the pencil out of his hand and bring him back to bed. If Will can't sleep, he draws.

Every day feels special, but June fourteenth is a gift.

Will and I paddle to the strip of shoreline where we sat together almost a year ago. Unlike then, the sun glitters off the lake—not a single cloud interrupts its rays. Sunglasses are necessary. Will has packed a picnic basket and a bottle of champagne, and we raise our plastic cups to the anniversary of the day we met.

We relax with our feet in the water and our pinkies linked in the sand, reminiscing about that June fourteenth. When the breeze picks up, it blows Will's hair across his brow, and my breath catches. I've convinced him to grow it out a little, and he looks just like how he did at twenty-two. Relaxed and rumpled and gorgeous. For the thousandth time over the past year, I think I might be hallucinating. It's hard for me to believe that we're finally here together, for good.

I took a leap when I showed up on Will's doorstep last August. I told myself if there was one person worth fighting for, it was Will, and if there was a relationship worth the effort, it was the one we had started to build. Because even though we hadn't put a label on it, Will and I were building something. I told myself we could make it stronger.

When the sun gets hot, Will pulls off his shirt, and I stare at the ridges of his stomach and the grooves of his hips and the black of his ink until he tosses his V-neck in my face.

"What?" I laugh.

"Your tongue is hanging out."

"*Pfff*. I was simply admiring the art."

Will pulls me to my feet, and I take his hand and press my lips to the newest tattoo, a small fern frond on the inside of his wrist, but then Will begins to unbutton my shorts.

"Let's swim," he says, planting a kiss on my nose.

We wade out to where the lake is deep and cool and float on our backs, shutting our eyes to the sun. Eventually Will pulls me toward him and we kiss as the water dances around our waists, and he slips his finger under the edge of my bathing suit and does the thing with his thumb.

After we've dried off and finished our sandwiches and the lemon squares Peter knows Will likes best, I begin packing our things into the canoe. I set the basket in the middle of the boat, and when I turn around, Will is kneeling in the sand, a tiny green velvet box in his hand. But before he says anything, I throw my arms around his neck and tackle him to the ground. I kiss him through tears and he murmurs something about not having said anything, but I'm too overcome to care, because Will Baxter is my favorite person, and I'm going to keep him forever.

"Don't you want to see the ring?" Will says, laughing. I tell him I don't give a rat's ass about the ring. All I want is to hear that happy sound bursting from his mouth every day of my life.

"It's kind of meaningful to me," he says.

I pull back, blinking at Will underneath me, my throat tight.

He holds my face between his hands. "Stand up for a second, okay? There are things I want to say."

I get to my feet and Will kneels in front of me, holding the sand-covered box. A plain gold band sits inside. I can't believe I didn't notice he wasn't wearing it.

"I had it resized," he says, taking his grandfather's ring out. "It's the most important thing I own, and I didn't think you'd want anything sparkly."

Will tells me how lucky he is to have met his soulmate eleven years ago, and even luckier to have found me again. He tells me I'm his best friend. He tells me he never thought it was possible to be as happy as he is now, with me. He tells me I'm the bravest person he knows. He tells me he loves my loyalty and my playlists and my nose. He tells me he loves me best of all. We kiss and we cry and we hug, and we tumble around in the sand until a group of teenagers in a boat start whistling and honking their horn.

There's a group of people waiting for us on the dock. I squint as we paddle closer, trying to make out their shapes. Sofia is obvious. I can see her purple shirt, the one she and Will tie-dyed, from way out on Smoke Lake. We're far from shore, but she's already jumping and waving.

"I could only keep so much a secret," Will says when I turn

around from my spot in the front. "You know what Annabel's like."

I do know what Annabel's like. From the moment we announced that Will was moving here, she's been plying me with bridal magazines and links to floral designers and Pinterest inspiration boards. She likes an occasion almost as much as Jamie does, and once she has a hankering, she's impossible to deter. She's more stubborn than Will, and though she'd never admit it, she's as protective of him as he is of her. I told her planning a wedding was the last thing on my mind, and more important, I didn't want to do the bride thing, ever. I'm not opposed to marriage, but weddings? I thought the vein in her forehead might burst.

I turn back to face the resort. We've drifted in a little, and I can spot Annabel as well as Peter's bulky frame. Jamie's there, too, standing beside Whitney and Cam.

They reach for us before we've even tied up the canoe. Sofia wraps herself around Will's waist once he's out of the boat and Annabel gives him a one-armed hug, pulling me in with the other.

Someone else curls around my back, and I can tell from the smell of her shampoo it's Whitney.

"Get in here," she says, and I feel more arms lock around us in a jumbled group hug.

"I'm throwing you an engagement party," Annabel says. "Just try to stop me."

The girls want to take the canoe out, and as the crowd disperses, Peter and I watch Will help them climb in.

"I think I got a good one," I say to Peter. I know he agrees. Since Will's moved here, not a week goes by when Peter doesn't deliver us some kind of lemony dessert.

"You both did," he says. "Well, I better get back to the kitchen." He gives my forehead a kiss. "Congratulations, pea."

As the girls begin to paddle, Will and I sit at the edge of the dock, where we were supposed to meet ten years ago. Annabel and Sofia go around and around in circles—neither one of them has got the hang of canoeing.

"They have no idea what they're doing," Will says.

"No, they really don't," I agree, grinning as Sofia leans over the side to splash her mom with her hand. Annabel shrieks and edges over on the bench. The boat rocks.

"They might tip," Will says, and I pat his knee.

"They're not going to tip," I tell him. "And if they do, we're here."

Then, with a wicked smile, Annabel raises her paddle and swooshes it through the water, drenching her daughter. Sofia squeals in delight. Will laughs and brings his arm around me, tucking me tight against his side.

We sit there, together, until the girls get bored with the canoe, and they wander over to the beach.

We sit there, my head on Will's shoulder, until the sun sinks low in the sky, painting the lake in purple and gold.

We sit there for hours, Will Baxter and me, making plans for the future, the dreams that we'll share.

I look at our feet dangling in the water, then up at Will. "Sometimes I can't believe we're here," I tell him.

"I know the feeling," he says. "But here we are, Fern Brook-banks. Right where we're supposed to be."

EPILOGUE

I'm not sure how to begin. I've never kept a diary before.

Will says I should think of it less as a journal and more like a letter. He says there's no way you won't find it one day and read it.

I guess, in that case, I shouldn't call him Will. I should call him your dad.

I can't see my feet over my swollen belly, but it's still hard to imagine one day you'll be here soon. Our daughter.

Your dad thought it might help to talk to you. He puts his nose to my stomach and sings lullabies or gives art history lessons, but I feel silly whispering to my stretch marks. So I think I'll do this instead. I'll write about all the people you'll meet once you get here. Peter and Whitney and Jamie. Annabel and Sofia. Mr. and Mrs. Rose. The incredible man who I call Will and you'll call Dad. And I'll write about the people you won't. I'll tell you all about this little world you'll live in.

And then, one day, I'll give this book to you. I'll make coffee—please tell me you'll drink it—and we'll wander down the path to the pair of old metal chairs by the water. I'll sit in Mom's old spot, and you'll sit in mine. We'll watch the waves crash against the rocks, and I'll share everything with you. It'll be our place. You and me, at the lake.

ACKNOWLEDGMENTS

I'm sitting here on my couch in Toronto trying to decide how much to tell you about the challenges of writing *Meet Me at the Lake*. It's a moody day in October—the peak of fall color—and the clouds are slate gray. Every so often the sun comes out, making the treetops glow orange, red, and gold. Tomorrow, I'll drive north with my husband and two boys to Barry's Bay for Thanksgiving. It feels like the ideal time to write my acknowledgments— there's so much to be thankful for.

At the top of the list are my readers. I don't have a thank-you big enough for your incredible response to my debut novel, *Every Summer After*, and for the countless messages of anticipation I've received in the lead-up to *Meet Me at the Lake*. The way you devoured *Every Summer After* and then told your friends and family to do the same was truly humbling and completely surreal. I know many of you want more of Percy and Sam. I get daily requests for Charlie's story. I love how much you love those characters, and I hope Fern and Will have won a similar place in your hearts.

It was easy to tell you about writing *Every Summer After*—the experience was one of pure joy. I was working full-time as a journalist, had a young child at home, and was pregnant with my second, and yet it took just four months to pen the first draft. In my late thirties, I felt like I'd found my calling.

Discussing the creation of *Meet Me at the Lake* is more difficult—but you've given me so much, and so I'll give you honesty. I spent at least five times the hours on this book than I did on *Every Summer After*. There were many rounds of edits and revisions. I rewrote almost half the book during the second draft (and had a blast doing so). With each draft, *Meet Me at the Lake* grew closer to being the story that it was meant to become. But the first draft knocked me about.

Before I began, I remember looking back at the notebook I'd kept while writing *Every Summer After* to try to figure out how I'd managed to write a novel. It seemed like an impossible thing to do again. *Every Summer After* must have been a fluke. It must have been magic.

Every day when I sat down to write the first draft, I waged a battle against the chorus in my head telling me I had no idea what I was doing, that my writing was terrible, that there was no way my second book would be as good as the one that came before it. It hurt. I kept going, and eventually I had something. It wasn't great, and the *Meet Me at the Lake* you've just read is a far better book. But I'm as proud of the final product as I am of that earliest, messy version. There may have been a little magic in writing *Every Summer After*, but drafting *Meet Me at the Lake* took grit.

As you've no doubt guessed, this book required tremendous editorial guidance and support. Amanda Bergeron, please know that I'm currently in tears trying to come up with words that express even a fraction of my gratitude for you. It's unreal that we have yet to meet in person, but I'm starting to think that's a good thing because I'll probably hug you too tightly and for too long and then I'll start sobbing, and it will be weird. You are brilliant.

I'm spoiled to have the wildly talented Deborah Sun de la Cruz in my corner. Deborah, I'm thrilled you live in Toronto and therefore I can hug you at semi-regular intervals, mostly without losing my cool. A massive thank-you for helping me bring Maggie into sharper focus and give deeper meaning to the book's title.

Taylor Haggerty, if these acknowledgments were a playlist, your song would be Bette Midler's "Wind Beneath My Wings." You're my hero. And because of you, I can now start sentences with the words, "My agent says . . ." Please see note to Amanda re: tear-filled hugs IRL. (For you, I may also bow down.) Jasmine Brown, I'm coming for you next. Thank you for all that you do.

An enormous, slightly more professional thank-you to the masterminds at Berkley—Sareer Khader, Bridget O'Toole, Chelsea Pascoe, Erin Galloway, Kristin Cipolla, Craig Burke, Ivan Held, Christine Ball, Claire Zion, Jeanne-Marie Hudson, Vi-An Nguyen, Anthony Ramondo, Christine Legon, Megha Jain, Joan Matthews, LeeAnn Pemberton, and Lindsey Tulloch. I'm so happy to call Berkley home.

I warned the good people of Penguin Canada that because I'm now writing full-time and no longer have an office of colleagues, they are all on the hook. Kristin Cochrane, Nicole Winstanley, Bonnie Maitland, Beth Cockeram, Daniel French—it's such a gift to work with you all. Emma Ingram: I adore you and your dresses.

Whenever I worry about book stuff, I think about the extraordinary people I'm surrounded by. Holly Root, I once heard you describe literary agents as wearing cardigans and sending emails. I don't remember the context, but sometimes when I'm anxious, I picture all you smarty-pantses at Root Literary in cute button-up sweaters, and I'm instantly soothed. Heather Baror-Shapiro, thank you for bringing my books to international audiences— what an absolute dream. Speaking of dreams, Carolina Beltran— it is a total pleasure to work together. Thank you, thank you, thank you!

To Elizabeth Lennie, whose paintings have now appeared on

the cover of both *Every Summer After* and *Meet Me at the Lake*: Thank you for bringing the lake to life.

Thank you to Dr. Jonathan S. Abramowitz for speaking with me about postpartum OCD in men and non–birth parents. Your work and expertise is greatly appreciated.

One of the coolest things about being a published author is that you get to pretend that you know other, more fabulous authors, since sometimes they're kind enough to mention you on social media, or blurb your book, or participate in an event with you, or respond to your DMs. Thank you to Ashley Audrain, Karma Brown, Iman Hariri-Kia, Emily Henry, Amy Lea, Annabel Monaghan, Hannah Orenstein, Jodi Picoult, Ashley Poston, Jill Santopolo, and Marissa Stapley for making me feel like part of the club. And also to Colleen Hoover, who mentioned *Every Summer After* on Instagram twice and now people think I can introduce them to her. (The jig is up: I'm not that connected.)

To the Bookstagrammers, BookTokers, reviewers, journalists, podcasters, librarians, and booksellers: Thank you for your passion, dedication, and creativity. I'm in awe of the work you do to build communities of readers. The book world is better for it. A special thank-you to the earliest adopters of *Every Summer After*—you shouted loud, and whoa, people listened. (Yes, Lianna, you were the loudest. No contest.)

Thank you to Sadiya Ansari, Meredith Marino, Courtney Shea, and Maggie Wrobel for reading this book in its earliest, shaggiest form, and for all the support and encouragement on this roller-coaster ride.

Lianne George, thank you for your mentorship, your friendship, and especially for the coffee dates. The kick line is for you.

Robert Nida, I will treasure my time at the cottage forever. You have my eternal gratitude.

Thank you to the Ursi and Palumbo families for the enthusiasm, excitement, and carbohydrates. Grace, thank you for your faith and the countless hours you look after the boys. (Can they sleep over tonight?)

To the Fortune family: Our song is obviously Tina Turner's "The Best." I think the New South Wales Rugby League will share it with us. Thank you for instilling in me the value of hard work, and for proving that home isn't the walls in which we live, but the people within them. Mom, I'm so lucky.

Marco, I know you suggested I devote this entire acknowledgment to how great you are (you are so great!), but I dedicated the book to you and I'm making steak for dinner, so hopefully that does the trick. Thank you for not letting me talk myself out of quitting my job. Thank you for taking a year off from your own work so I could write this book. You were a rock star stay-at-home parent. Thank you for being as prepared to celebrate with me as you are to pick me up when I fall. We don't have a song, but I think that's because we have them all.

And to Max and Finn: I love you beyond measure. May you one day grow into men who'll read their mother's books but never touch her diaries.

MEET ME
AT THE
LAKE

Carley Fortune

BEHIND THE BOOK

A note to the reader: Thank you so much for reading Meet Me at the Lake. *I hope you were transported to Brookbanks Resort and to the Toronto I so love. Most of all, I hope Fern and Will's story leaves you with a full heart. Parts of this book are deeply personal to me—they are the subject of this "Behind the Book" essay. I want you to know that I'm going to talk about some tough stuff. If you're not in a place where you want to read about reproductive rights, anxiety, and disturbing intrusive thoughts, then I encourage you to save it for another time.*

The earliest inklings of *Meet Me at the Lake* came to me like far too many of my ideas do: in the middle of the night. It was several weeks following the birth of my second child, and I couldn't sleep. Sleeping has never been a skill of mine, but I developed chronic insomnia during my pregnancy, and it continued after Finn was born. As I lay awake, I found myself wondering what I was going to do about my next book. Writing my debut novel, *Every Summer After*, in 2020 was a joyful experience, and I was brimming with ideas for future stories. But in the spring of 2021, I was empty. I was also in the midst of my second bout of postpartum anxiety.

I find writing similar to reading in that I get to travel to wherever my characters exist. That night, I asked myself where I wanted to *be*. I shut my eyes, and I saw it: a classic lakeside resort in Muskoka, with a hilltop lodge and cabins overlooking the water. And I saw Fern, reluctantly running the place following the death of her mother. I thought of Maggie's diary, too—how it would recount her own romance but ultimately show a mother's love for her daughter. I wrote *Every Summer After* partially as an escape from life in 2020, but I created Brookbanks Resort to give myself a world to escape into. (Smoke Lake does exist, by the way, but it's slightly east of Muskoka and inside Ontario's famous Algonquin Park. There are no resorts on its shores.)

There are pieces of me scattered throughout *Meet Me at the Lake*. My parents owned a restaurant and inn when I was growing up. I gave Fern my insomnia as well as my fondness for both the city and the lake. Maggie received my dedication to my career and my worries about not being very good at anything outside of work. And to Will Baxter I bequeathed the quiet, invisible terror of postpartum anxiety.

Meet Me at the Lake has evolved over the course of writing, but from the earliest conversations with my editor, it was always about how life doesn't always turn out the way we expect. But I didn't set out to explore the ways parenthood shapes us—perhaps that's what happens when you begin writing a book about a mother and a daughter a few months after having your second baby.

During the late stages of editing *Meet Me at the Lake*, the US Supreme Court overturned *Roe v. Wade*, and I began to worry that the two unplanned pregnancies in the book (and the fact that both Maggie and Annabel decide to become mothers) would be perceived as an endorsement of that ruling. That is not my intention. I firmly believe the choices to continue a pregnancy and to become a parent are exactly that: choices every person with a uterus should be able to make. Reproductive rights, including access to contraceptives and safe abortions, are fundamental to individual well-being and to society at large. I've always considered myself pro-choice—becoming a parent only strengthened my stance.

There was a moment when I was in labor with my first son, when my hospital room was suddenly swarming with doctors and nurses, their faces tense, that I thought I might die. It wasn't my life at risk, it turned out; it was the baby's. Long story short: He needed to get out of my body as quickly as possible and was born via a brutal forceps-assisted delivery. It took fifteen minutes of active labor for Max to come into this world, and an hour and a half for the doctors to stitch me back together.

From that day to the first weeks and months of the baby's life, it felt like I was fighting for survival—my own and the baby's. There were many intense challenges in those early days, and coping with them was made more difficult because my mind had become a very scary place. As a journalist, I've written about some of the struggles I faced as a new parent, but I've never publicly spoken about my postpartum OCD.

There's a good chance you've heard of baby blues and postpartum depression but not about postpartum OCD—I know I hadn't. (During both my pregnancies, no medical practitioner mentioned it to me.) It's a serious but treatable anxiety disorder with symptoms so horrifying, few of us are comfortable talking about it—it's often misdiagnosed and unreported. Despite its name, it can affect not only birth parents but adoptive parents and anyone in a parenting role: people such as Will.

I didn't experience compulsions, but like Will, I was bombarded by recurring intrusive thoughts and images. I made a conscious decision not to describe Will's thoughts—I didn't think he'd be ready to share them with Fern, and to be honest, I was worried you'd judge him. It took me months to tell my husband what was happening in my head. Years to tell my mother. The thought of putting it out into the world makes my chest tight. I don't want to burden you with what plagued me, with what made me afraid to be alone with the baby every day, with what made me certain I'd be institutionalized if I told anyone. But the reason I'm writing about it (and as vaguely as possible) is in case you find yourself in a similar position. If you become terrorized by thoughts of harming your baby, if the same horrible images keep flashing through your mind, if kitchen knives or stairs or subway tracks fill you with terror, you are not alone. The thoughts are just that—*only thoughts*—even though you dread the possibility of losing control. You won't. In fact, I've been told people who experience these kinds of thoughts tend to be highly contentious. You will be okay—your baby will be, too—but you need to tell someone. In fact, telling someone is the first step to being okay. We go through our darkest moments alone, but we emerge from them with help.

My postpartum anxiety was different the second time around. I had a few episodes with intrusive thoughts and images, but I was better prepared to acknowledge them, see them as a nuisance, and send them on their way. My anxiety, however, was almost debilitating. I've experienced anxious thoughts before, but nothing compared to the spring of 2021. It was like every problem I could possibly face for my entire life needed solving. Getting out of bed each morning took immense effort.

Tearful conversations with my mom (about how I sucked as a mom) and my husband (about how terrified I was for the future) helped. Walking helped. Therapy helped. Will and Fern helped.

In the epilogue to *Meet Me at the Lake*, we learn that Fern is pregnant with a baby girl. I don't believe I'm a more fulfilled person because I'm a mom. When someone tells me they don't want children, I get that. Sometimes I envy that. But for this story, I wanted to give Fern the opportunity to forge her own path as a mother—to decide what elements of her relationship with her mom she wanted to preserve and what she would do differently. Perhaps most of all, I wanted to show that Will's anxiety had not stopped them from having children, that mental health struggles don't preclude you from being a wonderful parent. I like to think that when Fern and Will discussed having children, they did what my husband and I did before we had our second child: They talked about the possibility that Will's intrusive thoughts may resurface, and they came up with a plan to ensure he'd have support.

What I admire about both Will and Fern is that they love hard. It's not easy for either of them to open their hearts—to risk rejection, judgment, failure—and they stumble along the way. Near the end of the book, Fern gives Will a chance to explain his actions. She decides to reach out her hand. This, I think, is one of the bravest, most challenging things to do in the early stages of any relationship. It's also what makes them stronger. We all make mistakes. We experience trauma and loss and plain old bad days. We all fly, face-first, onto loose gravel. But with any luck, someone stands beside us, reaching out their hand.

DISCUSSION QUESTIONS

1. Fern and Will develop a close bond over just a day. Have you ever felt that kind of strong, fast connection with another person, whether platonic or romantic? If so, what do you attribute it to?

2. How do Fern's and Will's life stages play into their friendship when they first meet? Do you think they would have been as drawn to each other at another time in their lives?

3. In chapter 5, Fern thinks to herself that secrets are a key ingredient in close friendships. Do you agree? Do you think Fern still believes this by the end of the book?

4. How did you see Whitney and Fern's friendship evolve? Have any of your long-lasting friendships had similar ups and downs?

5. What do you make of Fern and Jamie's relationship, in both the past and the present? Do you think they would have stayed together if Fern had never met Will?

6. Will learns that his sister is pregnant after the twenty-four hours he spends with Fern. Do you think their time together affected his decision to move back to Toronto and help his sister with the baby?

7. In her thirties, Fern is on hiatus from relationships because she doesn't think they're worth the effort. But she decides to give her relationship with Will a chance despite his actions and the secrets he's kept. Would you have done the same?

8. Fern carries around a lot of guilt when it comes to her mother. What do you think of Maggie and Fern's relationship? Do you think Fern's decision to stay on at the resort is driven by guilt or something else?

9. Do you think Maggie and Peter's love story is a sad or a happy one?

10. The fact that life doesn't always work out as we plan is a theme of this book. Does your life look like you pictured it when you were younger?

A FEW BOOKS I READ (AND LOVED)
WHILE WRITING *MEET ME AT THE LAKE*

A Hundred Other Girls by Iman Hariri-Kia
Book Lovers by Emily Henry
The Heart Principle by Helen Hoang
Twice Shy by Sarah Hogle
Something Wilder by Christina Lauren
Exes & O's by Amy Lea
The Road Trip by Beth O'Leary
The Dead Romantics by Ashley Poston
The One That Got Away by Charlotte Rixon
Seven Days in June by Tia Williams

CARLEY FORTUNE is the *New York Times* bestselling author of *Every Summer After*. She's also an award-winning Canadian journalist who has worked as an editor for Refinery29, *The Globe and Mail, Chatelaine,* and *Toronto Life.* She lives in Toronto with her husband and two sons.

CONNECT ONLINE

CarleyFortune.com
CarleyFortune
CarleyFortune

Ready to find
your next great read?

Let us help.

Visit prh.com/nextread